The Weekends
of You and Me

ALSO BY THIS AUTHOR

French Relations
Kiss Chase
Well Groomed
Snap Happy
Between Males
Lucy Talk
Lots of Love
Tongue in Cheek
Four Play
Love Hunt
Kiss and Tell
The Love Letter
Sealed With a Kiss (Ebook short story)
The Summer Wedding
The Country Escape
The Woman Who Fell in Love for a Week

The Weekends of You and Me

FIONA WALKER

SPHERE

First published in Great Britain in 2016 by Sphere

1 3 5 7 9 10 8 6 4 2

Copyright © Fiona Walker 2016

The moral right of the author has been asserted.

A CIP catalogue record for this book
is available from the British Library.

ISBN 978-0-7515-5617-9

Typeset in Plantin by M Rules
Printed and bound in Great Britain by
Clays Ltd, St Ives plc

Papers used by Sphere are from well-managed forests
and other responsible sources.

MIX
Paper from
responsible sources
FSC® C104740

Sphere
An imprint of
Little, Brown Book Group
Carmelite House
50 Victoria Embankment
London EC4Y 0DZ

An Hachette UK Company
www.hachette.co.uk

www.littlebrown.co.uk

To my rock and my soulmate,
and to the second decade of you and me . . .
and the forever after of us.

PROLOGUE

2014

Music: Paolo Nutini

*Car: 2010 Mini Cooper Countryman,
mildly dented and very dusty*

Season: Summer; heatwave

FRIDAY EVENING

The Arrival

Harry's choice of music for a weekend of arguments was a deliberately growling, sexual and melancholy anthem. *Caustic Love* had played through twice in the car, and Jo knew that it would be this year's background music in the cottage too. When Harry discovered an album he liked, he listened to it incessantly. She'd sneak in the odd old favourite, but whenever the iDock went unguarded, he'd change it back.

First came the Friday-night rituals: the Best Indian Takeaway in Shropshire had to be visited to order more than two people could hope to eat; they patronized the Six Tuns while they waited for their food, and ordered a plastic flagon of local ale to imbibe later. The narrow lanes of Castle Craven had to be walked and shopfronts studied, closures noted, the high street's higgledy-piggledy, half-timbered history admired. And then – cardboard box wedged between coats and bottles in the boot, its corners softening from rising steam and leaking sauce – they drove the ten miles on to the cottage, winding through tight hedge-hugged lanes then climbing high above the valley into which they dropped briefly to roll along its side, like a roulette ball. They rattled over the potholes and the cattle grid on to the track, climbing higher again, scattering sheep, cursing the deep ruts left by the farmer, back wheel spinning as they lamented the sale of Harry's beloved Range Rover. At last the tyres gripped hard-core for the final hundred yards beside the roaring brook and they drove into the woods to find Morrow waiting. As soon as he saw it, Harry's face burst into the smile that he seemed to have held back all year.

Even after a decade, Jo struggled to remember her way through the narrow lanes of the south Shropshire hills to the hidden valley that the cottage overlooked. She could never have found Morrow as instinctively as Harry did. Summer, winter, daylight, darkness, snow, rain or sun, he forged the straightest line to the place he had loved since childhood.

The arrival rituals were also deeply ingrained. The only things they carried inside were the takeaway, the ale, and wine for Jo: her taste for hops had faded after she'd hit forty. The stove had to be lit, even in a heatwave, although the back boiler no longer bubbled into life with eerie ghost farts from the tank housed in a bedroom cupboard: the ancient solid-fuel system had given way to eco-friendly biomass. But the wood-burner was still a vital part of their arrival: its crackling glow brought the cottage to life, with fat candles that smelt of hot dust and flickered as Harry gathered plates and glasses, grumbled about how the place had been left by other visitors, put on music loudly and flipped forward to his favourite track. He was so excited to be there that he had almost forgotten Jo was with him.

She felt a familiar tightening of her sinews, the irritation of the neglected wife. Morrow was always Harry's gig, even though he complained that it was hardly recognizable these days. It didn't matter how many hints Jo dropped about needing a cosmopolitan weekend of culture to remind them that there was intelligent life beyond hamster-wheeling, hard-working parenthood: Harry wanted to go to just one place.

The takeaway was spread on the pockmarked table – it

had been sanded and waxed by a restorer in recent years but was still as deeply grained and liver-spotted as an old man's hand. The ale was poured, the wine uncorked and the stove flues closed to calm the kindling as it ignited seasoned logs. Paolo was singing his heart out through 'Iron Sky', Harry's phone like a little tombstone in its iDock. There had been a time when the phones had stayed in the car, Jo remembered. There had been no point in bringing them in, so far from any signal. But we had talked to each other then, she thought bleakly.

She watched Harry devour the food, still complaining about the paying holiday guests and the housekeeper who came from beyond Craven Castle to clean and strip bedding on changeover days: 'Why fold the tip of the bloody loo roll?'

'People like that sort of thing. It's boutiquey.'

'It's all about authenticity, these days. Give them a stack of ripped farm-auction catalogues hanging on a piece of string.' His eyes narrowed as he spotted a bare nail poking from the wall above the door. 'She's put away the stag's head again.'

'It is a bit scary.'

'Brian's been here since the seventies. He sees off evil.'

'The cottage has been here since fifteen hundred. It can see off evil on its own.' Even your bad temper, she added silently. Morrow always soothed it away, eventually, although it took longer each time they came. And I'm not sure I want to wait any longer, Jo's silent voice added.

He was studying the visitors' book, tutting and snorting at any critical comments. '"The ice tray is cracked" . . . "Could do with fluffier towels" . . . They should have tried coming here when you had to start the generator to turn on a light. "The cafetière leaks coffee grounds, and please mend the broken shaver sockets. It was most inconvenient that we couldn't charge our toothbrushes." Well, screw you, Barry and Debs Newton from Reading.' He reached across and crammed a blade of poppadum into his mouth. 'I hope the coffee grits are still giving you hell between your unbrushed teeth.'

My heart leaks love, Jo thought wretchedly. She imagined writing in the book: 'Please mend my broken marriage and charge it up.' Morrow had always obliged before, but now she couldn't see how it might possibly help them. Once, Harry's extraordinary warmth and generosity, which had melted her heart from deep-frozen cynicism, had counteracted his anger. Now it eclipsed any affection and the frost had returned. She was suffocating with unhappiness, trapped beneath the slow-moving glacier of co-dependent domesticity. Visiting Morrow had once been a magical escape, but now it was as much of a routine etched with mutual rancour as loading the dishwasher.

'Man alive, people are unoriginal,' Harry ranted on, dropping lime pickle on the page he was reading. 'If I had a quid for every time someone writes, "The food at the Hare and Moon is very good", as though they were the first to discover it, I'd be able to send every local hare round the moon on their own purpose-built rocket.'

'They're being kind.' Guess how much I love you? Jo looked at his face, the deep frown softened by candlelight, remembering the book they'd read to the children as babies. The answer used to be, 'To the moon and back.' Now it rarely made it up the stairs to bed.

'They're stupid. People are stoopid.' He reached for the ale flagon to top up his mug. Harry always insisted on drinking his beer from the same mug, a running joke that dated back to the year the cupboard with the glasses in it had fallen off the wall, its weight too much for the damp old lime plaster.

Jo watched the beer foam into the mug. It always surprised her how many of her life choices had depended on tiny triggers. The decision to make a life with Harry, to move away from London, to have a second child, had all revolved around practical catalysts, straws balanced on a camel's back.

Now he picked up the little plastic tubs containing the pickles – the Best Indian Takeaway in Shropshire made their own, sweetly spiced Utopia for the taste buds – and scooped out the rest on to his plate, then looked around for something to load them on to. Jo had counted six poppadums when she was putting them out. Harry had eaten four. She had had one. If he takes the last without offering it to me, our marriage is over, she decided.

He looked across at her, beer foam and crumbs in the summer-holiday beard she'd thought so sexy the first year he'd grown it. Unsmiling, he reached for the plate.

PART ONE

2006

Music: Howlin' Wolf, John Lee Hooker,
Kaiser Chiefs, Arctic Monkeys

Car: 1990 Golf GTi, very battered

Season: Spring; sunny

FROM THE VISITORS' BOOK, MARCH 2006

What a rare find! When something is this beautiful and unspoilt, taking it for granted for a minute is unforgivable, and years of neglect are a capital offence. I plan to revisit regularly. And also come back to the cottage.

Harry Inchbold, London

FRIDAY AFTERNOON

The Journey

The car was screaming along to 'Smokestack Lightning'.
Jo was convinced a part of the exhaust had fallen off somewhere near Oxford.

'It's my sister Titch's banger,' Harry explained, as they
trailed a snake of fumes on the M40. 'She never uses it.'

'Can't say I blame her.' The Volkswagen was roaring
like an amorous elephant seal. I'm escaping from London
for the weekend with a man I barely know, she reflected
happily, as she studied Harry's profile, enthralled by its
unfamiliarity. All she knew for certain about him was that
he was sensational in bed, and that he made her laugh non-
stop. As Muddy Waters took over the airwaves, proclaiming
that he had his mojo workin', she shared his sentiments
entirely.

They'd met at one of Fi and Dom's dinner parties in the
Islington love nest, a regular diary date since the couple's
wedding, with guests reunited by the dozen to admire the
new twelve-place Denby tableware. Newly-wed Fi possessed
a Cupid urge to set up unattached friends with Dom's
banking buddies, however little they had in common.
Recently reclassified as single, Jo was towed across the sea-
grass carpet upon arrival to meet a tall, handsome-but-dull
thirty-something futures trader called Matt, who regarded
her with polite indifference despite – or possibly as a result
of – their hostess's gushing introductions: 'You're in for

such a treat, Matt, because Jo's a *hugely* talented artist who runs her own company and still finds time to globetrot to the world's most glamorous beaches.' Translation: arty-farty overachiever with skin like leather. 'Matt is a *brilliant* "scalper" with a mind like a razor, who climbs mountains on his days off.' A.k.a. an adrenalin junkie with something to prove. Poor Fi. It was like introducing two noble gases and hoping for chemistry. As far as Jo could tell, Fi's sole criterion for their compatibility had been height; it would have been more honest had she said: 'Matt and Jo, I think you'd suit each other perfectly because you're both ridiculously tall. Go and start a super race!'

Jo was still far too raw to be in search of love. She saw little of Fi these days, so it wasn't Fi's fault that she had added Jo to her singles database while her split from Tom was still in progress, the scar tissue painfully shared. Fi wasn't to know how delicate a process it was to dismantle a long-term relationship in which one half had gradually become sole breadwinner, social secretary and housekeeper. Three months after they had officially called it a day, Tom was still occupying the spare bedroom of the flat they had shared for five years, working his way through his stash of birthday and Christmas malt whisky as he watched National Geographic and played poker online, stubbornly in denial, dependent and depressed as his world crumbled beneath him. To avoid being at home, Jo accepted every invitation that came her way.

Now that she was back at the start in the dating game, she'd lost all faith in it. It was a snakes-and-ladders fairy-tale for the young based on castles in the air, priapic beanstalks bolting from cold frame to hothouse, familiarity and infatuation growing too fast on the same vine. She knew from bitter experience that the rot set in eventually under the weight of expectations. But, right now,

Jo wanted to do something she had never done before, something born of uncharacteristically cool cynicism, and it didn't involve being set up with husband material at dinner parties. In her twenty-year active sex life, Jo had never had a one-night stand. She'd never wanted one until now, but a bloody-minded horniness had gripped her during those sleepless post-Tom nights. Her body was firm from working through her anger at the gym, slim from weight loss caused by break-up stress, and she was eager to take pleasure again. She wasn't looking for a date or even much of a conversation. Instead she was determined to have one final fling before resigning from the game indefinitely.

And that night in Islington, she'd heard a man's laugh across the room, a sweet, feral sound that made her pulse points tighten.

Craning to see who it was, she'd casually asked Indifferent Matt whom he knew there. He'd reeled off a list of Dom's usual City-boy suspects, adding, 'And my disreputable brother is the prodigal guest leading our host astray. Bad form to muck up Fi's numbers, but Harry's staying with me right now, and I don't trust him on his own.' He made it sound like he'd got an unruly Labrador in tow.

The unruly Labrador turned out to be lounging on a sill with Dom. They were smoking out of the open sash window as that fabulous laugh rang out. With his mop of blond hair, black linen shirt and houndstooth bags, he stood out in a room full of sharp suits, a devilish Disney prince with an over-eighteen certificate. Glancing over his shoulder, his hair buffeted by the sharp February wind, he'd spotted Jo and shared with her a smile of such unbridled sensuality that she sensed her long stint of piety might be under threat. It was about time: her vintage copy of *Fear of Flying* had been by her bed for a while now, Janis Joplin's

17

'One Night Stand' on her iPod, and her mind was made up. Jo Coulson needed to flirt again.

'You're brothers?' she'd asked her companion, incredulous that one was as louche and languid as the other was frosty and formal.

'I'm afraid so.' Matt looked pained, as their hostess darted between them to top up glasses and check the chemistry.

'Dom says you Inchbold twins were once known as the Saint and the Sinner,' Fi conversation-hijacked brightly. 'And I know what an angel you are, Matt, so I don't need to ask who the Saint was.' She'd cast an encouraging look at Jo.

But Jo's gaze had strayed back to the man by the window. She was more interested in sin. As their eyes crossed once more, her lock was sprung. The mutual attraction was intoxicating.

A social gathering with Fi and Dom usually cast Jo as inadvertent comedy-fashion turn, never more so than at their big church wedding the previous year, where her striped red fifties' dress had resembled a lifebuoy amid the grey, teal and cream sea of morning suits and dresses. Within her own circle of friends, Jo was the vintage-loving conformist, but in Fi's world she was the opposite: a scruffy bohemian imposter, her hair always longer and wilder, her lipstick redder, and inevitably a head taller than almost everyone. For the newly-weds' dinner party she'd toned down her style, with a dark grey wraparound dress, hair blow-dried straight, her cuffed highwayman boots low-heeled, but one look around the room had told her she still stood out as alien. The other women were all in high-necked, figure-hugging pale tailoring, matched with high-maintenance glossy bobs. Jo's dress kept flashing her raspberry-coloured bra and was one badly tied bow away from a full frontal. Yet when the blond stranger had looked at her again and continued looking, she was grateful she stood out. And when he started to make his way over to her, she'd found heartbeats starting up in parts of her body she'd forgotten about . . .

Now Jo turned to look at him in the driver's seat, a latter-day James Hunt cutting through the motorway traffic, his profile ridiculously well proportioned, the long dimples that ran from his laughter lines to his jaw constantly animated with flirtation and amusement. Late thirties, self-assured and in possession of eyes so dark blue they were almost black, Harry Inchbold was, quite simply, sex on legs, and he knew it.

The fact that he'd clearly been half-cut on the night they'd met had done nothing to diminish his charisma. Acutely aware of his presence as he'd moved towards her through the room, Jo had tuned into his voice – the same husky timbre as the laugh and slightly transatlantic – responding to a barrage of 'How the devil are you?' and 'How's America?' from other guests, all of whom appeared to know him.

The closer he'd got, the more Jo had found their eyes catching. She'd forgotten how good it felt, that unspoken overture. His gaze was so seductively predatory, it was as though he was regarding her across a few inches of creased pillow, not a crowded room. Although equally tall and athletic, he was clearly a world apart from his neatly barbered brother Matt, who hadn't looked her in the eye once, talked in a nasal monotone and finally introduced her to Harry as 'Jane'.

'It's Jo, actually.'

As he landed a kiss by her ear – most men had to stand on tiptoe, but Harry Inchbold bent his head – he smelt intoxicatingly of Terre d'Hermès and danger. The tiny hairs on the nape of her neck had done a Mexican wave.

'Enchanted to meet you, Joactually. I'm Basicallyharry.' It hadn't been the greatest joke – and he'd slurred his words slightly – but the ripped-silk voice and come-to-bed eyes meant that pretty much anything he said sounded fabulously intimate. 'How d'you know Dom and Fi, Joactually?'

'Fi and I shared a flat once, Basicallyharry.'

'Joactually, that's really interesting.'

'It's not, Basicallyharry.'

With this silly patter, the smile they were sharing across an imaginary creased pillow grew ever more conspiratorial.

'As I'm sure my brother's told you, I'm gate-crashing.' He'd dropped his voice.

'I've said no such thing,' Matt said starchily. 'You know everyone here.'

Now, encouraging his guests towards the table, Dom was standing beside them. 'Harry's just moved back after a decade wowing the States as their *enfant terrible* of branding,' he explained to Jo.

'What brought you home?' she asked.

'I fell out with my boss,' Harry said lightly.

God, but his smile was disarming. She hardly took in Dom's sympathetic aside to Harry: his boss had apparently pulled the purse strings so tight she'd must have been hoping his balls would drop off. From the message she was seeing in Harry Inchbold's eyes, his balls were still firmly attached.

When they'd made their way to the table, one saintly Inchbold twin had moved ahead to hold out her chair while the other placed a sinful hand on her back to steer her towards it, his thumb turning a barely perceptible circle on the bare skin above her neckline. It was a sensation she would never forget, bringing with it a physical bolt of response so sudden and exposed that every other guest seemed to be playing voyeur. Jo understood only too well

20

how sexual attraction had the power to bring down empires. Her own little empire had already fallen, so it hardly mattered that she already wanted to sleep with Harry Inchbold without knowing who he was or caring where he went. Final flings needed no interview or job description.

Now the Volkswagen engine roared a bass note as John Lee Hooker sang 'Bang Bang Bang Bang', and Jo watched Harry squinting at a passing road sign, the creases around his blue eyes surely engraved more by laughter than frowning. His laugh was so good that she sought it now like a fix. If they were going to share just a few hours of each other's – long, happy and separate – lives, they were going to do so with aching ribs and no regrets. He glanced across at her and the big, easy smile slotted the little tanned jigsaw pieces together at his temples, fragments of a deliciously dissolute past.

The thought of the same blue eyes looking up at her from between her legs just a few hours earlier made the pulse there quicken. This was about sex and empowerment, she reminded herself. I'm in control here. It felt incredibly good.

'Does that say M42 east or west?' Harry squinted at another road sign.

Unbothered that he couldn't read it even at close range, Jo told him it said west. When a man's expert hands could drive one's body over its pleasure edge as repeatedly as Harry's had, Jo trusted him to drive a car to Shropshire.

'That's the one.' He veered across all three lanes.

'You need glasses.'

'I have glasses. I've lost them.'

'What's your prescription?'

'God knows. Half blind. Too much wanking as a teenager. Short-sighted, I think.'

'I have mine here.' She fished for them in her bag. 'I'm minus five in each eye.'

21

'Cold-eyed bitch. Hand them over. Fuck, they're strong.'
The tyres roared as they drifted over the rumble strips.

'You're probably better off without them.'

'I like seeing life through your eyes.' He laughed his class-A laugh and put a hand on her thigh, drawing his fingers back and abstractedly flipping between pad and knuckles as he drove, a gesture guaranteed to make her pulse rocket as she remembered the things those hands had already done to her. Jo had no idea how much further Shropshire was – she had a vague feeling it was near Birmingham – but she hoped they'd arrive soon. She'd never experienced that sort of animal attraction until now. Tom hadn't once made her feel like this, not even in the early days when they were at it all the time.

The hand was creeping upwards, thumb sliding beneath her hem to her knickers. The car was swerving wildly. A vehicle behind them beeped.

'You do something crazy to me.' He laughed again. 'You are unbelievably sexy, Joactually.'

'Keep your eyes on the road, Basicallyharry.' She grinned, fighting the urge to grab the wheel and steer them into the nearest service station to do something immediate and illegal on the back seat in the car park.

In Islington, the twelve place settings, banked flowers and ornate candlesticks separating Jo and Harry had seemed like an impenetrable jungle through five agonizing courses showcasing Fi's gourmet skills. Despite the complicated artistic division of twelve perfect portions into a baker's dozen, Fi was clearly thrilled to have Harry on a wing chair to her right, holding court, while Jo was trapped between Indifferent Matt and a boiling hot radiator.

She had edged the taller tableware aside and her eyes had met Harry's in an ever-faster silent repartee, an intense private conversation nobody else could penetrate. She hadn't

22

been able to help herself: physical attraction at its most shallow could feel surprisingly deep. The radiator to her left had made sweat run beneath her dress while she feigned polite interest in Matt's monologue on his achievements in futures trading and mountain-peak scaling. The couple opposite, whose names she hadn't caught, retreated behind the readjusted flower arrangements as he moved on to his property portfolio.

The only question Matt asked Jo all night was about her flat, his face briefly losing its indifference when she told him that, yes, thanks to her parents having lent her the deposit ten years earlier, she owned a very small slice of Crouch End. (She didn't mention that her ex occupied the spare room and was demanding a quarter of the equity.) At this, Matt had outlined yield comparisons between his buy-to-lets in north and north-west London; he was clearly a mathematical genius, his finances were copper-bottomed, and his manner corroded by arrogance. Basking in the Mediterranean warmth of Harry's blue gaze, Jo wondered why he could be labelled 'Sinner' while Matt was 'Saint': surely it was a sin to be so boring.

She'd caught only fragments of the conversation at the other end of the table: a book everyone had read, a discussion of which Greek island was best – the consensus was Naxos – and a ding-dong about Hollywood and American politics in which Harry refused to participate. All the time, his eyes flirted with hers around the guttering candles.

In frustration, she'd brazenly asked Indifferent Matt to tell her more about his brother, but he was tight-lipped, eyes averted. 'Harry needs to sort his crap out, basically. More Chablis?' Because Matt was a Square Mile fine-diner who only ever poured a centimetre, Jo had held up her glass until he was forced to pick up the bottle again and add more.

Looking back now, as she watched a piece of rattling

23

dashboard fall off in front of her, she realized that knocking back so much wine and jumping into bed with the prodigal guest had been shamelessly disrespectful to her hosts. At the time, though, it had felt absurdly perfect. It still did.

While puddings had circulated, debate had struck up at Harry's end of the table about how long the property bubble could keep inflating. Dom was holding forth so loudly about hedge-funders pricing out the Home Counties that all eleven guests could hear. 'They say everybody's looking for a new Cotswolds bolthole. Tell me, Inchbolds, do you still have that little wreck of a place near Ludlow?'

'Morrow Cottage.' Matt had become animated with the wider table talk, his mouth full of *tarte Tatin*.

'Aren't there more Michelin-starred restaurants in Ludlow than there are in the Square Mile?' trilled one guest. 'Do you ever let friends stay there?'

'Morrow's the other side of Clun, on the Welsh border,' Harry had said, his husky voice tinged with irritation. 'Not really in the Ludlow catchment.'

'Close enough,' Matt countered. 'And *of course* friends can stay there. The place hardly ever gets used now.'

'Isn't it halfway up a mountain?' The guest giggled.

'Pretty much,' muttered Harry, picking up a fork to prod at a poached pear.

'I love places like that,' Jo said. She'd always harboured a bit of a Grizzly Adams fetish for forest huts, log fires, wildlife and week-old beards. That earned her a hot glance from Harry and an exasperated sigh from Matt.

'It's sliding down it from neglect, these days. I've got a lock-up-and-leave apartment in Ciutat Vella, which is much more practical and has a twenty-per-cent yield.'

'Why not just sell Morrow if you never go there?' someone asked.

'I do,' Harry snapped, fork rattling.

'When?' Matt had given a derisive snort. 'You've been living in the States for almost a decade.'

'I was there for New Year.'

They all looked at him in surprise.

'You flew here without telling anyone and went to Morrow?' Matt seemed stunned.

'"Tomorrow, and tomorrow, and tomorrow, creeps in this petty pace,"' Jo had breathed, realizing too late that this was clearly audible because everybody else was silent.

Harry had leaned forward, though, and turned to look at her along the table with a slow smile. 'Seven points. Sing as Little Orphan Annie for a three-point bonus and I'll love you for ever.'

'For ever's a very long time.' She'd given him the benefit of her cynical Bacall face. 'I know the words to "Will You Still Love Me Tomorrow" better.'

'The Shirelles or Amy Winehouse version?'

'Bee Gees.'

Harry's laugh was straight-in-the-vein.

Beside her, Matt explained to the table at large: 'Morrow Cottage has a Welsh name, which, as kids, we could never pronounce, so Dad renamed it after the stream that runs past. We used to have family competitions to recite things with "tomorrow" in them, from Shakespeare to Bob Dylan, with awards for the most obscure.'

'"*Cras amet qui numquam amavit, quique amavit cras amet,*"' Harry quoted, in the times-table voice of one who has learned by rote.

'Meaning?' Jo asked.

Still looking at her as though only the two of them were in the room, his seductive smile had widened. '"Tomorrow he shall love who has never loved, and she who has loved will tomorrow love again."'

'That's beautiful,' sighed the woman to his right. 'Is it Catullus?'

'Cat Stevens, you mean,' joked a man opposite.

Harry had lifted his glass in a toast to Jo. 'I prefer "Hard Headed Woman".'

'"The First Cut Is The Deepest".' She lifted hers back.

Their eyes had gone to bed together at that moment and hadn't got out since.

That had been yesterday. They hadn't slept all night. Now they were driving to Morrow.

She turned to the car window, heat in her cheeks. They were miles from London in a clown's car that was collapsing around them, the blues replaced by Arctic Monkeys – whom she absolutely failed to get – as they finally exited the motorway, bald tyres clinging on to the slip-road camber. And she'd never felt so carefree. Her one-night stand was going on tour.

Late last night, crammed between Indifferent Matt and the scalding radiator, Jo had been desolate to see Harry lifting a hand to wave farewell as he took his leave early. His eyes had stayed fixed on hers for a long time. Peeved, trapped and overheated, she'd looked away. The fact they'd barely spoken yet she felt so betrayed by his departure had shocked her.

The dinner party had ground on through an interminable round of coffee and cognac before Jo had finally felt able to thank her hosts and bid everyone farewell, deflecting Indifferent Matt's stiff-jawed, watch-checking offer to see her into a cab. 'Or we could share one if you're heading in my direction?'

'I'm fine,' she'd told him firmly, only discovering how drunk she was when she stood up. 'I have a travelcard.'

'You should get an Oyster. I have several.'

'I don't think aphrodisiacs will help us here.'

'It's a new travelcard,' he said, in his sinus drone. 'I'm surprised you haven't heard of it.'

'It's a joke. I'm surprised you didn't get it.'

'Ha-ha!' He'd shown remarkably good teeth and asked for her number. She gave him her work one.

Outside, reeling towards Angel tube, Jo had switched on her mobile phone. A text from an unfamiliar number had been sent an hour earlier: *Come to Birdcage on Upper Street. I'll wait there. Harry Inchbold.*

Sliding to a halt by the Underground turnstile, jostled by revellers heading for the last tube, she'd felt as though a dose of adrenalin and caffeine had been injected straight into a main artery . . .

Harry was now negotiating a series of roundabouts on the edge of an industrial West Midlands town, asking her to shout out each road sign as they passed it. When they hit a long stretch of dual carriageway, he sang along loudly to 'I Bet You Look Good On The Dancefloor', hands hammering in time on the steering wheel. He had a remarkably good voice, Jo thought.

'My brother's seriously pissed that I went off with his date last night,' he said.

'I wasn't his date. Fi just sat us together. And I left alone.' She indulged herself by reliving the moment that leaving alone had gained an unexpected bedfellow, a delicious buzz running through her erogenous zones.

'Matt knows my MO. He gave me a hard time when I said I was taking Titch's car this morning. She keeps it in his basement parking space – his is too big to fit in it.'

Now unable to think about anything but sex, Jo found this stupidly funny and battled a cramp of speechless laughter, her raging libido adding to the head rush of silly humour.

But Harry's addictive laugh didn't play along. He pushed

the borrowed glasses up on to his forehead as he negotiated a busy bypass. 'Matt's the clever, successful one,' he insisted. 'He's a good man.'

'I'm not interested in him, and he's not remotely interested in me.' She was disconcerted by the Sinner's fit of conscience.

'He always plays it cool.'

'You play it cooler.'

'If you've had your fingers burned as badly as I have, you keep them in ice all the time.'

Jo was more than happy with sub-zero commitment: she was a frosty cynic. For all the molten passion bubbling over right now, she would not allow herself to get burned again. Harry Inchbold came with a health warning, and she was still dangerously raw.

Sleazily old school by the mid-noughties, Birdcage had been the trendiest late-night drinking hole and pick-up joint in N1 during Jo's single days, its martinis her undoing on more than one occasion. Walking in again had been like stepping into a time warp. Harry was sitting in a booth at the back reading a trashy novel, his unmistakable golden shock of hair and long, lean body marking him out. Jo paused by the door, absorbing a kick of sexual energy and pure freedom.

Then he'd looked up, and the kick went G-force.

'I stole this from our hosts' pin-board.' He held up one of her promotional postcards: it was acting as his bookmark. Her mobile number and email address were printed beneath her business logo. 'And this from their bathroom.' He lifted the book to slot in the postcard. 'Fantastic garbage, full of unlikely sexual encounters. Like this one.'

She'd slid in beside him, a move that somehow threaded their fingers together with a slam of body warmth, their faces turning to start a conversation that died on their lips, eyes unblinking.

'I am very drunk,' she'd warned him, as she studied his mouth, anticipating it meeting hers. 'I don't normally behave like this.'

'Contrary to everything you've no doubt heard, neither do I.' His lips moved in.

Jo had kissed a lot in her life, from the soft good night of her mother through puckering up for great-aunts, the covert learning curve of snogging as a teenager, with lots of tongue action, the niceties of cheek-mwahs on the social scene, the thrill of sharing long, passionate kisses with boy-friends and lovers, most latterly and exclusively Tom, with whom kissing had gradually receded to farewell pecks at the door or routine foreplay in which she tried not to mention that they hadn't cleaned their teeth and she had an early start.

This kiss was different. Without affection or affecta-tion, it was visceral and urgent and the sexiest thing she could remember. Harry Inchbold's mouth, lips, teeth and thoughts had melded with hers as they'd both known they were going to end up in bed together.

They hadn't talked much after that, except the briefest breathless conversation about where they would go. Her flat was out – Tom would be hanging tough in the spare bedroom sending disgruntled texts about the washing-up – and, wherever Harry lived, she had no desire to bump into his brother on the landing at three a.m. Still kissing, in serious danger of undressing one another at the back of the Birdcage bar, they had agreed to find a hotel.

Until that night, Jo had never imagined herself the sort of person to book into a hotel to have sex with a stranger. Signing in and getting from foyer to room seemed totally surreal: the weary, knowing look the receptionist gave them when she asked whether there was any luggage, then issued breakfast and checkout details they didn't take in, the body-slam as soon as the lifts closed and they were kissing again, spilling out moments later and ricocheting along an endless corridor to swipe the door card and fall inside, already tearing off each other's clothes.

Now Harry exited a roundabout too fast, bringing Jo briefly back to the present with a jolt as her body tipped into the car then back towards the door. They were passing a derelict red-brick mill, the sort that would be turned into million-pound flats in London or a boutique hotel. Theirs had been some sort of industrial conversion beside the canal. When she'd held the sill of the peephole window above their bedhead for balance, Harry deep inside her, she'd stared out at the moon on the water.

Her face against the passenger's window grew hotter as she relived the previous night, her body – which should have been sated for ever – already hollow with desperation for more, the memory so vivid of sixteen hotel-room hours' pure physical pleasure, without shame, that she could close her eyes and feel it afresh.

They hadn't gone down for breakfast or checked out. Neither of them had a clue what the room rate was. They didn't even know their room number.

'This will end when we leave here,' Jo had insisted, at which Harry had tutted, covered her lips with his fingers, disappearing to do things between her legs with his tongue that she'd never imagined possible.

After plundering the mini-bar snacks, they'd slept, slotting together perfectly in crumpled sheets. Jo had woken to find him sitting in the chair across the room, watching her. No amount of full-throttle sheet-shaking could diminish the instant, craving need she felt when she saw him.

'Come to Morrow,' he'd said.

She'd stretched luxuriously, smiling. 'I'd quite like to come again today.'

'To Morrow.' He'd said it very carefully this time.

It took her a moment to remember the cottage halfway up a mountain.

'When?' she'd humoured him.

'Now.'

A car horn made her chin jerk up. Her eyelids were heavy, her head lolling. She stifled a yawn as they finally shed the industrial town and drove out into open countryside, the car exhaust deafening. Harry was wearing her glasses on the end of his nose, which seemed to give him optimum focus as they ate up the rural miles.

'Do you want to sleep?' he asked.

'Sure.' She reached down to adjust the seatback a notch and it immediately clunked into a full recline, throwing her horizontal, so she was looking up through the sunroof instead of the windscreen. She might have been at the dentist's, about to have root-canal work.

'Sorry. I should have warned you about that. Titch meant to get it fixed.'

Jo unhooked the seatbelt from her shoulder to struggle upright. 'How did this ever get through its MOT?'

'I don't think it has one. You sleep. I need you rested for Morrow. I'm not going to let you sleep much there.' His hand drifted to her thigh again, making every nerve ending hum for action. Lying back made it ten times more acute as the hand slid up the curve of her body to squeeze her shoulder.

Jo was certain she wouldn't sleep while she felt that horny. When she closed her eyes, she went straight out, as if she'd been anaesthetized.

FRIDAY AFTERNOON

The Rituals

Jo woke up on her horizontal car seat to find Harry kissing her throat, a pleasure so exquisite that she didn't at first think to care that he might lose control of the car. Then she realized that they'd stopped, the engine ticking hotly.

She joined in and the kissing got noisier and more urgent, their eyes meeting as the familiar body rush kicked in. Jo pulled him on to her lap, feeling the eager press of him against her belly, twenty fingers stealing between them to draw back clothes, a warm welcome already clenching inside her.

Vaguely aware that this was public indecency, she put up a reluctant protest. 'I love nothing more than road head, Harry, but we can't fuck in . . . ' she read the neon sign over his shoulder ' . . . Glyn Pugh's car park.'

'Trust me, we're not the first.' He kissed her harder. They were both well aware that they'd do it anywhere right now, the urge too overwhelming to censor.

There was a tap on the window.

'Are you two dogging?' said a small voice with a strong accent, muffled by the glass.

Looking up, they saw a boy pointing a Curly Wurly, standing by the passenger door.

'Just testing the airbags,' Harry told him, as they pulled apart and straightened their clothes. 'You're right,' he breathed regretfully, into Jo's ear. 'We can't fuck in Glyn's car park. This is practically Wales. I need to take you up

32

the aisle first.' That addictive laugh broke out, creasing his eyes. 'Let's get a trolley.'

He got out of the car and strode around to open her door for her, a gesture that would have struck her as affected in most men under fifty but she found hugely appealing in Harry. He seemed to do it without thinking, his lips brushing against hers as she got out. 'Do you have a pound coin?'

Glyn Pugh was a co-operative supermarket that stocked everything from Coco Pops to sheep dip in a hangar-like warehouse behind a discount petrol station. Harry steered Jo inside with the expansive air of an old Hollywood roué taking his latest squeeze to Spago. 'You'll love this place. They sell bacon sliced as thick as Welsh slate and the best walking socks in Shropshire. I'll buy you some.'

'Why would I need walking socks?'

'Morrow's all about walking and talking.'

'I'd rather just have sex.' Jo was shocking herself with her brazenness. She hadn't planned on getting out of bed much, although she'd brought some designer wellies that had been a Christmas gift from her mother, which meant the odd country stroll was covered.

He pulled her behind a pallet of bagged compost by the entrance to share a kiss that seemed to draw their deepest laughter from diaphragm to lips. Fearless, wired and capable of making each other melt with one well-placed finger, they were both high on pheromones, a couple of lust junkies, who found it hard to behave normally in public places.

Emerging to find several voyeuristic shoppers feigning interest in a handwritten Day-Glo orange sign, boasting two for one on dog wormers, Jo mentally fast-tracked from cosmopolitan anonymity to country curiosity. Just three hours earlier, they'd been lying on crumpled sheets in a London hotel, sharing vegetable crisps and vodka, and now they were trolley-pushing together in a hillbilly cash-and-carry on the Welsh border. Agreeing to come along had been so instant that she'd had no expectations beyond the desire to share a bed with Harry for a little longer. Rebellious excitement still caught in her throat each time she breathed. She was never usually so impulsive. Seven years with Tom, five of them cohabiting, had made her risk-averse, and Harry was the perfect therapy – a short, sharp shock of sexual chemistry and high risk. Now even walking socks seemed the sexiest things on earth if Harry was in them.

He was piling a few two-for-one fleeces into the trolley, with long johns, several big bags of kindling and a shrink-wrapped super-king duvet. 'It gets seriously sub up there at night and the beds can be damp until the stove's dried the house out. It's a long way from London.'

Jo imagined pulling it up to their chins against a sub-zero chill as they shivered beneath, dressed in matching long johns and fleeces. She wasn't normally good with extreme cold or artificial fibres – she'd loved the heated luxury and Egyptian cotton of their hotel – yet the thought of lying in bed in walking socks with Harry Inchbold was already exciting the hell out of her.

And as he towed her around the utilitarian aisles, she found it hard to think about anything but being in bed with him. They kissed by a display of mops and, smiling roguishly, Harry brushed the hard pips of her nipples through her dress as they loaded up with bacon and sausages in the chilled section. She slipped a hand beneath his sweater and traced her nails along his spine as they selected freshly baked bread. He pulled her tight to his pelvis as they bent over a freezer choosing ice cream. She cupped the bulge of his crotch as they picked up tinned beans and ketchup.

'We take food very seriously at Morrow,' he said, his hand

covering hers and pushing it tighter against him. 'I can promise the best breakfast in bed you've ever tasted. I hope you have a big appetite.'

Jo felt a sensual kick from taste buds to belly via every erogenous zone. 'Cooking and eating are two of my favourite things.'

His fingers slid through hers as he steered her to a wall cobbled with long-life cartons in a deserted aisle. Pressing his lips to her shoulder, he slipped his free hand beneath her dress. 'It's time to ask how you like your eggs.'

She groaned, delight and bad-joke protest combined.

'Now that I've taken you up the aisle, it's the honourable thing to do,' he dead-panned.

'This practically being Wales,' she agreed solemnly, eyes dancing with his.

Curling together with silent laughter, they felt another hot rush of lust and his fingers briefly slipped under her knicker hem to trace her sweetest contour before sliding reluctantly away as another shopper's trolley rounded the corner.

As they studied a box that boasted the best free-range speckled hen eggs in Shropshire, Jo stretched up and breathed a kiss into his mouth, nipples now like cattle prods against his chest. 'Come with me and I'll show you exactly how I'd like my eggs.'

Taking his hand, she led him to the healthcare display to gather together an ambitious selection of condoms.

'Fuck you.' He cuffed her ears as they shared a laughter-filled kiss.

'That's the general idea.' Again, Jo felt the unfamiliar kick of empowerment.

Eyes narrowing as he spotted a familiar blue tube on the shelf beside the Durex, he tossed it into the trolley. 'We'll need this.'

'I think you'll find I'm pretty well oiled.'

'Not where I'm planning on going.' The kiss was proprietorial now, his smile hard against hers, and her stomach flipped.

Harry paid for everything with a big wad of cash, dismissing her offer to go halves. As they pushed the trolley out to the car, he reached across to stroke her neck, thumb running along her carotid. Her pulse rocketed. Her one-night stand, on tour in a clown car, in bedsocks with speckled eggs waiting, was the sexiest gig of her life.

The low winter sun was starting to set, blinding red on the dusty windscreen as they drove into a town with a ruined castle silhouetted above it, like a painted scenery backdrop. Harry parked at a bad angle on a narrow street, old timbered shops and houses leaning over them, each as different as wizened faces. The place was just a handful of sawdust away from a costume-drama clapperboard.

'The cottage is here?' Jo asked, in surprise, having got the impression it was far more rural.

'Miles away.' He leaped out to open the car door for her again. 'It's Inchbold tradition to take the Ganges' finest offerings to Morrow in greeting, like sacrificing a goat.' He indicated a half-timbered building behind him with elephants etched discreetly in the window glass and a framed menu beside the door. When he led her inside and a wall of hot, spice-infused air hit her, Jo hesitated. She wasn't remotely hungry. The smell of frying cardamom reminded her uneasily of Tom, a curry aficionado who had first seduced her by recreating the food he'd tasted travelling in southern India.

Harry placed their order without glancing at the menu, politely refusing the lager on offer while they waited for the food, instead taking Jo's hand and leading her back outside. 'There's only one place to drink round here.'

In the sharp cool of fast-falling dusk, he led her to a cobbled high street with tatty bunting criss-crossed overhead and old-fashioned shopfronts missing letters, the dusty windows of traditional butcher, baker and greengrocer too covered with posters advertising folk-music nights and postcards offering tree surgeons for her to see inside. The costume-drama location manager would have his work cut out preparing it for Judi Dench to bustle along in a bonnet and hoop skirt. At one end, a medieval inn, the Six Tuns, leaned drunkenly against its neighbour, the girth of its ground-floor cob walls bulging like a beer belly, no two beams parallel in its heavily timbered upper-floor frame.

Inside, it was as crowded as any London pub after office hours, yet the fug of warmth, beer fumes, tobacco smoke, talk and laughter was sweeter and more welcoming. Voices rose and fell, open fires crackled, bodies jostled.

Having swigged water all day to detox, awash with good intentions, Jo willingly broke rank and asked for a vat of sauvignon. But when Harry turned back from the bar, he was holding two brimming pints. He handed her one and clinked rims. Hops filled her nose, another smell that reminded her uncomfortably of Tom. 'I asked for wine.'

'And I ignored you. Try it.'

Had she been on a first date in London – a prospect she'd tentatively revisited in recent weeks – Jo would have been tempted to tip it over his head. Ordering food without consulting her was one thing – he was paying, and she wasn't hungry – but she badly needed wine, disliked real ale and resented being bulldozed. Yet eyeing Harry's golden hair and trying to imagine it doused in beer, she found herself unable to shake the memory of it cool and sweet-smelling in her face, then against her shoulder and sliding across her chest as she came. Smiling, she looked down at the frothy head in the glass.

Harry stepped closer, dipping his face towards hers. 'Shropshire hops fuel everything round here – hay-making, hero-making, baby-making, love-making.'

Cynical London Jo lifted an eyebrow, sensing the line was off pat. But when she glanced up at him, withering remark at the ready, she found that lovely, sexy welcome waiting, a direct challenge to lie back and take the love-making option instead of making trouble.

Not taking her eyes from his, she lifted the glass to her lips and downed the pint in one, then wiped the foam from her lips with the back of her hand. 'Now can I have a glass of wine?'

His laugh made her shiver with victorious pleasure. Its husky sound got her right in the solar plexus. Jo felt the connection between them tighten. 'I'll be right back.' She handed him the empty pint glass and threaded her way to the back of the room, where she found the Gents. The Ladies was by the bar, so she had to push her way to the front again, past a grinning Harry and into a tiled sanctuary of whirring hand-dryers and reflections of a tall, startling brunette, with stubble rash and savagely cropped hair.

Since she'd had her hair shorn, Jo still sometimes struggled to recognize herself. Gone was the long dark cloud that had framed her face since her late teens with only subtle variations in length and colour as fashions changed – straight cut or layered, skunk stripes giving way to under-tinting, a long fringe one year, a topknot the next. Here was something so totally different that her features seemed to have changed, the brown eyes huge, the straight nose longer and less feminine, the mouth stronger and harder, the line of her chin more chiselled, emphasizing the length of her neck and the sharp jut of her shoulders. Her mother hated it, especially when it was matched with the frameless glasses she often wore, although she was too kind to say so, instead making pointed remarks about Jo looking 'intelligent' and 'strong'. Close friends insisted it took years off her and marked her out as fashion forward. Tom seemed scared of it, which was good. Jo had still to get used to it, but she loved how powerful it made her feel.

Today, tufty after so much sex and hurried showering, the eyes beneath it sparkling with secrets, lips swollen from kissing and chin as pink as her cheeks, she decided she liked what she saw. This face – with its familiar lines, freckles, moles and wary smile – was having an adventure. It was the face of a woman with no strings attached.

She looked up as the door swung open, a wall of muscles clenching deep inside her as she imagined Harry dragging her into a cubicle, unable to hold back a moment longer. But it was just a girl with unfeasibly magenta hair who disappeared into a cubicle.

As Jo headed into the one alongside to pee, she suspected the local brew was stronger than it looked. She tried to read a sobering sign on the back of the door, telling chlamydia sufferers they were not alone, but her mind was already drifting back to the hotel bed. Harry's body, so hard and naked and uninhibited, was heaven to explore and bring pleasure to, a new toy she knew she could trade in for something more permanent when she got bored. The Sinner was exactly what she needed right now.

When she returned to the bar, he extricated himself from a group beyond the smoking line. He had a bottle of wine tucked under one arm, a plastic flagon filled with ale under the other. 'Come up to the castle before we lose the light.'

It was a steep climb through narrow, winding streets and along an uneven path skirted with benches for tourists who ran short of puff *en route* to the ruin. Breathless, they abandoned the grog at the bottom of a flight of narrow stone steps and scaled the crumbling battlements to admire the view, a misty panorama of fields, hills and mountains, the last pink rays fading on the horizon.

Arms wrapped around her, chin on resting on her shoulder, Harry pointed at a distant hill, its top still dusted with snow above the treeline. 'Morrow's there. Right on the border. Part of its garden's in Wales.'

'That's a long way.' She pressed back against him.

'Twenty minutes at most.' His hands slipped beneath her coat, fingertips already drawing the beat from her heart to her skin. She could feel him swelling against her, and turned to kiss him. Twenty minutes' drive felt like eternity. And yet they kissed on, not noticing the sun sink away or remembering their takeaway sitting on a counter, still kissing as dog-walkers pulled their sniffing charges away from the abandoned booze, and a rusting Golf left on a sidestreet, its handbrake not fully engaged, rolled gently back into a lamp-post and lost its bumper.

FRIDAY EVENING

The Arrival

Harry drove, possessed by the foot-down, homing-missile recklessness of one who knew exactly where he was going. Jo held on to her seatbelt as they rattled along a confusing series of high-hedged, hilly single-track lanes. The Golf's headlights bounced off overgrown verges and occasional salt crates, its wheels almost lifting off the grassy tarmac round endless twisting dog-legs. She half expected to take off completely and find a few meteors and satellites glancing off the wing-mirrors. It was far too dark to see any of Morrow's surroundings when they took a sharp left and rattled across a cattle grid on to a track that led up through a field, ghostly sheep shapes bleating away, the black silhouette of forest high above them as they snaked up an unmade track.

'Almost there.'

Jo had absolutely no idea where she was, but she knew they were a long way from civilization. All she cared about was getting there soon. The tension that had been building since London was now at melting point: they had only to brush fingers to feel a body rush. Right now, she felt as though she was sitting on several sex aids and a washing-machine in spin cycle as the car slithered and bounced beneath them.

The incline grew steeper and the engine groaned along deep ruts, wheels spinning over mud and loose stones, splashing through puddles, almost grinding to a halt several times as Harry changed gear, cursed and hammered the throttle. At last, they were skirting the woods and a gate appeared. As Harry jumped out to open it, Jo could just make out the corner of a stone building balanced between woods and hill. They drove behind it and parked. Apart from the headlights illuminating a crumbling stone porch, it was completely dark.

Leaving the headlights on, Harry crossed in front of the car and opened Jo's door. He took her hand, his grip tight and warm. 'Welcome to Morrow.'

'Thank God.' She whistled with relief, smiling up at his shadowed face. 'There was a point back there when I thought tomorrow would never come.'

Harry didn't laugh.

As soon as she stepped from the car, he was kissing her. His passion took her breath away. They kissed in a blind dance to the door, at which he stabbed random keys until it opened and they fell inside.

Harry groped for a light switch, but nothing happened. Jo hardly cared as he pulled up her skirt and lifted her to his hips, kissing her throat and carrying her to something that might have been a bed or a sofa – it hardly mattered. Cold upholstery, a knot of brocade, a scratch of wool blanket. Tipped back on to it, she was perfectly positioned for him to unbuckle his belt, roll on a condom and slide straight in.

The relief was ecstasy, too intense for anything more than throaty laughter as she turned her head into the heavy damask.

Harry stayed inside her for a long time afterwards. Senses intensified by the dark, Jo could feel their heartbeats slowing in tandem, his warmth sinking through her. The lumpy cushions beneath her backside were cold, and there was a strong smell of damp, but the heat and aroma of Harry's body were as comforting as a hot, pine-scented bath.

'Welcome to Morrow.' He lifted his head from her shoulder and she could just make out a glint of blond hair and a smile in the half-light. 'I'm a much better person here, I promise. Stay right there and I'll light a fire.'

He wrapped her in the scratchy blanket from whatever they were lying on and crashed around the room. Tempted to say that she didn't need him to be nicer – the Sinner was perfect company for this weekend – Jo pulled the blanket tighter, realizing just how cold it was in the cottage. 'Is there a power cut?'

'Trip's probably popped again,' he explained, falling over something.

'Is there a torch anywhere?'

'There are lots of torches here. Just no batteries. Ah!' The familiar rattle of a match box was followed by a strike and a low glow illuminating his hand as he held out the flame towards a shelf where wax-encrusted candle-holders jostled with hurricane lamps. Several match strikes later and the shelf was glowing with light, revealing an old stone wall, an oak ceiling veined with gnarled beams, and an inglenook fireplace into which Harry now stooped to wrestle open the door of a wood-burning stove. 'We need heat.' He looked around, then headed outside again, the open door letting in a rush of cold air and a slant of angled light from the car's headlamps, brighter than the fast-flickering candles. Jo saw chiaroscuro furniture briefly revealed like sleeping zoo animals before the door banged shut against the wind, shadows fell and the candle flames guttered.

She stood up, straightening her clothes beneath the blanket, breathing in the tang of mildew, far stronger now Harry wasn't close, undercut with the sharp reek of wood ash and disturbed dust. The deep windowsills had battered old shutters closed over the casements. She wasn't sure what she'd expected Morrow to be – not quite roses-around-the-door, but certainly somewhere she could see her way around. Yet, at this exact moment, she didn't want to be anywhere else.

When Harry came inside with a bag of kindling and a pile of *Evening Standard*s to light the fire, she crouched behind him to scrunch paper into tinder.

'I should explain the rules now you're here,' he said, as they crammed newsprint balls into the stove.

'Rules?' She sat back on her heels, seeing his blond hair glowing in the hurricane lamp, face shadowed. 'If it involves masks, ropes and safe words, it'll take a lot more than a blue tube of gel from Hugh Pym's to get me involved.'

'It's Glyn Pugh,' he corrected, a hint of that magical laugh gruff in his throat. 'And I promise I'm not into trussing women up like chickens.' He laid kindling on top of the paper and wedged in a firelighter. 'I'm quite good at trussing chickens like chickens, if Efon, the grumpy farmer, brings one for the pot, and I can cook a mean guinea fowl – they run wild round here. In fact it's mostly wild round here, but Morrow has a few house rules.

'There's no phone here and no television, and definitely no mobile signal. The outside world stays outside. It's always been that way.' He lit a spill and looked at her over it, his eyes reflecting the flame, doubling it back at her. 'That means no baggage you unpack can be taken home, Joactually.'

She smiled gratefully 'I always pack light.'

The spill caught against the paper. 'Emotional baggage.'

'That's what I mean. I'm not looking for anything long term, Harry.'

'Then we're a contradiction in terms, you and me.' His eyes glittered, as they slid towards hers.

Jo watched him closely, assessing the handsome, deadpan face, the fire's shadows playing against deep grooves that ran from the corners of his eyes to his jaw. She was pretty certain he was joking: there was a devil somewhere beneath the allure, as dark-humoured as he could be disarming.

'Work *always* stays outside,' he went on, the Sinner laying down the law. 'At Morrow we eat a lot, drink more, rest as much as we want and play hard. We're allowed to play dirty, but what's said between these walls stays here, and nobody betrays another's confidence.'

Jo felt a liberating uplift of relief to have it laid out in the open, grateful to know there'd be no repercussions, although she still found Harry hard to read, his seductive intensity at odds with hippie house rules.

Soon a roaring orange light brightened the room from the hearth, revealing a tatty red woven rug littered with old plates and bottles.

'Somebody should have fucking tidied this shit,' Harry cursed, gathering them up.

'Who was the last one here?'

'Me.' He stood up and headed through a door into a dark room, which, from the sound of a hollow metal bin lid clattering on flagstones, was the kitchen. He marched back in, grabbed one of the hurricane lamps and disappeared again.

Reluctant to leave the fireside until her bones felt warmer, Jo edged closer to the stove, determined to keep her head cool even if her body craved heat. She had divorced mind from body during her long, slow separation from Tom. And that body, so long neglected, wanted every bold inch of Harry Inchbold. It was this weekend's sole purpose. The secret was not to think about anything else. Be selfish for once.

A light came on overhead: Harry must have reset the trip switch. She had a brief snapshot of a room that could have come straight from the set of the gloomiest Thomas Hardy epic before it was plunged back into darkness and she heard a loud curse from behind a wall.

The fire was already burning itself out. Having aced at fire-pit building on far-flung beach-party retreats, Jo grabbed the protective mitt and opened the door to feed in some more kindling and firelighters, blowing on it all encouragingly, then closing the door and sliding the vents as far open as they would go. There were a couple of logs at the bottom of the basket beside the stove and she grabbed one to feed in, opening the door again. A fireball of her own making leaped out, blindingly bright and hot against her face. She let out an alarmed shriek and slammed the door. The smell of singed hair was overpowering. Her crop was already short enough.

'Jesus! What happened? Are you okay?' Harry rushed in, accompanied by more clattering of falling bin lids and furniture.

'Fine. Just over-stoked the fire.'

He leaned down with the hurricane lamp held aloft and examined the damage. 'Does it hurt?'

'No.'

'Did you have eyelashes before?'

'Very long ones!' She was offended he hadn't noticed.

'They're not now, and your eyebrows are pretty much gone.'

'No!'

'It's a very sexy look.' He kissed the charred remnants.

'Where's the bathroom? I need a mirror and a light, and quite possibly an ambulance.'

'Behind the kitchen, but there's no power here until I find fuse wire. I hope you're not afraid of the dark.'

'Of course not,' she covered his eyes with her hands, 'just of being scarred for life . . . and wearing long johns.'

'They'll keep you warm, unlike eyebrows.' He started kissing her wrists. 'You taste fantastic.'

'Flame-grilled?'

'Slightly caramelized.' He took a firm hold of her wrists and laid her back on the hearth rug. 'Christ, I'm famished.'

Kissing Harry was like drinking pure chocolate, the most moreish of pleasures. Eventually they came up for air. Laughing, Jo freed her wrists. She was starving too.

The much-stoked fire was soon hissing with damp logs, and they settled in front of it to feast on the Best Indian Takeaway in Shropshire, forked straight from the trays, mouths exploding with spices. When Harry couldn't find a corkscrew, Jo caved in and drank more beer, which complemented the peppery sweet heat perfectly. She couldn't remember eating so greedily in years. It was slightly shaming.

Harry ate just as indulgently, feeding her, kissing her, sharing the joy of the feast until it no longer felt shameful but simply the most aphrodisiac meal she'd ever eaten. 'Who needs Ludlow's Michelin stars when you have this?' she said, pigging out on butter naan.

'I've always loved the first night here.' He fed her a forkful of Malabar chicken. 'We need music.'

'There's no power.'

'That's pretty common here.'

He took a hurricane lamp and disappeared through a doorway set in thick wooden panels on the opposite side of the room to the kitchen, narrow stripes of light dancing behind its gaps and knots until he emerged with an old wind-up gramophone. 'The needle's probably buggered, but we always used to play this when a fuse blew.'

A scratchy Bach concerto was soon hissing as much as the logs.

'Is that a wooden wall?' Jo studied the panels' deeply veined grain, so beautiful in the firelight.

'Oak plank.' He nodded. 'You used to see them a lot in old Welsh cottages, but most were ripped out. Morrow's hardly been touched since a shepherd was shacked up here three centuries ago.'

'Have you been coming here long?'

'Not three hundred years.' He looked at her, fire-lit face speculative, one cheek hollowing as he caught it between his teeth with a sucking noise. 'But that's my baggage.'

'We're here for the weekend, Harry. We have to unpack something.' She sucked in both her own cheeks, comedy-faced. 'All I'm asking about is the cottage's history.'

He cracked the last poppadum and gave her a piece. 'Dad and his brother bought it for loose change in the seventies, along with a friend. It belonged to the local estate before that.'

'And you came here a lot as a kid?'

'All the time. Every holiday and most weekends in summer. I love this place. There was a period in my twenties when I practically lived here. Just not recently.'

'Since you moved to the States?'

'I've definitely left that bag outside.' His face darkened.

She held up her hand. 'You're clear through Customs, sir.'

'Don't break the rules.' He rubbed his forehead on his arm and looked up at her though his lashes.

She wasn't sure if the gesture was deliberate or not, but she sensed from his stillness that it was more defensive than coy. Either way, it made her insides twist with desire. He was beyond beddable. 'A weekend's a long time to talk about oak panelling.'

'We'd better stop talking, then.' His lips met hers.

Their bodies were as warm as toast now. With the roaring fire throwing out heat, and spices smouldering inside them, Harry laid Jo bare on the plush new duvet and stopped her talking for a very long time, forcing her mind and body far apart. If she'd stopped to question what she was doing – and the irresponsibility of doing it with a near-stranger – she might have doubted, but Jo wasn't about to stop to think while she was so full of Harry. This was her one-night stand that refused to fall. They were both on the rebound, at its highest apex, both knowing that they would crash down again, neither wanting company when that plunge came. They were riding the curve of a purely tem-porary arrangement. The fact they were in the same place on life's battlefield made the connection extraordinary. The sex was the most passionate and uninhibited she'd ever had.

When Harry came, that angry intimacy, he cried out a name – not hers – and she curled her arms around him, tight and reassuring.

'Fuck – sorry.' He jerked away. 'That was unforgivable.'

'I'd be much more freaked out if it had been my name.'

His face turned back towards hers, cheekbone glowing in the orange light, his eyes black shadows as he ran a finger across her lips. 'You are amazing.' He kissed her brows. 'Remind me what yours is again?'

She hit him over the head with a cushion. 'It's Don'tfuckmeoff, Basicallyharry.'

When they finally curled and nudged their way back to back on a fireside bed fashioned from sofa cushions, antici-pating sleep, he reached a hand over his shoulder, fingertips finding hers. 'Whatever we unpack this weekend, our crap stays here when we leave. Agreed?'

'I'm only planning to unpack a toothbrush, Harry.'

'Good girl.'

As they were dropping off the ledge towards oblivion, she added sleepily, 'And I should point out that I have no crap.'

'You so do.' He sighed, sleep claiming him as Jo found her eyes wide open again.

SATURDAY MORNING

The Cooked Breakfast

Jo woke freezing cold, her back aching and her neck cricked. It was very dark and very quiet. She rolled over, finding herself tangled in the twisted duvet on the floor. Light was stealing in through the gaps in the planked window shutters, illuminating columns of dusty air. Kicking her legs free, she groaned at the twinge shooting from her much-parted hips to her battered vertebrae. No amount of power yoga could prepare one for so much sex followed by sleeping on a hard floor. At eighteen she might have got away with it at music festivals and student parties, but she was twice that age now with a twelve-hundred-thread Egyptian cotton addiction and an old netball injury that flared up in the cold.

Eyes adjusting to the gloom, she made out a Welsh dresser laden with chipped plates, high shelves sagging with pottery, and a scrubbed table surrounded by spindle chairs. The room's rough stone walls were chequered with small, heavy-framed paintings at contrary angles, and the rugs on the flagstones were more weave than wool. The flabby camelback sofa – scene of last night's first blind, breathless coupling – was spewing its horsehair stuffing beneath layers of threadbare throws and blankets. Jo decided she liked it a lot: it had history, heart and, most importantly, Harry Inchbold.

Sitting up, she stretched stiffly, wondering where he was. The curry containers were still piled on a tray in the corner, attracting the attention of a brace of sleepy flies. The strong smell of damp and woodsmoke was now cut through with Indian spices and beer. The stove had gone out and cold draughts were chasing each other around the room. Jo had goosebumps, burned eyebrows, stubble rash from her chin to her thighs and she reeked of sex, but she couldn't remember waking up feeling so carefree in years, and she was also as horny as hell.

'Harry?'

When no answer came, she went in search of a bathroom, passing through a gloomy kitchen in which battered worktops, shelves and butcher's blocks leaned against one another like seasick sailors, the misty, deep-silled windows revealing dark tree trunks just inches away. A warped door in a whitewashed stone wall led down precarious wooden steps to a freezing cell of a bathroom. The smell of damp was almost asphyxiating there, and an ominous sound of rushing water was coming from the floor, along with scratching overhead. The power was still off, but a tiny moss-blotched window cast enough light for her to examine her face in the rusted mirror above the basin as she washed her hands and face in icy water. Harry was right: her eyebrows – expensively threaded arches of perfection yesterday – were as tattered as the rugs on which she'd slept, her lashes abbreviated with pale curled ends, like miniature shepherds' crooks, her nose and forehead glowing as red as her chin. It wasn't her greatest look, but her eyes shone like onyx and her smile wouldn't budge as she spat and rinsed.

Shivering, she headed back to find more layers.

Her case, still packed, was on a scuffed Windsor chair, only raided for her toothbrush last night, its contents as twisted and jumbled as her conscience should have been. Stooping beside it, she brooded over Harry's comment about emotional baggage staying there, if it was unpacked, and his swift rebuff when she'd said she had none. Had he seen right through her final fling, past the no-strings passion to a heart still on ice? Well, she could hold a mirror right back at him, she decided, lifting her chin. They could both be vampires with no reflection this weekend.

She had goosebumps the size of pebbledash. Cursing her speed-packing, she burrowed past her sexiest undies, but unearthed nothing more substantial than Joseph joggers and a few colourful ballet wraps. She put them all on, then turned her attention to the stove, cramming in newspaper and kindling to get it going again. Leaving it to putter brightly to life, keeping what was left of her eyebrows at a safe distance, she set about pulling open the shutters, anticipating more close-up tree trunks.

'*Chrrrrrist!*' She gaped through a filthy window in astonishment, then rushed outside.

Peeping out of the edge of its camouflage of woods, Morrow seemed to defy gravity as it looked across the valley beneath. The views were a staggering panorama of green disappearing into the misted depths far below, beyond which the Black Mountains rose in a beckoning quest to gather magical rings, slay dragons and find the last unicorn.

She turned back to the cottage, guarded by its army of trees, like a warrior warlock, its handsome stone face the tawny colour of a brindle blue greyhound. To one side, a stream tumbled through deep stone banks, which explained the gushing sound in the bathroom, its course careering just a few feet away from the cottage walls. To the other side, the track they had driven along in darkness last night curled away through the gate and on around the edge of the woods, where it dropped out of sight as though inviting suicidal drivers over a cliff. No wonder the Golf had struggled up it – Harry must have driven like a rally pro. She wandered across to admire the tyre marks.

That was when she finally registered that something was missing.

'*Oooooo*kay,' she muttered to herself. 'There's no car.'

Jo's ability to stay cool-headed was legendary among her friends, although in truth she was simply better at hiding panic than most, with a practised line in self-denial and sarcasm.

She tightened the knots on her triple layer of ballet tops and ran a brief thirty-something-woman-stranded-in-the-middle-of-nowhere-with-lots-of-flimsy-underwear scenario through her head, quickly dismissing it. While Harry had struck her from the start as excitingly reckless, this place was clearly very special to him, far more so than Jo was, and he was unlikely to abandon it to her.

Teeth hammering together uncontrollably, cold sinking into her bones, Jo headed inside to wrap a blanket round her shoulders and add a log to the fire in the stove. She pulled the rest of the shutters open, each revealing a mile-high view of dawn breaking over Wales that made her feel like an air hostess whipping up blinds in a jumbo jet. She dodged dropping dead flies and spiders as she prised apart the warped old wood.

The cottage was transformed by light spilling in, awakening it from its rest, revealing that the dozens of picture frames at wonky angles on the walls contained photographs, not paintings, as she'd thought, all apparently taken by the same person.

She moved between them, captivated by the saturated colour. Here were intimate, funny family studies taken with warmth and a remarkable eye for composition. At art school, she'd loved learning about the creative innovators, and had developed a fondness for the work of New York photographer Elliot Erwitt, whose ironic, absurd black-and-white vignettes of everyday life peppered the walls of her

Crouch End flat. These little pictures struck her as Erwitt in colour. They made her smile as she moved between them around the room.

Her ears had tuned into the constant rhythm of noises floating in from outside now – birdsong, lambs bleating, the wind through the trees. It was far from the silence she thought she'd woken up to and, instead, sounded like one of the relaxation CDs sold out of jukebox-style display units at garden centres.

She stroked the beautiful old wood of the oak dividing screen as she opened the door leading through it, so low that she was forced to duck, and found herself in a room walled with bowed bookshelves, hammocked with spiders' webs and crammed with faded, woven hardback spines, a clean square amid the thick dust on a leather-topped desk marking out where the gramophone had been sitting. It was obviously some sort of study. There was a huge, mad-eyed stag's head over the fireplace and mouse droppings on the checked rug. She backed hastily out.

A narrow stone staircase beyond the fireplace wound upstairs in such a steep, tight twist it was like climbing up through a tree trunk. Here, two interconnected rooms in the eaves of the cottage roof had tiny low windows at ankle height. The first room was almost entirely filled with an old carved-oak bed, beckoning naughtiness from its ticking mattress, the second tightly packed with two little brass ones. Ducking through the dividing door, Jo saw the cruck trusses, which bowed overhead and had to be half a millennium old; ancient arches that had protected shepherds from Shropshire winters for centuries. The dividing beams were littered with medieval carpenter's marks, like runes. On the doorframe between the two rooms she spotted far more modern marks, deeply carved notches striping their way up the bevelled wood.

There were initials scratched alongside them. Jo ran her finger along one, wondering whether they belonged to Harry's sexual conquests.

Hearing an approaching car engine, accompanied by the familiar boom of the Arctic Monkeys, she stooped to look through the tiny *Alice in Wonderland* window. The battered Golf was rallying its way back up the track, fish-tailing madly. There appeared to be two dinner plates wedged on the dashboard. At the wheel, Harry was ducking flying bacon rashers as the car bounced through potholes on the final ascent.

By the time she made it downstairs, he was carrying the plates inside with a debonair swagger. 'Full English, courtesy of Owen and Cerys at the village B&B.' His voice was distorted because his teeth were clamped on something. 'As I can't get the power on to cook you breakfast in bed,' he went on, 'this is the best alternative. And they gave me this.' He gestured to the piece of wire in his mouth, like a tango dancer's rose.

'Do you need to pick a lock? Floss?'

'It's fuse wire. It'll turn us on.'

She stretched up to take the wire between her own teeth, a modern-day Carmen. 'I think we're pretty good at that without electricity.'

As their lips brushed, the click was almost audible, as though an unseen hand had pulled down a lever on several thousand volts of sexual energy.

The breakfast slid off the plates as they slammed together and five ballet wraps came off in quick succession, a stumbling waltz taking them to the lumpy sofa where her joggers slipped away as more twisting, kissing and undressing moved them to the duvet abandoned in front of the hearth where the stove had already burned its morning logs to embers.

'You have no idea how hard it was not to wake you up and do this earlier.' He pulled his sweater over his head.

'I love it that you wanted to bring me breakfast in bed.' She laughed, rolling over to unstick a slice of toast from one buttock.

'Breakfast's on me.' He removed a bacon rasher from under one elbow. 'And on you.' He kissed away the toast crumbs and butter as, together, they enjoyed the full monty without eating a scrap.

Although she was driven to the very edge of bliss, Jo couldn't come, her body still deep-set with cold and stiffness. Harry was willing to keep trying for as long as it took – she had a feeling he'd be more than happy to go all day – but they were both famished and caffeine-starved. 'It honestly was wonderful. You are just the most amazing lover. Were you kidnapped by the sex trade at a young age?'

'I was married for ten years,' he said simply, rubbing her goose-bumped shoulders.

Jo hugged herself for warmth, shrugging back into her ballet wraps. The mention of a marriage had been like an Arctic blast, changing the atmosphere in the room. Her mind was racing with questions – how old were you? What was your wife like? What went wrong? – and she felt illogically jealous, but she had enough self-control to quash such knee-jerk gaucherie.

Harry said nothing for a long time. There were flints in his eyes, the dark grooves in his cheeks like scars in the gloomy light. Eventually he stood up. 'I'm going to hot-wire this place and make us coffee.'

His already blackening mood disintegrated at lightning speed when he discovered they'd dropped the fuse wire amid the abandoned breakfast. The torrent of expletives made Jo turn to him in surprise, then growl under her breath as she heard the C-word. 'Whoa!' She held up a hand. '*Nobody* says that around me unless they have one themselves.'

'I have a foul temper. I'm sorry.' He turned to her. His eyes were apologetic, but the flints were still in them, their focus sliding away. 'I just need that wire.' He cursed afresh as he stooped over the floor, scanning it for a glint of metal. 'I can't believe I fucking dropped it. Fucking twat!' The expletives started up again.

'You're right, you've got a filthy temper.' She got up to help him look. 'And, no, being one does not count. Nor does being a twat, for that matter.'

'They're the same thing, and, much as I love to feast on yours, I need hot food,' he snapped. 'I get bloody-minded without it.'

She was irritated by his anger, but wary enough to underplay it, sensing this might be a trace of smoke over a very active volcano. 'So start by eating your words. This is a short-order love affair, Harry. Forget breakfast.'

For a moment he stared at her intently, and she thought she'd made him think, but then she realized she'd merely given him an idea. 'Maybe you swallowed it. You had it in your mouth.'

'Are we talking about sex or the fuse wire now?'

'Fuck! It has to be here!' He kicked the sofa hard, sending up a cloud of dust into the streaks of sunlight, then carried on shouting at the floor as his eyes raked it.

Jo began gathering her clothes. His violent mood swing unsettled her, reminding her that she was in the middle of nowhere with a stranger, their physical intimacy no substitute for trust. She didn't know Harry Inchbold at all, but the 'Sinner' nickname should have been a giveaway. She sensed his boredom threshold was low and, with such a hot, reckless head, it made him potentially ruthless. If he got this angry about missing breakfast, how did he react to the big stuff?

She went to her bag to grab fresh knickers, wondering whether it was time to stage a quick exit. Spotting her best underwear, she hesitated, craving more freefalling, lost-weekend seduction.

Then she cocked her head. While he was still illogically angry, Harry was now yelling, 'Bacon! Eggs! Black pudding! Sausage!' with increasing frustration. 'Christ, I'm hungry!'

Zipping up her bag, Jo weighed her options. While her body was still popping for pleasure, she badly needed ibuprofen and a shower. She was holed up in the middle of nowhere with a foul-mouthed Sinner who made her laugh and come, the connection between them as hot and fragile as the little wires housed in the fuse box he couldn't mend. She didn't want to lose it, but she didn't want to give it a chance to burn through.

Harry gave up searching for the wire. 'Fuck it, we'll go to Rossbury. The market's on today. You'll love it.'

Jo picked up her weekend bag, the alarm bells now doubling at the prospect of some sightseeing that sounded uncomfortably date-like. 'I might jump on a train there.'

He took her bag from her, head brushing close, making Jo wonder how he could still smell so good now they'd practically gone feral. 'You didn't come,' he said, in a husky undertone, not moving. 'You can't go until you've come.'

'It's fine. I'm easy come easy go.'

'Then I'll make it very easy for you.'

Click. The power lever went down again. Before she could check herself, Jo turned her head to breathe in the scent of his blond hair. Then his lips landed with force against hers.

How could kissing somebody she knew was so bad feel so good? And how could she let Harry take over totally between her legs with his tongue and fingers, doing things that brought her to the very edge of her comfort zone yet took her body over the apex of its sexual ferris wheel, plunging weightlessly down faster and harder than ever before?

Jo had to hand it to Glyn Pugh's long johns. They were easy access and Harry wasn't going to let her stop coming now that she'd started.

'Do you really want to go back to London today?' he demanded, straightening up, fingers still curling in and out of her, making the ferris wheel spin ever faster.

'No – yes – no – oh, fuck, fuck, fuck.'

'Now who should eat her words?'

SATURDAY LATE MORNING

The Market

As they drove away from Morrow, Jo caught her breath at the plunging descent. Now in sharp spring sunlight, she could see the full, twisting length of the track they had climbed up in the dark, a deep scar cutting through acid-green pasture, the brook racing downhill alongside it in a slalom between rocks and grassy hummocks on which sheep kept sentry, watching them pass.

Jo looked up at the trees to her left, above which a steep stony peak curved to a dome, like an egg in a knitted green cosy.

'What's that big hill called?' she asked Harry, who was riffling through CDs in the doorwell, the car veering towards the brook.

'Mawr Vron.'

'Meaning?'

'It roughly translates as "big hill".' He glanced up and straightened the steering wheel just in time to stop them careering into the water. 'They're nothing if not literal around here.'

He slotted a CD into the stereo and the Kaiser Chiefs started singing 'Everyday I Love You Less And Less'.

It made Jo think about Tom and his spare-room siege, a blade of dread working its way beneath her ribs, like a knife shucking an oyster shell, as she contemplated returning to Crouch End. She looked back at Big Hill as the car rattled over the cattle grid and on through the slalom lanes, suddenly longing to climb it. Then it disappeared behind the trees and they drove through a village – if half a dozen cottages and a chapel could be counted as such – with a small stone pub called the Hare and Moon perched prettily on a riverbank.

'I'll take you for a drink there later, if you're still around,' Harry promised. 'It's been owned by the Thomas family for as long as I can remember. As kids, we used to lead the landlord's boys astray with our wicked London ways. Roy, who runs it now, still hasn't forgiven me for the night I tried to pass off one of my uncle's unfiltered Gitanes as a Camberwell Carrot.'

'When I was a student, I once gave my parents my flatmate's hash cakes by mistake,' Jo remembered, grateful for nostalgia. 'Mum kept having to stop the car on the A4 because she was giggling too much to drive.'

'I bet you were sweet as a student – all jumble-sale clothes and oversized glasses.'

'You were spying on me,' she grumbled. 'I was a late starter with a flat chest and big braces. Does that count as emotional baggage?'

'Just a vest or two. I like it. We're in a car. You have your bag with you. Might as well look through it to pass the time.' He glanced left and caught her eye. 'I'm particularly interested in your underwear. Stay another night and show it off.'

Jo drank in his face, the dark blue eyes intent with sexual promise. They both knew why they were there, she reminded herself. She had no desire to walk away from this adventure just yet. Harry was addictive to be around, and she longed for a repeat of the sensational thing he'd just done to her in the cottage. 'How can I resist a night at the Hare and Moon?' she said lightly.

'Unpack something else.' His lazy, husky voice made it sound more like a smooth sexual command than small talk.

'I told you, I travel light.'

'So unpack light. What are your parents like? Apart from being hash addicts, obviously.'

She looked across at him curiously, wondering what he was playing at. The music was so loud she practically had to shout her answers, but that made it seem less intense than tell-me-about-yourself date talk, abbreviating everything to soundbites. It felt strangely liberating, which she suspected was half his intention.

'One of each. Dad was an engineer, Mum a district nurse – the old-fashioned sort who drove round the countryside seeing patients.'

'You didn't grow up in London, then?'

'Just outside Bath. Mum still lives there.'

'And your dad?'

'He died last year.'

'Christ, I'm sorry.'

Jo stared out of the window. She was grateful that he didn't ask more. Shouting, 'Huge heart attack out walking the dog – would have been almost instant, they say!' over the Kaiser Chiefs predicting a riot was not a sexy soundbite. 'Your turn,' she muttered. 'Where did you grow up?'

'Highbury.'

She waited for more, but it didn't come. 'That's not even a sock! Is this like a game of strip poker in which one loser takes off their jumpsuit while the other removes an earring? In which case, I don't want to play.'

He said nothing, driving on with the music blaring, the black mood still circulating. In unpacking terms, Jo realized, Harry was emotional lost luggage.

*

Occupying a river valley where Shropshire met Powys and Herefordshire, Rossbury was on a different scale from Craven Castle, its tall Georgian buildings grouped along wide thoroughfares, a street market stretching from ornate clock tower to corn exchange across a wide square.

Harry made straight for a van selling bacon rolls and ate two in the time it took Jo's to cool enough for her to bite into it. The smile that burst out of him as soon as he'd eaten was like arc lights over a stage.

'I'm afraid I always chew people out when I'm hungry.' He wiped his lips, watching her indulgently. 'That was almost the best thing I've tasted all day,'

'You didn't chew me out.' Flustered, she abandoned her bacon roll half eaten.

That intense look again. 'My appetite for you won't change however much I eat, as you'll find out later.'

'I might go home, remember?' she said, still smarting from the car journey.

With his intoxicating laugh ringing out, Harry took her hand and steered her along the market stalls. 'My parents, Viv and Gerry, still live in the same house I grew up in,' he told her, without prompting, 'with books piled up the stairs, and attic rooms so crammed with old LPs and clothes that nobody's been able to get in there since the late eighties. They're cava socialists. I grew up to the sound of wine corks being pulled and pen nibs clicking over a fresh *Guardian* crossword. Dad still teaches part time, Mum works in market research. They refuse to retire or to move, much to Matt's irritation. Dad has MS,' he explained. 'The house is totally unsuited to his needs, but he thinks adapting is giving in. When they put in a stair lift, he bolted a wooden veg box to it to carry drinks up to the drawing room.' His tone was sardonic but admiring.

As they paused to test different-flavoured fudge slices, Jo felt curiosity steal through her once more. 'You're one of three children?'

'Yes. Titch is an actress posing as a waitress and a pain in the arse. Matt, as you know, is the golden boy. You?'

'I have an older sister. She's a lawyer on a baby break. They live in Harrogate.'

We're unpacking cotton basics, she thought, starting to relax again. Safe little items of no great personal consequence, the been-there-got-the-T-shirt bullet points of middle-class upbringing. After ripping off one another's underwear so often in quick succession, it felt strangely polite and formal to chat about education, music, pets and foreign travel – small-talk smalls – subjects that occupied them from stall to stall, sampling chutneys and flatbreads and cured meats.

'Dog called Amber . . . You?'

'Cat called Tab, who loved acid house, as did I . . . You?'

'I was an Enya-loving sad act, but "S-Express" was the print-room anthem at Goldsmiths College . . . you?'

'Dropped out at sixth form when Bon Jovi was still "Livin' On A Prayer".'

Beneath striped awnings, the stallholders of Rossbury market sold everything from fresh fish to lampshades, home-made cakes to dog beds, quince jelly to jewellery. Wandering between the stalls, Jo and Harry neatly unpacked and folded parallel childhoods, yet their desire for one another's bodies remained far stronger than any interest in the fabric of their lives.

The joint shopping trip no longer felt uncomfortably like a date: it was a delicious debrief. This is who I'm sleeping with, Jo realized, a sardonic, clever Londoner, whose laugh and lust I seek out, like a cat's purr. Nevertheless, the increased familiarity made her jumpy about proprietorial displays in public, however closely locked together their bodies were in private. When Harry put his arm round her, asking if she was warm enough, she shrugged it off awkwardly. 'Toasty!'

Having rejected the fleece-and-long-johns combo in favour of her ballet wraps, cord skirt and the trendy parka she'd worn down from London, she should have been freezing, but being with Harry gave her a charged glow that pumped out plenty of kilowatts.

They unpacked more small facts as they shared their love of cooking. Jo was an inveterate traveller who tried local food wherever she went and picked up recipes and ideas, no spice too strong, no meat too exotic. Harry had been brought up on fresh local produce, a farmers'-market nut whose years in America hadn't obliterated his belief in short food miles, quality stock and strong provenance: 'The farmers around here produce the most fantastic meat and cheese. Just taste the fresh air in this.' He fed her a sliver of Shropshire Blue, as sharp and salty as the taste of a lover's skin. His eyes were looking right into her, tasting her too, until they were forced to step apart and move on, overpowered by an attraction they couldn't yet control.

Nor could Jo control her body, sated and aching after bending every which way with his. As they ducked between canopies, her back muscles locked.

'I'm not sleeping on the floor again,' she muttered, trying to maintain her dignity while croning along at forty-five degrees to the ground.

'You're not sleeping much at all tonight.' He ran his hand beneath her buttocks making her straighten up with a yelp. Osteopaths take note, she thought giddily.

They tracked down a stall selling bedding, admiring the garish displays of duvet covers, pillow slips and quilts, their eyes getting into bed together again, laughter infectious as

Harry added the tackiest black satin covers he could find to their pile of Egyptian cotton, along with a sequin-trimmed mosquito net. Jo stifled a jaw-breaking yawn as he paid.

'We need the coffee-bean man,' he steered her onwards, 'but he's only ever here first thing. My parents used to get up at dawn to come and buy six months' supply to take back to London. They swore he ground his arabica with uppers.'

'Could be right. You can hide narcotics in coffee grounds to fool sniffer dogs. Most crack dens probably smell like Starbucks. I bet you grew up with a cafetière on the go in every room.'

'Two,' he admitted. 'My parents have very different opinions on coffee strength.'

'I rest my case. Makes my lot's hash habit seem small fry. No wonder you were peddling Camberwell Carrots as a kid.'

'I like the way your twisted mind works.' He laughed, knuckles stroking her jaw.

Jo smiled and looked away. 'I prefer the way our bodies work. My mind's not out for tender.' She felt a spark of empowerment. Doormat Jo was making her stand – one night, two nights and counting – and she was walking taller, coming faster and laughing louder.

Humour was today's aphrodisiac, from bad disco memories at the CD stall to two pairs of streaming eyes sharing the joke as they sampled Scotch bonnet chilli jam, then cramps of laughter while trying on granny berets and pervert fedoras at the hat stall. Looking on from a distance, Jo the cynical realist would have sneered at the cliché of herself playing out a Hollywood-romance montage, but to be a living, breathing part of it was no fast forward to a happy-ever-after. This was just short-term seduction, fuelled by physical not emotional need. She noticed Harry's gaze on her body more often than he looked into her eyes.

She also noticed the way women looked at him: the following stare, shy double-take and elbow-nudging call to arms, instinctive reactions to good-looking charisma. There were better-looking men out there, but his sex appeal and self-possession made him intoxicating to watch. It was like seeing a lion pad around a cattery, totally unaware that he was different. When he bought a big leg of lamb from a local farm's stall, she half expected them to throw it down for him to pounce on.

Eyes evaluated Jo too, questioning her credentials, another involuntary female response to this blond alpha male with his honeyed laugh. Jo had always possessed the sort of quirky looks that divided opinion – leggy, tall and contradictory, the feminine long neck offset by wide, bony shoulders, the slim midriff by the flat chest, the doe eyes by narrow lips. Monstrously self-conscious as a teenager, she'd lived in leggings and oversized sweaters with the sleeves pulled over her hands until studying art at Goldsmiths had finally made her rethink the way beauty worked, seeing it in every shape and form. To her astonishment, the fashion-design department had grabbed her at every opportunity to model at their shows. Embracing her own vintage fusion of glam rock meets Doris Day, her twenties had been one long dressing-up box of boho eccentricity, comedy-fashion statements and ever higher heels until she'd fallen head over them in love with Tom, who at five foot eleven got swamped if she strapped on madder platforms. Since they'd got together, she supposed she had toned things down, from flamboyant art-school muse to cardigan and tea-dress vintage. She clubbed less and partied less, trading exhibitionist culture for more intimate gatherings. There was no real need for peacock feathers and high heels at a National Theatre matinée, especially if it was standing room only.

Being with Harry made Jo feel as though she was back

in her slinkiest, most feathery cat-suit again, sliding into a bar to flirt her arse off for fun. As they wandered down another long run of stalls – his fingers threading in and out of hers, his arm around her shoulders, hand in her hair, knuckles stroking her neck – Jo felt the pulse between her legs already thrumming again. Casting her come-to-bed smiles, he bought more food, a thick cardigan for her, a dress she admired and a chunky pewter pendant shaped like an owl in flight. The stallholder watched indulgently as Harry fastened it round her neck. 'You remind me of an owl. Beautiful, wise and solitary.'

'And I can turn my head right round and puke up mice.'

He pressed his forehead to hers. 'Don't be ungrateful.'

'I'm sorry. I love the necklace. How now, Brown Owl.' She gave a Girl Guide salute, although she knew it was the compliment she'd struggled to accept, not the gift.

'You have the most exquisite throat.' He kissed its hollow and she felt molten heat run through her. This instant on-switch wasn't normal, surely. In public, it made her feel like a naked exhibitionist.

'Let's buy that fuse wire!' she said, still channelling the Girl Guide vibe, acutely aware that the stallholder was still looking at them. Harry followed in amusement.

In the high street, they tracked down an extraordinary hardware store that was part Arkwright's, part Miss Havisham's bedroom, with an old-fashioned cash register and narrow aisles packed floor-to-ceiling with domestic necessities Jo had forgotten existed, like moth balls, ironing starch, Jeyes Fluid and the all-important fuse wire. Next door was an art shop – Jo's addiction – and she lost herself in shelves of coarse paper, racks of paint tubes, the smell of oil pastels and wood canvas-stretchers.

'Stop it!' she whispered, when Harry piled almost everything she touched on to the counter.

'I want to spoil you.'

'I can spoil myself,' she snapped, feeling cursed like Midas, however seductively, unable to touch anything simply for the pleasure of it. The debrief date had started to feel overdressed again.

He regarded her with familiar amusement, undercut with sexual tension. 'I'm sure you can. But so can I, and I will.'

Unable to stop him buying it all for her, Jo selected a gift for the cottage.

'A visitors' book?' Harry eyed the fat, leather-bound volume suspiciously, its gilt-edged pages heavy and blank. 'Morrow doesn't have many visitors, these days.'

'I think I qualify. Every holiday cottage should have somewhere guests can eulogize about the place, as well as offer constructive criticism about the lack of fuse wire and dry logs.'

'"God pulled his bleeding fingertips through gold leaf to create the evening sky above Mawr Vron. Unfortunately the beds were lumpy. Jo from London."'

'I haven't seen the evening sky or tried out the beds.'

'You will tonight.'

That look again. Her pulse points went crazy. 'If I stay.'

'Might see a murmuration,' the shop owner suggested cheerfully, as she packed up their purchases.

'What's a murmuration?' asked Jo.

'When thousands of starlings gather together at dusk,' Harry explained. 'Happens once or twice a year round here.'

'There's a local superstition that if you see it the devil will take you, unless your conscience is clear,' the shopkeeper told them.

Jo shuddered as a warm train back to London became tempting once more.

'I've never witnessed it, but apparently it's one hell of a sight,' said Harry. 'I'm starving. Where can we eat?'

Jo was starting to understand that his appetite for food and sex were both gargantuan, although she had quiet doubts about his conscience. The flints in his eyes were back.

Tipped off by the art-shop owner, they found a gallery café in a side street. It was filled with local artists' work, presided over by a short-breathed maître d' with a greying bun as large as a cottage loaf, who asked if they'd like a guided tour of the work on show before ordering.

Jo found it all very mediocre, but Harry was charming about every exhibit. He was particularly taken with a painting upstairs of a Rubenesque nude redhead posing amid a lot of elaborate foliage.

'The artist can't draw hands.' Jo dismissed it in an undertone.

'I wasn't looking at the hands.' He tilted his head. 'Extraordinary bush.'

'Everyone says that,' their guide enthused, breathless from climbing the stairs, bun slipping. 'It's a wimberry. They grow wild on the moors and you can pick them in August. Ray Mears sells a special comb for them on his website.'

'Yes, I can see a comb would be useful.' Harry caught Jo's eye. That look was getting out of hand, laughter laced with so much sexual promise that she was struggling to walk straight, her face flaming. She needed to cool down. Leaving the bunned one sharing her wimberry pie recipe with Harry, she went back downstairs, headed straight for the card display and leafed through it with deft fingers.

Eventually Harry appeared on the other side of the rack, spinning it round and eyeing her through the wire shelving. 'See anything you like?'

'It's what I do for a living,' she explained. 'Greetings cards. I always look.'

There was at least one of her own on display, looking dubiously dusty, but she was too embarrassed to show it off. Instead she picked up a stunning pen and ink sketch of an owl. 'I love a theme. I'll send you this as a thank-you.'

He stepped closer to lift the pendant resting against her breastbone. '"The Owl and the Pussycat".'

'You are not a pussycat.'

'How do you know?' His gaze lifted, trapping hers. She remembered the lion in the cattery image. 'I'm at sea with you.'

'That's what happens with ships that pass in the night.'

'And if they drop anchor?' He eyed the back of the gallery where the tiny deserted café lay in a glass-covered courtyard. 'I have to eat.'

Still lead-bellied from her half bacon roll, Jo planned to watch him feast, but Harry crowded the table with so many treats that it was impossible not to join in with his infectious appetite. Sucking caster-sugary fingers, they became increasingly flirtatious, legs twined together beneath the table, eyes once again reliving the past thirty-two hours. Jo had had no idea that being fed Welsh cakes could be so erotic. Really they were behaving appallingly, she realized, casting a glance at the gallery curator, who was dusting a display of hand-thrown plates nearby and ogling Harry furtively.

'I think it's time to unpack something else,' he said.

'No emotional baggage.'

He shook his head. 'Just work overalls. Tell me about your business. Blue Barn, is it?'

She was surprised he remembered the name. It had been on the card he'd first taken her number from. She wished Fi hadn't exaggerated so much when introducing her to everyone that night. 'Blue Barn isn't my company. It belongs to a woman called Caro Roachford. She's an illustrator, a really good one – you may have heard of her. She had a cartoon strip in the *Telegraph*'s "Weekend" section for years.'

He shook his head. 'A Tory Steve Bell?' he asked, mouth full of cake.

'A lot less full-on. Think Labradors eating Cornish picnics. When she started out, her studio was in a blue-painted barn at her farm in the Chilterns, hence the name. That's her kids' playroom now, but Unit Seven, Chinnor Business Park doesn't have the same ring.'

'So you design greetings cards?'

'I did once.' She was grateful for the safe ground, comfortable in her professional role. 'My first job when I left art school was covering for Caro while she had a baby. It was all homespun in those days – limited-edition prints and cards, mostly selling to local gift shops. Caro thought she'd be back in the studio within a few weeks – that's typical of her. I learned everything on the job – orders, artwork, distribution – mostly sitting alone in an unheated barn with a lot of rodent life. Caro was fantastic at giving me free rein, and when she got pregnant again, she more or less handed over control. These days, we have twenty artists, including me, signed to us. They create exclusive illustrations, and we sell to hundreds of independent retailers as well as big garden-centre chains. We're still trying to crack a supermarket, but I'm this close to being in bed with Waitrose.' She pinched her fingers then crossed them.

'I am obscenely jealous of Waitrose,' he fed her a chocolaty lump of his choc-chip cupcake, 'and seriously impressed by you. What's your web presence like? Do you sell online?'

'I want to develop that side, but there are a few issues.'

'Iron them out. E-commerce is the only way forward for print media.' When Harry talked work he was seriously sexy. He had a different way of focusing, the humour muted, the dark blue eyes hardening and staying on her face, instead of wandering all over her body. Jo listened, enthralled, as he pitched a brilliantly pithy, convincing case for dotcom.

'Caro thinks we're as big as we need to be,' she admitted, feeling disloyal, but grateful to be able to talk to somebody who understood. Wasn't Harry some sort of international marketing hotshot?

'Sounds to me like you should break free and start your own company.'

Jo's guilt tic twitched. 'I couldn't do that to her.'

'But you've thought about it.' He took a teaspoon and filled it with creamy butter icing, feeding it to her. 'Is Caro still involved in Blue Barn on a day-to-day basis?' His voice dropped lower. 'You have no idea how much I want to fuck you right now.'

Mouth full of sugary cream, Jo decided that perhaps he wasn't entirely focused on her head, after all.

'I pretty much take the helm,' she said, watching him refill the spoon. 'She only interferes occasionally, usually when her husband David's home. He's an army officer.'

'I'd interfere with you non-stop if you were running my company.' He offered the spoon to her again.

Aware that the gallery curator was edging ever closer with her duster, Jo sat back, crossing her arms and legs and refusing to play along, despite a sudden rampant image of Harry seducing her on a boardroom table. 'I'm happy with the way things are. I run a business I love with almost total autonomy. Caro and David have four kids and a second home in France. It's a sweet deal.'

Caro was one of the few people Jo had confided in. Her future plans depended a lot on her ongoing support. No maverick brand-maker was going to rock that boat.

But as Harry ate the spoonful of icing, not taking his eyes

from hers, she had the distinct impression that he was in the same imaginary boardroom with her, their agenda very different from this conversation.

'You reinvent companies for a living?' she asked.

'I did.' He watched her across the table, unsmiling. 'Right now, I'm reinventing myself.'

'What is the new-brand Harry?'

'You're looking at him.' He didn't blink.

Jo stared back, thinking about her own reinvention, far more life-changing than her ambitions for Blue Barn. Perhaps the Sinner was seeking a wholly different future too. Was this also his final fling?

She had to call a halt to it: she was getting too fascinated. She couldn't risk her plan. 'I think I'll jump on that train from here, after all.'

He leaned forwards, eyebrows curling together in apology. 'You could try, but they move pretty fast. They closed the station fifty years ago.'

The gallery proprietor had shuffled up to remove the empty plates, fixing Harry with a make-or-break stare. 'I can offer you ten per cent off *The Wimberry Nude* for cash. No more.'

'I'll think about it.' Harry flashed his big smile. When she'd shuffled off with a cupcake stand, he turned back to Jo. 'I don't think you travel quite as light as you make out, Joactually.'

Furious with herself for feeling such a rush of light-headed, horny relief that she couldn't bolt back to London, Jo crossed her arms again defensively. 'I'm not unpacking any more. Not unless you empty an entire portmanteau.'

'For you, I might just do that.' They looked at each other, the mutual attraction almost overwhelming.

Click. Without warning, the sexual-power lever slammed down to maximum. Jo felt her nerve endings sizzle.

Harry's eyes darkened. He called the gallery keeper back. 'I'll take the nude! Can you export-wrap it?'

'Of course, sir!' She huffed up, cupcake stand still swinging in hand. 'What's export wrap?'

'Three layers of padding and cardboard on the corners.'

'I'll just check if we have enough bubble wrap.' She wheezed off, climbing the stairs painfully slowly.

Grabbing Jo's hand, Harry led her through the service door that led to washrooms, where the kiss he landed on her was straight to the point.

'Tell me to stop.' He pulled up her skirt, pressing her back against the wall.

'Why should I?' It felt absolutely fabulous.

Eyes locked with hers, sharing the brazen risk they couldn't resist, he lifted her higher, creating an angle of such sublime friction that she thought, in those brief moments of stolen nirvana, she might be quite happy to unpack totally with this man.

SATURDAY NIGHT

The Pub Night

No bigger than a farmhouse kitchen, the tiny Hare and
Moon was a comforting mix of heavy beams, stone walls,
planked floor and scrubbed tables.

Drunk on each other long before their first drink of
the day, Harry and Jo spilled inside already laughing at
a private joke. It was 'Open Mic Folk Nite', and in front
of a roaring inglenook, a bearded man in a leather jerkin
was singing 'Myfanwy' to half a dozen regulars. Behind
the bar stood a large, rubicund *patron*, whose arm-span
stretched from his draught ale lever to his cider tap, red
cheeks glowing beneath a monk's doughnut of prema-
turely greying hair.

'As I live and breathe, if it's not Half Inch!' he boomed, as
soon as they walked in. 'And you brought the wife to meet
us at last!'

'One drink and we'll go home to bed,' Harry promised Jo
in an undertone, as he propelled her towards the bar.

Jo's fixed smile hid a sharp adrenalin spike at the word
'wife'. She quashed it hard, forcing her focus elsewhere.
'Why "Half Inch"?'

'I've grown a lot,' he muttered, already ducking a ritualistic head-cuffing as their host rugby-tackled him. 'Jo, this
is Roy Thomas, a.k.a. Half Mast.'

'We all had stupid nicknames as kids,' Roy explained,
beaming at her. 'We called ourselves the Half Moon Gang.
The twins were Half Bold and Half Inch. I was Half Mast,

from Roy Tho-Mas, see? There was Ned who was Half Wit, on account of his name being Whittaker.'

'And because he is a halfwit,' Harry pointed out, not unkindly.

'Done well for himself, though, from what I heard,' said Roy, coming through the bar hatch, like a shire bursting from a stable. 'And you have too, Half Inch. You're looking good, boy! C'mere. We've missed seeing you round here.'

The bear hug that followed incorporated Jo, burying her briefly in a hot, cavernous armpit.

'I hear you're from America.' Roy studied her excitedly when she was finally released.

'My wife's American,' Harry said, which didn't help.

'I'm not.' Jo flashed her eyes at him, realizing that he was enjoying the ruse. Adrenalin spiked again.

But Roy wasn't listening, eager to return to mysterious Ned, whose apparent success meant he was a topic of great fascination. 'You and Half Wit still close, then?'

Harry's expression darkened. 'We keep in touch.'

'Doesn't he build ugly skyscrapers?'

'Yeah, but he'd prefer you call them iconic architecture. Matt works in one of them in the City.'

'Well, Ned always did send him up something rotten!' Roy laughed.

Not in on the joke, Jo looked down as she felt something warm brush against her leg, and saw a smiling German Shepherd pushing his face into her hand. Her fingers curled beneath his soft ears into his deep neck pelt.

'That's Sinbad,' Roy told them.

'Does that make him Half Bad or Half Sin?'

Roy laughed even more riotously as he headed behind his bar to pour drinks. 'The Half Moon Gang disbanded in nineteen eighty-three, my love. No dogs, no Irish, no women.'

Jo looked at Harry, shocked, and his eyes apologized.

'There was a lot of in-fighting when my little sister wanted to join,' he explained. 'The committee couldn't agree whether to lift the boys-only rule.'

'Were you in favour?'

'Of course.'

'Always one for the girls.' Roy presented Harry with a huge, brimming tankard and Jo with a half in a glass.

'Jo drinks pints, Roy.'

'Ladies' measures in my pub.'

'What century are we in?' Harry laughed in amazement.

'The Half Moon Gang lives on, it seems.' Jo raised her glass. 'I take it your motto wasn't the "Better Half"?'

'Actually it was "Ask for the Moon".'

Harry took her drink and handed it back to Roy. 'You'll be seeing stars if you don't pour her a pint.'

'It's fine.' She reclaimed it, joking, 'I'm only half offended.' Had it been London, she would probably have argued the principle until it went to the Equalities Commission, but these were Harry's old friends, and she was a passing out-sider with no desire to turn the evening sour. She'd leave a blistering review on TripAdvisor if Roy did anything else sexist. Passive aggression had its uses.

Spotting Harry, the regulars by the bar were edging closer with a few grunts of welcome. The open-mic folk singer had moved on to a slow ballad now, miserably recounting the loss of his One True Love.

'Thought you'd moved to the States, Half Inch?' said an elderly man with the longest earlobes Jo had ever seen.

'I did. Now I've moved back.'

'You ever meet that Arnold Schwarzenegger fellow?'

'I didn't have that honour, no.'

Jo tried to tune it out, but her date data-analysis was locked on, gathering information about Harry's recent life, far more dangerous territory than the distant past they'd safely unpacked from their weekend bags.

A small man with a moustache sidled up to her while Harry was trying to explain to Long Ears where Connecticut was in relation to Los Angeles. 'You like it here in England?'

'Yes. I always have.'

'Lots more history than America.'

'So they say.'

He turned to call over the bar, 'Harry's married a looker, eh, Roy?'

They were all staring at her now.

Finding herself assessed like a prize ewe, Jo gave a stiff smile and looked across at him with eyes on high warning. 'I'm sure he did.'

Harry dipped his head, putting his arm round her, fingertips slipping idly along her collarbone. 'Jo and I aren't married,' he told the little crowd quietly. 'My wife is still in America. Jo is my . . . ' He looked at her, gaze amused, eyebrows raised, offering her the chance to fill the gap.

'Lover,' she said gratefully, shrugging off his arm.

As soon as she did so, Jo realized her mistake. It wasn't just the looks of total horror around her, a sharp reminder that in a small rural pub in a very traditional area 'friend' was the right cover-all-bases, it was Harry's flinty expression. Hands now plunged into his pockets, he was squinting and a muscle flickered in his cheek, the switch from good to bad mood instant. She knew him well enough now to guess that he wouldn't have cared if she'd announced she was his transsexual gimp. Yet she sensed his sudden detachment, and she knew why straight away. It wasn't what she had said: it was what she'd done as she said it. She'd been shrugging his arm off her shoulder all day, wary of the public ownership it conveyed, the clichéd romantic togetherness, determined to stay self-protective and independent. Harry had taken it in good humour, yet he constantly forgot, like an instinctive reflex, and they'd performed their own lop-sided dance around Rossbury market. And now they'd done it again, only this time it was different. This time it had coincided with the Arctic blast of his marriage being spoken of again, a cold, hard fact of real life that lay beyond their fantasy, and one that Jo sensed she must avoid if she was to walk away unhurt.

After a lot shoe-gazing and throat-clearing, conversation at the bar hurriedly moved on to Morrow and the shooting rights in the woods around it changing hands, clearly the cause of much local unrest. Grateful to be out of the spot-light, Jo hurriedly threaded her arm through Harry's and reached down for his hand, eager to recapture the adven-ture. Even though his fingers tightened round hers, she sensed his black mood lingering. She watched him in profile as he joined in the bar talk, admiring afresh the symmetry of his short nose and straight brow, reminding herself to sketch it while she still could.

After a while, they settled on a battered sofa closer to the fire with a small group of younger locals, cheering as a new face took to the mic, clearly a local favourite, a black-haired woman with a fabulously throaty, sensual voice singing in Welsh.

The Hollywood montage was back, Jo thought – the cosy country pub, fireside conversation and music. The director would no doubt have Harry in an Argyll sweater, her in a floaty dress, and give them lingering eye meets and knowing smiles, softened by the golden firelight. In reality, Harry had bummed a fag off somebody and was already looking worryingly half-cut, chasing his ale with Scotch as he joined in a heated debate about Brits buying up Welsh cottages as second homes.

Having deflected several questions about how she and Harry knew one another with a vague 'through mutual friends', Jo escaped to the loo. Being in a social situation with Harry made her ill at ease: she knew so little about him and they had no plans. It was like playing a role for which she hadn't auditioned or rehearsed. She still hadn't shaken off her corporate identity as one half of Tom and Jo, a trading name she'd used for so long it was rubber-stamped into her head. Her next joint identity would be an entirely different relationship.

Locked into the cubicle, she found she was straining to pee with nothing but a burning sensation to show for it, and let out a quiet groan as she recognized cystitis. It wasn't really a surprise after so much sex – and Harry was much better endowed than Tom – but it compounded her worry that tonight marked a seismic shift between them, the fall of the one-night stand.

Still paranoid that she smelt like a randy skunk, she washed at the basins as best she could, grateful for the hot water as she topped and tailed with vile pink liquid soap.

Harry was at the bar collecting another round, blond, dishevelled and every inch the dissolute, handsome Sinner, who had shagged his way through two lost days.

'Don't worry, we'll leave the car here and walk down to collect it in the morning,' he told her, handing her several drinks to carry. 'Efon the farmer's offered us a lift back – he has to check his ewes anyway. That pint you're carrying is his.' He pointed out a figure in a flat cap, swaying by the bar, who appeared so drunk he was only standing up by virtue of a sheepdog propped against each leg. 'I'll order us some food.' He looked up at the blackboard above the bar. 'They do fantastic steaks here.'

'I'll pass, thanks.' The teatime Welsh cakes were still clogging her arteries alongside the bacon roll.

'I'll order you one anyway. I can always eat yours if you don't want it.'

'Two T-bones, is it?' Draped over the food counter, like a car-show model over a bonnet, Roy's barmaid was desperate to take his order. 'You going to sing for us later, Harry? We love it when you sing.'

'Depends how much more I drink.'

So much for one quick drink and we'll go, Jo thought crabbily, as she delivered the pint to cross-eyed Eton and headed back to the group on the sofa, who regarded her warily, Harry's taciturn 'lover' with the dodgy personal hygiene.

Only Sinbad the German Shepherd seemed genuinely glad to have met her, stretching out in front of her and placing his chin on her feet. She stooped to scratch his thick ruff and he rolled over appreciatively.

'You have a dog?' asked a butch, skinny girl, her hair in a curly quiff, like an alpaca.

'Yes – no. Not for much longer. It's complicated.' The unofficial custody battle for Turtle, the scruffy wire-wool terrier that she and Tom had adopted two years earlier, had caused a lot of upset, and not just between them: Jo's parents had adopted Turtle's even scruffier litter brother, Rathbone, at the same time. In the grief and anger that surrounded her father's death, keeping both little dogs in the family had taken on huge significance. But after months of rows, Jo had finally agreed to let Turtle go with Tom, who was devoted to him. It was kinder all round, and suited her better. Yet it would break her heart to see him go.

'I like dogs more than people,' said the quiffed girl. 'Have you and Harry got kids?'

'Not together.' She had no idea if he had children. Like talk of his marriage, it was a truth that would start to draw her too far into his world to risk. Staying true to herself meant avoiding that.

'Do you want them?' The girl had the Welsh bluntness that, in another accent, might have seemed rude, but was instead full of singsong enthusiasm.

'Very much.'

'My sister Cerys is trying at the moment, but she's thirty-seven and it's not happening, and the doctor says they might just have missed the bus on this one. You don't want to leave it too late.'

'I've got that covered, thanks,' she said tightly, looking up as Harry joined them, carrying cutlery sets rolled in napkins.

The butch girl made space for him. 'I was just saying to Jo, you shouldn't leave it too late to have kids. She says you have a plan.'

'Harry's nothing to do with that,' Jo said quickly, as his eyebrows shot up.

'It's complicated, Lowri,' he said, sitting down.

'Like the complicated dog?'

'What complicated dog?' he asked Jo, who rolled her eyes, wishing they could change the subject. But a brace of locals to Lowri's far side seemed eager to weigh into the fray.

'Dai had a sheepdog that used to hurl itself at washing machines,' said one. 'He was bloody complicated.'

'When it wrecked the third Electrolux on the trot,' the other picked up, 'he took it to a woman who claimed she was an animal communicator. She told him the dog wanted to be called Nigel, eat more cereal-based food, sleep under an east-facing window and do that dog dancing he'd seen on the telly.'

'Dai just had it castrated and it was fine after that,' his friend told Jo. 'Might work for yours,' he suggested help-fully.

She thought about poor neutered Turtle, soon to be the victim of a broken home. Suddenly she wanted to be back in London, sharing the sofa with him while she still could, watching a trashy Saturday-night talent show, reading books about conception. She longed for a hot shower and a good sleep. 'I'm going outside to get some air. Excuse me.'

A few moments later Harry followed her, lighting a cigarette as he stepped into the shadows, hollow cheeks glowing. 'You okay?'

'Never better.' Jo tried not to let the ragged edges of tiredness and sadness catch her mood. He was her host and weekend lover, she reminded herself. She'd shared his reckless hedonism all along. Now that she suspected they'd both run out of stamina, there was no need to pick a fight.

She wandered across to a narrow stone bridge. 'Is this the same brook that runs beside the cottage?'

'Yeah.' He perched on its wall. 'We used to joke about sending orders ahead on Pooh sticks.'

'Should have sent one earlier. Four pints, four halves, four whisky chasers, two steaks.'

'One kiss.'

She loved his mouth against hers, even tasting of Scotch and cigarettes.

'Matt does morality statistics too,' he said. 'I told you he'd be better for you. Although he couldn't fuck you like I can.' He drew her into his lap. 'And that's all you want, isn't it?'

Jo pulled away and sat beside him on the wall, needing the loo again, guessing that it was just the cystitis fooling her. 'I'm certainly not looking for a morality statistician. What you and I had was perfect.'

'Had?'

'We go back to London tomorrow.'

Harry watched her. 'Tell me about your complicated dog.'

'It's not important. He's not mine any more.'

There was a long pause. 'I have two dogs in America that aren't mine any more.'

Don't ask, Jo told herself, turning away. But she was burning to know. 'How long ago did you divorce?'

'I'm in the middle of it.'

Jo winced, real life charging in again with a rush of adrenalin and burning interest as it made sudden sense. The temporary accommodation, truncated career, the reckless one-night stand. She could guess it was far from amicable.

He caught her hand, forcing her to turn and look at him. 'I think you're in the same place.'

'What makes you say that?' She let out a brittle laugh.

'We're both on the run. That's why this happens.' He turned her palm until it was open and buried his lips in it, turning her pelvis instantly liquid.

'That's just sex, Harry.' She dipped her head to breathe in the warm, scented sweetness of his hair. 'It's post-traumatic sex.'

'Precisely.' His teeth traced the delicate skin on her wrists and she had to bite her lip to stop a moan escaping. His touch had an extraordinary effect on her. 'We're so raw right now, it's like walking into a boiling hot room when you've been frozen solid outside in the cold for hours.' He moved closer. 'So why go back out into the cold?'

She shook her head, determined not to lose control and start blabbering on about her personal circumstances. 'I'm in a good place right now.'

'If you say so.' He untied her ballet tops and pressed his face to the flat plane of muscle beneath, breath hot against her skin, making it knot tight with longing. 'Tell me about the complicated dog.'

Her fingers snaked through his hair. 'He's just a dog.'

'Mine came everywhere with me, my allies and my slice of home. It killed me leaving them.' Harry was lifting her bra, thumbs running beneath the wires, his touch burning straight through her frozen shield.

She closed her eyes, trying not to think of her solid little pan-scourer companion snoring beneath her desk at work, skittering around after her on the stripped floorboards at home, sitting adoringly in the no man's land between his master and mistress on the sofa, loyal diplomat, relationship counsellor and baby substitute.

Backing away and rearranging her clothes, she turned to glare into the fast-flowing brook. 'You know nothing about me, Harry.'

He looked across at the pub, its windows glowing, a rat-titty-tattity drumbeat audible as another folk ensemble took to the mic. 'You're right. I shouldn't have brought you here tonight. It's too personal.'

'Is that why you're getting drunk?'

He rubbed his fingers through his hair. 'Eat, drink and be merry because tomorrow we . . . ' He laughed hollowly. 'I need to eat. I'll say something I regret if I don't.' He turned and walked inside, leaving Jo staring into the dark, rushing water, focusing hard on her plans. They didn't include Harry Inchbold or a complicated dog.

Big, bull-necked Roy was doing his wide-wingspan welcome behind the bar when Jo went back in. 'Beautiful women deserve beautiful drinks. I've got the cocktail book out in your honour.' He was already reaching for the peach schnapps. 'How about we start with Sex on the Beach and go for a Multiple Orgasm later?'

She shook her head, looking round for Harry. 'Mine's still a pint, Roy.' She was developing quite a taste for ale.

'Two halves?' Roy offered stubbornly.

'Whichever way you pour it, it still adds up to one.' She couldn't see Harry anywhere.

'Think he'll sing tonight?'

'I've no idea.'

'Not heard him sing in almost twenty years. Not since Half Wit pulled the plug on the band. I don't think Harry ever really recovered from it. You know what kids are like. Full of dreams. But, by God, he can sing, huh?'

'I only met him two days ago, Roy,' she said, in a stage-whisper. 'I know nothing about him.'

Roy's mouth fell open.

'You know about this, though?' He pointed at a framed photo above the bar in which three handsome youths were draped over rocks, one with a startling blond mop of hair flopping into his eyes in an eighties curtain. 'They were tipped as the new A-ha.'

'How could they fail?' She tried to keep the sarcasm from her voice.

'They didn't. Their first single sold a stack, went straight into the Top Ten. Ned wrote the songs, but Harry was the face.'

She squinted at the picture more closely, a vague memory stirring in the back of her mind, a group with a lead singer who had got girls at school hot under the collar in the common room. She'd been too heavily into Andrew Lloyd Webber musicals to take much notice.

'What were they called?'

'Glass Half Full.'

It rang no bells. 'What happened to them?'

'Ned's family didn't like what it was doing to him and called him out. There was a big fuss at the time – court cases, a lot of money to pay back. Harry was screwed up about it. But they were just kids. He's done well for himself since then. Seems happy now. Between you and me,' he dropped his voice, 'he always was the nicest one of the Morrow lot.'

'Can I have that drink, Roy?' Jo asked shakily, trying to shake the niggling voice that told her Harry Inchbold might need to pay excess baggage on his past, but that was why he lived so fearlessly for today.

She and Roy turned in unison as a voice started to sing over the loudspeakers, gruff and sexy, and far more in tune than any that had preceded it. Jo recognized the song: an old Bob Dylan number her mother loved. Straining to see round the audience, which was several deep now, she already knew it was Harry singing. He'd borrowed a guitar, fingers dancing across the frets with practised ease, totally lost in the tune.

'Now that's a turn-up.' Roy was so taken aback, he picked up a pint glass and started filling it.

They fell silent, listening to 'Just Like A Woman', sung with a fantastically sardonic edge, the bitterness clear in his voice as he told his lover they'd reached the end. He was slurring his words very slightly.

Jo took her pint and made her way closer to the fire where there were whoops and cries for more, finding Harry's eyes on her, as she stepped into clear view, gazing through his fringe, fingers deftly tuning the bass string from D to E.

'This one's for you, beautiful Owl,' he murmured.

Jo recognized the first refrain of 'Will You Still Love Me Tomorrow'.

Eat, drink and be merry, she reminded herself, suddenly filled with a huge head rush of Harry Inchbold's reckless spirit and something crashing away in her chest that was dangerously close to devotion. For the next twenty-four hours, she told herself, she was going to stop focusing on the point in the future that she was determined to reach and concentrate on the here and now, and the end of a glorious affair. To her shock, she found a tear in her eye.

Wiping it hastily away, she saw that Harry was staring at her, that irresistible smile spreading across his face, and she now recognized how generous it was.

'Bloody hell! He's as good as I always heard he was.' Lowri had appeared alongside Jo. 'They used to play up at the cottage, him and Ned. Cerys says it was like rock history in the making.'

'I hardly think "the next A-ha" is on the same scale as Def Leppard or the Who.' Jo covered her bursting heart with sarcasm.

She was blown away that Harry had a talent like this that apparently he never used. The little pub crowd wouldn't let him stop. They called for encore after encore. So what if he played a few bum notes and forgot lyrics? He was out of practice and being plied with free drinks. Harry was a born entertainer, his charm and voice unique, his generosity boundless as he sought to find forgotten melodies, accompany guest singers and please the folk purists. When he finally held up his hand to leave the stage, his fingertips were red raw.

Jo wrapped her arms around him, brimming with pride.

Now very high and very drunk, he kissed her in a way that made her heart roar so loudly her ears were deafened with the sound of rushing blood. She saw his mouth moving and half lip-read the words. 'We're going home to unpack.'

Blood still pounding, Jo shook her head, certain that for every truth she shared with Harry Inchbold, she would lose her will to walk away from him without a backward glance. She was determined that, instead, they'd lie together in a bed made up with market-stall black satin sheets, shameless and sinful and sated. 'You haven't eaten yet.'

His eyes moved between hers, challenging and impatient.

At the same moment, a penetrating shriek cut through Jo's blood rush and they turned as Efon lurched onstage with a mouth organ and a pint. Their designated driver launched into a remarkably controlled rendition of 'The Green Green Grass Of Home'.

'Fuck it, you're right.' Harry turned towards the bar. 'We need those steaks we never got. You must be starving, beautiful Owl.'

He was really very drunk. Jo already knew the flinty-eyed look of hunger-anger. Sure enough, when Roy apologized that the kitchen was now closed and the steaks they'd let go cold were now inside Sinbad, Harry stomped past him and insisted on cooking two more himself. Despite the impromptu chef's foul temper, it was one of the best meals Jo had ever eaten.

Much later, Harry groaned, semi-conscious, from the back of a rusty pick-up truck that was racketing off-road towards Morrow, as though he was suddenly aware of his surroundings for the first time since he'd climbed in. 'Why did we leave early? I was going to do another encore.'

'You did.' Jo battled to be heard over the engine. 'You sang "It Ain't Me Babe" accompanied by Efon on a mouth organ. There was a lock-in. It's past one.'

'Oh, yeah. Of course.'

'Before that you cooked steaks bigger than dinner plates and heckled a woman in a poncho singing Joni Mitchell hits.' She shifted, still unable to shake off the indigestion from eating a week's worth of food in a day. She appeared to be sitting on a bag of sheep nuts.

'I could drink a vat of you right now.' Harry slid across his hay-bale seat and started to kiss her shoulder, lips moving towards her throat and ear. Even rolling drunk, he knew exactly which spots reduced her straight to jelly.

'I'm vat-free and you're pissed.' She deflected him, acutely aware of Efon just a rear windscreen away, listening to bluegrass and driving remarkably sedately for a man who had just tried to start his car with his house keys.

'Trust me, I am never too pissed for sex,' Harry assured her. 'Our lift's got to check five hundred pregnant sheep before he drops us off. This is much more fun than counting them.'

Things were starting to get thoroughly out of hand when the pick-up bounced over a deep rut, propelling them apart.

Jo retreated behind a bale and looked up at the stars. Laying his head on the other side of it, Harry pointed at a sliver of curved silver overhead. 'New moon. Make a wish.' He closed his eyes.

Thinking he was asleep, Jo looked up at the moon and wished for the one thing she'd longed for more than any other in recent years.

A hand closed warmly round hers.

'Do you have children?' she asked, before she could stop herself.

'A daughter.' He sat up groggily. 'Orchid.'

Jo drew her fingers away gently and hugged herself, imagining his blond hair and blue eyes in miniature. Then she gripped the sides of the pick-up as it swung into a field, and Efon more or less fell out of the driver's door to clank through the gate with a searchlight, dogs at his heels.

The sudden silence was startling, the farmer's retreating footsteps and the tick of the engine amplified with their breathing. Jo lost her battle with curiosity. 'How old is Orchid?'

'Nineteen.'

She chewed her thumbnail, rearranging her ready-made assumptions. Not a little all-American toddler in the midst of her parents' messy divorce, but an almost grown woman. 'It's a pretty name.'

He propped his back higher against the hay bale, pulling up one long leg to rest an arm on, eyes closed. 'It started out as a joke because her mother used to call her "our kid". Tara's from Lancashire and it sounded like "Orchid". It suits her – she's a hothouse flower.'

'Do you see much of them?'

'Every few months, if I can. They live in Ibiza most of the year. Tara has a place there. She deejays in clubs.'

Realization dawned. 'Orchid's mum is Tara Riley?'

'You know her? She's great, isn't she?'

'Not personally.' The *enfant terrible* of 1980s Radio 1, with her crimped crazy-colour hair and legendary drug use, made an unlikely match with cynical maverick Harry, who must be twenty years her junior. Tara would be knocking on to sixty now. 'How long were you together?'

'One night.' He opened one eye, looking embarrassed. 'We met on a music show called *Deck 9*.'

'Camera angles that made you sea sick,' she recalled. 'Wasn't it on Channel 4 after the pubs closed on Friday night? We watched it as students.'

'Well remembered. You won't have heard of a band called Glass Half Full.'

'Not until tonight,' she said honestly.

'Don't tell me Roy got the picture out?' He groaned, both eyes glittering in horror, then disappearing as he rubbed his face with his hands, trying to sober up. 'Christ, he did. We were dire.'

'You looked the real deal.'

'We thought we were a post-New Romantic Pink Floyd, but we were just a bunch of North London schoolkids with pretty-boy faces and a few decent songs. Ned's dad was filthy rich in media, so he'd pulled some strings to get us signed. When the record label made us over to appeal to teenage girls and toured us around school halls and radio road shows, it was soul-destroying for Ned. I didn't care as long as I got out of bombing my A levels. Here's Efon.' He craned round to look into the dark field where a torch was bobbing back towards them.

Walking round the back of the truck, cigarette dangling, the farmer thrust something warm and shaking into Jo's arms. 'Hang on to that, will you?'

She and Harry were now sharing the back of the pick-up with an orphan lamb. As they bounced along a dark track, Jo clutched the warm little body, letting it suckle her fingers.

'You'd make a great farmer's wife.' Harry watched her through the darkness.

'You were telling me how you met Tara Riley.' She was burning to know now, shouting over the engine. 'Was it when you were in the band?'

He nodded, yawning. 'We'd had one song that charted – a totally forgettable teen dirge with a designer video – and very briefly tasted fame, if not fortune. We only got on to *Deck 9* because Iggy Pop's back went, and we were the last-minute replacement. Tara was coked out of her mind, really sweet and funny. I was the band's singer, so always got the most attention, and we were both serious flirts. After the show, a big group of us went to some fuck-off trendy bar, then we went clubbing in a warehouse some- where that Tara was deejaying in and I woke up in bed in her flat the next afternoon, and stayed there until the record label tracked me down in a panic because I was supposed to be in Frankfurt. Six weeks later, the band split because Ned – who had been offered a place at his father's college in Cambridge – said he didn't feel he was being taken ser- iously. Then Tara called to say she was up the duff.'

Jo cuddled the lamb closer, trying to imagine nineteen-year-old Harry, all floppy hair, blue-eyed smile, and fertile as hell. Had he been as good a lover then? Probably not. And certainly not ready to settle down. 'Our kid?'

'Our kid.' He nodded. 'Tara was thrilled. She was thirty-nine and single, her biological clock ringing out quarter-hours.'

Jo swallowed uncomfortably and held the lamb further away, grateful that she'd conspicuously used a condom every time to muffle her own chimes.

'She explained she wanted me in Orchid's life,' Harry went on, 'but that I didn't need to take any financial or moral responsibility. My parents freaked out a bit – my mother acted as though I'd been tied up and child-abused at first – but they worked it out. They were more upset about the fact I only had a handful of low-grade GCEs and a failed rock career to my name, with no ambition to oil the wheels of industry or devote myself to public service. Nothing much has changed there.' He held out his arms for the bleating lamb, which wasn't happy with Jo's unexploded-bomb hold.

'You're a brand-making genius now.'

'Ha!' He put his chin on the little head as he wrapped the animal in his coat. 'That was more by bullshit and balls than by design, which is fitting, given it's what my marketing career has been all about.'

Efon parked up again, falling out of the passenger side this time, torch bobbing away up another undriveably steep field.

Harry's head started to loll.

Jo wanted his company and his story. 'How did you end up in marketing? Did you go to college?'

'After school, I was pretty hard to educate or employ.' His voice was sleepy. 'My family packed me off travelling to keep me out of poor Tara's hair – I got a bit obsessed about my responsibilities, and convinced myself I should marry her. Then Mum pulled strings to get me a career.

She got me enrolled into a training thing her market research team was supporting – I half suspect it was invented for me – and I managed to last out the year reading demographics for free newspapers. I wasn't a lot of use to them, and I enjoyed partying far too much. I bummed around a few jobs, living at my parents' basement flat, and variously fancying myself a musician, a poet or performance artist, but it was all basically an excuse to go to lots of music festivals. You don't want to know all this. It's drunk talk.' He yawned, eyes closing again, the warm lamb asleep against his chest. 'Tell me about you, beautiful Owl. Hypnotize me.'

'You still haven't told me how a free spirit ended up reinventing companies,' she complained, eager not to break the spell and enjoying his husky, self-mocking drawl.

'Freeloader, you mean.' The yawns were jaw-breaking now. 'I bought a motorbike and posed about with Ned, who was back in London after graduating, along with lots of other friends joining *meedja* graduate-recruitment programmes, who invited me to hang out among their new work colleagues because I was good company and easy on the eye. I liked drinking and travelling and shagging, and I was getting a pretty bad reputation, thanks to the latter. I also didn't give a fuck about anything, which for some bizarre reason seemed to thrill them.'

'The Sinner.'

'Matt was holier-than-thou with his double first from LSE and his fast-track City career, although you can imagine how much our parents disapproved of him working in the corrupt world of corporate commerce. Titch is their angel – all tree-hugging, badger-saving sweetness, with occasional walk-on roles in off-fringe agitprop theatre. And I was always the Problem.'

Efon reappeared in a blast of torchlight, plumed with

cigarette smoke, and thrust another lamb at Jo. It was thinner than the last and pitifully cold. 'This one might snuff it,' he said matter-of-factly.

As the engine roared again and they slalomed on, clutching orphan lambs and side-bars, Jo prayed desperately that the little creature didn't die in her arms. 'Keep talking to me,' she urged Harry, who appeared close to sleep again. 'Did you come here in those days?'

'I brought friends up.' He yawned again. 'We had a few cracking parties. I moved into Morrow for bit when my parents wanted to rent out their basement again to raise some cash. That was great, but my then girlfriend pushed off when it got cold and the mice joined us. Then I ran out of money and was forced to head back to London to live with Ned, who'd bought a place in Fitzrovia.

'I loved living in the West End, but all my mates worked and I didn't, which made the days dead. I need to keep busy. I could argue black is white and talk myself into jobs easily enough, but keeping them was a grey area. Ned claimed I had an entrepreneurial streak and would pay him in holidays on my Caribbean island one day, but my father – who'd just been diagnosed with MS – went all working class on me and said that I must have a trade if I didn't have a vocation, so I enrolled in college for a bit, swapping courses from plumbing to car mechanics to find the right fit. I'm no more practical than I am academic. I used to fly into a rage and blame the tools. I'm all small talk and big concept. Perfect requirement for a career in marketing, basically. Branding was the buzzword among my drinking buds, and the edgier marketing agencies all loved a token wild boy on the team to shake things up. Thanks to some horrific Golden Square nepotism, and a lot of exaggeration about my market-research training, I got a job at one of the leading design agencies with no more of an interview than a bar-stool debate about a new television series called *Big Brother*.'

'That's how you got into it?' Jo stroked the little body in her arms, pressing her cheek to it, listening for breathing. It was still alive.

'The thing you have to understand about my industry is that it's all entirely emperor's new clothes. One day I'm an apprentice chippy and the next Harry Inchbold became a "brand and concept developer". The first thing I had to make up out of nothing was my own job description.

'The approach of the millennium had set everybody on a reinvention frenzy. Old brands needed a twenty-first-century makeover, and there were juicy corporate worms literally waving out of the ground to be plucked. Mostly, we were reinventing the wheel for the sake of it, but we got lucky with a few brands that went stratospheric. And because I was an arrogant shit, who thought outside the box and had no respect whatsoever for tradition, I had the Midas touch. Basically, I got away with anything as long as I was controversial enough. I was paid a heap of money to talk a load of bullshit.

'Today's market is much tougher – it's all about dotcom bubbles bursting and social media reinventing itself faster than plague bacteria, but back then you could let all the geeks bang on about statistics, the designers create some pretty logos, then take all the credit for something lame like "I see this totally unique new retail enterprise as Zen meets Baroque – let's call it Zoque!"'

'You thought up Zoque? My friends and I were all total Zoque slaves. We loved that shop more than Miu Miu.'

He lifted his head with an I-rest-my-case expression. 'By then I believed my own hype so much that I thought marrying a beautiful, ball-breaking American high-flyer was playing the final level in a Sim game. Instead I found myself in a ten-year hostage situation with guilt as the ransom. This is where

97

we get out.' The pick-up shuddered to a halt in the veil of the Morrow woods and Efon slid open the cab's rear window.

'Post the buggers through here if they're still alive.'

Jo's was bleating lustily now. She gave it up reluctantly, along with Harry's; both lambs settled between farmer and his brace of dogs. When Harry jumped from the tailgate, calling out his thanks for the lift, he lurched left and disappeared into some bushes.

'Be lucky to get him home in that state.' Efon chuckled, watching over his shoulder as Jo clambered out more carefully and went to help him up. Then the red taillights raced away in a belch of exhaust fumes.

When they finally reached the cottage, having stumbled up the last few hundred metres of track in almost total darkness, Harry leaned against the door, barring the way in. 'I want you to unpack everything before we leave here.'

Jo felt panic grip her again. 'It's late. I'm shattered. You're drunk.'

'I'll sober up and make coffee.'

'We have no power.'

He pulled a cardboard rectangle from his pocket that glinted in the half-light. It was the packet of fuse wire, which he pressed into her hand. 'Don't drop this. You light the fire and I'll sober up.' He sprinted around the front of the house towards the woods. A moment later, Jo heard a loud splash accompanied by a cry of shock.

'Oh, shit! He's jumped in!' She stifled a laugh, hurrying after him, and was just able to make out a broad-shouldered shape leaping though the water, like a bear catching salmon. He was singing Joni Mitchell's 'River'. There was a pile of clothes by her feet. Jo ran inside to light the fire and fetch a towel.

*

Teeth chattering, Harry got the power on and fired up every electric heater he could find to set up around the carved-oak bed upstairs, on which he layered duvets and eiderdowns until a princess would struggle to identify a pea. Their black satin bedding was still in the car boot outside the pub, but Jo was quietly relieved, given the fire risk represented by several thousand watts of glowing element just a sheet flick from reducing Morrow to smouldering timbers.

The warmth was heavenly. They were both zombies of exhaustion.

Significantly more sober, if close to hypothermia, Harry cleaned his teeth, then stumbled upstairs, while Jo boiled the kettle to make instant cocoa, and filled two hot-water bottles, then climbed into bed beside him. 'I'll be sweating like a consumptive all night,' she grumbled.

'Good. Sweat on me. You'll warm me up.' His teeth were chattering too much for them to kiss safely.

'Why did you jump into a freezing stream?' she asked, as he burrowed and thrashed his way to comfort.

'The urge to sober up is pretty self-explanatory. It's the urge to get drunk in the first place that requires greater examination.'

'And why did you do that?'

'I'll tell you in the morning.' His voice was muffled by the layers of bedding.

Jo listened to his breathing deepen and willed herself to sleep, but she felt as if she was lying on broken glass, fragments of truth that didn't add up together. She longed for the oblivion of that extraordinary physical connection to stop her playing with the jigsaw.

Then Harry's hand slipped between her legs and she turned a smile into his hair, opening them gratefully as her mind and heart put up Closed signs.

SUNDAY MORNING

The Hangover and Lie-in

Striped sunlight danced through the low windows like luminous ribbons. Jo basked for a moment in the total silence – no radio alarm clock, no traffic, no snoring dog, no booming bass from the flat downstairs. She was utterly relaxed, comfortable and warm. Very warm.

She stretched steamily. 'Either I have a high fever or there are way too many covers on this bed. Do you want a cup of tea?'

The lump beside her let out a groan.

Slipping her feet on to the blissful cool of the floorboards, she wrapped herself in one of the lighter duvets and headed downstairs to make mugs of tea, amazed that such simple pleasures as a mattress and electricity could make her feel so high.

'We have the power.' She danced from kettle to fridge. Inside she found a mountain of Glyn Pugh breakfast staples. Stomach grumbling, she set about transforming them into a feast with the aid of an ancient electric cooker and several rusting cast-iron frying pans that were as heavy as gym dumbbells.

Despite a frustrating five minutes in the bathroom trying painfully to wee, she felt happier cooking amid the stone walls and antiquated kitchenalia than she ever did in her small, ultra-modern Crouch End galley. Morrow had a charm that was totally infectious and other-worldly. The light stripes spilling between the trees were magical and the birds that hopped along the windowsills so fearless that she had to shake 'Snow White' fantasies, and remind herself she was in control.

Upstairs, the lump had barely moved. She held a mug of tea beside it. 'Rise and shine.'

His head emerged briefly, hair messy, blond stubble, bloodshot blue eyes flinty with hung-over hunger. He looked foul-tempered and absurdly handsome, but managed a muttered 'Thanks'. He sipped some tea and disappeared again – only the mug remained poking out. 'Christ, I stink. I need a bath. Please tell me I didn't jump in the brook last night.'

'I'd be lying,' she said, taking the mug and setting it on a little scrubbed-pine washstand. 'I think I've put the immersion heater on. There's a switch by the bathroom and a red light came on when I pressed it.' She headed back towards the stairs up which the smell of grilling bacon was drifting temptingly. 'I'm bagging first bath.'

'Toss you for it. Or you can toss me.' His voice was muffled beneath the covers. 'There's the mother of all morning glories down here.'

Her cystitis twinged. 'Maybe you should have a shower now while the water's still cold.'

'Only if you get in with me and rub my back with your goosebumps.'

'Let's have breakfast first. It'll be ready in five minutes.'

'I don't deserve you, beautiful Owl.'

Within minutes of tucking into a hot pile of eggs, mushrooms and bacon, Harry's hung-over sourness lifted, although he remained shamelessly single-minded, watching her across the table with a glint in his eye. 'Your nipples look amazing in that top.'

'They're cold. Do you only ever think about sex?'

'Around you, that's pretty much all I think about. And

101

food. This is sublime.' He poked his fork at the plate. 'Where'd you learn to cook?'

'At my mother's knee.'

'I'd like to spend time at your mother's knee. Is she as sexy as you?'

'She's sixty-four.'

'A fabulous age for a woman. I bet you'll be just as beautiful. I'd like to see you at sixty-four.'

'Isn't that a Beatles song?' she asked. 'Or are you suggesting a second date in twenty-eight years' time?'

'Do you have an evening free in twenty thirty-four?'

'I'll have to check my diary.'

'I don't think we should hurry things.'

'Agreed.' She pushed her plate away and looked around the room, feeling his eyes on her. She was aware of the strangeness of the situation, the fleeting, flirty domestic intimacy that might never be repeated yet felt so easy and so deeply sexy she was already sliding off the chair in anticipation, cystitis or not. 'Who took all these photographs?'

'Me.'

'They're amazing.'

'It's what I wanted to do as a kid.'

'Not music?'

'That's what I did as a kid. Briefly. I was more interested in becoming a photographer.'

'You're very talented.' She looked at him in surprise.

'Different lifetime.'

'They'd make wonderful cards.'

'Are you offering me a job?' His husky laugh revved her libido. 'I do need one.'

'We couldn't ever afford you. Are these people all your family?'

'No – all sorts of oddballs came here.' He drew across her unfinished breakfast and started on it. 'The North London intelligentsia – academics, politicos, bohos, musos, writers who stayed months to finish books that never got published. The broken-hearted healed, drunks drowned their sorrows, the exhausted slept. It's a safe haven where tomorrow is always a day away.'

'"Eat, drink and be merry for tomorrow we die."' She repeated the phrase that had been in her head last night.

'Five points. As far as I'm aware, nobody died here.'

'Or unpacked.'

'Oh, they all unpacked.' He looked at the pictures surrounding them, wonky frames of foxed happy memories, the faces gloriously animated. 'There were summers we kids couldn't hear ourselves think for the unloading of adult angst over a fourth bottle of Chianti after lights out.'

'And it all stayed here?'

'It all stays here. You are seriously sexy when you unpack.'

'You too.' She caught his eye and the chair she was sitting on suddenly felt made of twigs, barely steady enough to hold her up. His effect on her frightened her, the way it stormed in and overwhelmed her, no longer just physically any more. Listening to him talking last night, forcing him to stay awake and keep her company around the sheep fields, had ignited her imagination. Before she left Morrow, she was burning to know about the characters in the photographs, about the Half Moon Gang and the Inchbold family. She wanted to know about Harry's marriage and messy divorce, and why he'd been there alone for New Year. She wanted to know what made Harry Inchbold tick. And that was why he was making her feel so vulnerable just by looking at her. Because if she knew everything she wanted to know, she wasn't sure how easy it would be to forget it.

She stood up instead, determinedly self-protective. 'I'm going to run that bath.'

They shared the deep, soapy tub, although most of its contents slopped out while they washed each other, revelling in cleanliness and naughtiness, slipping around doing what they did best amid a lot of laughter, bubbles and teasing. The bathroom, transformed into a luminous green grotto by sunlight streaming in to meet the steam, became a lagoon of abandoned inhibitions and slithering fingers. Back in the bedroom, they'd barely started dressing before they ended up naked again, squeaky clean and still skin-clingingly damp as they tangled towels on top of the bed and made one another's hot, scented bodies sticky once more. They couldn't stop looking at each other, their eyes addictively joining their bodies in conversations that needed no words. If they'd expected the reckless vigour of their first forty-eight hours together to wear off as the weekend wore on, the reverse was true. The connection was stronger than ever.

'Let's bring that second date forward,' Harry insisted, as he slid in and out of her, hands gripping her ankles over his shoulders.

'What had you in mind?' Jo was poised deliciously close to the precipice, rippling with delight at how deeply she could feel him, all warning bells silenced in the wake of the pounding pleasure in her ears.

'Let's make it here at Morrow.' He let go of her leg, then spat on his thumb before it dropped down to bring her to climax. 'You name the day.'

She turned her head, laughed and gasped into a pillow. 'It can't come soon enough . . . and neither can I . . . '

'I'm coming right with you.'

They collapsed together in a clinging knot of pleasure. Jo could feel her heart positively hammering against her rib-cage, meeting his hammering back, like the 'Anvil Chorus', his breath rising as hers fell, his fingers curling and uncurling through hers.

'Let's go up to the Burf,' he breathed into her hair.

She pulled back her chin to look at him, eyebrows shooting up. 'Is that some sort of hard-core sex act?'

He laughed, kissing her hard. 'It's a hill fort on top of Mawr Vron. The climb's pretty extreme, but it's worth it.' He was already getting out of bed to look for his trousers. 'The views are fucking sensational.'

'The views – and the sensational fucking – look pretty good from here.' Jo admired his naked bottom. She was too full of cooked breakfast and sex to feel like any challenge described as 'extreme'. She generally confined energetic walks to a gym treadmill where she had total control over the incline, speed, weather and view. On Sundays, she liked nothing more than spending all day in bed napping, flirting and making love. It had been years since she'd indulged in that.

'Come on, Owl. It's not that hard a climb, I promise you. I've been doing it since I was six.'

She rolled over with a groan, catching sight of the notches carved in the knotted wooden doorframe that led into the small second bedroom. Getting up, she pulled the sheet around her and walked across to examine it, seeing the same three initials repeated: H, M, T.

Harry, Matt and Titch: she let her fingers climb from notch to notch, imagining the blond heads pressed there, a ruler on top to help mark their heights as they grew each year between visits to Morrow. She could almost feel Harry the boy standing in front of her, barely at her waist, not towering over her with his bad reputation and his mind-blowing ability to make her come, his life so recently turned upside down by the end of his marriage.

'If we unpack, everything stays here, right?'

'Right.' He stepped behind her,

'Then we go our separate ways.'

'If that's what you want.'

She turned to him: she couldn't leave without knowing more – it would be like reading only the last chapter of a book, then abandoning it. She always sneaked a look at the final few pages too soon, but she'd then go on to read all that came before.

She trailed the sheet across the room and climbed back into bed, settling cross-legged among the hillocks of duvets and eiderdowns where they'd just shared so much pleasure without knowing more than a few biographical details about each other. 'You start.'

He sat down on the side of the bed. 'What's his name? The lover you're leaving.'

Jo sighed. That wasn't what she'd meant: she wanted Harry to be the one to confess. 'How do you know I'm leaving him?'

'Tell me I'm wrong.'

'Tom. What's your wife's name?'

'Bree. How long were you and Tom together?'

'Eight years. You?'

'Ten. Did he have an affair?'

She shook her head. 'We just drifted apart. Isn't that what they say? We have nothing in common any more, not even friendship. We made each other depressed but we clung together because we were frightened of being lonely. You?'

'Much the same, but with expensive divorce lawyers. At least there are no kids involved.' He looked across at the initials carved on the doorframe, his face impossible to read.

Jo pleated the sheet edge between her fingers, a raw nerve close to the surface. 'Did you not want more?'

'Bree had cancer in her twenties, before I ever met her. It made her infertile.'

She looked at him in surprise, saw the regret etched deep in his face. 'That must be such a terrible legacy to live with.'

'She coped by refusing to believe it. When we got

together, she'd been to some crackpot healer who said he'd cured her. It was only after we'd been trying a long time for children that she finally admitted what the medics had said at the time of her cancer treatment.'

'You mean you didn't know about it when you married?'

'I didn't know much about my wife when we married,' he admitted. 'We didn't have time to unpack before the honeymoon. It was a pretty whirlwind romance. Fools rush in.' He looked at her with a half-smile. 'Whereas you are the angel who fears to tread, beautiful Owl.'

Jo thought about her three-year your-place-or-mine apprenticeship with Tom followed by half a decade cohabiting their way into bad habits, the carefully made plans that had come to nothing, their inability to deal with life's big dramas or decide upon marriage, too busy squabbling over the day-to-day minutiae and, latterly, money. Their parenthood plans had been blighted too, but that was packed too far out of sight to share. She envied Harry his openness, the way he saw things so clearly, unlike her muddle of anger, regret, pity and guilt.

'Didn't you and Bree think about surrogacy or adoption?'

He shook his head. 'Bree said she didn't want somebody else's child. I was pretty screwed up about it at first, but I loved her, and I saw how much she beat herself up over it. She didn't need me beating her too. Her denial is totally genuine. She believes her own myths. It's what makes her such a good saleswoman. Work is her real baby, and it became the drug that made me forget too. It's how we met and we were a very good team, even if we became a lousy married couple. It's hard to get off a wheel which turns that fast and drives a rut that deep. It was an exciting wheel.' He stood up. 'I need coffee. Stay there. I'll bring it up.'

Jo could sense how raw it still was. Yet she longed to

know more, realizing how far she might have misjudged him from the Saint and Sinner comment the night she'd met him. She stayed in bed, chewing her thumbnail, looking at the carved height marks, wondering what wannabe photographer H, five foot four, would have made of his six-foot-two-inch self. She now had the impression of someone much more self-critical than she'd first thought, much more generous and loyal, who was willing to put aside his own dreams for the sake of others.

He carried in a tray of coffee and plates laden with bread and jam, biscuits and the tub of Glyn Pugh ice cream. She smiled. He had his eternal munchies again.

'How did it all end with Tom?' he asked, making the smile fade. She didn't want to talk about Tom.

'Not with a bang but a whisper. We couldn't even be bothered to argue any more – just long, angry silences. After a three-day stand-off over something petty, I made him a cup of tea and told him I wanted him to move out. How about you and Bree?'

'Slightly more dramatic.' He grimaced. 'More bang than whisper. Never tell your wife your marriage is over when she has a gun in her hand.'

He underplayed it so admirably that Jo had to run the words back through her head. 'She tried to shoot you?'

'Scare me would be more accurate. Her father, C. P., has a private range,' he explained, buttering a slice of bread, the prospect of food lifting his mood as always. 'We were shooting targets – it's their idea of down-time.'

'Shoot-'em-down time?'

He laughed, breaking a biscuit to share. 'Not a good time to shoot one's mouth off about wanting out of the family firm. They're a trigger-happy lot.'

'You all worked together?'

'Bree's father is the C. P. Hunter behind Hunter Broadcasting. They say he's been in the Forbes Rich List so long, that C. P. stands for Cut and Paste. He claims it stands for Charlie Parker – he's a jazz nut – but nobody really knows, not even Bree. It's another thing she'll have to wait for him to die to get hold of. She basically runs the company, but he won't give her the CEO title. He jokes that she's his only vice.

'The fact that she spent our marriage drumming her gel nails against the desk waiting for her father to die cast a bit of a dark shadow on domestic bliss, but we politely ignored that. One of the advantages of a British husband is that we're frightfully good at ignoring elephants in the room. Ironic, given that Bree always thought she was the size of an elephant. She isn't. In fact, if she turns sideways, she disappears, like a knife.' He ate another biscuit.

He sounded totally different when he was talking about his marriage, Jo thought. An artfully practised English charmer, clipped and sardonic, not the man whose shaking body she'd held when he'd called out Bree's name. She sensed that this was the role he'd inhabited during his long marriage, one forced upon him by expectation and self-preservation in a family where emotions stayed hidden: the clever, witty British husband, with a genius knack for reinventing things. Perhaps Bree had hoped he would reinvent her.

'So did you married your American heiress for love, Harry?' She matched his clipped, ironic tone.

He laughed. 'Poor Bree thought she was getting the *Gosford Park* package, but all I ever had was half a room here.' He looked at the sagging beams, the tiny low windows and whitewashed stone walls. 'Not that we ever visited. If a room falls below seventy-two degrees, Bree thinks she's being cryogenically frozen.' He sighed. 'To be fair, she's remarkably grounded if you take into account that C. P.'s fifth wife is half her age with a tenth of her IQ, and that her brother – who became her sister – is big in reality TV, baring the family soul on network prime time twenty weeks of the year. All Bree cares about is money and status, which in a family as motivated by ego and fame as hers seems almost self-sacrificial. And, yes, I loved her, just as you loved Tom.'

Jo pulled the sheet tighter around her and thought of her years with Tom, a shared rhythm that was so hard to drum alone. Harry and Bree had been married a decade: no wonder the echoes of those impatient fingernails wouldn't stop ringing in his ears. 'How did you meet?'

'In New York in 'ninety-five. I was one of the delegation sent there to pitch at Hunter Broadcasting. Ours was a brand-management company that was an exemplar of style over content, all big-screen tile TVs and Chapman Brothers art in the lobby in Soho Square. Hunter had been on a spending spree to roll out DAB channels globally – Bree's brainchild – and giving it a European identity was a big scalp for my firm. I was the high-risk hotshot they always rolled out for key contracts, so I sailed in to shatter everyone's preconceptions. And I seduced the best-looking woman on their board to reward myself. Bree Hunter was a much bigger challenge than the contract. She was ten years older than me and had just got engaged.'

Watching him talk, already on his second coffee and halfway through the biscuits – the sugar rush made him breathtakingly honest – Jo was both fascinated and appalled. 'Didn't that bother you?'

'Not at the time. It does now our marriage is over. I was single-mindedly single then. We were having the mother of all affairs when she offered me a job – twice my salary, half the work. I said I'd only take it if she was part of the deal, never thinking she'd actually call my bluff – it was just a neat trick to get out of the situation.'

'Instead you married her?'

'Bree took an over-the-cliff risk in ditching her fiancé for me – he was a part of that whole East Coast power clique, big Republican movers and shakers whose family adored hers. Turns out he was also gay, but I only found that out a lot later.

'Nobody's ever shown me they love me like that. There seemed no greater statement of commitment and love. I'd have swum every inch of the Atlantic to be with her.'

'What's she like?' Jo started on the ice cream, needing comfort food as she took in Harry's hurricane love life compared to the three years of art-house films and budget travel it had taken her and Tom to decide they'd be better off with one council-tax bill and a shared toaster.

'Very tough, very beautiful and very clever.' He picked up a spoon and joined her in the salted-caramel raid. 'She's funny too – although she can't laugh at herself, which is a fatal flaw with a Brit. It took me a long time to work out that most Americans in my wife's world can't laugh at themselves. It's not their fault – it's probably their strength. At first I loved living there. I bought into the whole lifestyle, saw our future mapped out – the New York culture fixes, homespun Connecticut domesticity, long playful weekends in the Hamptons with our beautiful children, holidays skiing in Aspen and wine tasting in Martha's Vineyard. A big old American dynasty shot through with blood that Bree thought was blue, however hot, red and loyal mine was. But there were no kids. It was all work, work, work. We've been in different time zones for half our marriage. They called us a power couple, but we were mostly on travel chargers.' He smiled sadly. 'The more money we made, the less love we made.'

Jo looked at the crumpled sheets around them, more familiar with the libido-killing effect of an argument about lack of money than excess.

'We both started drinking too much, flirting with other people, destructive patterns. Her father was a constant shadow over us, controlling, bullying, attention-seeking. I was happy to take him on – we had glorious battles in the early years – but Bree had begged me to stop. I think she knew I'd win eventually, and she couldn't bear it. Instead, I was set the labours of Hercules for Hunter Broadcasting, starting with rescuing the DAB investment that C. P. had totally overextended himself on in countries whose names he couldn't even pronounce. I did it, along with a host of other big shake-ups, to bring his global empire into the twenty-first century from Europe to the Far East, but it killed our marriage. I felt at home working away and a stranger in my own home. Work, work, work.

'The fights were toxic. Bree can fight very dirty, the retaliation far more brutal than the crime. I could never forgive her for covering up the fact she couldn't have children, and she could never forgive me for already having Orchid. That was what finished the marriage off in the end.'

'They didn't get on, you said?'

'Bree didn't want anything to do with her. She only let Orchid come to stay with us once. I always visited her in Europe. They met just twice in ten years. It's such a shame – she's a wonderful kid.' His gaze softened into hers. 'Tara never wanted me around playing daddy, and looking back, I can see I would have been hopeless, but I've always tried to be there for them. We get on pretty well nowadays, although Orchid's inherited my bullshit charm. She wants to be a television presenter, so it might not all be wasted. The one time she came to the States – I guess she'd have been fifteen or sixteen – Bree spent most of her time in the office. C. P. was the one who played the magnanimous host, letting us access all areas. It was great being able to show Orchid around the studios and feel I was helping her out in life at last. I've never had a problem with family nepotism – it would be bloody hypocritical if I did, being married to a Hunter.'

They'd finished the ice cream. She licked the spoon as Harry put the tub back on the tray and stretched out alongside her on the bed, head propped on one hand. 'Am I boring you?'

'Don't you dare stop telling me this,' she warned, rolling on to her front. 'What happened between Bree and Orchid that ended your marriage?'

'Bree did nothing to her personally, apart from wanting to protect the family cash-pot,' he said quickly. 'When Orchid turned eighteen, I planned to give her a trust fund – something that would get her through university and on to the housing ladder. I've always bunged funds across to her mother when I could, but it was never formally agreed, and Tara's fantastic, but crap with money. Turns out I'm no better. I assumed I'd earned the right to make a gift to my daughter, but Bree clamped down totally when I told her what I wanted. I've made a fortune for Hunter Broadcasting, but my reward was mostly in company shares that I couldn't cash, so while our lifestyle was lavish, my independent wealth was zero. They're a notoriously tight-fisted lot. There were bigger rows than ever. Eventually C. P. got involved and pulled rank, insisting no money would go to Orchid unless she came to stay with us as a part of the Hunter family Mafia. You can imagine Bree's reaction, but C. P. talked her round. She's always done what the old creep tells her.' His face twisted angrily.

'I suppose I was so keen, and pushed so hard for it, that I didn't stop to question motives, even though I knew it would crucify her mother – Tara and Orchid are incredibly close. But I selfishly wanted Orchid with me, wanted to get to know her better, give her that first break. It was all arranged. Orchid would come and have an internship at Hunter Broadcasting that most ambitious media students can only dream of. Even Bree was coldly supportive, kept in line by Daddy. It finally seemed that something might bring us all closer together. Instead it's what called time on our marriage, at gunpoint.

'When we were at the target range, I used C. P.'s personal laptop to check for an urgent email because mine was out of battery. He'd stopped using a password because he was the only one in the company who could never remember them. He's almost certainly got low-level dementia, which in men that powerful is like a runaway tank with its missiles primed. His desktop was such a mess – I could see the pictures of Orchid stored on it straight away, all scanned from holiday shots of mine. Orchid in a bikini, topless, laughing, pissed, pulling V signs, pulling faces – my beautiful kid, my little baby, all lined up for C. P. Hunter to drool over.

'I wanted to kick his head in, but Bree stopped me. That was when she pulled a gun on me, telling me she'd shoot me if I hurt him. She admitted she'd had her suspicions that her father was obsessed with Orchid, and that my daughter was being lined up as my future mother-in-law in his power-crazy old mind, but she insisted it was harmless. She even thought I should say nothing and let Orchid come. When I told her I wanted out of the family, she threatened to shoot me again.'

'She didn't want you to leave.' Jo was blown away by the high drama.

'She didn't want me to get a penny of the family fortune,' he corrected. 'I pointed out that the fifty-page pre-nup should have that covered, and the gun was lowered.'

Jo thought about her final rows with Tom again, many of them financial, which had felt as passionate as Shakespearean tragedies at the time: her angry protests that

Sky Sports was not a 'total essential' on their tight budget after he'd stopped working; her pleas for him to get a part-time job at least, if he was going to insist on buying only organic and free range; her late-night tears of frustration over whose turn it was to put the bins out; the furious stand-offs about who'd left a tissue in their jeans when they'd put them into the washing machine. They'd had no pre-nup or even an inventory – the vicious exchanges about ownership of the pouffe, the steam cleaner and the Tarantino DVD collection were still ongoing, mostly debated by texts sent between master and spare bedroom. Since their decision to part, Tom had written Mine and Yours lists, ranting letters, poems and even one rather alarming suicide note, which he'd left in the bread bin. When she'd called his parents in a panic, he'd said it was a joke. But at least he had never held her at gunpoint or issued death threats.

'We agreed to part there and then,' Harry told her, rolling on to his back and staring up at the ceiling. 'It was surprisingly amicable. We're cut from the same cloth in many ways. Stubborn, inexhaustible and willing to put up with any amount of pain for those we love. Which is why she is standing by her father and I walked away with nothing but my pride and a disgruntled daughter, who won't speak to me for disappointment. I won't lie and say I don't still love Bree in some way, but it's twisted and cankered and skewed in a way that no longer functions. And now I have this weekend, which has cheered me up so much I can't tell you.' He turned his head towards her, his eyes glittering.

Jo bent her head to kiss him, a taste that was so much richer and sweeter now. As she did so, she was aware of a shift in her chest, a budging aside of vital organs to make room for his heart alongside hers. They kissed on, longer and harder. Her pulse points had all started up, along with the familiar thrumming between her legs, but something louder was drowning them out, insisting on a stronger beat. However hard she resisted, it was happening now. Her heartbeat was so hard it hurt, the lump in her throat as solid as polished flint, the tears in her eyes embarrassingly mawkish and, illogically, she was slightly jealous of the passion and drama, and of Bree's decade with a man like Harry. So loyal and tireless and positively sensational in bed.

She reached down and drew him out of his still unbuttoned jeans, feeling him harden to smooth rock in her hand, then letting her sheet fall away as she climbed on top of him and tipped towards the bedside cabinet for a condom.

'The feeling's mutual,' she assured him, as she rolled it on, not taking her eyes from his, sharing their power-lever smile. She was already slippery in welcome. It felt glorious to slide down on to him and ride to his spectacular climax. She could never tire of that Harry finish, so unbridled and explosive.

Breathless, she curled into the crook of his arm, her ear against his furious heartbeat, holding his hand and keeping his arm firmly around her shoulders.

They lay in silence for a long time, but the conversation hadn't stopped; sex was emotional punctuation in baring souls now. Jo hadn't needed to hear a name cried out to know who Harry was thinking about.

'Bree's totally screwed up because she thinks everybody's after her father's wealth,' he said eventually, 'and yet she buys people.'

'She bought you.'

'I loved her. And maybe she did buy an element of that, but I got out for free. That's what counts. Orchid's a lot more valuable. My freedom's a lot more valuable. So is yours.'

'Leave me out of this,' she scoffed, but there was a

heartfelt edge in his husky voice that made her curl tightly against him.

'It's your turn to unpack.'

Jo felt the ice cream curdle in her stomach at the prospect. She hardly thought custody of the pouffe and Turtle the terrier compared to his ordeal. He'd laid out a lifetime of colourful disguises, battered armour, bulletproof vest, flight masks and sharp suits. She just had a few vintage dresses, lots of sloppy joes and some long-neglected party shoes. And the patterned wellies she'd brought at Harry's insistence, she remembered with relief.

'I think I need that walk after all.'

SUNDAY AFTERNOON

The Walk and Talk

Harry pulled on clothes faster than a lover who'd heard the jealous husband's key in the door, 'You'll love the Burf. It's magical. We'll come back past the pub and pick up the car. You can talk as we walk. Inchbold tradition.'

Dressing reluctantly, aware of his mood swinging again, her cystitis pain raging, Jo didn't want to talk; she didn't want to bare her soul. It seemed Harry had lived life at full throttle, veering from fast lane to off-road, his foot permanently on the accelerator, while she'd been stuck in traffic, barely edging out of her parking space.

It didn't help that he laughed his head off at the sight of her wellies, which were emblazoned with sweets. 'You're not seriously planning to hillwalk in those?'

'They're fine. We've covered miles together.' Discreetly, she tugged off the label.

An hour and a half later, after an uphill forest trek incorporating several painful attempts to wee behind a vast log pile and a lot of long silences, her feet were already sweating and blistered. She'd managed to avoid walking and talking by virtue of being too puffed out to speak after the first ten minutes. She liked to think she was pretty fit, but it was a murderous climb.

They finally reached a few nondescript stones on the brow of the windswept hill as the sun dropped to a low, golden glow that cast their shadows out as far as they would go, transforming them to long, slender giants. It was bitterly cold, the icy remnants of winter snow still underfoot. The ballet wraps and trendy parka did little to keep out the chill as the wind howled past, like a series of deranged, whip-wielding jockeys flying along a finishing straight. But the views were indeed breathtaking, the valley beneath them, misted in cloud, resembling a white, rolling sea of surf.

'It's not Stonehenge,' Harry patted a boulder, 'but that's crawling with tourists. We have this place completely to ourselves. Which is why I can do this.' He pulled her closer, starting to unbutton her flies.

Jo had barely caught her breath, yet the response lever slammed straight down as she got off on the whole sacrificial pagan ruggedness of it. She reached for the condom in her pocket, spots of high colour at her lusty pre-planning providing much-needed warmth to her cheeks. 'Is this an Inchbold family tradition too?'

'Only very recently. Starting today.' He laid her on the boulder. 'We'll do it again next year. Are you sure this won't hurt?'

'If it warms me up, I'll take the risk.' She tried to stop her teeth chattering as the wind sliced through her. It felt sensationally tribal being spread-eagled on a standing stone, and she could feel herself coming with almost indecent haste as soon as he ran his fingers between her legs, but it was bitterly cold.

Harry wrapped her in his huge padded coat, inside her in an instant, the eye contact impossible to drop away from now, the satisfaction they were taking entirely shared.

Afterwards, they stood up wrapped in the same coat, leaning against the stone. Harry was warm as a furnace. Jo folded her arms and legs around him to draw him to her.

'This is something else, you know that?' He kissed her face, her eyes and her mouth with tremendous tenderness.

Jo knew it, but she couldn't say it. Admitting it out loud

was throwing herself under its rollercoaster wheels, and she needed to wait for the ride to stop and get out on the platform. It was almost time.

'Talk.' He clutched her tightly. 'Tell me about Tom.'

The jockeys rode past again, whipping hard as the wind got up. Jo hugged Harry closer. She had none of his eloquence, his ability to spin an anecdote and transport her there, as though telling a bedtime story. Her truth came in snatches, a lifetime of polite, slightly sarcastic repression making it impossible to articulate something that was still hurting so much.

'There's not much to say. Most people who meet me assume I'm married to my career, even though I've been cohabiting for five years. It's been a bigamous relationship. In the end, I chose my career.'

'Did you send Tom a card to let him know?'

She laughed, grateful for the break in tension. 'I told him in person. Now it's over. That's about it.'

He slipped a knuckle under her chin and lifted it so her eyes levelled with his, the honesty between them impossible to look away from. Jo knew that when she'd said, 'You first,' and he had jumped so honourably, she was duty-bound to follow.

'Tom's a good egg and I'm a lovely bird, but our nest was built on a cliff face. We met the day I split up with someone I thought I loved. I'd had a very rocky relationship history up until then, and Tom was a safe harbour.' She paused, thinking hard, trying to be as heartfelt and lyrical as he'd been with her.

Harry was looking at her curiously. 'Is he some sort of marine ornithologist?'

She laughed again. 'He worked for a charity. I thought he was the kindest man I'd ever met. Even his name is safe. Tom Nice. He's Mr Metrosexual. He bakes bread and recycles. He wanted babies, our babies, and he wanted to raise them as a house husband so that I could keep working. At the time, I thought he was my forever-after.' She backed away, suddenly racked with guilt at spilling all this on a hilltop with her final fling when her faithful partner of eight years was still laying siege at home, refusing to accept it was over.

Harry took off his coat and wrapped it around her. 'What changed?'

Jo thought briefly about the day when everything had changed, then forced her mind away. 'An analyst would no doubt come up with a load of stuff about me losing Dad last year, but if anything, losing Dad so suddenly made me realize that I couldn't tread water any longer.'

'So you decided to swim for shore?' Harry leaned back against the stone beside her and they both looked out at the horizon.

She watched the sun dropping lower, deep gold now. 'Tom came along just as all my friends were settling down, and I thought I should follow suit. By the time I turned thirty, my life looked perfect. I had a great job, my own flat, a long-term relationship that was casting its eyes towards a bigger house somewhere quieter and towards parenthood. And we shared four healthy sixty-somethings revving up for the role of grandparent. Then we –' she couldn't say it, still unable to admit the real truth behind the beginning of the end ' – we decided to put off the big move and babies for a year or two and travel more instead, see more of the world while we still could, really get to know one another. We both love travelling. It's the mutual interest that first brought us together.'

She turned to Harry for a reaction.

His eyes were narrowed and he was looking at the horizon, hair buffeting madly. 'I hate travelling. I like being places. Is Tom, the all-round backpacking Mr Metrosexual nice guy, good in bed?'

He's jealous! she realized.

'He's a great travel companion,' she deflected, 'but whenever we came home, it felt like more and more was missing. We snarked a lot. We had less and less sex – he's quite inhibited in bed and he's always struggled to make me come, but it had gone downhill really fast after – ' she stopped herself again, emotion muting her ' – after Blue Barn expanded and I was simply too shattered most nights. Tom loves his downtime. He started cutting down on work hours and talked about doing a doctorate, taking over the flat with his mess. He'd stopped wanting to go out at night. I found myself reacting by turning into a workaholic adrenalin junkie who avoided being at home.

'Then last year Tom gave up his job completely because he said he was unfulfilled, yet he didn't do anything towards starting the PhD he's been banging on about for years. He just stayed in bed until midday, watching TV. The flat was a tip. We argued all the time. I can see now how depressed he was – we both were – but it didn't make me want to reach out to him. I was too angry. He'd become completely dependent upon me financially without discussing it. I couldn't afford to take time off any more, yet he still talked about children and being a house husband as though it was a realistic option.

'I cried every morning in the shower and every night after he'd fallen asleep. What hope did Tom and I have of becoming good parents together? We'd more or less stopped having sex, so how could we make babies? We no longer had anything to say to one another, so how were we going to survive decades of marriage and family life? If he drove me to head-butting, knuckle-chewing tears of fury just by the way he left his socks balled together in the laundry basket, how would we get through the big stuff? I didn't even want to go home to him any more, let alone travel or procreate with him. After eight years, I knew we'd been earning loyalty points for two different dreams, a huge emotional investment with nothing to show if we cashed it in. I'd only confided in my very closest friends about it, but they all agreed I had to break free.' She stopped. She'd made herself hoarse, the wind and raw emotion ripping at her throat. She'd never talked like this before in her life.

The sun was almost down now. A cluster of birds was gathering just above the tree line in chattering anticipation of dusk.

Harry's hand reached across to take hers. 'When did you break it off?'

'Just before Christmas. We were supposed to be going to his parents and I wanted to try to hang on until New Year to spare everyone's feelings, but in the end I just couldn't. Once my mind's made up about something, I have to do it. There were a lot of tearful scenes. We talked all night and all the next day, but I stuck to my decision. It was the most incredible feeling of relief I've ever experienced.'

They watched the black silhouettes of the birds above the trees swoop and cluster together, their numbers growing, the shrill calls intensifying.

'It's been hell, if I'm honest. Tom refuses to leave the flat. He's moved into the spare room and plays a lot of Nickelback very loudly, saying he technically owns a share of the property because he helped pay some of the bills. I've offered him money – more than he's ever paid in – but he's demanding five times the amount. That would wipe out my savings and I need them.'

'You're being far too kind. Tell him to fuck off.'

She turned to him, loving the outrage in his face. 'You sound like my mother. I know Tom will be all right. Women love him. He'll have a family one day and he'll make some-body very happy. Just not me.'

'And what do you want, Joactually?'

She turned back to watch the birds on the horizon, more and more gathering now. 'Are they crows?'

'Starlings. You haven't answered my question.'

She thought about her plans, all so clear-cut and care-fully laid out, with Caro already on side to support her at work, her mother at home; her savings – if she could keep them from Tom – would pay for it all.

Standing up and stepping in front of her, Harry wrapped his arms around her shoulders and pressed his chin on her head in the most comforting hug she'd had all year.

'I've made plans,' she told him quietly, 'I know what I'm doing next. I've signed up with an agency. I'm going to have a child, if I can, as soon as I can.'

'You're adopting?'

'Donor insemination. I have enough money to try for a year.'

Harry said nothing. The silence stretched on. She could hear the birds over the woods chattering and gathering in force and the wind whistling past. His arms stayed tightly round her, his head above hers. She was still wearing his coat. If she listened very carefully, she could hear his teeth chattering – or was it his heart beating?

She wanted a child on her own terms. It was all she'd thought about for months. The prospect had seen her through the bitter, unhappy end with Tom. What she'd found here was too transient to trust. As Harry had pointed out from the start, their baggage got left behind.

Still he said nothing. She could sense his anger from the tension in his body, already so familiar in its every contour and plane, her perfect partner for the grand finale of all final flings.

124

Jo now wondered in a panic if he thought she'd been shagging him all weekend to try to get pregnant on the cheap. Hardly likely, given the number of condoms they'd been getting through, but it seemed best to clarify the point.

'Before I go ahead with this process, I decided to have an affair,' she told him. 'Just short. Just for sex. Just to know that I could. You're it, Harry.'

His arms slid lower, hands cradling her backside to lift her up against him until she was level with his face. His blue eyes were telltale flinty. 'What about our date?'

She cupped his face in her hands. 'We both know that's never going to happen.'

'Give me a year. Give us a year.'

She tried to look away, but his eyes had hers trapped. 'This might be my last chance, Harry. I can't throw it away.'

Even as she said it, she knew she was doubting herself. The thought of parting, of letting this go, was like sharpened steel across her throat. Harry Inchbold had started to conquer her head and her heart as well as her body. They were two cynics who had learned from their mistakes. That could make the best combination. A year was nothing compared to the eight she had lost with Tom, so much of it spent bickering, so little of it happy. Being at Morrow with Harry had made her happy, from making love in a blackout to taking confession over ice cream on a crumpled bed. The cottage was fairy-tale perfection, like the witch's lair that children find in enchanted forests, but which was gone when they searched again.

'Tell me honestly that you don't think you and me is worth trying.'

She found she couldn't answer, because the honest answer would turn her life upside down again. She'd made a plan: she was going to stick to it.

His mouth landed against hers, possessive and sensual. Jo started to protest – he was gripping her so fiercely, she could hear the coat ripping – but it was seriously sexy, and before she could stop herself she was kissing him back. Now she was perched on the rock again, the kiss deepening to the soul-swapping level she had only ever known in the past forty-eight hours.

The birds above the woods were chattering louder than before, a screeching white noise.

They kissed on. She wound her fingers through his hair, the other hand cradling the stubbled precipice of his jaw. How could someone she'd only just met make her feel so much?

The sky around them was darkening now as the birds congregated in ever larger numbers, from a few hundred to a thousand or more. The noise was deafening.

Still they kissed, locked so tightly together it seemed they might fuse into one.

And then, as the noise got too loud to ignore above even the loudest of roaring hearts, they turned and gasped: the starlings they had last seen in their several hundreds now flew together in their several thousands. The sky was alive with a geometry that seemed made of black smoke, spiralling and tunnelling, a constant swirl of animated shapes, like a giant monotone kaleidoscope.

'It's a murmuration,' Harry breathed, as the huge cloud of ever-shifting black specks danced in front of them.

Jo wondered for a crazy moment if she was dreaming. It seemed impossible that the little black birds should gather in such numbers and fly in formations that no child with a Spirograph, however ambitious, could hope to replicate. It seemed born of another world, inexplicable and magical, black chiffon drawn across the sky by a giant's hand.

And then, just as quickly as they'd arrived, the birds disbanded and were gone.

Harry folded his arms around Jo as she curled against him for warmth and mutual wonder. 'Now we have a year or the devil will take us.'

FROM THE VISITORS' BOOK, MARCH 2006

God pulled his bleeding fingertips through gold leaf to create the evening sky above Mawr Vron. The beds were lumpy. Nevertheless, I fully intend to be back next year. Don't change a thing.

Jo Coulson, Crouch End

PART TWO

2007

Music: Amy Winehouse, Norah Jones, Miles Davis

Car: Jo's ancient Mini

Season: Spring; raining

FROM THE VISITORS' BOOK, MARCH 2007

There are secrets everywhere; some are
kept, others forgotten, and some have yet
to be discovered. To have found this one
is something I'll never take for granted,
and waking up to it is among the greatest
feelings in the world; going to sleep inside it
is even better.

Harry Inchbold, London

FRIDAY AFTERNOON

The Journey

Dirty spray landed on the windscreen in waves, a filthy ride of car-on-wet-motorway, wipers slicing brown snakes aside, teardrop eggs re-forming and morphing into ever bigger serpents.

Inside, heaters blasting and music pounding, it was a warm, throbbing incubator of anticipation. Harry had the passenger seat pushed right back, his long body folded up in the front of Jo's Mini, like sexy origami.

'I never was, I'm always to be,' he said. 'No one ever saw me, or ever will, and yet I am the confidence of all. What am I?'

'Tomorrow.' She knew the riddle.

'Ten points, Owl.' He reached across to tousle her hair, now long enough to form a Beatles mop that was Juliette Binoche chic on a good day, Richard III on a bad.

'Here we are, same time next year.' Jo plunged the car into a fast-wipe cloud as a pantechnicon passed them. She'd been dreaming about going back to the cottage for weeks, and now it was finally happening, her senses were heightened so that every raindrop seemed sharper, every blade of grass greener.

Harry eyed the speedometer. 'How come you always drive so bloody slowly?'

'This journey deserves savouring.'

She glanced across at him. The stomach-melt impact of his eyes meeting hers made her foot float away from the pedal.

133

'I still think you should have let me hire a car to drive you there – I know a company that has a fantastic fleet of vintage open-tops.'

As he said it, the Mini was almost knocked sideways by another riptide from a passing lorry. They started laughing, Harry's amusement so catching that she was lifted with it to a breathless silliness, the rumble of the hard shoulder line shaking the car. Jo forced her eyes back to the road.

'I think savouring the moment may register on AA Road Watch,' he said, side-waves lapping them in a steady rhythm as a procession of impatient cars overtook. 'Let's play I Spy.'

'You always cheat.'

'I just use my mind's eye. I Spy with my little eye something beginning with *n* . . . and the clue is, it's a part of your body that's sticking out and exciting the hell out of me right now.'

'That'll be my nose.'

As Harry spied parts of her body well out of view and Norah Jones sang 'Come Away With Me' seductively through the car's speakers, Jo tried to concentrate on the carriageway ahead, but his focus was making parts of her tighten, cleave and soften in anticipation of Morrow's isolated intimacy. He knew every inch of her. Twelve months of new-found land had left no uncharted territory. Seeing past Harry's third eye into his head was another matter.

'Does it feel strange going back to Morrow?'

'With you, Joactually, everything feels just right.'

Jo smiled, staring out through the sheets of rain and loving every wet inch of motorway leading them to the cottage. She'd almost forgotten about the silly Joactually/ Basicallyharry joke. The chemistry had started there. It was still combusting spectacularly. She couldn't wait to get to Morrow. She accelerated into the middle lane.

Propping a foot on the dashboard with a wince, Harry stretched back in his seat. He'd nicknamed Jo's car the Zit at first because it was small, uncomfortable and an ugly shade of yellow, but Jo adored Minis so he'd learned to tolerate it. 'If you love me, you're heartless, but if you hate me you're full of kindness. What am I?'

'One of the many slogans I rejected from Blue Barn's Valentine-card suggestions?'

'Caro's lucky to have you.'

'It's nothing.'

'Right answer. If you love nothing, you're heartless. Hating nothing is kindness. You are the latter, which is why I love you.'

'I hate ten-pin bowling and nail art,' she pointed out.

'That just makes me love you more.' He gave a gruff laugh, raking his free hand through what had recently been a blond mop, now shorn to an urban clip, honey tufts darkened by an office life away from the sun.

'I love you too.' She reached across and their fingers briefly curled together before she had to grab the wheel to hold the car on line through a slew of standing water.

From the very start, they'd found it easy to say they loved things about each other: bodies, minds, sex, quirks. To say 'I love you', in all its abstract simplicity, had taken many more months. Looking back, it was impossible to know who had said it first – one's declaration echoing the other's, the biggest unspoken truth they'd left till last to share. Now there was almost nothing Jo wouldn't tell Harry. They could spot secrets at twenty paces, which was more than could be said for road signs.

He squinted up at a passing slip-road marker. 'Does that say Kenilworth or Kidderminster?'

'Shit!' This was their exit. She swerved left.

'I love it when you drive badly. There's nobody I'd rather

die with.' That laugh rang out again, drawing hers breath-lessly alongside.

It was a running joke, which Jo had been the first to make because Harry was so reckless behind the wheel. Because he had no need for a car, the joke had shifted to her granny-driving.

A year together. A year of teasing and flirting, believing and depending. A year of getting to know one another, learning when to trust and when to doubt – Harry realizing that Jo always took too much on herself and was tirelessly kind, hilarious when drunk, and that she cried the moment she heard the opening bars to the *Out of Africa* theme. A year, during which Jo had never quite known which of Harry's stories were hard fact, which embellished to enter-tain her, and had discovered that he would stay awake all night to make her come. A year of breaking apart from others: his divorce had now neck-locked him beneath a guillotine of court orders, taking Harry and Bree Inchbold from soulmates to stalemate; her split from Tom had dragged on through early summer, formal proceedings executed at the kitchen table, a household item and petty recrimination at a time. Yet all their regrets and the guilt at two failed relationships had been eclipsed by the huge, fast-growing magical world that was now exclusively theirs. It had been a year focused around one promise they had both kept. Same time next year. And now they were escap-ing to Morrow.

When the yellow Mini eventually pulled into Glyn Pugh's gateway entrance, the car park had turned into a lake and the rain was coming down in stair rods, now hammering on the car roof so loudly that they couldn't even hear the car engine and music stop.

They stared out at the downpour, then looked at each other, eyes alight. They didn't need to say what they were thinking. Contorting themselves in their seats, hot breath against ears and necks, bodies hard against one another, they faced the back seat where they'd crammed coats and clothing. With a groan of effort, they took what they needed quickly before twisting back into their seats with a sigh.

As Jo struggled to pull on her patterned wellies, accidentally beeping the horn several times, Harry opened the door to make space to lace up his heavy-duty nubucks. 'I'm buying you some walking boots.'

'I'll add it to the list.' Jo fished a piece of paper out of her pocket, then shrieked in protest as Harry snatched it away and threw it behind them.

'This is Morrow. No lists, no agendas.'

Carrying his coat over his head, he leaped out and dashed around to open Jo's door for her. Then, holding hands, they ran towards the entrance, shrieking with laughter as the puddles splashed up over their knees.

FRIDAY EVENING

The Takeaway

'I'd forgotten how good this tastes.' Jo dunked another poppadum and held it up to Harry's mouth. Curled up together in front of the wood-burning stove, the room infused with the smell of curry and smoke, she couldn't remember a moment of feeling quite so complete, a circle that had closed to make a whole.

Her heightened senses were in nirvana. Everything was utterly perfect. The beer tasted like sunlit dewdrops on hop leaves, the shadows danced like spirits along the glowing walls, the oak panelling was melting chocolate and the ceiling beams were fat cinnamon sticks. This was their spiced gingerbread house. Morrow was so much prettier than she remembered, the tapestry upholstery a perfect contrast to wood, stone and whitewash, the threadbare rugs as soft as pony muzzles. Its decrepitude was exquisite.

'Why did we leave it a whole year to come back?'

'That was the deal. Never welsh on a deal, especially so close to Wales.' He chased the last vestiges of lime chutney from the pot and fed it to her, followed by a kiss, then another and, 'I love you,' which she repeated back in the same shared, mouth-watering breath.

'I could live on these poppadums,' she moaned greedily.

'It would make a change from Fruit 'n' Fibre.'

'I'm a cereal monogamist.'

His rented houseboat in Little Venice had just one small food cupboard, which was largely filled with her cereal

138

packets. Although Jo didn't live there, half her clothes had a timeshare in his single wardrobe while half of his were draped over her bedroom chair in Crouch End. Neither really liked the other's choice of home – Jo found the boat noisy, cramped and unstable while Harry complained that her flat was too far from a Tube and too minimalist. Her decision to rip out Tom's wonky shelves as soon as he'd gone and paint every room white had, on reflection, probably been an overreaction. In London, Harry and Jo were minute and hour hands chasing the time between N8 and W9. Here, it felt like the clocks had stopped.

'No one's been to stay here this year.' He pointed to the fire-making basket, brimming with Sunday papers dating back to the previous November when he'd brought his friend Ned to cool off during a marital blip.

'The cottage's mysterious co-owners could have come every weekend and brought their own papers to burn,' she pointed out. 'Or not lit a fire.'

'Christ, you're sexy when you're logical. Except that if they hadn't lit a fire, we'd have found their frozen, desiccated bodies here. This place gets seriously cold in winter. I'll bring you in summer next time. It's magical.'

Jo decided she definitely wanted to see it in summer: it was the most unspoiled of all love nests. And she was with the most wonderful of all men.

'I love you,' she said, licking butter chicken from her fingers.

He took her hand and kissed it, briefly rolling his tongue against her palm, the sensation of its firm, swirling promise hypnotizing her, hunger vanishing. 'Let's go to bed.'

That first stolen weekend at Morrow, when they'd bonked so much they'd used a catering pack of johnnies and she'd got cystitis, Jo couldn't imagine the sex getting any better. Yet now it was in a different league, a year of addiction to one another turning into a deep-set intimacy. They knew each other's bodies and minds so well, sharing every button and sweet spot, learning the exact pressure, the rhythm and angle, uncovering the fantasies, endearments, dirty talk and soft flattery that melted inhibitions. Tonight they were fearlessly tender, wrapped up in each other as the rain hissed against the windows and the candles guttered.

SATURDAY MORNING

The Cooked Breakfast

The cup of tea slid on to the bedside table, soft kisses moved from forehead to cheeks to mouth, followed by the familiar whisper of, 'Ssh, you sleep longer.' Jo had never been good at waking up; Harry was the best alarm clock she'd ever had.

Her senses, so overloaded last night, gradually came to life. The rain was hammering on the roof so hard and the trees shaking so ferociously that it sounded like white noise being piped into the room. Starfishing her way beneath the new duvet and into a luxurious stretch, she could smell bacon grilling and hear a crackling record playing on the old gramophone beneath the floorboards. It wasn't yet eight. She buried her face in his pillow and breathed deeply, a slow smile forming before she rolled off the bed and hurried downstairs to find Harry.

Both Harry and Jo loved food and music, sharing their tastes with enthusiastic generosity and impatience. They fell over one another in the two small, impractical London kitchens where they created feasts, making increasingly ambitious dishes for one another and for friends and colleagues, griddling and blending through simmering marital tension, new romance and office politics. Above all, they enjoyed cooking for family, from the first summer deck barbecue for their parents – not a resounding success, given the strident argument that had struck up between the senior Inchbolds about Blairite politics, only silenced when Jo's mother's dog, Rathbone, had fallen into the Thames and had to be rescued – to the Christmas Eve monkfish tails that had been declared a triumph, washed down with so much Gavi that a mellow truce had prevailed. Harry's little sister, Titch, always came loaded with home-made vanilla vodka and a doggy bag, and Matt brought a succession of tall, blank-looking girlfriends with no appetite. They'd tried out vegetarian recipes for Tara and Orchid when they were over from Ibiza, both getting wildly drunk and hugging Jo a lot, telling her she was so much lovelier than Bree the bitch.

To Jo and Harry, it was as though their lives were one jigsaw, the box of which had been lost years ago but all the pieces remained. Some had been with Jo, some with Harry. They couldn't see the picture yet, but they knew it all fitted together totally, half sky and half earth. Harry was impulsive, generous, mercurial and explosive; Jo was self-controlled, kind and unshockable. Her plans were as practical and long-held as Harry's were abstract and changeable: she wanted a child before she was forty and a house in the country before she was fifty; Harry wanted them to start having as many children as they could as soon as possible, filling up an enormous house with music and friends. Jo was happy in her job as long as she could afford the finer things in life; he was totally unmotivated by money, but he was ambitious, most of all for her talent, which he thought was wasted. His own talent was in high demand, securing him a high-flying job among former London colleagues in branding, where he spent all day ruffling feathers and was constantly threatening to leave.

It amazed Jo that he had lasted so long at Hunter Broadcasting, but when she'd broached the point, he'd said simply that he'd done it for love. Harry Inchbold would do anything for the one he loved.

'I think we should open our own restaurant,' he said

now, kissing her good morning over his shoulder as he fried mushrooms, and growling with approval when she slipped a hand between his legs to give his balls an affectionate stroke through his boxers. 'A cliquey greasy spoon off Aldwych banging out twenty-quid Eggs Benedict to media types – or a gastro-pub with a micro-brewery somewhere pretty in the Home Counties where you can drop sprogs into Moses baskets while I drop fat cod fillets into beer batter. There's a mug of tea for you there.'

She went to find it. 'Isn't dropping babies supposed to be bad for them?'

'I'll be there to catch them as they come out. We'll put you in one of those birthing pools in the kitchen and they'll bob up. If our firstborn's a boy, we'll call him Bob. And, indeed, our second-born.'

'And if we have a girl?'

'Also Bob.'

'Along with the dog and cat?'

'All Bob, yes.'

Silly jokes delighted them, often gripping them in silent tears of shared laughter in their private world of mutual obsession. Playing the career-change daydream game was a favourite lazy-day flirtation – last week Harry had fixed on the idea of retraining as a carpenter to create a line of artisan furniture made out of old tun barrels; before that they'd both become very excited by urban pop-up galleries, and before that an online swap-shopping empire co-ordinated from a warehouse in Shoreditch where they'd have endless sex on a smoked-glass boardroom table. Lately, their hypothetical children had joined their conversations on an increasingly regular basis, much giggled over for unlikely birthplaces and derided for their silly names.

Being entrepreneurial parents and cohabitors were fantasies, but pinning Harry down to anything more concrete was impossible, and Jo was getting increasingly jumpy as their year together sped to an end with no proper plans in place.

Recently a pregnancy scare had elevated the baby conversations from idle jokes to something much closer to parenthood. Jo had never been great at remembering to take her Pill at the same time of day, and she'd paid the price for constantly living between flat and boat by missing three on the trot. Harry, a fatalist who feared nothing, insisted they shouldn't wait any longer. When her period had arrived, along with an unexpectedly sharp sense of disappointment, they'd drowned their sorrows and made a drunken pact. She'd stopped taking the Pill altogether. But it was life-in-the-fast-lane family planning, Harry-style, and Jo knew she was out of control, with too much at stake to be so reckless. Harry's ability to make anything seem possible was addictive.

At thirty-seven, Jo's relief that her meticulously planned route to single motherhood had veered off course to join forces with Harry's unswerving determination to be a father was matched by fear of trusting to Fate. Her D.I. Daddy Designer Baby, as Harry called it, was a dream she'd owned and organized, its chances of failure carefully analysed, along with her private coping mechanism should it go wrong; she alone would take responsibility and make decisions. Now it was a shared experience that twisted together two fates to try to make a third, and while she longed to bear Harry's child, she was secretly terrified she'd let him down. A donor father would have made no judgement about the child she bore him, and would feel no disappointment or anger, should it be less than perfect. Harry deserved to know, and urgently, one of the few facts she'd never shared about what had poisoned her relationship with Tom and their own baby plans, yet she still couldn't bring herself to talk about it.

Jo found Harry's total belief that they would be parents together as daunting as it was reassuring. Harry never planned ahead because he'd inevitably already set off. For a details-obsessive like Jo, the logistics of living between a small damp boat and the same top-floor flat she'd owned since she was a student worried her. Weren't babies supposed to happen after you'd moved in together, redecorated the smallest room in suspiciously neutral tones, freebased folic acid for months and kept a mountain of pregnancy guides by the bed, like Fi and Dom, who were now expecting a boy in May? Jo had come off the Pill three weeks ago, her hormones and thoughts still in turmoil, and nothing had been properly planned or discussed, however excited they were at the idea of having children and living together.

She was determined to talk about it this weekend.

'How would you like your eggs?' Harry asked now, reaching for the box. 'Apart from pursued by many tens of thousands of my sperm?'

'I might just have a slice of toast.' The smell of frying mixed with last night's curry and woodsmoke was making her queasy. Her stomach was crying out for wholemeal ballast and the sweet energy rush of honey. She knew she had to start getting healthy for conception, cutting down on rich food and booze.

Unable to wait for the ancient grill, she leaned over the table, elbows propped as she started to butter a slice of bread. Harry moved in behind her, his lips dropping to the top of her spine, the length of him hard against her as he lifted her T-shirt hem.

'I hope those aren't four-minute eggs,' she smiled into the honey pot, 'because mine take a lot longer than that.'

'I turned the heat off them so I could turn it on you.' He dropped down to his knees and kissed the curve of one buttock then the other before his mouth plunged between them, making her jerk back in delight, the knife clattering from her fingers.

Table-top sex was among their favourites, perhaps unsurprising for two such enthusiastic cooks, although their capacity to break furniture was becoming a private legend. The legs on the ancient Ikea drop-leaf in her flat had been repaired so many times they'd eventually thrown it out and bought a sturdier painted Victorian one. When that had given way, they'd opted for heftier plank-board. They were currently trending the industrial look in the minimalist white-cube flat with a steel workbench bought from a local builder who was dismantling a factory canteen.

Having driven Jo to a gloriously full-on orgasm for a sleepy, hung-over morning, Harry turned her towards him, so that he could look her in the face when he came inside her. He was a gratifyingly open-hearted lover, confident and generous, if sometimes extremely kinky, belying a long track record that Jo's own relationship history fell far short of. She was still prone to pose and check her angles, messing about with half-baked fantasies and jokes to mask her self-consciousness, whereas Harry lived in the moment and shared it all. With Harry, seduction was a natural pause in conversation. Sex came effortlessly to him. He also had the most spectacular finish of any man she'd ever known, a powerhouse of passion, his head dipping to her chest in a heavy counterweight of hot breath and noise as he exploded inside her.

Jo curled her fingers into his hair and felt their heartbeats collide, that now familiar barrage.

'I love this place.' He pulled out, cupping her in his hand. 'I love it.'

Jo didn't care if he was talking about her body or Morrow. Being here made her feel a part of his history, the place he loved most. Having somewhere so important was magical.

'Now I *am* hungry,' she said, ravenous for a bacon sand-wich. Pulling her T-shirt down, she went to gather some kitchen towel to clean herself up, then stooped to examine the delicious-smelling contents of the grill. 'I've decided to sell my flat,' she said after a moment. 'We'll buy that place together we keep imagining.'

There was a long pause. Jo glanced over her shoulder and saw that Harry was fiddling with a wonky table leg that was now almost hanging off. 'I have no money to put in, Jo.' His voice went even huskier when he was tetchy. 'We've talked about this.'

Having witnessed her fury and despair at having to pay Tom off with almost all of her baby savings, Harry was incredibly protective of the independence Jo had earned for herself. He was also ridiculously generous. When he talked about their sprawling house full of children, it was always Harry who was going to buy it for her. He currently earned a very fat salary, but he'd been left with nothing when he walked out of his marriage. Ten years of being kept had made him very jumpy.

'And I've told you to stop being so proud about it. My flat's trebled in value since I got it and the mortgage is tiny, so we have a big deposit. We'll get a joint mortgage. We both have good jobs.'

'I'm not planning on staying in marketing for long, Owl. You know that.'

Jo switched the grill back on and cranked up a hotplate: he needed hot food. Hunger always made Harry mood-flip. But she couldn't wait to share something she'd been think-ing about all week. 'Maybe we factor that into this move. A business start-up.'

'What did you have in mind?' He stood up.

Jo pressed her hands together under her chin, convinced Harry the ideas man could make it happen. 'I was thinking of a retail opportunity, somewhere we can sell all the Blue Barn cards and merchandise under one roof in a single collection. The Blue Barn Shop.'

He smiled uneasily. 'And you want me to be its shopkeeper?'

'Its innovator and creator.'

'Creating a Mecca for ageing Tory housewives looking for jolly Labrador cards to send their friends to thank them for kitchen sups?' The tone was jokily light, but the smile dropped away.

'Exactly! I bet we'd have a cult on our hands in six months.' She watched him cross the room to fetch plates from the rack.

Harry had always had the highest praise for Jo's talents, and he was endlessly charming to her boss, Caro, but he'd never entirely got Blue Barn, its middle-class cosiness and small, safe margins at odds with his love of risk-taking and reinvention.

'Ooo*kay.*' He still sounded sceptical, but he could never resist conceptual empire-building, lobbing out breakfast alongside her as he talked. 'With a business model like this, you absolutely can't rely upon till receipts from merchandise alone to turn over enough to justify retail space. The Blue Barn website is your biggest direct sales tool, so this is all about offering something unique to build loyalty and to give your customers something back. You need this to be the place where you launch new products and roll out exclusive treats – limited editions, personalized items. It could have a café or bar attached, plus a gallery of the card artists' originals on sale and an exhibition. You could have workshops and special events that fit in with the brand. Caro would ideally need to have a personal presence, with appearances and talks scheduled in so it's as much of a fan hub as a shop, the glamorous store front while Unit Seven in the business park does the hard work.'

Listening to him, the husky voice mesmerizingly persuasive, Jo had a sense of why they kept offering him more money to do what he did, even though he longed to do something else. The man who came out of the shower at half past seven on the dot every weekday morning, smelling deliciously of Terre d'Hermès, dressing in rebelliously tweedy suits that hung beautifully because he was so tall, and kissing her thoroughly before heading into the office to reinvent things, was talking to her now, his blue gaze compellingly direct. Harry, her lover and cooking partner, was the sexiest man she knew, but Harry the marketing guru spread-eagling her on a boardroom table remained the sexiest fantasy.

He was talking about the website now. She knew she should concentrate. '. . . needs to be revamped, plus a refocus on social media, like Facebook and the new one, Twitter. That's not really going to appeal to Caro's diehard fans yet, but it'll be huge in a couple of years, trust me. Meanwhile there's a very loyal Blue Barn following to harness so they can spread the word on the ground. They all love Caro's early stuff, don't they? I know she won't sell the originals, but they could be on show.'

'She has nowhere to hang them at home – they'd be perfect,' she agreed, already seeing it vividly. Once he struck upon an idea, Harry could lift anyone into the warm thermals of his pitch for it. She was already desperate to talk to Caro and get the ball rolling. 'I'm loving this. They could have a permanent home at the Blue Barn Shop. This is so brilliant, Harry.'

He landed the plates on the now wobbly table and sat heavily, hand raking the hair he kept forgetting had been cut so short. 'It's your idea, Owl.' He forked up some of

149

his breakfast. 'I'm just playing with it. Frankly, you'd be better keeping it all online. Or, if you want to create a retail shrine for the diehard Caro fans, reclaim the original Blue Barn and use that to keep the overheads down, with limited opening and special events. Her kids must have outgrown it by now. When did you start there? Eighteen, nineteen years ago?'

'Fifteen, and you know full well Caro has four children, the youngest of whom is seven. Barnaby loves his play-room.'

'And Mummy and Daddy will be sending Barnaby to boarding school when he's eight, so the room's about to become vacant.' He didn't hide the disapproval in his voice: he thought Caro and David were educational dinosaurs.

Jo let it pass. She adored Caro, but was under no illusions that her boss was anything but a dyed-in-the-wool Sloane Ranger. She was the only woman Jo knew who still wore an Alice band and tasselled loafers. 'Couldn't we take a lease on a little shop in Farnham or Guildford or somewhere?'

'You're about to have a baby, Owl.' He sighed. 'Put Blue Barn on the back burner. Let Caro do some of the work running her own company for a change.'

'I'm not giving up my job. I love it. Caro's practically family.'

'I know. I'm sorry.' As the food went in, the blue eyes started to soften. 'And I want to look after you and our family. Cook. Fuck. Simple things you can taste and feel. Harry and Jo welcome you to the Michelin-starred country inn and micro-brewery.'

'We're not bringing up the Bobs in a pub.'

'So let's buy them a house.' He took her hand, running his thumb along her palm. 'Where we break a lot of kitchen tables. I'll stick with what I'm doing for another year,' he promised. 'No pubs, pop-ups or gift shops. Just a house, the two of us and lots of baby-making.'

Looking into his eyes, Jo knew this was her chance to tell him about her baby-making worries, but she didn't want to spoil the moment. There was something about being at Morrow that made the worries, which had stopped her sleeping for weeks on end, fade into insignificance.

They shared a bath after breakfast, talking up their plans until the house went from a modest terrace in an affordable London borough to a commuter-friendly watermill they'd convert themselves, complete with working wheel, lavish personal workspaces and open-plan family living for the Bobs. Watched through the small, steamy window by a fascinated guinea fowl perching on the log-store roof, they soft-soaped one another every which way as they laughed, daydreamed and scrapped over mod cons.

'Won't you mind selling the flat?' Harry asked.

'I can't wait,' she said truthfully. She knew she'd sub-consciously depersonalized and decluttered it in readiness for this. Harry had never liked it, and no longer did she. In the past year, she'd far preferred staying in the houseboat, which had become seductively associated with him, for all its impractical, cramped damp and bad plumbing, much like the cottage. The thought of finding somewhere dry, safe and well plumbed that was all their own made her tingle from head to foot. She half expected the bath water to form into whirlpools. It did when Harry stood up with a great rip-tide, like Neptune, reaching for a towel to wrap her in.

'Let's go to Rossbury and buy champagne to celebrate. We'll call in on the pub on the way back.' He enfolded her so that her arms were pinned to her sides. 'But we'll eat here tonight. I want you all to myself.'

*

151

Outside, the rain was still pounding down, the view hidden by clouds, sealing them in.

Jo's yellow car – which had only made it up the track the previous evening because Harry had taken over the wheel for the hill climb and burned half a tank of petrol coaxing it out of the ruts – was miraculously clean and sparkling, only its caked alloy spokes belying its off-roading debut.

'God's carwash.' Harry held open her door for her, huge umbrella aloft, like Vettriano's butler.

As he made his way round to get into the driver's seat, she looked at the cottage, its magical face exquisite, stone walls glittering like the pebbly base of a stream. 'Do we really have to go back tomorrow night? I can blag Monday off.' If she had longer, she might be able to broach the secret she was harbouring.

'Much as I'd love to tell them to fuck this Monday breakfast meeting, I don't think I'd have a job by lunch-time if I did.' He fastened her seatbelt for her as if it were a child's. 'And if you want me to pay the mortgage on a million-pound doer-upper, I can't risk that.'

'I'm happy with something a lot more modest.' She looked at him earnestly: they'd got far too carried away in their forward planning. 'Somewhere like this cottage. Only in Dulwich – although that would probably make it a million-pound doer-upper.'

He laughed, stretching across to kiss her. 'This cottage is going to be here for us wherever we end up. And it's definitely not a doer-upper. Nobody's allowed to touch Morrow. It's where my soul is.'

Jo said nothing, knowing how much the place meant to him, but secretly hoping his soul would relocate to the home they were going to have together.

SATURDAY, LATE MORNING

The Market

Harry loved shopping. Rain-hammered Rossbury market had been sensibly deserted by locals and most of its stallholders, its few remaining striped awnings tipping waterfalls on to the cobbles. But holding his huge umbrella that kept turning inside out overhead, Harry found treats to lavish on Jo as she laughed in protest, her wet-sleeved arms filling with flowers, cheese, a vintage handbag, *pain au chocolat* for tomorrow's breakfast, handmade soaps and a little wooden doll's house no bigger than a shoebox, yet carved in intricate detail with tiny casement windows in its Georgian front wall, which swung open to reveal minuscule furniture.

'Our first house. It's mortgage-free and carbon-neutral.' He took her other shopping bags as he presented it to her. 'Welcome home. I'll carry you over the threshold later.'

'I love it.' She laughed.

In turn, she bought him a new umbrella and a Miles Davis CD that looked suspiciously pirated. On impulse, they bought a huge sea bass for later, hoping it would fit into the tiny Morrow oven to cook. Jo hoped it wouldn't make her car smell. Its briny whiff was already making her regret trying so many cheese and fudge samples in quick succession.

'I think I could do with a coffee.'

The gallery and café in the side street had a big sign in the window: UNDER NEW MANAGEMENT. Inside, local artists' work had been replaced with boxy canvas photographs and prints featuring purple-skied landscapes, along with a lot of Thai sculptures, New Age clothing, dreamcatchers and scented candles that made Jo's stomach heave even more as she carried her fish through to the deserted café area at the back. At least that remained unchanged, its glass walls misted with condensation, rain sounding like ball bearings on the plastic roof, the same tattered fake flowers on the tables.

Despite the new management, the same slow-moving curator-cum-waitress with the bun shuffled slowly up, wheezing heavily, to take their order. She didn't seem to recognize them, complaining breathlessly about the weather and pointing out that the soup of the day was French onion with 'cretins'.

Jo and Harry, who remembered her well, locked eyes with relish.

Predictably Harry was already famished again, reeling off an order that involved simply reading the entire menu. Jo took her weighty bag of seabass to a far corner to leave it on a chair out of sniffing distance and escaped to the loo. Sitting down, she pressed her hands on her boobs, which were aching uncomfortably, as though her period was due. Coming off the Pill had mucked up her cycle totally. She'd Googled it, and knew to expect a bleed within two to four weeks of stopping. She hoped it held off until they were back in London. The feature had also said it was technically possible to get pregnant within days of stopping contraception, but she thought it far from likely at her vintage. Last time, it had taken six months and then she'd vomited from day one. But she wasn't going to think about last time.

Nonetheless, while Harry was tucking into a massive pile of local 'crempog' pancakes swimming in honey and butter, she said she needed some fresh air and headed back out into the rain to cross to the little pharmacy on the corner of the high street, where she bought a big pot of folic acid tablets, a bottle of luxury bubble bath to replace the last dregs they'd used up this morning, a box of tampons and a pregnancy test, which she thrust deep into her handbag.

Jo usually told Harry everything – they were compulsive sharers – but she already knew she wouldn't confess this, just as she hadn't yet confessed what had happened before they met, because to do so was to make the disappointment and worry all the more acute. This test was just to prove she was right in thinking that nothing had changed

Harry was waiting outside, brolly back up, one hand weighed down by bags as he peered into an estate agent's window next door.

'What about your pancakes?' She clutched her bag of booty closely to her side. 'I thought you were still eating?'

'Crempogs are so much more than pancakes, but I lost my appetite. Even I can't eat with that much patchouli and sandalwood up my nose. Let's lease the gallery and liberate it from tie-dye.' He squinted at the houses for sale. 'Rhona, our waitress, says the tat shop is on a three-month lease only. The building's owners are looking for a long-term tenant.' His eyes slid towards hers.

'No.' She looked at him in horror. 'Rossbury isn't the right place for the Blue Barn Shop.'

'Of course not. That has to be inside the M25. But *this* could make an amazing restaurant.' He turned to look at it from across the road, a piece of half-timbered medieval history, picture-perfect Georgian townhouses to either side as pretty as the miniature. 'Apparently the building has full A3 restaurant–business use. We could turn Rossbury into the next Ludlow.'

'No.' She shook her head firmly.

'The town has a famous folk festival, more church bell-ringers than a box set of *Midsomer Murders* and an award-winning library that was opened by Glenys Kinnock.'

'We agreed no pubs, pop-ups or gift shops.'

'And this isn't any of those – well, it's a pop-up tat shop right now, but—'

'We're going to buy a house, Harry!'

'Exactly!' His handsome face was wreathed in smiles. 'We'll live in Morrow. Buy all the others out. It will be our home. Can you imagine a more idyllic childhood for the Bobs?'

Jo stared at him in shock. This was her fault. 'Somewhere with a reliable power supply, a driveway and neighbours for a start.'

'We can extend, Owl. Build a conservatory and a garage. Put up some decking.'

'You said it wasn't a doer-upper! You said you'd—' She stopped. She'd spotted the teasing glint in his eyes and his obvious delight in her reaction, despite the Oscar-winning sincerity. He was winding her up. Jo grabbed her flowers and bashed him with them until they fell into a kiss so long and sweet and private beneath the drumming timpani on the umbrella that it might have been a tent in a remote field. Finally they turned, laughing, to race back through the puddles to the car. It was only when they were inside shaking the rain from their hair that they remembered they'd left the huge fish and the doll's house in the gallery.

'I'll get them.' Harry opened the door and splashed away, head bowed.

As soon as he was out of sight, Jo pulled the pregnancy test from her handbag and hastily read the instructions. 'Don't think about it,' she told herself, thrusting it back, heart pounding. Then she flipped down the sun visor to check her rain-spattered reflection in the mirror. Her face looked damp and shifty. She had to tell Harry the truth.

Now she'd let her hair grow, it curled over her ears and collars, long since transforming her from urchin to something more womanly. She tried to tuft it up a bit, but it was too heavy with rain, plastered to her head. She pouted, telling herself it had Chrissie Hynde sex appeal.

She had to tell him.

Flipping the visor up, she clicked on the ignition so that she could put in the new Miles Davis CD, lying back to let it soothe her, eyes closing, already composing the news in her head. 'Hey! It's almost definitely nothing, and I'm sorry I'm making a habit of this, but I'm having a bit of a pregnancy scare again. It's not that I'm very likely to be pregnant – almost certainly not – but I'm scared because we need to get more organized. Be a bit less random and fateful about it. Buy a house. And before that, I have to tell you something that I've never told a soul, not even my best—'

'It's bloody hard carrying a sea bass and a doll's house at the same time.' Harry had wrenched open the boot behind her, making her jump out of her seat as he lobbed in the weighty fish, which landed with a corpse-like thud. 'Are you sure we didn't buy a shark by mistake?'

'As long as it tastes good with black butter, samphire and vanilla, who cares?' Even thinking about it made her stomach heave afresh. She buzzed down her window.

'Are you feeling okay?' He appeared beside it.

'I will be in a minute.' She closed her eyes and girded herself to say something before she realized he'd got out of the car again. He opened her door, umbrella shielding her from the rain.

'Let me drive.'

'I'm honestly fine.'

'No, you're not. You need to lie down. We'll skip going to the pub.'

'I want to go to the pub,' she said, starting the engine, a plan forming. She'd do the test as soon as they got there. Get it over with, prove that she was being paranoid and that nothing had changed, that they had time to buy the dream house and decorate the spare room in suspiciously neutral colours, that she could still get drunk without feeling guilty that she wasn't treating her body as a temple. That she had time to tell him every last secret.

He looked at her worriedly. 'If you're sure you're okay.'

'I'm honestly fine,' she snapped, fear making her testy. 'Just stop asking.'

The open window and Miles Davis restored her equilibrium as she drove back into the warren of lanes that threaded through deepening floods, then climbed rivers of water into the hills. By the time they swung into the car park at the Hare and Moon, Jo felt almost silly to have bought the stupid test at all. Of course she wasn't pregnant. She was in her late thirties and barely off the Pill. Who was she kidding?

SATURDAY, LATE LUNCHTIME

The Pub

They were greeted over the Hare and Moon bar by jubilant, back-slapping Roy, who had grown a stubbly designer beard, trimmed like two crossed scimitars to counterbalance his bald pate. 'It worked for Connery.'

The pub was rammed with lunchtime trade, which Roy proudly explained was down to his new website, offering hill walkers the ultimate soup-and-sandwich lunch-stop, complete with complimentary foot-spa, blister pack and Thermos refill.

'I swear we had Clare Balding and Janet Street-Porter in here last week.' He filled Harry's tankard. 'Bloody Lowri says it was just the Clun Ramblers, but I know what I saw. Sod's law my camera was out of charge. You seen Ned lately?'

'He's building a hotel shaped like a bottle in Dubai.'

'What they calling that, then?'

'The Bottle.'

Accepting her lady's half-pint without complaint, Jo left them catching up and took it to the loo with her where she tipped it down the sink, hastily rinsing it out before locking herself into a cubicle and – sending up a silent apology to Roy's hygiene procedure – peeing in it. She dropped in the test stick and stared at her watch, fingers drumming. After a minute she took it out, crammed it into the reader and eyed the window warily. No line. She gave it another thirty seconds. Still no line.

Happiness. Sadness. Relief. Regret. Guilt. They all ran through her, but as she heard somebody coming into the Ladies, she was already too busy covering the traces of her crime to dwell on its emotional aftermath. She capped the stick, looking around for a sanitary towel disposer to ditch it in. There was none, so she hid it deep in her handbag and hurried out to wash her hands, finding herself beside a curvy blonde who was applying make-up at speed.

The blonde turned as Jo washed her hands. 'You're Harry's girlfriend.'

'Hi there. Yes, I'm Jo.'

'Cerys.' A steely smile.

Somewhere in the back of Jo's distracted mind she remembered a Cerys being talked about a year ago. Harry had begged fried breakfasts and fuse wire from her the first morning they'd been here. Owen and Cerys. And hadn't Cerys's gruff, funny little sister spoken candidly about their struggle to conceive? A twist of irony caught in her windpipe before she smiled into the mirror, registering that the palest of grey eyes – now rimmed with thick black kohl – were far from friendly. 'You run the B&B, don't you? With your husband?'

'I run it without him now,' Cerys said, uncapping a red lipstick to paint on unsmiling lips. 'We split up.'

'I'm sorry.'

'Don't be.' She smacked her lips together and recapped her lipstick before raking her fingers up through her hair to tease it out. She had a faded blue tattoo on the back of her neck, Jo noticed: the word 'OWNED' with little stars around it. 'He's a waste of space. I'm footloose and fancy-free. I just need someone to fancy.' Her voice was deep and dry, with a seductively sardonic Welsh borders curl to it. 'Do you have any mascara? Mine's all clotted.'

'Sure.' She fished in her bag, unwittingly pulling out the

mascara-shaped pregnancy-test phial and offering it, then realizing what it was just as Cerys's fingers closed over it. Whipping it away, face burning, she dug deeper for an old promotional giveaway. 'This one's better.'

Cerys was mercifully oblivious. 'Thanks. Oh, I love Clarins.'

Sharing make-up with a stranger after panic-weeing on a pregnancy test transported Jo back to her student self in a nightclub twenty years earlier. Deciding she should make an effort too, she found some lip gloss, her reflection wider-eyed than ever as it shared the secret of the cubicle, still letting it sink in, that collision of relief and disappointment at no line.

'I like your hair,' Cerys said, her pretty face now almost painted out. 'That boyish look's so hard to get away with if you have an hourglass figure like mine. I'd love to try it out, but it doesn't really work with tits, does it?' There was a spiky backhand to the compliment, pulling Jo's attention away from the snowstorm of emotions in her head.

'I had to have it cut for prison,' she deadpanned.

But Cerys's expression was benignly amused beneath the warpaint as she handed the mascara back. 'You're such a tease. Harry always did have witty girlfriends. I love your top. Karen Millen, is it?'

'Thank you. Yes.' She checked her reflection one last time and pinched her cheeks to add colour. She and Harry were living for the present and planning the future. His past of witty exes wasn't part of her life. She felt much more herself again. Not yet pregnant, not yet panicking. 'I'll see you out there, Cerys.' She hurried back to the bar to order a celebratory pint. The teetotal folic-acid campaign could begin tomorrow.

When Roy reached out to refill her empty glass – recently peed in – she whipped it aside. 'Let's settle this once and for all, Roy. I'd like a pint in a pint glass. Put a sparkler and an umbrella in it if it makes it more feminine by all means, but mine's a pint. And whatever you're having.'

She could hear Harry's husky laugh moving in behind her, feel his heat against her spine and his lips trace the nape of her neck as their bearded landlord resignedly pulled a full pint, scraping off the head with a beer mat before placing it on the bar. He then reached beneath the counter to pull out a fat cigar. 'Will you be wanting one of these to go with it? Public smoking ban comes in next month, so I've got the Cubans on half price. For now, you just have to stand to the left of the line, see?' He nodded towards a thick stretch of blue tape marking the area where smokers were allowed to congregate.

'Thank you, but I'm not crossing any lines today.' She smiled, turning back to Harry and whispering, 'Let's get plastered.'

She felt strangely, tearfully elated. Her adrenalin was still racing crazily from doing the test, the secrecy of it shameful. Harry took the cigar from Roy and sniffed it appreciatively. It made him look as though he had a big brown moustache, yet he was still ludicrously handsome, like Robert Redford in *Butch Cassidy and the Sundance Kid*. Only Harry could look that good with a handlebar.

She watched him as he ordered a bottle of tequila, her heart spinning with a curious blend of love and unfamiliarity, knowing that they would never behave like this in London. According to the clock above the bar, it was just after two in the afternoon.

'I hope you'll stay on for the karaoke tonight.' Roy handed the bottle across with two shot glasses. 'The lot from the new caravan park like it. Cerys does a mean Christina Aguilera, don't you, love?'

Appearing at the bar, the little blonde's face was now a

mask of kitten eyes painted wolf and cherub's mouth turned poison apple.

'Hello, Half Inch.' She glanced up at Harry then looked quickly away.

'Half Cut.'

Jo eyed Cerys with new-found respect. Wasn't the Half Moon Gang male-only?

'You keeping well?' Cerys was staring down at her Uggs.

'Never better.' He was looking fixedly at the brass bar rail. 'You?'

Jo knew she was oversensitive this afternoon, but her radar was now on high alert as she picked up the tension. She looked to Harry, waiting for an introduction that didn't come.

'So-so.' Cerys was still admiring her footwear. 'You heard me and Owen have split up, I suppose?'

Jo saw the split-second reaction in Harry's face and felt a tic of nerves start up in her throat. He looked happy.

She leaned forward, fed up of being ignored. 'Can we buy you a drink, Cerys?'

She glanced at Harry, giving him another opportunity to introduce them, but he was staring fixedly at Cerys while she made up her mind about the drink.

'No, thanks.' She smiled politely at Jo. 'Got the place full this weekend. There's a big wedding on up at the castle and they've left the bathrooms swimming in hair lacquer and bronzer. I'll be back later for the singing. Will you be joining in? I heard you were great at the folk night last year, Half Inch. I was sorry to miss that.' Her voice had a tiny crack through it, hairline thin, revealing something molten beneath the accent.

Harry hesitated.

Tell her we have a sea bass! Jo stared at him silently. We agreed it would be just us at the cottage. I don't want to watch you reading Kylie and Jason lyrics off a screen while reliving some eighties romance with the hourglass blonde.

Still Harry hesitated, and Jo waited through the pause. It felt long enough to recite a Shakespeare sonnet in, to play a chess move or phone a friend. It spoke of secrets.

She could sit it out no longer. 'We're eating at the cottage,' she said, in a strangled voice. 'We bought a sea bass.' As soon as she said it, she knew how pretentiously London it sounded. At least she hadn't mentioned the samphire and black butter.

'Shame.' Cerys's grey eyes, incandescent through the make-up, stayed watching Harry's blue ones. 'I might sing "Don't Stop" for old times' sake. How many points does that get?'

'Eight.'

She played the Morrow game, Jo registered, as her mind processed faster than a search engine: Fleetwood Mac, 'Don't Stop Thinking About Tomorrow'. Cerys even looked like Stevie Nicks. Just how much a part of Harry's secret past had 'Half Cut' been?

'See you around, Inch. Ask for the Moon.' A hand went up, nails bitten to the quick.

'Not if I see stars first, Cut.' He nodded, turning away and raking the mop of hair that was no longer there.

Jo picked up her pint and set it down again untouched, telling herself she was being paranoid, overloaded with haywire hormones and her own secrets. But she couldn't let it pass. 'I thought the Half Moon Gang had a strictly no-girls policy?' She tried to sound casual.

Harry didn't look at her. 'Cerys had honorary life membership,' he muttered, unscrewing the tequila-bottle cap, his expression hardening. 'She was always Half Cut.'

Jo found she didn't want to get drunk any more. She and Harry could sniff out secrets like old detectives, and right

164

now her nose was twitching on a scent so strong her eyes were running. She was already battling not to erect imaginary scene-of-crime tape around their recent encounter.

She knew she had to keep control. Harry had a lot of history, none of which he'd ever tried to hide from her. Part of her own history was still hidden from him, and that was far worse a crime. She had to tell him the truth before it was too late. If tonight's scare had taught her anything, it was that she would fear the thin blue line with mortal dread until she had.

But when they did settle on the cracked leather fireside sofa, with Sinbad the Alsatian underfoot and a pair of ramblers slurping soup opposite, Jo's mind wouldn't let Cerys go, those painted wolf eyes alight in her head.

'So is Cerys's surname Cutthroat or Shortcut or something?' she asked. She knew she sounded catty but she couldn't stop herself.

'It's Jones. Cerys and Owen Jones.'

'What was it before she married?'

'Jones.'

'She married a relative?'

'Not as far as I know. There are so many Joneses around here, it's impossible to keep up with them.'

He was already working his way rapidly through the tequila, she noticed, his gaze telltale flinty. He wasn't looking her in the eye much. He seemed distracted and tetchy, classic guilt tics. Her scene-of-crime officers were moving in, dipping beneath the tape, forensic magnifying glasses out.

'What's her husband like?'

'Honest. Hard-working. Not the brightest.' He eyed the ramblers' soup enviously.

'Why do you think they've split up?'

'I have no idea. Why are you so interested in Cerys?'

165

'You've obviously known her a long time.'

'Her father farms the land around Morrow.'

'Efon?'

'That's right. She got the name Half Cut because Efon's such a boozer.'

'Shouldn't that technically be Quarter Cut? Or was her mother a boozer too?'

'She had a tough time as a kid. They're not a nice family. You don't know the half of it.'

'That's because I'm not in the gang,' Jo muttered, then looked up in surprise as the bar waitress appeared with two huge steak baguettes. 'You ordered food?'

'We didn't have lunch.'

'What about the crempogs?'

'Elevenses, and I didn't finish them. You'd buggered off looking ill. You need to eat.'

'I'm in very good health.' No blue line, she thought wretchedly, then forced her mind elsewhere, distraction not hard to find. 'Why didn't you introduce me?'

'What?' he asked, mouth full of food.

'You didn't introduce me to Cerys. "Cerys Jones, this is my girlfriend, Jo Coulson. Jo, this is Cerys, honorary life member of the Half Moon Gang" sort of thing. It's not like you.'

He seemed baffled. 'I didn't think it was that sort of conversation.'

'It was still rude.'

'I'm sorry.' He put down his sandwich and reached for his shot glass. 'I had no idea you were so hurt.'

'I wasn't hurt, I was offended.' She watched him pour another tequila measure, knowing she should leave this alone now, but unable to. 'You acted like I wasn't there.'

'That's feeling hurt.'

'I know the difference, Harry. They're my emotions.

Offended is not being introduced to someone you once shared a kids' gang with during school holidays. Hurt is not being introduced to someone you once fucked.' Where had that come from? she wondered in horror.

Then she saw that Harry was staring at her with an expression that made it plain she'd just scored a direct hit.

Instinct is a terrible thing when it makes you unearth still-warm bodies, Jo thought. Her inner detective might be leaning back against the Panda car now, highly satisfied that another uncanny hunch had led to a surprise confession, but she wished she'd never been assigned to the crime. Now she had to deal with the truth.

The ramblers, feet still plunged into the soothing vibrations, eyed them with interest over their coffee cups as they started speaking in urgent whispers.

'When were you together?'

Harry slugged back the contents of his shot glass. 'You couldn't really call it being together. It was just before I met you.'

'That recent?'

'It was New Year. My marriage was over and I was in a bad state. I'd spent Christmas with friends, but I was far too raw for more company. So I came here and drank myself stupid.'

'I saw the empties – you really should learn to recycle,' she reminded him. 'I take it Cerys offered you a shoulder to cry on?'

'Actually she pointed a shotgun at me.'

'Must have felt familiar.' Jo laughed, adrenalin pumping hard now. Ancient history was one thing. Recent history was another. 'You obviously have that effect on women.' Where's my AK47 when I need it?'

'She thought somebody had broken in. She'd seen the woodsmoke and wanted to check who was using Morrow –

nobody ever stayed there, especially not in winter. We got talking. Correction, we got drunk. I already had a serious head start on her. Turned out her marriage was pretty decimated too. She told me she and Owen had been fighting on and off all Christmas and he was spending New Year with the lads to spite her. Then she told me she'd always had a crush on me. We ended up in bed. That's that.'

Jo glanced at the ramblers, who were rapt, feet going wrinkly. She glanced at the half-empty tequila bottle sitting beside her untouched pint. Her eyes darted here and there before finally landing on Harry and staying put. 'That was it?'

'Yes.' He picked up his sandwich again.

The jealousy worm was too deep in Jo's ear for her to believe what she was hearing. She couldn't wipe away a mental image of them together in the cottage. She knew this had happened weeks before she'd even met Harry, but she still felt totally unprepared for the hurt she felt, the brutal reality of his angry-eyed collaborator, all set to step on stage tonight and sing about it.

She felt geysers spurt, volcanoes erupt, a tsunami roll in as she remembered their very first morning together at Morrow. 'You went to see her the weekend we were here. You came back with breakfast!'

The ramblers flexed their toes in the bubbling water and leaned forwards.

'I went to warn her that I was here with you, that you were somebody special. I didn't want her turning up.'

'I think she's in love with you, Harry.'

A piece of steak flew out of his mouth and hit a rambler, who was too engrossed to notice. 'That's absolute crap.'

Her eyes narrowed. 'Just how close were you back in the day when she was Half Cut and you were Half Inch?'

'She and Matt were together.'

Jo stared at him, taking this in. 'She was with your brother?'

'That's right. Cerys and Matt were the Cathy and Heathcliff of Mawr Vron. That's why she got honorary membership in the gang. They were inseparable. They wrote to each other every day during school terms. She was the love of my luckless brother's life from six to eighteen. That's longer than my marriage.'

'What went wrong?' Jo could already guess. Long-distance love stretched to its limits as Matt went to university, the prospect of settling down just a dot in the distance while home-loving Cerys grew tired of waiting. Then she'd met Owen Jones, with whom she had so much more in common than just a surname.

But Harry was glaring into the fire. 'I'm what went wrong.' He raked his fingers through his hair, face dipping into the crook of his arm. 'Cerys and I did much the same thing as we did that New Year twenty years ago, except without the failed marriages under our belts.' He turned his head to look at her, eyes dark with regret. 'The only thing under our belts was the very thing stopping our brains functioning.'

'Why did you do it?'

'Same reason. We were both drunk.'

Speaking so softly that they could barely hear each other, let alone be overheard, the intensity of the conversation nonetheless amplified every word in Jo's head as Harry talked on.

'There were a load of us staying down here that week – the Half Glass Full boys, some other school friends, some hangers-on. We were having a party at Morrow the night it happened. Cerys and Matt had had a huge fight. I've no idea what it was about, but it must have been bad because they never usually argued over anything, and he'd taken

169

the car and driven home. Cerys got off her face, clearly miserable as hell. I wasn't far behind – I'd smoked a stack of weed and downed a quart of Jack Daniel's because Ned was acting up about the band – he'd just told me he didn't want to do it any more. I ended up in bed with Cerys. I can't pretend I was something better than I was, Jo. I was a drunken teenage stoner. I don't even bloody remember it. I just remember waking up with Matt's fist in my face.'

'How did he find out?'

'He walked in on us.'

Still speaking in whispers, they could have been on a sofa adrift in an ocean, for all the care they took of their surroundings. They didn't notice that the ramblers had silently re-laced their walking boots and long since stolen away, like spectators at a bonfire who had noticed it was full of gas canisters.

'We all thought Matt was driving back to London, but it turned out he'd just been belting round the lanes like a rally driver to vent his anger. When he came back and caught me and Cerys in bed together, it was over between them. Matt never came here again.'

Jo felt unforgiving, hormonal jealousy setting her morality gauge at its most Mary Whitehouse sensitive, and her sarcasm to max. 'At least you and Cerys still get together occasionally, though, hey.'

'It was a once-off, Owl.'

'Technically it's a twice-off.' She stood up and stomped to the bar for a glass of water. Her head was throbbing, her boobs aching more than ever. She couldn't remember feeling so murderously pre-menstrual in years. She was terrified that she had just built castles in the sand for a year and was now kicking them all to pieces.

'What can I get you, sweetheart?' A rugby type was propping up the bar beside her, getting a round in, pale green eyes too close together over a zigzag broken nose. 'Wine? Cider? Cocktail?'

'I'll buy my own, thanks.'

'C'mon, don't be rude. I'm celebrating. Take a drink.'

'Thanks. I just want something soft.'

'I shouldn't think "soft" is in any man's thoughts around you, eh, Roy?' he growled.

'Jo drinks pints, Owen.' Roy raised his red brows in despair. 'She's one of these feminists.'

Jo looked sharp right, eyes taking a split second to run along the stranger's broken-nosed profile, like a scanning laser. Messy greying cherubic curls, thick neck, wide shoulders, beer belly, stout legs. So you're Owen Jones who married Cerys Jones after she'd betrayed the Saint for the Sinner, she thought wildly, head in a fast-boot mainframe of logic now. *Did you know your wife and my boyfriend have fucked each other? That must put us together on some sort of sexual network, like cousins twice removed.*

'I always say feminism is God's way of identifying women who are not having enough sex,' Owen was declaring bombastically.

'How funny,' Jo muttered. 'I always say opinions like yours are God's way of identifying men that women will never have good sex with.'

'Told you.' Roy reached for the pint glass with a sigh.

Owen turned his full seventeen stone of magnetism on her. 'You are one sexy firecracker, sweetheart.'

'My name's Jo.' *Your wife and my boyfriend. Not once, but twice. Twenty years apart. Star-crossed stuff.*

'You are one sexy firecracker, Joanne. Are you busy later?'

'Yes.'

'Right answer! You and me are going to be busy making love all night.'

'Fuck off.'

171

'Hey, steady on!' He laughed. 'That's not very nice. I'll fill that mouth with something far sweeter than swear words if you let me.'

Jo heard a husky voice speak behind her. 'You heard her, Owen. Fuck off.'

Not looking round, she held up her hand. 'I can deal with this, Harry.'

'Yeah, let the lady deal with this, Half Inch.'

'Just leave her alone.'

'I said I can deal with it!' She turned to glare at him. His eyes were deep blue seas of apology and regret.

'This one with you, Half Inch?' Owen laughed. 'Might have guessed. Heard you like gobby bitches, like my ex-wife.'

'Take that back.'

'Wife-ex my like bitches gobby like you heard.' Owen ran the sentence in reverse, clearly a party trick, which somehow made it sound ten times more offensive.

'Owen, wanker fucking a you're.' Harry snapped straight back.

Across the bar Roy was looking between them in confusion. 'Is that Welsh?'

Owen faltered for a moment, then lifted his big square chin. 'Nobody round here likes you, Inchbold. That cottage of yours is falling apart, and you still think you're some sort of pissing rock star, rolling up here once in a blue moon with a leggy tart and acting like you—'

Jo was aware of the cool air whistling past her face a heartbeat before she realized Harry's fist was slipstreaming it, and that his full weight was behind it. Her reflexes were lightning, and without thought, as she threw herself in front of him, screaming, 'STOP!'

Harry had shipped the best part of half a bottle of tequila and had far slower reactions; Owen was a committed rugby

172

tackler who could headbutt a ball out of a scrum swimming in mud. Being caught between them was like being trapped in a slamming bank-vault door.

'Oof!' She fell, grabbing at a bar stool to stop herself crashing to the floor. Harry's arms were around her in a moment, lifting and cradling her as he asked whether she was all right and told Owen he'd kill him if he'd hurt a hair on her body.

'*You* punched her, you twat!' Owen wailed accusingly.

'You were the one who bloody punched her!' Harry's voice was hoarse with concern, not looking away from Jo's face. 'Jo, please say you're okay.'

'I'm fine!' Jo insisted overbrightly, batting him away. 'I want to go back.' She struggled up.

'I'll drive you.'

'Please don't bother. Stay here and sing "Eye Of The Tiger" for Karaoke Night. I'm sure Cerys would love to see you perform again.' She stormed out, mortified that tears were already starting to spill. She was shocked to find it still light, having somehow forgotten it was only mid-afternoon.

Harry charged after her. It was still raining, the stream a torrent beneath the bridge, Mawr Vron hidden in cloud. When she wrenched open the driver's door, the car reeked of fish, making her stomach heave. She couldn't stop shaking, shock and anger and fear colliding.

'I'm sorry, I'm sorry, I'm sorry.' He crashed into the passenger seat as she started the engine, raindrops flying. 'I should have told you about Cerys. I fucked up.'

'Good of you to defend her to her husband.' She reversed violently, almost tipping him off the seat.

'I wasn't defending her, I was defending you!'

'I can defend myself. I have a black belt in gobby bitch and firecracker.' She dabbed at her nose and discovered it was bleeding.

'Christ, you're hurt!' He saw it too. 'Stop the car, Jo.'

'I want to get back to Morrow.'

'At least let me drive.' He was fishing in his pockets for a handkerchief to stem it, pulling out old receipts, flyers and cash.

'You're pissed.' Jo pinched her nostrils together, blood dripping from them. She couldn't drive one-handed.

'Everyone drink-drives around here. Once we're off road, I'm fine.'

'Not if you kill me or a sheep.'

She was never normally as angry as this. The post-Pill, pre-menstrual mix was acting like crystal meth in her blood, yet she felt totally justified, an overwhelming self-preservation instinct kicking in. There were too many secrets, her own included. She could smell secrets on Harry when they were close to the surface, and she was certain there was more to tonight's revelation than he'd admitted.

She set the car into gear and rattled over the bridge, hearing Harry's alarmed intake of breath as they almost went straight into the river. Blood dripping into her lap, Jo made it less than a third of the way up the track before the car got stuck, wheels spinning in a river of mud. It had sunk to its hubcaps, too deep to shift. Filthy and sodden, they were forced to abandon it and walk through driving rain.

Not waiting for Harry, his Vettriano umbrella and string-bagged gifts, Jo cradled her enormous fish and waded on ahead, unable to control her anger, which was raging crazily now, King Lear ranting on a cliff, Kate Bush scratching at windows, the Hulk turning green. She wanted to earth it, but it was totally out of control. There had been no blue pregnancy line, and no lines in the sand before that. Now she couldn't draw the line on her anger.

SATURDAY EVENING

The Romantic Meal

Crashing into the house, grateful the door was unlocked, Jo dumped the sea bass in the kitchen sink and stormed back into the sitting room to screw up newspaper and cram it into the now cold wood-burning stove, last year's headline's crumpling, marking three months' wasted time about to go up in smoke, and nine months before that. A year of Harry. A year delaying the baby who could not wait as her body decayed from incubator-ready to incapable. She'd had it so well planned before meeting him, the father of her future child selected purely for his genetics, not his ability to make her laugh and come, love and hurt. She would have been ready and fit and well read by now. She would possibly have become a mother already. Not be wrapped up in love with a man who could tear her heart apart at will.

Harry burst in, dripping rain and dropping parcels everywhere, tequila head slowing his movements but not his heart. 'What I was is not what I am now. You have made me want to be better.'

'I can't change you, Harry.'

'I don't want to change. I don't need to change. Have I ever let you down? Have I ever lied to you? I love you more than I thought it was possible to love anyone.'

'I love you too. More than. Too much.'

He was across the room in seconds, inside her moments later. It was the most intense sex they'd ever had, coming together in an angry, passionate, grateful mess of tears

175

and aftershocks that kept them tied together for a long time, unable to talk. They just clung to one another in rucked-up, rain-soaked clothes, trapped in breathless, heart-hammering closeness, still quietly livid.

Eventually they had to peel apart. The door was still open, banging gothically and letting in lashing rain. It was freezing cold. They finished lighting the fire in silence, uncertain where the apology should start or stop. Upstairs, they peeled off their wet layers, towelled damp skin and changed into dry clothes, listening to the rain overhead and the ongoing silence, no longer angry or sulky, but sinking into a dark, mute void as something shifted between them. Neither of them understood it, but both hated it, desperate for it to pass, bodies brushing close enough to seek comfort, pride then bouncing them apart, like polar magnets.

'Let's cook,' Jo suggested desperately. She wasn't sure if she'd ever feel hungry again, but she needed something to do.

The fish saved them. Crammed with lemons, capers and herbs, the huge sea bass was a monster that they brought to life, chopping and seasoning, tasting and basting. Cooking soothed them, and they shared a rhythm and a silent language, the spoon in the sauce, flavour drawn through teeth-sucking lips to cool it, more salt, a fresh spoon shared, compared, more lemon juice, a smile and a nod.

As incredible cooking smells filled the cottage, Jo's appetite raced back. She and Harry boiled potatoes and rinsed samphire, playing chef and sous seamlessly, fingers nimble together as they slid through the water, each touch practical, reassuring and highly charged.

Harry watched her a lot, blue eyes wary, no longer fighting to be heard. This was the cottage. Whatever they unpacked stayed here. And as he watched, his control came back, his body leading the kitchen dance. He was drinking

176

water and sobering up fast. He folded his body along her spine as she stretched up for plates from a high rack, his fingers bumping up her ribs beneath her sweater before his hands cupped her oh-so-sensitive breasts. 'Marry me.'

She stared at him in shock.

They hadn't spoken for over an hour. They had fallen out so badly, she had thought right up until this moment that it might be over. He'd even punched her – admittedly accidentally. Was this the man she wanted to spend the rest of her life with? Would he want to spend his with her once he knew the risks involved in having children together?

Jo had now hesitated long enough for Harry to know she wasn't about to say 'yes'. His ego put on a good show of *sangfroid*. He shouldered the door, eyebrows raised. 'How about we eat, drink and sleep on it?'

Jo nodded, feeling guilty and angry, loving and confused.

He put on music – not the scratchy gramophone, but the dusty CD player in the sitting room from which Amy Winehouse sang 'You Know I'm No Good'. The sultry, knowing voice and sexy, jazzy swing beat pulled at her hips and libido as she danced towards the table with the cutlery. He knew just how to play her.

If secrets and hormones were a toxic mix to Jo, guilt, cooking and hormones was a curious aphrodisiac. She danced across to him, covering his lips with her fingers, eyes sparring with his, all anger dissolved. 'No drinking. Not much sleeping. *Lots* of eating.' She lifted her eyebrows and looked down.

'You filthy firecracker.' He grinned as she dropped to her knees.

But as 'Me And Mr Jones' came on the stereo, she lost her enthusiasm.

'Surely you can see the funny side.' Harry's dark blue eyes widened pleadingly, not wanting her to stop.

She sat back on her haunches and crossed her arms. 'I know there's more to you and Mrs Jones, Harry. Or was it when she was Miss Jones?'

There was a pause. 'Miss. It was a long time ago, Jo.'

'So tell me.'

He zipped himself back into his trousers and crouched down angrily. 'What good would it do?'

'I need to know.' She couldn't explain. She couldn't explain that it was different with him from what it had ever been with Tom or others before him, that once she sensed a buried truth about Harry she had to see it, hear it, defuse it, as if it were a bomb.

'Let's at least eat.' He raised his eyebrows questioningly.

She nodded and found she was kissing him.

'What's that for?' He laughed.

'Because I love you. And I love your honesty most of all.'

Then they kissed for so long the potatoes boiled dry. Harry's capacity to make her jealous, make her forgive, make her tender and make her horny broke all boundaries. That was why she loved him so much. But secrets were their mortal enemies.

As they ate, he spoke humbly and quietly of another lifetime.

'About three months after the party at Morrow, Cerys called me and told me she was pregnant. She was in a terrible state. Matt still refused to talk to her. She didn't know whose it was, but the odds were fairly heavily stacked my way – Matt's very conscientious. We'd been too drunk to care.'

'What happened to the baby?' Jo closed her eyes. She already sensed the answer. And she'd inadvertently stumbled upon her own unconfessed secret.

'Cerys had made up her mind she didn't want it and nothing I could say would change that. She just needed the money to have a private termination. She didn't want her family doctor involved – she was terrified of her father finding out. She came to London the following week and I paid for it all and held her hand. And before you ask how an eighteen-year-old had the sort of money to pay for a Harley Street abortion, Glass Half Full's first hit had out-sold Madonna and at that point it was all still being kept hush-hush that it would be our last. My face was, briefly, everywhere. At the time everyone assumed I'd earned my place in that discreet eau-de-Nil waiting room beside Premier League footballers reading inch-thick glossies while my underage girlfriend had an unwanted pregnancy dealt with.'

'You thought it was some sort of rite of passage?' Jo gasped, appalled.

'Christ, no. My head was all over the place. Tara was six months pregnant with Orchid at the time. I was already about to be a daddy with one woman who didn't want me around.'

'Did Matt ever find out?'

He nodded. 'We've always been lousy at hiding things from each other. I managed to keep it quiet until after he'd taken his exams. And by then Cerys had met Owen – they were the talk of the Moon. It was whirlwind stuff with a ring already on her finger, so it took the heat off my misde-meanours. That and Orchid arriving. I guess Matt being a teenage uncle to a baby photographed at Glastonbury with Elvis Costello was preferable to being an uncle to his ex-girlfriend's firstborn. To his eternal credit, he forgave me. He's put up with a lot from me. He even forgave me for seducing his beautiful date at a dinner party twenty years later.'

'I was never his. And we're not talking about me.'

'I only want to talk about you right now, Jo. I want to talk

179

about your eyes. I love your eyes. You have the most beautiful eyes.' His voice was getting huskier, his gaze moving around her face now, a practised seduction that would so easily entrap her if she let it.

'Stop it,' she warned, waving her fork at him.

'Your lips. I'm just mesmerized by your lips. The things I imagine your lips doing are probably largely illegal. They're fabulous lips.'

'I warned you!' She threw a samphire strand at him, starting to laugh. 'You have no idea how clichéd this sounds.'

'Your wrists are beautiful,' he said quietly. 'The first time I met you, at that awful dinner party, I kept looking at your wrists.' He took one now, turning it over to examine the soft side, running a finger along it. 'So delicate, the veins like marble. Every time you reached for your glass, I watched for your wrist, thinking it the most beautiful thing I'd ever seen.'

Jo could say nothing. Because she knew he was telling the truth. And looking down at her wrists, she found that, for the first time in her life, she thought they were beautiful too.

Much later, after a hot bath and slow love-making, she lay awake curled beneath Harry's arm, listening to a fox bark, thinking about her own secret. She had to share it, however much it hurt.

SUNDAY MORNING

The Lie-in

The *pains au chocolat* had been soaked to a strange sandbag consistency when they had carried them through the previous day's rain. Ten minutes in the oven simply hardened them to roof tiles, but Harry was utterly enchanted when Jo presented them to him in bed, along with a pot of coffee, a bowl of Greek yoghurt rippled with honey and a big bunch of grapes, which he picked up questioningly. 'I'm not ill.'

'You don't eat enough fruit.' She took one and popped it into her mouth.

'Will you forgive me if I eat more fruit?'

'Maybe,' she hedged, then shrieked with laughter as he rolled her over and started to eat fruit from the most divine and sinful of places.

'You *cannot* put a grape there!' became her increasingly astonished, aroused cry.

They were still having fabulously lazy, laughter-filled Sunday-morning sex when a familiar battered pick-up snarled into view outside towing their muddy, abandoned car. Pulling on his boxers, Harry headed outside to pacify and pay off Efon Jones. Furious that he'd almost tail-ended it when checking his sheep last night, Efon stopped shouting at Harry when he spotted his flagging glory wilting in his boxers. 'Better use that before it goes to waste, boy. Men are like tractors, see. We haul and shovel shit all our lives, then when you get to my age, you can't always rely on the hydraulics. Call it a tenner for the tow and we're quits.'

Jo heard the exchange through the window as she ate a pastry from the tray on the sill, wiping crumbs from her chin and listening in fascination as the farmer launched into a long lament about the years he'd been known as the Loins of Mawr Vron.

'Jones men are always notoriously good lovers, Harry boy. Very potent, see?'

'No wonder there are so many of you around,' Harry said, with polite bravado.

'Exactly. We spread our seed well. Children are the future, Harry, mark my words.'

'Thank you, Efon. It makes a refreshing change from people telling me it's smartphones.'

When Harry finally made it back inside, his sexual hydraulics were well and truly shot, and he was in the curious sugar-rush mood Jo had yet to really understand. 'Are you okay?' he asked. 'Not feeling ill?'

'I'm fine. The *pains au chocolat* were a bit soggy but otherwise fine.'

'You feel sick?'

'No.'

He sat beside her on the windowsill, wedging them together in a ludicrously tight fit. 'I nicked a tenner from your handbag. I hope that's okay.'

'Sure.'

He watched her face closely for a while. 'Efon says a load of chavs from the campsite hogged the karaoke microphone all night singing Eurovision hits. Who camps in March?'

'Eurovision fans camp it up all year round.' Jo wished she hadn't just eaten three pastries. She was feeling seriously bloated.

They were going to bruise quite badly if they stayed crammed into the window recess together, they decided, so they squeezed out like two corks and settled on the floor instead, backs to the bulging wall, toes lined up, like a small crowd watching their faces, one low-browed and guarded, the other increasingly green.

'Let's walk up to the Burf,' he said, polishing off the last flat *pain au chocolat*.

'It's still pelting down.'

'I like rain.' His toe crowd mingled with hers. 'We have excellent boots.' He'd bought her a ludicrously expensive pair of Merrells from the outward-bound shop in Craven Castle while they'd waited for their Ganges takeaway, still languishing in a plastic bag in the kitchen.

'I feel a bit sick,' she admitted truthfully.

'Do you want to lie down?' He took her hand.

'Actually, the fresh air will do me good. There's something I have to talk to you about.'

To Jo's horror, her stomach chose that moment to reject three doughy French pastries and a lot of grapes. She only just made it to the bathroom.

SUNDAY, LATE MORNING

The Walk and Talk

When Jo laced up her boots and zipped up her waterproof to step outside, the rain hadn't eased, but she badly needed a sharp dose of mountain air. She was burning hot and boob-throbbingly uncomfortable, her stomach still churning. No amount of teeth-cleaning could remove the sour taste from her mouth and the deep, hot bath Harry had run for her had just made her feel like she was stewing in her own juices. She needed her period to start, and fast.

They squelched up the track, over stiles and across fields, feet sinking into peat, sheep bleating away, heads bowed against the rain.

Jo kept working her way up towards saying something about planning better for pregnancy and learning from past mistakes, but she found she couldn't. She'd forgotten how hard the climb was – she was astonished that Harry could claim his family walked and talked up Mawr Vron when she longed for an oxygen tank and a pack mule to carry it.

As they paused for breath by a forestry log pile, she willed herself to start the conversation. Instead, she found herself saying, 'We need a dog.' She still missed Turtle. If it took a long time to conceive, or if it didn't happen, a dog would help them.

Harry looked surprised. 'We can get a dog. Labradors are great with kids.'

'And without kids,' she pointed out.

On they trudged, awaiting another abbreviated exchange.

His hand slipped into hers. 'Let's not live in London,' he said.

'Your work's there.'

'I can commute. Where would you like to live?'

'Dulwich.'

'Always makes me think of Dull Witches.'

'Or Cockfosters,' she muttered, which shut him up.

They plunged into the woods, grateful for the cover of the pines, the soft bounce of the loamy ridge between the ruts in the forestry tracks.

'I want a big kitchen.'

'Me too.'

'And views.'

'Dulwich has great views.'

'Over Dulwich.'

They climbed the steep, slippery banks between trees, breathless again now. To Jo's embarrassment, she needed to wee urgently, forced to high-step her way through the brush and get nettle stings on her bottom. 'Too much coffee!'

When she came out, he'd disappeared.

'Too much coffee!' came a call from behind a log pile on the opposite side of the track.

I could grow old with him, she thought. We match. We laugh. He's generous and thoughtful and honest under pressure. He sympathy-pees. And I fancy every last inch of him. Oh, but his past stinks ... and drama follows him round with a clapperboard calling, 'Action!'

As they walked on, the soap opera of Harry Inchbold's life bothered her more and more. She wanted to stop obsessing, but she couldn't.

'Tell me about Cerys again,' she said, as they broke out of the trees and found themselves in thick mist, walking into the raincloud. 'Did you fancy her when she was with Matt?'

'Not like I fancy you.' He sighed, clearly weary of the

cross-examination. 'For years, she was just Matt's sidekick. She was an honorary boy in a Blondie T-shirt. I honestly didn't see her any differently from the rest of us, even when the wet dreams and wanking started. I fancied her mum more – until she ran off with a sheep-shearer. I was sexually precocious, you know that. I've told you I was on the case by fourteen. Matt was a seriously late starter by comparison, and so was Cerys. I'm still not sure anything much happened between them beyond kissing. But by the time they had that New Year row, she'd grown fantastic tits and I guess I was all too willing to show her what it was all about.'

'Until you found out she was pregnant.'

He said nothing, his hand tightening in hers.

'Why do you think she went to bed with you again twenty years later?'

'Because I was there. Because she was drunk. Because Owen had been messing around. She wanted it to be Matt, but she got me.'

Jo had a feeling it was more complicated than that but she couldn't get her thoughts to settle in the right order just yet. 'How will he react to the fact her marriage is over, do you think?'

'Equably. Things run deep with Matt. He never met Owen, but he knows he's a prat. You saw him. And Matt works in numbers – he'll see the pattern. They met at eighteen. By twenty, they were married. Now they're divorcing before forty. No kids to glue them. Like me and Bree, you and Tom.'

Jo knew that this was her cue. She couldn't keep the secret to herself any longer. Walking blindly into a raincloud, it felt like stepping over a cliff.

'I got pregnant,' she said quietly.

'I know.' He reached for her hand.

'You know about Tom getting me pregnant?'

'*Tom!*' The hand fell away.

'Five years ago, we were expecting a baby. A little girl.'

Harry's hand found hers again, anchoring her to a halt. 'Tell me.'

'We started trying for a baby about a year after we moved in together.' She spoke in staccato sentences to stop her voice breaking with emotion. 'We took it very seriously, reading the books, quitting alcohol, eating the right food, jogging round Alexandra Park – I was super fit. I'd have whizzed up here.' She stared up at the steep incline. 'When I got pregnant, we were so excited. We thought it was the start of family life. Instead it tore us apart eventually.'

'You lost the baby?'

'We terminated the baby. It was a mutual decision.'

'Why?'

Jo tried to frame the explanation simply in her head, but the memories it brought back were too painful to speak. As her face crumpled and tears came, she tried desperately to turn away and hide the full shame of her pain. But Harry had already caught her in his arms, pulling her closer, comforting and firm. 'Tell me. Just tell me.'

At first, she could only explain in abbreviated bursts, like a crackling old Pathé news report, her sobs creating jump cuts between pieces of information '... decided to keep it a secret until the twelve weeks ... waiting for a scan with the other expectant parents ... so thrilled to see the little grainy person we'd created on the screen ... nurse called in a colleague ... We knew something was wrong ...' She wept into her hands, angry with herself for grieving so much still. With a monumental effort, she pulled herself together, forced herself to stick to the facts.

'Our baby had thanatophoric dysplasia. It's a skeletal disorder that leads to underdeveloped limbs and lungs. "Thanatophoric" is Greek for "death-bearing". We were

187

told she wouldn't survive long, if at all. We were very calm about it, about the decision to spare her suffering. Tom saw it as a *fait accompli*, without seeing how much of me felt like I was dying with her. Those days and hours leading up to the termination were suffocating. Selfishly, and perhaps stupidly, I wanted to wait for her to be born, to meet her, to bury her if she died. All the time, I had this crazy belief she might survive, that she would be the one to beat the odds. Some people with the condition *do* survive. I researched it. I tried talking to Tom about it, but it was like I'd offered him salvation only to take it away again. Looking back, I think he was absolutely panic-stricken by this alien monster that had hijacked my body, and who might come out and ransack our minds. He wanted our lives back to normal. We were so shiny and newly nested and perfectly matched. And I didn't want to let him down.'

He wrapped his arms more tightly around her. Pressing his lips into her hair.

'Harry, you have to understand that I would NEVER make that decision again. A joint decision is a coerced decision if one person feels much more strongly about it than the other. I fought, argued and debated for our daughter to have a right to be born and live, however briefly, but it was always academic and abstract to Tom. It came down to a simple choice: Tom or our child.

'Five years later and there's no contest, but at the time I had none of the strength I have now. I had no idea how mutually soul-destroying our lives together would become. I still talk to my thirty-year-old self and scream at her for choosing Tom, but back then I thought we'd try again. I thought my career would become safer and his more supportive. I didn't know he'd give up work, or that we'd stop having sex or that I'd hate him just a little bit – a lot – for the rest of our time together because he became the baby, the needy one, and every time I saw a severely disabled child, I folded up with love and loss, wishing I'd known our daughter, let her live her life, however brief its lease. Instead, we stayed wrapped up in my guilt and his need for seven years.

'That's why I wanted to have a baby on my own terms now I'm older and riskier. I had it all planned. I wanted this choice to be my own. But then you walked into my life, with your egg-chasing sperm and shitty track record, and your opinion counts just as much as mine because I love you. I love you so much I can't do this without you.' She reached into her pockets for a tissue, now utterly blind with tears, grateful for the white cloud around them and the silence that greeted her, the warm hand still in hers and not letting go.

Eventually Harry drew her hand to his mouth and kissed her pale angry knuckles. 'Our child will live, no matter what, no matter how.'

Jo felt a part of her break in the mist, cracked through with love and loss, so played out by telling him her deepest truth that she was utterly flat-lined emotionally, and so grateful for his strength and comfort that, for a moment, she imagined she might stand here in his arms for ever, taking root like the trees around them, a twin-trunked monument to love.

When she forced herself to step away, a self-protective pragmatism kicked in, making her sound artificial and brittle. She blew her streaming nose. 'Not that any of this matters if I'm infertile.'

'What are you talking about?'

She turned to stumble on through the wet mist, heading vaguely upwards.

'I'm thirty-seven, Harry. I'm not your safest bet. You have to think what life might be like without children, if that's what you really want. Just me and no family.'

'I want whatever we have together.'

They were breaking out into clearer air now, a strange sunlight filtering through the mist as they climbed above the cloud and treeline to find the Burf stone cast in bright sunlight, clear sky above. They rested against it.

'I want us to be married.' He turned to her, drawing her into a kiss that seemed to lift her up into the blue above them. She felt his confidence thread through her, pump into her veins, reassure her crazed pulses, calm her heart. 'I'm old-fashioned enough to think it counts.'

'I'm modern enough to think it doesn't matter,' she said truthfully. 'But I'm open to persuasion. Let's start with your divorce and our joint mortgage and work our way up to calling the banns.'

'God, I love it when you're practical.' He laughed as he kissed her, lifting her into his lap. 'I guess we'd better hurry up and buy this house.'

'And have a lot of sex to try to make a child to bring up in it.'

He paused mid-kiss, his eyes on hers. 'I saw the test.'

'What test?' She tilted her head back.

'In your bag. The pregnancy test. When I borrowed that tenner. I saw it.'

'Better luck next time.' She hung her head. 'I'll take folic acid, quit booze, give my body time to get over the Pill. No more random chance.'

'What exactly is it about being pregnant this time that you don't trust?'

She looked at him curiously. 'The not-being-pregnant part, perhaps?'

'I saw the test, Jo. It's positive. Come back to Morrow.'

'Forget tomorrow.' She was suddenly terrified by how much this lopsided conversation was making her hope. 'Let's go back now.'

Slipping and sliding their way back through the mist, trees and rain, they careered into the cottage and upended her handbag, like looters, its contents spilling out across the flagstones, pregnancy test and all. Then Jo froze. In her panic to get an answer, she couldn't have waited long enough last night to let the result develop in the little window. Even at this distance, a short-sighted woman the wrong side of thirty-five could see a line. A strong blue line.

FROM THE VISITORS' BOOK, MARCH 2007

Climbing up Vron Mawr through a cloud
is a magical journey. When the amazing
views are hidden, they no longer
distract you from the beauty of what is
so close by: the Burf stone isn't a plain
monolith, but a rugged, many-textured
thing of exquisite complexity. The can
opener is broken and the kettle leaks.

Jo Coulson, Crouch End

2008

Music: 'The Wheels On The Bus' (stuck in car CD slot), Amy MacDonald, Kings of Leon

Car: Jeep Cherokee with baby seat and pull-down sunscreen

Season: early Autumn, an Indian Summer

FROM THE VISITORS' BOOK, SEPTEMBER 2008

Never underestimate the endurance of something that was built with love, however humble it purports to be: it's a palace for those who value it, with a welcome like no other. Fill it with laughter and happiness. When it empties out, fill it again.

Harry Inchbold, Wiltshire

FRIDAY AFTERNOON

The Journey

'Sell.'

'Rent.'

'Stay.'

'Rent.'

'Sell.'

Jo and Harry had been running around the same trio of options since Warwick services, and were still no closer to a solution. It was like a maddening, good-natured game of Paper, Scissors, Stone with no victor. There was no point in arguing the pros and cons any more. They knew them all. It was simply the decision that had to be made.

'Rent,' Jo said decisively. 'Final answer.'

'Stay,' Harry contradicted.

'How can we?'

'Sell, then,' he said. 'Last word on the matter.'

They glanced at each other irritably, then laughed to avoid an argument, both aware that there was no right answer, just the wrong move that had put them in this position in the first place. That had been a joint decision they hadn't argued over at all.

Jo put on the radio to give them a break from the stalemate and they fell gratefully silent, toes tapping to 'Love Shack' on Eighties FM. Harry was definitely playing the tolerance card in listening to her favourite channel without sarcasm, Jo realized, stretching back and closing her eyes tiredly. He was clearly eager to get her onside and swing this decision in his favour. Or perhaps he was building up some favours ready to cash in over the weekend of passion they were anticipating. Of course what was most likely, she thought guiltily, as her head lolled towards a nap, was that he was just being loving – he often took the piss out of her taste in music, but that didn't stop him joining in the Bananarama dance around the kitchen island, in the same way she funked alongside him to the Kooks. But now, as she listened to the radio playlist, drifting in and out of sleep, she started to half suspect that Harry had prised out the nursery-rhymes CD that had been stuck in there for three months and planted his own subliminal compilation collection: Paul Young singing 'Wherever I Lay My Hat That's My Home' was followed by Madness's 'Our House', then Shakin' Stevens's 'This Ol' House' and now the Cars asked 'Who's Going to Drive You Home?'.

Head propped on her rolled-up cardigan, Jo opened her eyes and glanced at Harry again. His profile was that of a Greek bust at the steering wheel, albeit with rimless glasses and a very funky haircut, his face dusted with stubble as a remnant of the beard he'd grown over the summer – it had been streaked with silver and she'd found it absurdly sexy.

She didn't want to take the dilemma unresolved to Morrow. She needed this weekend to be as stress-free and relaxing as possible for both of them. Harry had been enormously tense all week, and she knew how much he needed this break. They'd both agreed that their home situation was no longer practical as it was, which ruled out 'stay', and Jo had tried every which way to make the figures add up better for 'rent', but they were not in her favour. That left the one option she'd prayed they wouldn't have to take again.

'Sell,' she said quietly. 'Now let's not think about it.'

He reached across and squeezed her hand, his grip tight with relief and regret.

But Jo knew she wouldn't stop thinking or feeling over-emotional about it, in the same way that she couldn't stop thinking about what else they had just left behind.

John Lennon started singing 'Beautiful Boy'. She snapped off the radio, choked with sudden tears. 'Since when did music start being about my life?'

'It always has been.' Harry squeezed her hand again. 'But now you can hear it.'

FRIDAY AFTERNOON

The Supermarket Ritual

A new Waitrose had opened on the outskirts of Craven Castle. Harry adored Waitrose, and this year they had forsaken Glyn Pugh's fat bacon slices and crusty white in favour of hickory-smoked streaky and sourdough. Determined that they would enjoy a gourmet weekend of treats, he wandered off with his barcode reader while Jo twitched briefly by the baby-food section, breasts tingling and hormones raging. Although nine-month-old Wilf had been guzzling puréed bananas and carrots for weeks, with formula replacing most of his daytime milk while she was at work, her fuel tanks still refilled with painful regularity and she had frequent inconvenient urges to cry, which Harry found as endearing as Jo found it embarrassing. At thirty-nine, sobbing uncontrollably at the sight of loo-roll commercials was far from dignified, but at least it went hand in hand with her frequent, inconvenient urges to pee.

The sight of a tiger-face soother identical to Wilf's made her swallow a sob. It was ridiculous to feel so emotional when she'd been looking forward to this weekend all month, yet she was already a wreck of homesick, baby-missing need, and they'd barely travelled further than her usual round trip to the office. Even being in Waitrose made her wistful, their familiar Saturday ritual echoed in Shropshire, although a standard trolley had replaced the baby-seat one, its contents luxury deli food instead of essentials and eco-nappies, a breezeblock tower of which she now faced like a weeping wall. This time, she failed to catch the goat-like bleat of yearning that escaped her lips, causing the shopper beside her to look up in surprise from a jar of organic rice pudding.

Hurriedly, Jo refocused her mind on food to blot out Wilf's gummy, bunny-tooth smile, and went to find Harry.

She had read somewhere that firstborns resemble their fathers in order to bond with them, and once they'd known they were having a boy, she'd spent a lot of her later pregnancy anticipating a blue-eyed son with a killer laugh. As she rounded the chiller cabinets, though, she struggled to match her fat-wristed, dark-haired little chunk of tantrums and cuddles with the lean whip of sex appeal currently eyeing cheeses while several female shoppers discreetly eyed him. Even in weekend clothes, Harry looked as though he'd just sauntered out of a gourmet coffee advert, the self-confidence of success infusing the air around him, like freshly ground Kopi Luwak. The smile that swung in her direction was pure buy-me packshot. The more tired and stressed Harry felt, the more forcefully charming he became. Now, jet-lagged from a punishing few days in China, he kissed her cheek in a supermarket aisle as though she'd just breezed into a party instead of catching up with him up by Continental Cheeses.

'Didn't you say you were going to get a newspaper?' He noticed her empty hands.

'Oh, yes. Of course.' She'd quite forgotten, her mind seemingly incapable of retaining the most basic tasks. Accustomed to speed-grazing, she lobbed a net of mini Babybels into the trolley.

He hooked them straight out. 'We're going on a Grand Tour of European cheeses,' he told her, looking into the trolley. 'Spanish Manchego, French Brie, Swiss Gruyère and Italian Taleggio. There's a lot of seriously good blue

I want to share. That part of the tour won't necessarily involve a dairy product.' He turned to her and suddenly eight aisles shrank to his single-track thought.

Jo didn't doubt she'd get into the mood as soon as they were at Morrow, but right now she felt absolutely exhausted at the prospect of sex. She struggled to think about more than one thing at a time these days. At the moment it was food. 'Crackers.'

'What?'

'For the cheese. I'll get crackers. Or oatcakes.'

'Oh. Right. Make it spelt thins – the ones with fig.' Foodie Harry knew more about the Waitrose range than most of the supermarket's staff did.

He liked to take charge of catering when they went away. They'd managed to escape once with Wilf in the summer, sharing a French gîte with friends, and he'd created mind-blowing feasts while Jo slept, napped, yawned and slept again. She'd never known it was possible to be quite so tired, the indulgent zombie half-life of a new parent, too besottedly in love to remember that not everyone's lives revolved around a small baby and his sleep patterns or the contents of his nappies. For his first few weeks on earth, Wilf had suffered chronic croup and colic, after which he had settled into a routine of only sleeping when Jo needed to be awake and bellyaching constantly in her few brief opportunities for rest. Harry was magnificent, if short-tempered, but he was away a lot with work, jet-lagged corporate hours taking a different toll, his powers of recovery swifter, his empathy less resilient. By turns joyful, inconsolable or furious – but never predictable – Wilf was a baby who resisted routine utterly, not helped by his family's living-out-of-suitcases circumstances after three house moves in a year.

As she went in search of biscuits for cheese, Jo reflected

that she probably knew her way around any given super-market better than she did her new neighbourhood. She still regularly dreamed she was living in Crouch End, only to wake struggling to remember where they were now. Disturbingly, she often dreamed that she was still living with Tom or her old flatmates before that. She sometimes worried this was because Harry was so seldom at home that they were already drifting apart, but her pragmatic mother, Di, insisted that it was perfectly normal and she herself had been 'emotional blotting-paper' for the first year of motherhood ('I had a recurring dream that your father was jumping out of the window'). She maintained that being so much older and unmarried, Jo was bound to feel vulnerable. 'It's no wonder you cry a lot – you're almost forty, you've just had your first baby and you haven't seen your hair tongs since you packed them in Crouch End. I'd be *very* stressed.' Di meant well, but it didn't make Jo feel any better about herself. They'd become closer since Wilf's birth, her mother a reassuring presence who had been there and done it before, and whose confidence that Jo would learn as she went along was a helpful counterpoint to Harry's breezy belief that she was instinctively brilliant already.

Forgetting that she was supposed to be fetching crackers, she wandered back along the spine of the shop, breathing in the scent of freshly baked bread, childhood memories hijacking her, making her stall at the junction between the deli and Homeware. Her mother had baked bread twice a week; Jo and Harry had a machine that created a dough brick the texture of sofa-cushion sponge while they were at work. Lots of things happened while they were at work, like their son smiling for the first time, repeating the *b* sound and cutting his first tooth.

Jo had never anticipated that having a baby would expose the long-lost child in her, a vulnerability so terrifying that when they'd brought Wilf home she'd instantly seen the naivety of her carefully made plan to be a brilliant mother. First, she didn't automatically understand what this incredible, forceful little new being wanted, and second, she was so overwhelmed by love that it wiped away any practical, logical thinking.

The cheese section was now unusually crowded with female shoppers eager to offer advice on Cambozola as Harry plotted his Grand Tour's route home through Germany and Holland. It was a geographical route with which he was very familiar after six months of global commuting hell; European city-hops were now easy days out compared to the pages of Harry's diary, cross-crossed with trips further afield, the International Date Line killing off any hope of date nights. A succession of back-to-back long-haul business trips meant he'd rarely been home for more than one day a week recently, if at all, which was why this weekend away together was so important, although it felt horribly strange without Wilf. They'd both agreed that trips to Morrow would remain theirs alone, at least until Wilf was old enough to appreciate his surroundings. Morrow was their grown-up sanctuary.

Looking at Harry now, Jo felt hormonal tears rise again. She was filled with gratitude for his boundless good humour and goodwill in the build-up to this escape. In a flood of emotional hubris, she could overlook the constantly changing ideas and the impulsiveness, his recent black moods and flashes of rage, mostly directed at his work. He put so much into a job he disliked in order to provide for them; he was their rock and she was going to treasure this weekend, kept sacred among recent madness. As he laughed at some unwanted advice being offered, showing that big white smile and deepening the grooves than ran from the points of his cheekbones to his jaw, she felt her heart turn over. *Now* she saw Wilf. When Wilf laughed, it was a gurgle so infectious it felled all nearby. Both father and son were utterly irresistible when they laughed.

Jo was familiar with the effect Harry had out shopping – when he had Wilf strapped to his chest it was something close to middle-aged female mania, an Athena postcard coming to life. Supermarkets were missing a trick: they should place good-looking men and babies in every aisle to bring in shoppers.

Jo felt another sharp pang of homesickness for Wilf. She reminded herself that she was supposed to be getting something – what was it? She caught sight of the newspapers at the far end of the aisle and remembered.

As she walked past the displays of sumptuous interior-design magazines, she blanched, remembering how she'd lapped them up in waiting rooms during the endless round of hospital and surgery appointments, first with a growing bump, then a baby car seat. She'd wasted hours poring over *Period Homes*, seeking inspiration for the new family nest, obsessing about what designer linen to reupholster the nursing chair in. Before that had come the mother-and-baby magazines, imagining the birth, the magical first year, the snuffling joy of quiet hours together feeding and bonding. In reality, the nursing chair had been little used, her milk largely expressed into a noisy pump to leave at home while she focused on slicing minutes off her commute. She called that her guilt trip. Guilt for wanting to escape the endless cycle of food, sleep, non-verbal communication, regurgitation and defecation; guilt that it was so much easier to function on the days she left Wilf with her mother in Wiltshire instead of taking him with her to work; most of all, guilt for her growing resentment that Harry jetted around the world in business class with no more than cabin baggage while she carried piles of baby paraphernalia wherever she and Wilf went, hurriedly spooning sieved vegetables into him from plastic mini pots between meetings. Yet, unlike Harry, she loved her job. Combining it with motherhood had always been the dream, and now she was living it. Harry joked that she would have worked through the birth if she could, and while that was definitely not the case, she wished she'd known what a mess Caro would make of running her own company in her deputy's absence.

She eyed the card selection as she passed, gaze critical and appraising. Blue Barn had lost all their supermarket orders in the past six months, but that was relatively minor in the short, destructive reign of terror resulting from the company's founder retaking the reins. When Caro had begged Jo to come back early from maternity leave, explaining that she was struggling to cope alone and offering to look after Wilf three days a week – 'I do babies better than I do business' – it seemed the ideal arrangement. The drive was hideous: there was nothing commuter-friendly about the M4 in rush-hour with a Baby on Board – but it suited Wilf, who slept better in the car than anywhere else. 'Fairy-godmother' Caro doted on him, adoring his solid pugnacity, clearly enraptured to have a baby in the house again. 'They're lovely as teens and tweenies, but you can't beat the warm weight of a tot on your hip.'

Jo knew that the warm weight of the telephone receiver in one hand and computer mouse in the other was no substitute for Wilf, but she had found returning to work a great boost because – for a few hours a day, at least – she knew exactly what she was doing. She was no longer spending every waking hour with a small person incapable of saying how he felt. Neither was she faced with a domestic treadmill that never stopped. To her surprise, she barely thought about Wilf during working hours. That must be how Harry coped. It was only when she gathered her baby back at the end of the day that the walls enclosed her again, imprisoning her in protective love. Or when she left him behind for the first night since he'd been born.

Looking at the supermarket's first-birthday cards made Jo well up again, heart roaring, confusion reigning. Right now, she missed Wilf like a vital organ, yet craved freedom. That contradiction was something she couldn't square up. She picked up a card featuring a terrier puppy in a hammock, the image splitting into two puppies, then four as tears rose again.

A warm breath on her shoulder made her turn into the big sea-wave lift of Harry's gruff laugh, full of surf roar. 'We'll get one eventually.' He tapped a finger against the picture. 'A big, soppy one that who pushes you, me and Wilf into a tiny corner of the bed, but will defend us like a lion.'

'One day.' She put the card back. A dog was definitely one complication too many right now, and it shocked her that as a lifelong dog lover she found herself ultra-protective whenever one came near Wilf. It had taken her a long time of jumpy heart-leaps to trust her mother's scruffy little terrier around the baby, yet soft-hearted, dopey Rathbone was in far more danger from Wilf than the other way around.

She selected another, featuring an Old Master still-life. 'Do you think we should send a card to Matt?'

'Why?'

'Because he's going through a hard time.'

'He's a tough guy, he'll cope. Nobody's died, Owl. We don't do that sort of thing in our family.'

'Well, I'm in your family and I do.'

Jo's many thank-you cards, gifts and emails were something that the Inchbolds took good-naturedly, although they rarely remembered a birthday, let alone sent a handwritten card simply to cheer someone up. Viv and Gerry were terrifically entertaining, but they were rather shabby grandparents who seemed to want little to do with their first grandson beyond admiring him briefly upon arrival. When not trading insults with one another, their favourite pastime was long, clever conversations that left Jo feeling far more knowledgeable and intelligent than before, if exhausted from having to think so hard. Harry was a natural father – loving, demonstrative, funny – but it seemed this gift hadn't been handed to him from either of his own parents, although they laid claim to his creative flair and culinary skills; theirs was the most culturally crammed house she'd ever been in, with by far the largest cookbook collection.

Jo adored all the Inchbolds, in particular growing close to Titch, who was screamingly funny, kind and, like her brother Harry, knew no fear.

But it was once-indifferent Matt who had surprised her most, because while he was difficult to get to know and socially awkward – and they were never entirely comfortable in one another's company – he had turned out to be an incredibly loving and indulgent uncle. His generosity when Wilf was born in starting a small trust fund for him and buying him a beautiful Victorian silver rattle had touched Jo deeply, along with armfuls of brightly coloured toys for his nephew to stare at, cuddle, throw and now chew. When Matt was with Wilf, her brother-in-law smiled more than she had ever seen before. To Jo, Matt remained a frosty enigma, but he showed flashes of something far deeper and warmer that made her long to get to know him better and to worry that he was miscast by his family as the strong, silent loner. Now, more than ever, he needed their support and understanding.

Harry's twin was currently pacing the many square metres of his latest warehouse bachelor pad in which the walls must feel as though they were closing in on him.

Earlier that month, the financial crisis had taken Matt Inchbold from safe bet to high risk almost overnight, his City career in tatters, his bank tipped to be the next to go under, the blame laid firmly at the feet of their big traders, which included 'scalper' Matt. And that week his cool, commercial-lawyer French girlfriend had walked out on him, their six-month romance all too swiftly followed by a six-storey exit in the lift when the going had got tough.

Jo was very worried about Matt, who hadn't turned up for his father's birthday lunch last weekend – most unlike him – and was no longer answering texts or emails. 'Well, maybe you could try calling again this weekend,' she suggested to Harry.

'I'm not climbing halfway up Mawr Vron to hear his voicemail message. He never picks up.'

It was Titch who had discovered the arrival of a mobile-phone signal at Morrow during a recent stay with a short-lived boyfriend, who fancied himself an erotic poet. Two days into his passionate struggle with erections metaphorical and physical, she'd roamed across the surrounding hills to find one precious bar and text Matt to come and rescue her.

Poor Matt, so loyal and stoic, yet so off-puttingly aloof. No matter how many times Harry told her not to worry and dismissed her fears as hormone overload, Jo had an uncomfortable gut instinct that things were very wrong. 'Losing your job and being dumped by your girlfriend in the same week must be hell.'

'I lost my wife and career in a day,' Harry said lightly. Then, seeing her glum expression, he wrapped his arms round her. 'It's great that you care, Owl – really kind. But Matt won't thank you for drawing his attention to his biggest life fuck-ups with a card.' Stepping back, he took it gently from her and put it back on the shelf. 'And he will be fine. He has his property investments, and plenty of admirers at work and play. Things will pick up.'

'We'll be climbing up the hill to make calls to Mum to check Wilf's okay.' Jo reached down to gather a fan of broadsheet newspapers reporting the latest banking-crisis losses, her conscience still pinching. 'We can at least try his number while we're there.'

'This weekend is about us, Owl.'

'We are family,' she reminded him, suddenly infused with a deep throb of disco sentiment as Sister Sledge rang in her ears.

'No talk of family, work or houses. Just us.'

'But that's all we talk about.' She laughed. 'That and baby poo.'

'Definitely no talk of that.' He tutted, eyes brimming with affection as he kissed her and the newspapers slid to the floor, fanning apart, like opening swan's wings, around them. They only parted when someone nudged them aside to make a grab for a *Castle Craven Echo*.

FRIDAY EVENING

The Takeaway Ritual

After the Bags for Life had been packed into the boot and the short trip made into Castle Craven's tourist-clogged town centre to order a takeaway at the Ganges, the stroll to the Six Tuns was punctuated by long, pirouetting pauses while Jo tried to get a phone signal to call her mother and check how Wilf was doing. She ignored Harry trying to herd her along.

'Wilf's had two explosive nappies and is very red in the face,' she whispered, covering the mouthpiece, already breaking the poo-talk rule. She didn't care: worry gripped her. 'I've asked Mum to take his temperature. If it's high, we'll have to go back.'

'I'm sure he's just teething,' he soothed, glancing long-ingly towards the pub, where his annual local ale fix was waiting. 'The Bro will be fine, Owl, trust me.'

'The Bro' was the nickname they'd given Wilf in embryo – originally 'the Bryos', then 'the Bros', then the singular – and Harry remained fondly and forgetfully attached to it. To Jo, 'The Bro' and Wilf were two different entities, one as conceptual as the other was sentient. She ducked away, speaking urgently into the phone: 'Are you still there, Mum? Is he crying more than usual?'

'He'd need a third lung to do that,' Harry muttered, as she waved him away, mouthing that she'd catch him up.

Assured by Di that Wilf's temperature was normal and that she should relax and enjoy her weekend, Jo rang off

209

reluctantly. She stared blankly at the shop window in front of her, where fliers advertised everything from mobile pig roasts to life coaching, a great well of fire in her chest.

She knew that Harry struggled with her overprotective logic, not seeing how leaving Wilf in someone else's care was fine while she worked by day, but a night away wasn't as easy. Di could sleep through a hurricane after a G and T. Since Wilf's arrival, Jo had found her protective reflex, so overpowering and instinctive, was often out of tune with Harry's. He was accustomed to being away from his son overnight – it was increasingly the norm – whereas this was her first time. It felt a world apart from entrusting Wilf to a different carer for a few daylight hours.

Yet Harry was surprisingly bothered by Caro looking after Wilf so regularly, complaining that she had practically adopted him as her own in her Sloaney, old-fashioned Nanny-knows-best way. Jo trusted Caro totally, and saw no harm in a baby enjoying the ride on an earth mother's hip. She also trusted adoring, super-careful Titch. Harry, though, seemed permanently terrified that she would leave Wilf somewhere, like Miss Prism. Yet Jo found Harry's total trust in her as a mother equally confusing when she almost constantly felt she had no idea what she was doing.

One of the fliers in the window was for Craven Castle Mums and Tots Club in the Baptist Church Hall, and Jo felt a strong pang of longing for the other mothers she'd met through the NCT and now lived too far away to see, for all her old London friends she called so seldom, and for the groups in her new area to which she was too busy to take Wilf. She barely recognized the gregarious, self-possessed Jo, who'd imagined breezing into working motherhood with the same confidence she'd always tackled life, spinning the social, work and domestic plates. Instead, her plates were still in packing cases, along with much of her old life, and she was juggling sippy cups and plastic bowls, veering between mother-love and cabin-fever.

Harry believed her insecurity had to do with loss: their first scan had revealed twins, but by the second there had been just one baby. Wilf was their ferocious little survivor, which to Harry made him all the more precious, but to Jo meant that her body had let down Wilf's sibling. She was now equally terrified of letting down Wilf. It made her feel lost and passive sometimes, something she struggled to explain to Harry, as though Wilf was in charge and would tell her which way to go. Di called it 'a mother's instinct'.

Yet Harry's faith in her gave her the strength and determination to get it right; their dancing-to-the-radio moments helped her see past the storm to the blue sky ahead. Now she tilted her face up to the warm evening sun, hearing Sister Sledge in her ears again, this time 'He's The Greatest Dancer'.

She headed towards the pub, the sun blinding her for the first few yards until she stepped into the shadow cast by its thatched roof and discovered she was walking directly into the path of the best-looking man she'd ever seen, the hard blue focus in his eyes so unequivocally fixed upon her that she felt butterflies behind her ribs.

Harry enveloped her in a tight hug. 'I'm sorry. We'll drive straight home if you're worried.'

'No. You're quite right – he's teething. I'm just overtired and anxious. Let's go to Morrow.'

'Or stay here all weekend?' He took her hands and held them between their mouths, his smile widening.

Laughing, she looked at the double sunset of his eyes above their tightly knotted knuckles, so brimming with love and a sparkle of lust. 'Take me to Morrow, Harry.' Her fingers tightened in his, eyes flirting back. 'And the next day, and the day after that . . . '

FRIDAY EVENING

The Arrival

The trees around Morrow were just starting to turn, not yet fully red-headed, but faintly burnished, like nervous salon customers who had asked for subtle lowlights. The cottage's pretty stone face was in shadow, but its roof was tiger-striped with orange from the sunset that was dropping behind the tall trunks banked above it.

Jo battled joyful hormonal tears when she saw it. She'd forgotten how isolated and unspoilt it was.

'You've never seen this place in autumn,' Harry said, as they racketed up the track. 'This is only the beginning. In a month, the woods will be like glowing coals, all reds and oranges. We always said Morrow looked on fire in an October sunset. It was Dad's favourite time to be here. We'd come for half-term and pick and prick a million sloes for Christmas gin. It's too early for those, but we'll get the black-berries and mushrooms. When Wilf's old enough, we'll teach him all the edible ones, like the chanterelles that grow round the birches by the stream. Posh omelettes are a cinch here. He's bound to be a fantastic cook, like his parents.'

Harry came alive when he saw Morrow.

Jo loved the easy way he always talked about Wilf grow-ing up. The past year had been so changeable that at times she found even planning into next week a mind-warp, yet Harry still never stopped looking far into the future and seeing reason to celebrate. They would find a better work-life balance, he kept insisting, along with the perfect place to live, more time for friends and freedom. They would get a dog, host magnificent parties, have a vegetable garden, take a road trip across America; Matt would find a wonderful wife; Titch would bag a role in *Torchwood* that would propel her to Hollywood. Most joyful of all, Wilf would be practically superhuman, along with his as yet unborn brothers and sisters.

'I propose we spend the entire weekend in bed. We've brought more than enough food. In fact we could stage an FP Love Siege.'

'What's an FP Love Siege?'

'In the seventies, my parents had two married actor friends, Frank and Pru, who used to come here and never go anywhere. We arrived one summer holiday and they were still here from Easter. They'd told their respective spouses that they were doing rep in Pitlochry.'

'I thought you said they were married?'

'They were. Just not to each other. The FP Love Siege became legend.'

Right now, Harry's enthusiasm was at its most infectious, making it easy to forget the day-to-day difficulties. With Morrow to escape to, those difficulties were no more than trifling details in the pictures he painted, his childhood and Wilf's intertwined. Harry saw no difference when looking back from looking forward. Here, reality altered. Harry's connection with the cottage was timeless, seeing past its decrepitude, and Jo found it easy to follow him.

The same dust, faulty electrics, damp wood and swollen shutters greeted them, now so familiar and welcoming Jo wanted to bottle the smell. The wood-burning stove spat like a furious llama. The house groaned and moaned as it warmed up and stretched in the air. The takeaway tasted deeper, sweeter and spicier than ever. A single glass of wine was enough to make them feel drunk and silly. All the time,

Harry spun dreams and Jo wove them further, their future glowing as brightly as the flames lighting them, laughter chasing every mouthful.

'This is for you.' As he broke the last poppadum to share, Harry placed something on top and held it up. It glinted gold in the firelight.

For a moment Jo's mind raced uncomfortably fast. Perhaps it was a ring. They'd talked about marriage a few times since Harry's proposal, but she'd thought it was something abstract and non-urgent that he was no longer so hung up about. Wilf was as big a commitment as any vow, they'd agreed. Proposing on a poppadum was a total shock, even given Harry's unpredictable fondness for odd-ball romantic moments. Then she saw it was a key.

'It's for this place,' he explained, looking up at the dark wood beams. 'My heart's here and I want you to know you have total freedom of it.' He stood up, dropping a kiss on her head as he stepped away from the debris of cartons.

'That's beautiful.' Those tears again.

'We will find our forever home.' He dropped down on his haunches to look at her.

She knew he was trying to make her feel better, but it just made her more tearful: she understood what they were going to give up now the stay-rent-sell decision had been made.

'We'll always have this place.'

'A forever home from home.' She managed a wobbly smile, pressing her hand to his face. 'Thank you. I know how much this place means to you.'

'You're tired out, my beautiful Owl. You must sleep. I'll make up the bed.'

Hearing him creaking around overhead, loudly cursing the damp mattress and musty duvets, Jo studied the key, newly cut and shiny as twelve-carat gold. And suddenly, childishly and guiltily, she found herself wishing he'd been offering her a diamond engagement ring after all, a full down-on-one-knee (with poppadum) proposal. She knew it was ungrateful and contrary, but since she'd had Wilf her attitude to marriage had started to shift, a reactionary voice kicking in, along with an old-fashioned romantic desire to feel cherished and honoured, to prove to the world that she and Harry were for keeps.

She kissed the key, loving Harry all the more. Because she knew that, for him, giving her a key to Morrow meant she was for keeps.

Sleepiness, sentiment and curry dragged her deeper into the chair, like anchors. She yawned again as Harry thundered downstairs, complaining that Titch had left all the windows open up there and the bed was unusable.

'The rain's got in and the mattress is still damp. We'll have to camp by the fire tonight, Owl. Or I can take you to a hotel?'

'I'm going nowhere. This is an FP Love Siege, remember?'

'I can't even offer you a new Glyn Pugh ten tog and sexy sheets this year – just sexy me.'

'Sounds perfect.' Jo was too grateful at the imminent prospect of the shared curl of sleep to care, reaching up for his hand as he passed behind her, their fingers cogging through one another, sensual and familiar. She swallowed another yawn, stood up and gathered the last of the takeaway remnants. The thought of making love was fabulously abstract, at once desired and yet insuperable. Her heart was beating in all the best places – chest, wrists, between her legs – but it was slow and faint, her mind already making its escape in PJs and a sleep mask, clutching its hot-water bottle.

They kissed in the kitchen doorway: his meant business; hers was an apology.

Since Wilf's arrival, the intense sensuality they had always shared felt like an out-of-body experience to Jo, even when she was at her most wide awake. Sex-mad during pregnancy, it had taken her weeks after childbirth to recapture the insistent twinge of longing to feel Harry inside her, and it still remained nebular and impossible to predict, her ability to come no longer guaranteed – sometimes it was almost instant, at others she was too distracted or tired, no matter how close Harry brought her. Now his indulgent gaze ran over her at every turn as he made up their *ad hoc* bed while she cleared the path, his eyes full of intimate promises, while Jo sensed her own viewpoint float ever higher above them to watch from afar, seeing the handsome optimist she loved planning to seduce a lactating, exhausted pessimist who longed for sleep.

When she came back from cleaning her teeth he'd banked up the fire and lit candles, she noticed, with another deep clench of anticipation, wondering if it would kill the mood to suggest a strong coffee and a Berocca chaser.

'Let me rub your back,' he offered, helping her across the soft stepping stones of seat cushions.

'I'll fall asleep,' she warned, leaning into him.

'That's what I want you to do.'

'Don't you want to make love first?'

'Right now, I love you beyond anything I could imagine. Why make more?'

She leaned against him for a long time, her love and gratitude sinking through her skin into his. Then, full to the brim with butter chicken, Morrow's comforting woodsmoke smell and Harry's love, Jo stretched out on a bed improvised from rugs and sofa cushions in front of the stove and let his fingers ease knots from her shoulders. She was asleep within seconds.

SATURDAY MORNING

The Lie-in

Apart from the repeated theme of living in Crouch End, dreams had proved elusive to Jo of late, stolen away, leaving transient smoke trails through the fog of interrupted sleep and blackout exhaustion. But now she dreamed vividly of her father, not the grey-faced death mask that had haunted her long after losing him, but the ruddy-cheeked, lively eyed protagonist who told her off for not having a painting in the Summer Exhibition and who raged that Tracey Emin's bed wasn't a patch on her *Sweet Pea in Evian Bottle* (painted when she was thirteen and proudly hung above his desk at home). In her dream, she sketched Wilf for him, the thatch of dark hair, jutting lower lip and pink cheeks echoes of his maternal grandfather's. When she handed over her creation, the truth suddenly occurred to her: 'You're dead, Dad. You took yourself away.' He just smiled, immensely reassuring and kind.

She awoke filled with a sense of loss and love.

Two years ago career-girl Jo Coulson had sworn she would never sleep on the floor at Morrow again, feeling like the princess and the pea after a night on a Giant's Causeway of sofa cushions in front of a dusty wood-burning stove. Working-mother Jo, by contrast, had slept like the dead beneath two blankets and a slightly moth-eaten duvet, her body dovetailed against Harry's for mutual warmth. Aware that the warmth beside her had gone, Jo rolled on to her back and breathed in the dusty, fusty Morrow smell, a mule kick of sexual *déjà vu* tightening her buttocks and lifting her hips as her legs lolled apart, remembering that first visit and its glorious excess of lovemaking. Then, from outside, she heard a sheep bleat, so like a baby's cry that her body jolted in response. In an instant, the languid nostalgia had gone as she checked her watch. It was almost nine. She stumbled up to scrabble for her phone, heart leaping.

'Harry?'

The bathroom door was shut, water gurgling inside.

Pulling on a T-shirt and stepping into her trainers, she dashed outside, blinking against sharp sunlight and terrifying a small clutch of guinea fowl – Christ, there were more than ever – as she hurried towards higher ground.

'Mum? Can you hear me okay? The reception's— Oh, shit!' Losing the signal, she climbed higher, chest burning. 'Mum? How's it going? Is Wilf okay?'

Her mother's answer was cut short as Jo felt a cold sensation thrust between her legs and let out a shriek, dropping the phone and the call.

A collie smiled up at her, tail wagging delightedly,

'What are you doing, you stupid bitch?' came a roar in a thick Shropshire accent as a bent figure in a leather baseball cap and overalls appeared around a hedge.

'Calling my mother.' Jo picked up her phone and squared up to him defensively.

'I was talking to the dog, my love.' He took off his cap respectfully, gaping at her legs.

Jo recognized Efon, the farmer from the pub, a man of few teeth and fewer words, although he appeared to be more verbose when sober. 'Nice day for it. You're wearing your shoes on the wrong feet.'

She looked down and saw it was true. Apart from her wrong-way-round shoes and Harry's T-shirt, she was wearing nothing but a scant pair of Sloggis. She tugged down the T-shirt hem. 'Right . . . thanks.'

'Very skimpy, jogging things, these days,' he said, although it took Jo a while to decipher his accent.

'I wasn't – quite. Yes.'

'Staying down at Morrow with one of the Inchbold boys, are you?'

'I'm Harry's girlfriend, Jo. We've met. You gave us a lift once.'

'Always brings pretty girls here, Harry.'

She felt her ire rise. 'This has been our first chance to come to the cottage since our son was born.'

He went misty-eyed, still talking to her legs. 'Remember when my two were nippers. Babies are no trouble. They stay at home and sleep a lot. It's when they're all grown-up you've got to worry.' He sighed, then whistled his dog back. 'I'll leave you to your run. Tell Harry I'll call by later with something for the pot.' He trudged off with a wave over his shoulder.

Jo hurried back to the cottage, too distracted to remember to put her shoes the right way round or to notice that there was a large mattress balanced on the roof of the Jeep.

Harry was in the bathroom, checking the temperature of a soufflé bubble bath, scented steam swamping the air. 'There you are, Owl. Hop into this. Breakfast won't be long.' Morrow had already cast its magical spell over him, taking his eyes from dull granite to bright blue, the smile inches wider. He was always at his kindest here, possessed by a zealous need to spoil her.

She stood breathless in the doorway. 'Mum says you phoned already?'

'Yeah – a couple of hours ago. I checked that the Br— that Wilf's okay.'

'Why didn't you wake me?'

'Because he's doing fine.' He kissed her nose. 'And because you needed sleep.'

'Thank you,' she said uncertainly, fighting an illogical crossness that felt like indigestion. Guilt that Harry had woken first and been the concerned parent while she snored on, resentment that her mother was clearly doing brilliantly and that Wilf had slept better than he had in weeks, and pique that Harry looked just ... so ... damned ... sexy ... while she still felt sleep-creased, stubbly and morning-breathed, and was now also covered with burrs and bramble scratches.

She'd forgotten how small and deep the bath was, like a hot well. The green grotto bathroom was darker and clammier than ever, the moss and ivy now tangling completely across the window. Beyond the stone wall to her right, the stream bubbled at a low ebb. Several wild guinea fowl appeared to be line-dancing on the slates overhead. She closed her eyes and tried to put Wilf out of her mind. He was, as Harry and her mother had both confirmed, doing just fine. She'd been too wound up about Harry calling her mother and not waking her to tell him about meeting Efon. The odd-shoes-and-jogging comments were just the sort of story he loved, although she wasn't so sure he'd like the leg-ogling element.

She looked at her knees poking up through the foam, like two bald clown heads. Wiping the foam from her thighs, she examined the stretchmarks at their very tops, running her fingers along them. Her baby battle scars.

None of the many expert books Jo had read in the build-up to motherhood had warned her that her body – an erstwhile shrine to personal grooming, sexual pleasure and good health – would be exposed and undermined by pregnancy and childbirth in a way that would change the way she looked at it. It was no longer exclusively Harry's and hers. This weekend was about the two of them, yet carrying Wilf had changed her, a temporary ransack that had left a permanent brand way beyond the silver stretchmarks.

Before pregnancy, smear tests and bikini waxes had been Jo's litmus test for professional exposure, and she'd endured the indignity by necessity, grateful that Harry exclusively accessed all areas where others simply checked and groomed. But now that had changed irrevocably: clinicians had peered and smeared, nurses had scanned and swabbed, and an amazing new life had forced his way out of ten centimetres' dilation in full view of the man who had fathered him, the partner she loved, the lover who had all too quickly wanted to re-enter that now public exit point, expecting the tight, sweet welcome of old.

Jo sank back in the water and washed hard, trying to conjure the knee-parting sexual nostalgia she'd felt upon waking as she ensured she was squeaky clean. She was determined to fix her mind's eye upon this weekend, not recent months' living from boxes, her old sex drive still packed away among the ornaments of her previous life, the new one an unpredictable voyeur, watching her from a great height.

She could hear music strike up in the kitchen, could smell posh Waitrose bacon grilling. She closed her eyes and breathed deeply, soaping more gently now, remembering the way she and Harry had pinballed their way around the cottage that first weekend here, then the deep sense of togetherness on their second visit, Wilf already tightly bedded within her. Pleasure was starting to soak in like heat. But now her hand stopped as she remembered that his twin had been inside her then too.

SATURDAY MID-MORNING

The Breakfast

Wrapped tightly in an old towel, hair turbaned, she picked at a huge cooked breakfast while Harry wolfed it. 'Do you want to go anywhere today?' he asked.

She shook her head. 'Love Siege is good by me.'

'Perfect.' He grinned, cheeks bulging with bacon. 'In that case, we'll leave the mattress on the car roof. It's almost dried out already. Unlike me.' He lifted a glass of red liquid. 'Are you sure you don't want a Bloody Mary, Owl?'

'I'm happy with Virgin.' She tapped her fork against her own glass, brimming with untouched tomato juice and spice.

He sank half a glass with a contented gulp, then forked up cubes of blackened local sausages. 'Very overrated, virgins.' The blue eyes locked on hers: Harry the Sinner inviting her to play now it was grown-ups only.

Sensing seduction coming, Jo could already feel herself stepping away from her body, floating up to watch it prepare for action, clean and polished, an expectant beat now starting to tick between her legs.

Harry helped himself to her leftovers, washing down fried bread with the rest of his drink and looking at her with an intensity that made her hairs prickle. 'I want you to promise not to get dressed all day.'

Reclaiming a sausage with a smile, Jo didn't have a problem with that: she was still struggling to do up her old pre-Wilf jeans; it would be heaven to have a day without a waistband digging in.

Chewing a piece of toast, he stood up and headed through to the sitting room. The sound of drawers rattling and cupboard doors banging was followed by a victorious 'Ah' and he returned with a chunky SLR camera that dated back to an era when Lord Lichfield had worn them round his neck, like medallions, to snap Pirelli calendar girls. 'You're going to pose for me.'

'Looking like I'm on a spa day?' She ducked her towel-turbaned head away from the lens with an amused huff. 'Get lost.'

'It's fine, there's no film.'

'So there's no point.' She poked her tongue out and he clicked and wound.

'There so is a point. The tip of your tongue is a perfect point. Poke it out again, baby.' His kitsch seventies David Bailey impersonation was spot on. 'Now pout, darling. I want to see some cleavage.' He raised an eyebrow as he looked at her over the camera, adjusting the settings.

Harry loved to play. Today it was testosterone-packed centrefold snapper and glamour-puss model. Indulging him, Jo pulled off the turban and shot him a dirty look, pouting as the shutter clicked.

'Beautiful, baby! Now let the towel slip.'

He'd always been fantastic at mimicry. As he barked orders and she posed, each time sillier and sleazier, Jo surprised herself by how much she enjoyed strutting her stuff and giving him lip, adopting a flat-voiced cover-girl drawl that made them both crease up, although it was never going to turn into the unbridled sexual fantasy Harry might have hoped for, hijacked by comedy and camaraderie.

Keeping up the Essex accent was starting to make her adenoids hurt, and Jo called a break, gathering up her towel and the breakfast plates.

'That's part of the set dressing,' Harry grumbled.

He lounged against the doorframe, camera slung round his neck, blond hair on end, still channelling Lichfield. He couldn't strike a bad pose of he tried. 'I think we'll get some table-top shots next.'

'I'll wash up first.' She started the water running.

'Leave it. Nobody cares here.'

'Let me put them in to soak at least.' The sink was a predictable bombsite. Harry was incapable of cooking anything without using every available pan and utensil. She could hear the camera shutter clicking behind her, but kept turned away, although the towel was slipping fast, gripped hard by her elbows. Even though she knew there was no film in it, the game made her feel self-conscious now, torn between laughter and a deep, vaguely familiar sexual kick that was outside her baby-friendly comfort zone, too selfish for safety.

'DIY Daddy wouldn't make me do this,' she complained.

DIY Daddy was a running theme that Harry had made up, and had evolved from the D.I. Daddy Designer Baby he'd teased her about when first together; a fictional sliding-doors character whom Jo would have chosen had they not got together; he was a computer-animated hieroglyph with zero personality.

'Which is why you have Daddy Harry,' he said, with a Clint Eastwood slide on the name.

'Ha.' She looked at him over her shoulder.

Elbows propped on the table now, forming an improvised tripod for the camera, he peered up at her through his fringe, sexy as hell. 'Be a good girl and drop the towel,' he teased, voice soft as angora.

'And if I don't?'

'A Dishmatic and rubber gloves will torment your young skin while I dry up.'

Looking down at the pans, Jo knew she didn't want to

tackle them. Her domestic-goddess auto-reflex was as hard to bypass at the moment as her breastmilk, but now another force had taken over, stealth-like beneath the laughter. She didn't know why she was fighting it. It wasn't the tentative, guilty excitement of sensual moments stolen within hearing of the baby monitor, and it was nothing like an out-of-body experience. This was Morrow. Different rules applied. She let the towel slip and turned slowly, unable to stop a rebellious sexual kick racketing right through her as she struck a pose.

Harry watched her, not touching the shutter. 'You're so beautiful, Owl.'

'How do you want me?' She tried for a Marilyn Monroe purr.

Harry shook his head, the camera body clunking down on the table. 'I'm taking you to bed.'

'Our mattress is on top of the car,' she reminded him, in a brief moment of grounded pragmatism before he lifted her off the floor and she shrieked with laughter.

'There are other beds,' he said, carrying her through the cottage and upstairs with determined effort, despite banging his head on every beam and almost tipping backwards round the steep landing turn when Jo got wedged at an awkward angle.

On a single bed in the furthest room, layered with old clothes and curtains, they reconnected at last, flirting and teasing, the laughter only falling away when their bodies slid off the edge of self-control. Jo didn't feel remotely detached when they came, sharing the moment, loving the pleasure in his eyes as he watched the effect he had on her.

Of all their love-making since Wilf's birth, so much of it hurried and disconnected, this was the first time they'd been able to lie together afterwards without a time limit. For long minutes on end, their breath rose and fell in tandem, oblivious to the smell of sex, damp and – in this room – mouse.

'I love being here,' Jo breathed. 'I love us here. I love you.'

He buried a kiss in her hair. 'Let's stay. Make Morrow our home.'

She pulled her head back and looked at him curiously, remembering his wind-up last year about buying the cottage outright. She could tell better when he was teasing these days. But he seemed deadly serious. He lowered his head and pressed a kiss to her collarbone. 'What do you think? We could try it out for a year, see how it fits.'

There was a long pause; she felt his lips smile against her skin. He was still inside her body, but their minds were shifting apart, like tectonic plates.

'Actually, I've been thinking Maidenhead.' She tried to make a joke of the truth. 'Cheaper than Twickenham, and the schools are good.' She sounded like a daytime-television property presenter.

'Childhood's about more than schools.' He propped himself up on one elbow.

'An education is the best gift you can offer a child.'

'Not a silver rattle and a trust fund?' he muttered. He hadn't quite forgiven Matt for stealing a march on the Most Generous Baby Gifts front, or her for writing him so many thank-you cards afterwards.

'Wilf would never see his grandparents if we lived somewhere this remote,' she humoured him.

'We have cars. And he would see both his parents sharing the role of bringing him up without contracting it out.' A flash of familiar flint hardened his gaze, lifting Jo's defences.

'Are you accusing me of farming Wilf out?'

'No,' he checked himself, 'but I want to be a bigger part of his childhood, not spend my life crossing datelines. I'm not bloody DIY Daddy, Jo. I'm Wilf's father. I love you both, and I want to be there for you.'

She turned her head away, unable to bear the frustration in his eyes, both of them hating the situation they'd found themselves in. 'We'll find a way through, Harry. We'll find a solution.'

'I've just given you a solution.' He kissed the back of her neck.

She opened her mouth to snap that it wasn't a solution, it was an idealistic pipe dream, but stopped herself. There was no point making their current predicament any more hurtful by baiting the anger he'd left at home for her sake. 'Let's take a long pause to think about it, hey?' She turned to kiss him back, and just for a split second caught a look in his eye that she hadn't seen in over a year: the dull opacity of a hidden truth. 'Is there something you're not telling me?'

The kiss deepened against her nape. 'I'll see if that bath's still warm enough to take a turn in. Bring me a coffee and rub my back.'

Lying alone, Jo closed her eyes for a moment, the pipe dream raging through her head too fast to catch it and make it real. Living here would be total madness. She knew Harry hated his job, however star-crossed it seemed to those looking on, herself included. His salary was triple hers, his hours half; he travelled business class and had fans of stiff, embossed invitations spilling from the top of his chest of drawers, along with loose change in several currencies and a small plastic mountain of hotel key cards. He got paid a fortune to think up buzzwords and concepts. Yet in his darker moments – usually after too much to drink – he said he'd sold his soul. He longed for the simple life, but his salary was paying the enormous mortgage on the house they should never have bought, and Jo's just about stretched to the rest.

It had taken them two years together to grasp that they were both equally random with money. She'd always been parsimonious with company finances, overly generous with her own. When living with Tom she'd trusted him as household cashier to keep her spending within limits; Harry was completely extravagant and simply relied upon the fact that he earned a lot – which he did – to mop up the huge monthly bills he ran up, of which a huge proportion was now borrowing against a house he spent no time in.

In the past year, they hadn't so much progressed up the housing ladder as thrown themselves from roof to roof, like urban street runners, their final leap of faith a stretch that had landed them in totally the wrong place. Neither of them wanted to move again, but there now seemed no way to avoid it.

When Jo had accepted a cash offer on the Crouch End flat from its first viewers eighteen months earlier, neither she nor Harry could have imagined that they would move house three times before their son could sit up. Back then, they'd seen their future in a little townhouse in Dulwich, but when it filled up to the sills with silt and sewage in the autumn floods, they lost their mortgage offer and pulled out of the deal. Not wanting to let her buyers down, Jo had been certain they'd find somewhere perfect long before Wilf was born. But by the time she'd gone into labour in December, they were living out of boxes in Harry's parents' basement flat in Highbury. The head-clashing battle of wills between 'Let him cry' Granny Viv and hug-him-tight Jo had guaranteed that this was a very temporary arrangement, a swift exit accelerated by the damp, and the bin-raiding foxes crashing around outside the security grilled windows at night.

Shortly after New Year, they'd ignored dark talk of a property crash and bought a Victorian terrace in an 'up-and-coming' North London borough at auction, pushed over budget by desperation and bidding fever, discovering too late that, as well as being crazy-paved with subsidence, it was impossible to find a parking space within half a mile, the neighbours were hearing-impaired rap enthusiasts and the nearest park was where glue-sniffers congregated to admire flashers and pit bull terriers. Both Jo and Harry had lived in London on and off for great sections of their lives and loved it, but with a baby they longed for somewhere safer, quieter and further from constant reminders that they had to grow up fast at almost forty. When the house was burgled twice in a month, thanks to opportunists scaling its scaffolding, they'd made a pact that they would move beyond the M25.

Overreacting, they'd spent a speculative day house hunting in Wiltshire near to where Jo had grown up; Harry was already in love with the area from trips to visit Di, and totally entranced by the idea of the village idyll. That day, both he and Jo had fallen hopelessly in love with the Granary, a big converted barn full of vaulted beams, flagstones and high-tech gadgetry, surrounded by three acres of garden – a future-proof forever home with more than enough space to grow into. It was four times the size of anything they could afford in London and ten times as beautiful. It would take all their money and all Harry's salary, but such was the passion they'd felt for it and the lifestyle it offered that they'd found ways of making the maths work. Harry would stay on in his job – he could live with the downsides; he and Jo would work from home more when she returned to Blue Barn; they'd take long home holidays together.

The Inchbold family, especially Matt, had tried to talk them out of it, pointing out the potential pitfalls in moving so far away from everything they knew and facing long commutes, especially with a young baby. They won each argument with adversarial conviction: lots of friends had started moving away from London with their families; they'd have childcare on tap based close to Jo's mother, Di; it would be like living at Morrow every day of the week, only with London just an hour away by train. But they'd never got on the train in rush-hour to find out how crowded and unreliable it was, and they'd never driven from the Granary to the Blue Barn offices to discover that the commute time Google Maps suggested was wildly out for one of the most congested, accident-prone and often repaired stretches of road in the south of England.

Desperate not to miss out on the Granary, they'd offloaded the Stoke Newington house's subsiding dilapidation at a bargain price to a property developer for cash, and within weeks they'd exchanged contracts on their mortgage-busting but heavenly barn conversion in a village near Chippenham. That same week, Harry's company had announced it was closing its Soho office and relocating its European base to Berlin, and Caro had called Jo in floods of tears saying she couldn't cope without her and she thought she'd 'made a few silly executive mistakes'. Those mistakes had almost brought the receivers in.

Since then Harry and Jo had spent few consecutive nights together. The cliché 'distance makes the heart grow fonder' didn't take into account a young baby, crazy commutes and family life still sealed in packing cases while they decided whether to put up another for-sale sign, this time on a house they both loved. Jo had cried inconsolable secret tears at the thought of leaving their forever home before it had seen Wilf walk or talk. The thought of leaving her mum, with whom she was now sharing so much of motherhood, made her cry harder. Di was a wonderful ally and granny who, for all her protestations at being a merry widow, had blossomed at having them so close. Jo had moved back home only to find it was too far away from her life.

She pressed the heels of her palms against her eyes. Their situation was impossible. Harry was besotted with a son he rarely saw; his hard-earned salary paid the mortgage on a house he seldom slept in; his clever, creative brain was constantly tasked with challenges of near-immoral triviality; he worked with colleagues he found unbearably shallow, and the deadlines were life-shortening. And his once indefatigable partner was a sleep-starved, antisocial, house-proud zombie, who hawked their son to the office like a laptop bag. Oh, God, she missed Wilf.

She curled into a foetal ball, pulling layers across her, now aware of the smell of damp on the fabrics above and below, a rank, salty sweetness in the air from sex wiping out any hint of mouse. A pulse still played within her, Harry having triggered the physical melt-through she'd never known with anybody else. And yet she felt suddenly, terrifyingly, more alone than she had in years.

She had no idea where they would head next, the displaced couple who worked between Berlin and the Chilterns and had never settled anywhere together for more than a few months. They might now agree Chippenham was totally impractical, however beautiful the house, but they couldn't agree on what would be better. They'd had the Granary valued, had been shocked to discover that it had already dropped below what they'd paid for it in the falling market, and that letting it wouldn't cover the mortgage. She and Harry had drawn a circle around Heathrow and the Blue Barn office, the epicentre of which they'd discovered was Staines. She was sure it was lovely, despite the name, but she didn't want to live there. She wanted to live in her beautiful barn in its acre of apple orchards near her mum.

Pulling on shorts and a T-shirt, she hurried outside to clamber breathlessly up the hill until she found a bar of phone signal. Di – interrupted while she and Wilf were taking a nap in front of *Saturday Kitchen* – was not at her most soothing, tetchily assuring her all was well and repeating her earlier entreaty that Jo must relax.

Jo perched on a stile, chewing a thumbnail, trying hard to relax and put everything in perspective. She and Harry had each other, Wilf and good jobs. They were incredibly lucky buggers. How much worse to be where Matt was, with nobody to share life's stresses with, no job to throw himself into.

On impulse, she looked him up on her phone contacts and dialled his mobile.

'Matt Inchbold.'

'Matt, it's Jo. How *are* you?'

'Erm ... fine.' There was a pause. 'Is everything all right? Is it Harry?'

'No, no, it's all great. I'm just calling to see if you're okay.'

'I said I'm fine.' Another long pause.

She chewed her nail again, wincing with embarrassment: self-protective, reserved Matt probably thought she'd called him to ask for a favour. But she was worried about him, her gut churning afresh with an instinct that the family Iron Man was under the greatest imaginable tensile pressure and about to break.

'We've just been thinking about you a lot, that's all.'

'That's kind. Aren't you and Harry supposed to be staying at Morrow this weekend?'

'You can get a phone signal on Mawr Vron now,' she reminded him.

'You climbed up Big Hill to phone me and ask if I'm okay?'

It would be rude to admit that she'd actually climbed it

to call her mother to check on Wilf and added him as an afterthought. 'You don't have to go all the way up – just to the second stile. And I have great stile, ha-ha.'

There was another long pause. His pauses were costing her a fortune.

'Well, I'm glad you're okay. Harry will be relieved to hear it.'

'Glad to be of cheer.' The line was abruptly cut.

Jo stared at her phone. He'd hung up on her. She found another nail to chew, sensing that she might have made things worse. She thought about sending Matt an apologetic text, but that would probably wind him up even more. Then, as she stood up to leave, he rang back: 'I apologize. I'm grateful for your call. It was rude not to say goodbye.'

'Hey, anytime.' She beamed with relief.

'I might hold you to that.'

It was her turn to leave the pause, uncertain whether to repeat the offer with a kind, sister-in-law/therapist tone or make a light-hearted joke about not having to puff up Mawr Vron more than once a day for him.

Before she could make up her mind, Matt said, 'That big house of yours in Wiltshire. Have you decided what to do with it yet?'

'We're selling,' she said flatly.

'Don't. If you must, let it. But don't sell – wait a couple of years for housing stock to drop before you even think about doing that. That way you get your money back.'

'The rental figures don't add up.'

'I'll make them add up.'

'Oh, Matt, if you could, we'd be so grateful.' The thank-you cards would rain through his letterbox.

When he rang off – saying a formal goodbye this time – Jo knew that the property advice was his way of saying thank you for calling him at a time of crisis. She was a long way off working out proud, awkward Matt, but she felt she'd drawn a tighter circle around him and Harry. Having Wilf had made her think a lot about twins, and about the bond they shared. Wilf had never had the opportunity to know his. She wanted Harry to feel his more strongly again. She'd never known anybody who could love as fiercely and loyally as Harry, yet he kept Matt at a distance, his own betrayal forgiven but never forgotten. She wanted to be the one to put it right. If Matt was going to help them hold on to their dream home, it was the least she could do.

SATURDAY, LATE MORNING

Sunbathing

As she slithered back down to the cottage through the scree, pursued by a small flock of guinea fowl, Jo was filled with renewed determination that she and Harry could hold on to their dream – the real one, not his pie-in-the-sky Morrow idea. They had talked themselves in circles too many times. Now it was clear.

She took him a cup of coffee in the bath and perched on the edge. Duffy was singing 'Mercy' from a crackling radio on top of the loo cistern. Harry had shampoo foam tufted through his hair and frilling his eyelashes, yet remained as masculine as cigar smoke.

'We have to keep the Granary. We love it too much to lose it, even if that means letting someone else live in it for a bit, or facing the guilt trip every day. We'll make it work for you, Harry, I promise.'

He disappeared beneath the water, leaving nothing but a halo of foam.

She waited, counting. By thirty, she started to worry, hand plunging beneath the surface to grab his leg.

Harry resurfaced with a great splash and a gasp. 'The company want to relocate me to China.'

It was as though a cold, heavy spade had swung round to knock her sideways. She stood up, gripping the basin. 'How long for?'

'They're offering a one-year contract, but my guess is longer.'

'What have you said?'

'There's a Mandarin saying: *"Rén wú qiān rì hǎo."*' He stood up, wrapping himself in a towel. 'It means, "There is no person that has a thousand good days in a row."'

'Does that mean you've said yes or no?' she asked, as he dripped his way past her and back into the kitchen, carrying his coffee.

He picked up a packet of biscuits. 'Did you know we've been together almost a thousand days, Owl?'

'I suppose that means we're due a bad one,' she said anxiously, following him outside to the car, thinking they'd already had quite a lot of those.

'Good. The mattress is dry.' He reached up and patted it. 'Let's sunbathe.' The next moment Kings of Leon was bursting out of the car stereo.

Jo wasn't entirely comfortable sunbathing on a mattress on the roof of a Jeep, but she could tell Harry was wound up like a spring, and she knew she owed it to him to be supportive. Having hastily fetched her bikini and sun cream, she settled alongside him, the bassline of 'Sex On Fire' making the car vibrate beneath them. It wasn't the sort of place one usually expected to have a life-changing conversation, but it was typically Harry. And it made a change from climbing up a small Welsh mountain.

For a while, they watched clouds scud by, talking about the practicalities of what he was being offered. It wasn't easy to be heard over the music – Harry had turned it up deliberately loud, Jo was certain – and every time a sheep bleated between tracks, her mother reflex made her sit up in shock, but she got most of the detail. She'd known Harry's annual contract was coming up for renewal soon, but it was also clear the company wanted to keep him and would offer him a lot of encouragement to stay; the difficulty was that there was almost no work for him in the UK, and very little in Europe, the global turndown pushing most key clients to India and the Far East, where Harry was currently flavour of the month.

'If I take it,' he said bleakly, 'Daddy Harry might as well be DIY Daddy after all.'

'And if you don't?'

'I can think of two people in the UK who will employ me at the level I'm at, and I won't work for either of them. I'll have to start again, doing something else.' He rolled over and kissed the hollow between her breasts. 'We should be sharing a spliff and making plans to become dotcom billionaires or hand-make artisan goat's cheese and live the good life.'

She wriggled away, too tense for affection. 'Is that what your HR department recommended you do if you turn down China?'

'They want to put me on a consultancy.'

Despite the hollowness of his laugh, this filled Jo with relief, like an airbag inflating, softening the whiplash of the crash she'd been experiencing in slow motion since he'd broken the news. 'That could work, couldn't it?'

'They'll still send me to China, Owl – just with no health insurance, and with double taxation hanging over me. This industry's pecked out my heart long enough. I want to make something, do something, use these.' He held up his hands.

His current contract paid for their home; a fledgling freelance career in whatever artisan trade he'd fixed on most recently would surely mean losing it. 'Please use this first.' She tapped his head, airbag now exploding in her mind so that she was sliding across the bonnet in a shingle of glass chips, too horrified to scream. Often perceived as cool in a crisis, Jo's level-headed rationality was pure knee-jerk politeness. The truth was that she froze in terror, became a clipped heroine of repressed emotion and glacial kindness, unable to say what she really thought. It made her seem witty and calm, but she clammed up what she was really feeling. It would inevitably burst out at a later point, usually alone, in the dead of night, the panic and pain erupting in a solitary meltdown. Recently, in the wake of post-pregnancy hormones, her private emotions had staged many more public appearances, but they tended to be very small eruptions and she was good at laughing through them to make everybody around her more comfortable with them.

Right now the meltdown remained quietly internal yet industrial in scale, a tinny Doris Day medley trapped inside her head, battling to be heard over Kings of Leon and the sheep bleats, singing that she needed Harry to be strong. He was her rock, the breadwinner and paterfamilias. The thought of him working so far away, and living there too, was awful: she wanted him home more. But she also wanted them to hold on to that home.

'A consultancy could be lucrative, surely,' she said.

'No pension, no bonus, no security, no benefits, no PAYE.' He kissed her throat between negatives. 'More money, but that's all the Inland Revenue's, especially on double taxation.'

'But you wouldn't have to be in China so much if you were freelance, would you?' she reasoned, ignoring the kisses because she needed to concentrate. 'You could take on other clients, British ones, like Blue Barn.'

'You want to be rebranded?'

'We could do with a spruce up,' she said vaguely, knowing the company was on the edge. She didn't dare tell him now that she couldn't risk taking a salary for a couple of months while she sorted out Caro's cash-flow crisis.

'Do you have any idea how much my hourly rate would be?'

'As the mother of your child, I'd expect a discount.'

'As you're my lover, I'm sure we can strike a deal.' He laughed.

'What does that mean?' She was too wound up to find anything funny. 'I give you a blow-job and we get a free consultation?'

'If you insist.' He tousled her hair and let it pass to keep the peace, but she could see the storm clouds gathering behind his blue-sky thinking. They both knew how much he longed to trade air miles for the fire and earth of physical work. Now that the pressure point had come, even the lucrative flexibility of a consultancy couldn't dent his determination to break free.

'Seriously, Owl, if I'm going to go self-employed, I'm throwing pots in Wiltshire or dry-stoning in Staffs. Or propagating rare alliums and making love to you every night.' He slid his thumb beneath her bikini top and around one nipple.

'Since when were you a plantsman?' She batted his hand away.

'I grew beans as a kids. I can mow grass.'

'What would your hourly rate be for that?'

'Peace of mind.'

'Well, here's a piece of mine.' She looked away, taking a deep breath to stop her voice cracking, the cool-in-a-crisis surface an enigma while the panic was bedlam inside, her body rigid with unexploded tension. 'You can't do this to us right now.'

Harry's hand found hers, firm and reassuring before it moved up her arm to the nub of her shoulder and on to the hollow of her neck. His stress cure had always been sex; her anger needed a more complicated code of truth and trust to defuse it. She was too wound up to speak, appalled by how easily he talked about ditching his career, as if he was still a teenage boy with a big music break he wasn't taking seriously, not a breadwinner gambling with his family's future.

It made her feel powerless, just as his hands all over her now made her feel reduced to a sexual comfort blanket. Wilf had a comfort blanket – it was a red fleece square that she kept as close tabs on as she did her work diary, knowing they both panicked the moment they were out of sight.

Suddenly she saw red – the red bills they would face, the red faces, the red eyes from crying. Most vividly of all, she saw Wilf's little red blanket.

Harry was kissing her neck. She tipped him back so she could climb on top of him, hormones spurring her into action before she could stop to question it.

'So you'll become a consultant if I give you a blow-job?' She tilted her head matter-of-factly, comfort blanket to child.

He looked up at her in surprise, the flints sharpening in his eyes. 'It would have to be a bloody good one.'

Something hardening against Jo's thigh told her that terms were being negotiated by a third party.

She slid back from the shooting-stick sprouting beneath her through his shorts and lowered her face to it, eyes fixed on his. 'It will be.'

'Are you trying to blackmail me?' His fingers slid through her hair, not taking her seriously at all, the big smile contradicting the hard-core arousal in his eyes.

'Take the consultancy.' She unbuttoned his shorts, letting him spring out, taken by surprise that the sight of him in full glory could turn her on in adversity.

'I won't last six months, Owl.'

'Let's see how long you can, shall we?' She slipped her lips around him, giving the negotiation every swirling, sucking, double-dip depth she could think of.

240

She focused purely on her task, finding it the sweetest of challenges. Jo loved Harry's familiar sounds when he was taking head, the groans and sighs, the 'Christ, that feels good,' followed by the 'Oh, yes,' and 'Don't stop.' His fingers were in her hair, raking it, tangling it, pressing her head down, lost in the soft, warm slide of her mouth around his cock. It was only when she felt him swell for a finish, knowing what was at stake, that Jo lost her rhythm. Don't quit your job, she prayed. Love us enough to let us keep our house. Harry's fingers tightened in her hair.

Then she felt him yank her head back, his torso looming up in front of her, his arms wrapping around her, the hands soft on her head now, stroking her hair down. 'Stop, please – God, stop. You don't have to do this, Jo.'

She could feel his heart hammering through his chest against her breastbone, her breath hoarse and angry.

'You don't have do this. I'll do anything for you, you know that.'

Jo's hormones smashed into her fear and love, tears already running.

He cupped her face, thumbs rubbing them away, drawing her head back so he could look at her. 'Don't be frightened, Owl. I'm not frightened.'

'You're not frightened of anything.' She laughed tearfully.

'I'll look after you.'

'I don't want to be looked after. I just want it to work. You, me and Wilf.'

The music had stopped, the sheep's bleating barely registering on her consciousness, just their breathing slowing and their trust growing. They looked at each other for a long time. They both knew absolutely what was going to happen next. Not tomorrow, or in coming weeks, or in six months' time, but here, on an old ticking mattress on a car roof in the warm autumn sunshine, they were going to live for the moment.

Jo moved into Harry's lap. For a long time it was languid, deeply pleasurably, incredibly connected. Then their rhythm accelerated to breakneck speed, Harry's spectacular finish on its way, expert fingers bringing Jo to join him, the mattress teetering on the edge of sliding down the windscreen,

They didn't hear the arthritic whine of the old quad bike until it was executing a handbrake halt alongside them, a wall-eyed collie barking furiously between the handlebars.

'*Bore da*, Harry!' Efon the farmer shouted, over his engine, face hidden beneath his scabby leather baseball cap as he reached down to cut the engine.

Harry sat up with a bellow, causing the mattress to tip off the far side of the car, which at least spared Jo's blushes as they both slid out of sight to make a soft landing on a sun-dried Posturepedic.

'Nice day for sunbathing!' Efon exclaimed, from the other side of the car.

Shielding Jo, Harry leaped up and glared at him over the running rails. 'What do you want?'

'Brought you a rabbit.' He slung a carcass on to the car roof with a thud. 'I told your lady friend I'd come round with it. We're out lamping round here tonight, so I thought I'd better warn you to stay indoors. Some of the lads will shoot at anything.'

'Thanks, but we're not planning on going out.'

'Bugger all to do round here. That's why Cerys pushed off.'

Crouching out of sight, Jo felt his goosebumps stud her skin as Harry asked where she'd gone.

'Cardiff University,' Efon said proudly. 'Mature student. Studying psychology. Whole new life.'

'Good for her.'

'Brave thing to do when she's knocking on to forty, but that runs in the family – her mother was the same age when she pushed off with that Kiwi shearer.' He was sounding quite chatty now, apparently unaware of what he'd interrupted. 'Flighty buggers, Jones women. I'm thinking of getting one of those Thai brides.'

'Oh, yes?'

'I was talking to Roy about it. He's organized one on the Internet. Bloody marvellous. See you've got yourself a nice-looking woman. Good she keeps herself fit with all that jogging.'

'Runs rings round me.' Harry laughed hollowly, looking down at Jo who mouthed, *Get rid of him.*

But Efon was leaning back against the Jeep's bonnet to roll a cigarette now. 'I'm proud of my Cerys, escaping this valley. It's tough on kids, even grown-up ones.' He launched into a tirade about the lack of opportunities locally, with youngsters unable to find jobs or afford housing.

Still crouching low, Jo almost star-jumped back up in shock as the collie goosed her from behind.

'Take this place.' Getting into his stride, Efon started reminiscing. 'When your dad and his brother bought Graig Ddu, nobody round here wanted it – now they couldn't afford it. Don't get me wrong, we're grateful to you Inchbolds – you're hardly ever here to cause bother. My cousin Osian sold a derelict cottage on his farm to a couple from London and they're there half the week with their paint pots and their vegetable patch full of funny-coloured carrots that the rabbits eat while they're away. We'd much rather have a quiet life with you lot.'

'Glad to hear it. In fact, we could do with a bit of quiet right now, if you don't mind.'

Not taking the hint, Efon relit his cigarette as he started

243

on a flight of fancy about his own property's value. 'I'm thinking I might sell it and buy a bar in Spain. I like the weather there, and the bullfighting. You're never too old for a fresh start, are you, Harry?'

Still crouched modestly in the shadow of the car and wrestling with a bikini top that had twisted its triangles under her arms, Jo had heard enough. Covering her boobs with her hands, she stood up. 'Thank you for the rabbit. We'll treasure it.'

Efon's cigarette fell from his mouth, as he stared at her in wonder, then at Harry, realization finally dawning that he might have interrupted something. 'Bloody hell! It's just like old times here.' He chuckled. 'You should have said, boy. I'll leave you to it. *Hwyl fawr.*' Touching his cap in farewell, he whistled for his dog and they set off on his bike.

As the quad revved away, Harry fixed Jo with a look she couldn't match up: his eyes were stormy but his smile was moon wide, the long dimpled grooves dark in his cheeks.

'Before you say anything, he's lonely. You'd be lonely if you talked to sheep all day, then got too pissed to have a conversation with anybody at night. Which, come to think of it, sounds pretty much like my career path right now.' He hauled the mattress on to his head to carry it back inside. 'But I, by the grace of God, have you, which makes me the luckiest man alive.' He tried to kiss her, but the mattress shifted balance, pitching him towards the cottage door at speed.

'*Touché.*' Jo sighed. Retrieving her bikini bottoms from the wing mirror, she made to follow him inside, then doubled back for the rabbit. 'What do we do about this?' She fought an urge to suggest burying it in a shoebox.

Harry was having some logistical difficulties getting the mattress through the door, which made her doubt his practical, artisan ambitions to build drystone walls or throw pots. He was brilliantly creative and talented, she reflected, but, really, he was a head man.

'I'll make it into stew.'

And he was a great cook.

'We're going to spend the next twenty-four hours in bed, Owl,' he called, over his shoulder, as he crammed the mattress through the door.

And he was a great lover.

Following him in, Jo found the mattress in the middle of the kitchen floor.

'A Love Siege needs a constant supply of heat and food,' Harry explained, taking the rabbit and putting it into the larder, then washing his hands beside her, their fingers slithering together around the same bar of soap. 'Now let's pick up where we left off, Owl. Where did we leave off?' Still their fingers slithered, faster now. Jo found it astonishingly arousing.

'You'd just said you'd do anything for me.'

'Ah, yes. And we were doing this.'

Jo loved the kiss that landed on her, and the kiss she gave back was packed with so much heart that they found picking up where they'd left off was no match for starting all over again.

Throughout the afternoon, the mattress travelled so far in action that it ended up shunted against the bathroom wall, neatly right-angled, like a student's futon. Jo and Harry pulled themselves upright on it, side by side and legs entangled, canoodling on a makeshift sofa. They'd lost all sense of time, but Jo could see the sunset streaking in through the trees and windows now, striping the kitchen, like a jewel vault protected by laser beams.

Tracing his finger around her face, Harry said, 'Remind me, what are we doing for contraception, these days?'

'We agreed we're safe while I'm breastfeeding.' She yawned.

They looked down at her much-sucked, much-stroked boobs, neither of them remotely mumsy this weekend, the milk switch off. Then they looked up at each other.

'We need to talk about this, Harry.' Suddenly Jo was wide awake, the excited freefall she only felt with Harry.

Harry was shaking his head. 'We need to do this, Owl.'

FROM THE VISITORS' BOOK, SEPTEMBER 2008

Don't worry if you can only get halfway up Mawr Vron. The views are still amazing. Sit on the second stile and, if you take the time, you see an entirely different angle on this beautiful place. The mattress was damp, and the mouse problem needs addressing.

Jo Coulson, Wiltshire 2008

2009

Music: INXS, Lady Gaga, Bon Iver

*Car: Jeep Cherokee with baby seat,
dented wings and keyed sides*

Season: late Winter, cold

FROM THE VISITORS' BOOK, FEBRUARY 2009

When you think you've lost something – a
key, a box of mementoes, your sex appeal –
the harder you look, the harder it is to find.
Don't panic. Wait for it to come to you. And
while you're waiting, flip through a book. You
can start with this one ... I have a feeling
it's about to get a lot more interesting ...

Harry Inchbold, Wiltshire

FRIDAY AFTERNOON

The Journey

Jo was accustomed to Harry living life at full pelt. It wasn't that he was a frantic go-getter or a stress head – in fact, his laissez-faire attitude often drove her mad – it was just that his world seemed to turn faster than anybody else's. The only place she'd ever known him really slow down was at Morrow, where living for today stretched back over four decades. At home, he drove obscenely fast, ate very quickly, worked at breakneck speed and made snap decisions that jettisoned everything into turbo-boost. And when he argued – which he and Jo had done a great deal more of in the last six months, most often about money – he did so at a pace that made her aware of just how sharp his mind was, and that he'd grown up in a family of lightning-fast debaters, who could pitch their case in the time it took most people to draw breath. Jo argued messily, tearfully, often illogically – especially when five months pregnant and under hopeless amounts of stress – and always with feeling.

Arguments and anger were two separate things to Harry, however. When it was something he truly cared about that made him angry, he couldn't argue very well at all. He swore appallingly, threw things, slammed doors and often stormed off. But if it was something he could be dispassionate about, like cash flow or card manufacturing, he was always infuriatingly, logically persuasive.

Despite Harry driving faster than ever to Morrow – Jo's pleas about speeding tickets only ever slowed him up briefly – they managed to fit in five separate ongoing arguments between Wiltshire and Shropshire.

Driving away from the Granary, where they'd clung on through one magical Christmas and now dreaded losing it all the more, they'd argued about which tenants to take on. Harry favoured the two lawyers, their children and dogs, who were returning after three years in Canada; Jo thought there'd be less wear and tear from the childless, cat-loving opera singer and his wife, who needed somewhere to live while they built a modern dream home out of glass cubes in a field near Bath, and who had flirted outrageously with both Jo and Harry at the viewing. Harry wasn't convinced they'd suit the Granary or keep its big soul alive, but he was very taken with the idea of the glass-cube house built far from prying eyes. 'I'm sure they're swingers. Never trust anybody who wants transparent loo walls. If the builders have tried anything like that at Morrow, I'll crucify them.'

'Having something that actually works would be an improvement,' she suggested, eager to be positive.

But at this Harry swore and shouted a lot about wrecking a beautiful piece of history, then ran a red light without noticing.

On the M4, they switched debating hats from landlords to tenants to have their second disagreement, this time about which house they should rent of the trio they'd now viewed and shortlisted close to airports and work. Jo had calculated that they could afford a modest three-bedroom house if they were going to live in the circle they'd drawn on the map, and she now felt panicky, her voice climbing scales as she pointed out that she needed to know where they were going to be living when the next baby arrived: she couldn't go through the same thing they'd had with Wilf. Harry, who had persuasive arguments for hating all three boxy, modern houses, wanted to ask Matt for a reduced short-term rent on one of his investment properties. 'It's the least he can do for us, given the way he's stabbed me in the back over Morrow.'

'He didn't stab you in the back, Harry. All the co-owners except you have agreed that it should be turned into a holiday let.'

'Well, they're all fucking back-stabbing bastards!' Harry ranted, flashing his lights furiously at middle-lane hogs.

Jo put on the Bon Iver CD to calm him down, hoping he took in the message in 'Skinny Love' about being patient and kind.

When they joined the M5, ignoring the warning screens telling him to slow down for ice, Harry cut through their third quarrel – predictably about his career – to put the case very convincingly for abandoning his consultancy role, which wasn't proving profitable enough. When Jo got a bit shouty and tearful, pointing out that this was because he'd alienated his biggest-paying client and become increasingly obsessed with the one he was working with for gratis, he argued that his 'gratis' input had helped hand Jo a golden opportunity now that a big card manufacturer wanted to buy Blue Barn. 'You can get out with a fat bonus from the sale proceeds. We both can. I expect a fee now I've made the company so desirable. There should be more than enough to buy Morrow outright and stop strangers trooping in and out all year round.'

'I'd rather try to keep Blue Barn.'

'We have the chance to save Morrow here, Owl!' He started ranting, cursing the other owners for not listening to him. 'The place will never be the same again.'

Calming down, now navigating his way around industrial towns and out into open country, he steered the fourth squabble – her career this time – by arguing compellingly that keeping Blue Barn independent would be a very bad idea in the current economic climate, and that Jo having another baby made it perfect timing for her to take a sabbatical. His rapid-fire points were almost overwhelmingly persuasive, and Jo could see the total sense in them all, but it didn't stop the fury, indignation and fear rolling over her in waves as she glared out of the window at the Shropshire countryside, bleakly stripped bare by winter.

The company Jo had helped build up for almost twenty years was as good as sold and now both their careers were under threat, their second child was on the way, they were about to hand over their dream home to strangers, they still didn't know where they were going to live – and Harry was more upset about Morrow getting a holiday-let makeover than he was about any of the huge worries hanging over them. It was the one thing he couldn't talk about without getting impossibly angry. While Jo lay awake panicking about their future, how they could provide for their year-old son and unborn daughter, how they could save their careers and their home, Harry thought about the hidden cottage his family had been escaping to for over thirty years, now being advertised on luxury holiday-let websites as the Ultimate Rural Retreat Coming Soon . . .

Their final argument, played out as they drove from Craven Castle to the cottage, the Jeep crammed with Glyn Pugh bags and smelling deliciously of curry, was about Matt. Harry was particularly caustic and articulate about the reasons to mistrust Matt's new fiancée, Rowena, whom Jo wanted to get to know better for the sake of family politics, but Harry argued wouldn't be around for long.

'I don't like her or trust her. She's a power freak. That's always been his type, unfortunately, but at least they usually have a career and no kids. He's obviously still on the rebound.'

'She's very clever and family-oriented.' Jo defended

Rowena, although she, too, struggled to warm to her. She felt it was important to try to nurture her for Matt's sake.

But then the argument inevitably drifted to the subject of Morrow, which Matt had put Rowena in charge of refurbishing: 'Who does she think she is? She's not even in our family yet. And why did Matt fucking well take her there in the first place? That's what started all this. He *never* goes there.'

Jo had a pet theory that Matt, who hadn't returned to stay at Morrow for two decades after his heart had been so badly broken by Cerys, had returned with Rowena because he'd finally found someone who could make him forget his first love and whom he cared about enough to see past those painful memories. But Harry thought that was total claptrap. 'As soon as Rowena heard about the cottage, she started banging on about holiday lets and asked to see it. Now she's ripping its heart out just as she will Matt's.'

When Harry and Jo had visited Morrow last September for the FP Love Siege, they'd had no idea that it would be the last time they'd ever see the cottage as it was. And when they'd discovered Jo was pregnant again, they'd planned this year's visit for Valentine's Day as a joyful salute to cliché, imagining a weekend curled up on the camelback sofa in front of the wood-burning stove with every candle alight, wrapped in Glyn Pugh's maximum-tog duvet, walking socks and thermals put to full use, almost certainly the only visitors the cottage would see all winter, apart from guinea fowl and mice. Instead it had been overrun by house clearers and heating engineers.

If Harry Inchbold was a quick mover in love and in life, his twin brother could be just as expeditious. The decision to let it to holidaymakers had been made in January, after a flurry of emails had passed between all the owners, spearheaded by Matt, whose New Year trip to Shropshire had seen him place a large diamond on his girlfriend's ring finger and a new property project in her care. Less than a month after that, the repair work had already started with a total rewire, and a renewable-energy team had put in a heating system that would dry the cottage out while the decorators, plumbers and kitchen fitters waited out the worst of the winter weather, which could make Morrow almost inaccessible. Matt had assured Harry that nothing much would change in the fabric of the place – it was basic refurbishment, along with improvements to the track – and he insisted that the owners would all take priority if they wanted to use it for breaks and holidays. But the suddenness had shaken Harry deeply, the ever-running hare for once overtaken by the sharpest sight-hound in town. The brothers turned forty next week, but were currently barely talking to one another.

Jo knew that Harry would get used to the idea of sharing Morrow eventually, and she could see the sense in making it into something that earned the family a little money and paid for its own repairs – Matt was covering the cost of the work and would receive a larger cut of the yield. It was still their hideaway. She'd been really looking forward to this weekend: they both needed to escape the stress and leave all five arguments outside the door.

But as they bumped over the cattle grid, headlights illuminating the multiple tyre tracks from all the vans and trucks that had been up and down to Morrow in recent weeks, Jo could feel the tension coming off Harry like steam. He slammed on the four-wheel drive and sped up the track through the ice and mud as fast as Jo could ever remember.

FRIDAY EVENING

The Arrival

The first thing Jo noticed when they opened the door was that Morrow smelt different: the familiar woodsmoky damp tang that always made her nerve endings tingle with memories and anticipation wasn't there. It smelt of pine cleaner and paint. And it was warm.

They flipped on the lights – the old round Bakelite switches replaced with modern white rectangles, the low-energy glow from the new spotlights gradually brightening to reveal a familiar room stripped of its familiar contents. Harry's photographs had gone. The bare stone walls had been partly painted white, startling and harsh. The gramophone was missing, along with all the many tens of Inchbold books; the dresser had been cleared of chipped plates and candles, its cupboards emptied of old seventies board games. The sagging sofas had been removed, along with the heirloom cushions that had carried scars from generations of Inchbold dogs chewing the corners.

'Fuck,' Harry breathed. It was only thing he said for the next twenty minutes as they wandered round, taking in the starkness. The study beyond the oak plank wall was now completely empty, apart from mouse traps and bait trays. Only the kitchen and bathroom remained much as they always had been, most of the wonky-doored, clutter-filled cupboards yet to be tackled, the gloomy grotto of lime-stained enamel still complete. Upstairs, all the old rugs had gone, along with the mountains of damp, mouse-eaten bed linen that had been crammed into trunks and carriage boxes. *The Wimberry Nude*, which they'd hung with such amusement in the bedroom on their first visit, was conspicuously absent. The antique beds had new mattresses, still in their plastic wrapping, ordered in especially because Matt had known Harry and Jo would be there. Harry stood in the doorway between the two rooms and stared at the marks in the wood for a long time, H, M and T carved in ever-higher rungs, the Hs and Ms always so competitively close, a half-inch making the difference between supremacy and inferiority in any given year.

A part of his childhood's gone, Jo thought, with a rush of compassion, watching the confusion of emotions crossing his face, like fast-moving clouds.

She raced across the room to hug him, and although he leaned against her, pressing his lips gratefully into her hair, his body remained rigid. He was finding it hard to shake off the ghost of the boy, whose notched H now reached only to his elbow, his memories packed into black bags and carried away to landfill.

For Jo, Morrow no longer felt like their bolt-hole. Being there was like moving house yet again, and they had already done that too many times. She felt suddenly exhausted, her swollen ankles throbbing. 'Let's light the stove and get the takeaway in,' she said gently.

Nodding, Harry stepped back, then placed a hand on her swollen belly. 'We made her here. Nobody can take that away.'

To light the fire, they tracked down a few logs in the old wood store that now housed a big biomass boiler, which roared like a domesticated dragon. There, packed in boxes marked 'Inchbold', they found Harry's framed photographs and the gramophone, along with other family objects. Covered with cobwebs, *The Wimberry Nude* was propped up against the stone wall behind a stack of new guttering supplies.

Harry's mood lifted enormously at the sight of her redheaded curves. 'She's coming back in.' He picked it up, then spotted the stag's head next to Jo, apparently looking up her skirt. 'So's Brian.'

His mood lifted further as the stove roared into life, Lady Gaga started up on the CD player, and the curry was laid out, the familiar Harry easing his way back into the room, albeit on a bloody-minded mission to get drunk. He'd worked his way through half the Six Tuns ale keg before Jo had finished a single poppadum. Harry wasn't prone to beer-fuelled rages, but she trod very carefully around his short fuse, aware of the five arguments that were only just outside the door in the February frost, itching to come in to hot up. Neither of them said much as they mopped up lazeez chicken with naan bread, flavours exploding in their mouths in place of that day's angry words. It could hardly have been described as a companionable silence, but there was something united about them that muted the panic Jo had been feeling since their last visit six months earlier.

She looked around the room, at the familiar gnarled beams and stone walls, the worn flagstone floors and the lopsided Welsh dresser. It was still unmistakably, ruggedly Morrow.

By the time they pulled the plastic wrapping off the mattress on the big bed and settled under the new Glyn Pugh discount duvet, Harry had drunk himself into a drowsy, benign state of arousal. Already sliding fast towards sleep, Jo shrugged him off, tucking the five arguments under her pillow, like worry dolls. 'Hold that thought until the morning,' she told him, snuggling into sleep spoons.

By then, she trusted there would be nothing under her pillow any more. Even ransacked, she was sure Morrow could work its magic. She fell asleep as though shot.

SATURDAY MID-MORNING

The Pub

Jo had always typed quickly and badly. She'd never learned to do so without looking down, which meant she still suffered long 'Where's N? Where's B? Where's W?' blanks, especially now that most of the keys had lost their letters. Today's blanks largely revolved around the words 'no bloody way'. The elderly laptop's fan was roaring in protest as it struggled to keep its cool on the table she was sitting at, which she'd edged closer to the big open fire that roared in the pub's inglenook. Above it, a blackboard had been written up with HARE AND MOON VALENTINE'S SPECIALS.

Jo didn't feel in a remotely romantic mood, although the day had started with a promising half-hour of Harry trying to coax her sleepy, crampy, puffy-ankled body into arousal while she soothed his hung-over one with fingertips that knew exactly where they were going. But the atmosphere had been ruined when he'd decided to spice things up by teasing her with a fantasy about the oh-so-stylish couple she wanted to live in the Granary, involving their own super-king bed, a second viewing and *Don Giovanni* on the room speakers. As he did so, one of the five open arguments had crept out from under her pillow.

'How do you know they're that kinky?'

'I can tell. I saw the way they looked at you. I think a

threesome would be on the cards. Given the way he looked at me, it could even be plus one.'

'I'm five months pregnant!'

She'd given up any hope of coming and gone to make a cup of tea instead. If Harry thought he could titillate her lagging second-trimester sex drive with a fantasy involving her preferred tenants in four-way sex, he was seriously off form.

Three more of the arguments had slid out from under her pillow and crept downstairs during breakfast, starting with another scrap over the rental houses they had to choose from, Harry pointing out that they didn't need to live close to Blue Barn if the company was being sold. This had triggered a nasty ding-dong about Harry's consultancy advice making it vulnerable, the tables in the temple of Tory housewives' favourite gift cards upturned so swiftly that it was all too appealing to a predatory rival: 'It was fine as it was. You pimped it!'

'You asked me to.'

'I asked for some advice – you took the whole place apart and reinvented it.'

'I can't help being good at what I do.'

'So why in hell do you want to give it up?'

They'd slid seamlessly into the third of the trio, a tirade only silenced when the newly rehung stag's head fell off the wall.

Jo was now taking her rage out on her laptop, courtesy of the pub's free Wi-Fi. *No bloody way*, she typed again, punching the keys so hard that one stuck and gave her a long line of Ys.

Prising it back up, she saw Roy table-wiping ostentatiously in her peripheral vision, eager to chat. The pub was quiet, just a couple of old regulars at the bar and an all-day-breakfasting couple polishing off coffee.

261

'More snow forecast, they say,' he told her, as he threw another log on to the fire. 'You need to be careful up at Morrow this time of year. I remember when the whole village was snowed in for a month and no one knew the Inchbolds had a friend staying up there. Unlucky bugger almost died.'

'Poor man.' She looked up. 'Was it hypothermia?'

'No, he stayed warm burning furniture. But all he had to eat was thirty-six Kilner jars of Gerry's pickled onions, and the dyspepsia nearly finished him off. When's the baby due?'

'Not until July,' she said. She rather fancied a pickled onion.

This time round, Jo's pregnancy bump was enormous and her appetite had been insatiable from the first blue stripe on the test kit, undeniably bold this time. She and Harry had thought she must be expecting twins again, but the scans had revealed just one baby girl, immediately nicknamed 'The Sis' by Harry, and now known as Thesis.

She turned back to her screen and typed a few more *no bloody ways*.

'You writing a novel?' Roy rubbed his beard, which had had thickened from ironic fluff to full-blown bear pelt since she'd last seen him, his waist expanding in tandem so that he could have been six months pregnant too.

'Resignation letter.'

'Unhappy at work?'

'It's not mine, it's Harry's.'

'He unhappy at work, then?'

'He loves it.' She hammered the keyboard some more.

'Still doing that stuff with logos and whatnot, is he?'

'In consultancy, yes, but the company he's been working with recently isn't happy. Has a cow of a boss.'

'Who's that, then?'

'Me.' She banged the return key, then looked up triumphantly. 'But he's just resigned.'

'Sounds good to me.' Roy cleared his throat and beckoned over a small, smiling woman with a far neater pregnancy bump than Jo's. 'You've not met my wife, Ping, have you?' He put an arm round her proudly. 'Jo and Harry are staying up at Morrow,' he told his wife, in a loud voice, with Marcel Marceau hand gestures that indicated she was either short-sighted and partially deaf or that English wasn't her first language.

Ping nodded eagerly at Jo. 'You there Christmas time.'

'That was Harry's brother, Matt,' she explained. 'And his, um, fiancée.'

When Matt had lost his high-flying job and high-maintenance girlfriend in the banking crash, nobody could ever have predicted that he'd be bringing a ready-made family to join the Inchbold clan six months later. At the time he'd slumped into a deep depression, hitting his nadir at around the time Jo had called him from a stile partway up Mawr Vron and received a polite brush-off. He'd stayed in bed for a week feeling, he later admitted, as though somebody had stolen his identity. His cleaning lady, who was the only person with a key to his Limehouse flat, had been the one to finally unearth him, with sharp orders to take a shower while she changed the bed and vacuumed under it. Matt had fired her. Then, realizing she was the only domestic he'd ever had who satisfied his high standards, he'd hurriedly re-employed her with a pay rise, and politely insisted he stand her a drink to apologize. Three cocktails later and, according to the newest Inchbold family legend, he'd discovered single-mum-of-three Rowena was his soulmate.

In a romance as whirlwind as his twin brother's –

almost deliberately competitive, Jo sometimes felt – Matt had brought Rowena and her children to Morrow not long after Christmas (although they hadn't slept there: as soon as Matt had clapped eyes on it for the first time in twenty years he'd declared it a pigsty and booked them all into the local spa hotel). The next day, he had proposed at the top of Mawr Vron – another uncomfortable parallel – and now a wedding of grand proportions was being planned.

When Harry and Jo had first met Rowena, they'd expected her to be an armour-plated tart-with-a-heart survivalist, but the truth was quirkier. She was an androgynous, tight-lipped academic, who had been widowed young, was OCD about cleanliness, thought a long time before she spoke, cooked inedible vegan dishes and mothered Matt in a way that made it clear she was besotted with him. Jo found it odd and rather endearing the way they acted as though they had been married for years, instead of meeting for the first time less than a year ago, although she worried about Rowena's children, the youngest of whom was only six and understandably quite mixed up. But Matt was very kind to the three, and a very old-fashioned, courteous fiancé, if sexist enough to make Jo's lip curl. He didn't want Rowena to work, so the Morrow holiday-let makeover was her 'Little Project' to occupy her now she'd given up cleaning.

The Inchbold family almost all thought Rowena a Very Good Thing for Matt; they'd started to despair that he'd find true companionship, let alone with a woman who shared his property passion. Only Harry doubted the wisdom of the match, disapproving of the iron will that had transformed his twin from confirmed bachelor to family man, so in thrall to his future wife that he was prepared to sacrifice forty years of hidden Inchbold history for the sake of a better energy-efficiency rating. That currently meant ugly photovoltaic panels glittering on Morrow's lean-to and a deep clean so industrial that half the crumbling beams were now in a hoover bag.

'Heard there are big changes up there,' Roy fished, clearly the reason he was hanging around.

'The family want to rent it out as a chic retreat. They're all the rage.' Knowing Rowena, a sludge palette of eco-friendly hessian and healing crystals beckoned. 'I hope it brings a bit of business your way.' She smiled at Roy and Ping.

'That's kind. Tough time to run a business. Doing some of the work yourselves up there, are you?'

'So it seems,' she muttered, still puzzling over that one.

After they'd given four of the five arguments a workout at the breakfast table, Jo had fully anticipated the Matt-is-ruining-Morrow rant to complete the quintet. Instead, Harry had announced his intention of fixing some guttering.

Jo was still somewhat shocked: she had never seen him show much enthusiasm for home repairs. Now she realized it was all to do with taking ownership, part of a primeval male DIY urge she'd never witnessed in him before.

Leaving him striding over the roof in rigger boots, waving bits of black plastic tubing with deliberate machismo, she'd retreated to the pub to lick her wounds and access Wi-Fi.

She looked at her laptop again, where the Wilf slideshow screensaver had clicked in: his adorable wide-cheeked face beamed out from muddy puddles, toy piles and his pushchair, showing off his increasing possession of small white teeth and a cheeky sense of humour.

'That your little boy?' Ping cooed admiringly.

'Harry certainly marks his stock.' Roy chuckled. 'Looks just like him.'

Wilf was so dark and delightfully thuggish, Jo sometimes still struggled to see the likeness, but other people always remarked on it, and when father and son dissolved into those addictive, all-encompassing laughs, they were doppelgängers.

'You brought this little chap with you?'

She shook her head. 'He's with my mum. They dote on each other.'

'You live with your mother?' Ping asked eagerly, glancing at Roy.

'Nearby.' Jo looked down at her fingers, on which she would soon reluctantly start counting the days until they moved further away. 'At least, we do for now.'

She looked at Wilf's face on screen again, so joyful and fearless. He loved the Granary, charging around its enormous open-plan floors, already familiar with the short drive to Di's house, during which he'd chant, 'Bone, bone, bone,' because he adored Rathbone the dog.

She nudged the touchpad to make the image, and its associated guilt, go away.

Her email was open and she could see a stack of Blue Barn messages to deal with from yesterday, all flagged up as urgent by Caro, who couldn't be left in charge for more than two days without a meltdown, particularly at the moment with so much at stake.

She braced as Thesis squirmed with a few kicks. Her daughter had made herself known early. Wilf had barely shifted until he was almost full term – Jo had been regularly gripped by terror that he'd died – but Thesis was womb Zumba champion. She was also turning her mother into a constantly bad-tempered eating machine.

'Is it too early to have a pudding?' she asked Roy and

266

Ping. Lunch service was still an hour away. She glanced up at the VALENTINE NITE SPECIALS board. 'I could murder a Sticky Toffee Double Love Handle.'

'Stick Toff Double Love Hang coming right up.' Ping smiled in greedy agreement, patting her own tiny bump, then hurrying off to the kitchen.

'Lovely girl, isn't she?' Roy sighed indulgently, watching her go. 'Not put an ounce of weight on that sweet little backside since she fell pregnant.' He turned back to Jo and nodded at her enormous belly. 'Are you telling people what you've got or keeping it a secret?'

'I'm very open about the fact I'm pregnant, slightly over-weight and I have piles,' Jo said, enjoying the blush creeping behind his beard. Roy was a mild-mannered bigot, but a bigot nonetheless.

'Ours is a boy,' he hurried on. 'Gethin Thomas. That's a Welsh name.' He gave a patronizing smile. 'Going to play rugby for his country by the time he's eighteen. How about you?'

'Harry was hell set on Gaylord – family name, also possibly Welsh – but it's a girl,' she deadpanned.

'Oh, well, at least you've already got a boy,' he offered sympathetically, moving away to wipe more tables.

Ping came hurrying back with two enormous slices of sticky toffee pudding, sauce steaming.

'One of those for me, my darling?' Roy called hopefully.

'You too fat,' Ping told him, settling opposite Jo and winking at her. 'This good for baby. Make rugby player.'

Grinning back, Jo decided she liked her. 'I'm hoping more for senior high-court judge or Poet Laureate. Or Mary Berry.' Her mouth watered as she smelt the sauce.

'One job best.' Ping scrunched up her face in confusion and held up her spoon. 'My mother work five job. No good. She come here soon. Roy build bungalow.'

Glancing up, Jo saw fear bleach the ruddiness from Roy's jolly, whiskery face. As he hurried off to wipe tables too far away to be a part of the conversation, she and Ping made orgasmic noises over the sponge, which was delicious. These were the first vaguely orgasmic noises Jo had made in several weeks, her bad-tempered, insatiable pregnancy having also killed off her sex drive. First had come almost constant nausea. Then vaginal dryness and restless-leg syndrome took over. Now that she'd added swollen ankles, piles and chronic fatigue to the mix, she'd choose sticky toffee over two-hour marathons with Harry any day.

But when Harry sauntered into the pub and Ping's dark eyes lit up, she guessed she was probably alone on that front. In the past six months, he'd put on five kilos – mostly Caro's home-made office biscuits – sported stubble more days than not and let his hair grow over his collar. Today he was dressed in an ancient leather biker jacket and red cords matched with one of her bobble scarves and beanies, yet he looked better than ever. Jo found it deeply unfair. She was wearing his jumper and had gained a matching amount of weight (most of it Thesis, she told herself) and looked like a grumpy cross-dresser. The extra pounds suited Harry, mostly bulking his shoulders and thighs: he did a lot of running and cycling now he didn't spend every waking hour on flights or in boardrooms – he was especially fond of hiking miles across country with Wilf in a toddler backpack, or mountain-biking with him strapped into the baby pillion seat. Neither Harry nor Wilf was remotely afraid of heights, speed or reckless descents, their outings terrifying Jo, who grew ever more crotchety and disapproving. Fear and hormones made an uneasy mix, no matter how deeply she trusted her fast-living, volatile and easily bored bedfellow. Harry was delighted at the prospect of being a father again, having adopted a more-the-merrier attitude to family planning from the off, but Jo fretted that it was too soon after Wilf, and that their personal and professional circumstances made the decision to have a second child selfish and reckless.

Harry's lucrative consultancy with his old firm had been short-lived. Having held them to ransom for contracts that kept him in the UK, his bluff had been called with the task of spearheading the hasty rebrand of a City bank with a very poor track record in staff relations. It had been spared liquidation by the skin of its teeth, thanks to a very questionable buyout. It was the same bank that had sacked Matt, whose position as top 'scalper' had been earned through hard work, maths genius and a steely nerve, but whose scrupulously honest reputation had been sacrificed in the mass sacking that had saved it. Harry's attempt to bypass the project for reasons of principle and personal interest had been stonewalled. He was ordered to put up, shut up and talk up one of the most corrupt financial institutions on Bishopsgate. Furious, he'd sent an email setting out his opinion of all that was wrong in his industry to his company director, cc-ing the entire staff. He was lucky not to have been taken to a tribunal. His acerbic, expletive-scattered, brilliantly crafted summary of why he no longer wanted to represent the company had circulated across the whole of London, then on through Europe and America, and had featured in *Private Eye*. For a short while, he was known as the man who had rebranded branding.

Jo only found out about it afterwards, and had been apoplectic that Harry hadn't warned her of what he planned to do. Yet the night he'd killed his career they'd had the best sex of their lives. It was the last time he'd made her come, she remembered. That had been nearly five months ago. No matter how hard they both tried now, she had a totally flat battery. With Wilf, the second trimester had been Mojo Central, but this time stress and uncertainty seemed to have beaten it down. Harry was endlessly patient, but she knew it was getting to him. With one baby following so swiftly on the other, they'd barely got their rhythm back, and now the music had stopped again.

Watching him, knowing how skilfully he made love, her baby-filled, pudding-heavy stomach flipped over, despite its sexual apathy and the five open arguments. Loving Harry sometimes felt like constant heartburn. Even in the midst of a two-day row, her loyalty burned like a fresh brand, the only one Harry now influenced. She was also constantly aware of her need to control her jealousy, always high voltage with Harry, and spiked to max through this bad-tempered pregnancy. He was helping himself to the last of Ping's pudding while she giggled and chatted in broken English, swooning under his charismatic sticky-toffee charm. When he had finished what was on the plate, Ping insisted on fetching another helping.

'Ready to go in five minutes?' He pulled his chair closer to Jo's, leather jacket still ice-cold from its rooftop morning as it brushed her arm.

When her eyes met his, it was as though they were both wearing self-protective safety goggles, their focus not connecting quite as sharply as usual, still wary of fragments of argument spitting up.

'Aren't we having lunch here?' She had no desire to go out in the chill again. Every time the pub door opened, it was as if Boreas, the god of winter, was slamming apart mythical saloon doors. 'There's a special Valentine's Day menu.' She pointed at another board – LIP-SMACKERS FOR LOVERS – with an ironic flourish.

There'd been no cards or flowers this morning – not that she'd expected them: she and Harry had rebelliously agreed at the start of their relationship that they were allowed to give each other spontaneous romantic gifts on any day of the year *except* 14 February – but she liked it that they both remembered to acknowledge this fact annually in her hypocritical Valentine's Day ritual.

'We'll grab lunch in Rossbury.' He had clearly forgotten the custom. 'The market packs up early in February, but it's the best month for bargains and I want to go to that hardware shop on the high street. I need enough duct tape and draught excluder to hold a year's worth of cottage guests hostage.'

The primeval DIY urge was still going strong, Jo realized. 'Can't we improvise with Sellotape?'

'C'mon, Owl. You love the market. I want to get a load of fringed lampshades and bobbly loo mats to piss off Rowena.' He glowered at the thought of his nemesis.

'Half Inch!' Roy appeared from the kitchen, weighing in with a back-slapping man hug. 'The lady wife said you were here. Looking good, boy!'

'Half Mast! Congratulations, husband and soon-to-be father.'

'Time I caught up – can't be the last Half Moon member without a gold strip on my finger.' As they exclaimed at the news about Matt, Jo started counting backwards, certain what was going to come next.

'Seen much of Ned lately?' Roy asked, settling into a chair at the table.

Jo smiled to herself. She had no idea what it was about Ned – apart from being very rich – that made him such an object of fascination here. His perpetually rocky marriage made it awkward for couple get-togethers so she didn't know him well, but the modish modern architect with a head for heights seemed a world apart from the Hare and Moon.

271

Leaving them catching up, Jo went to the payphone to call her mother and check on Wilf.

Di's voice was almost drowned out by background screams of 'Bena, bena, bena, bena!' as her grandson demanded his blackcurrant drink. She reported that, miraculously, Wilf – who was still learning to walk and tended to do so mostly into walls and over precipices – hadn't yet required antiseptic wipes or A and E. At hearing him, Jo felt a pang of yearning before it was eclipsed by a shield of relief that they hadn't brought him with them. It was far too cold, Wilf was far too wobbly, and his crabby parents had five arguments on the go, of which the Blue Barn one was inflaming her most.

Glancing over her shoulder, Jo pressed Carry-on Call and rang Caro, who answered breathlessly within one ring. 'You've just told him our idea!' The echoing music and grinding noise told Jo she was on her treadmill. 'What did he say?'

'I haven't mentioned it yet. It's not that easy. There's lots to do here.'

'You've had another row, haven't you?'

'We're row-surfing,' she confessed, in an undertone. 'It's like channel-surfing but you fight dirty over the remote control.'

Caro, who adored Harry with a borderline crush, had widened her big-sisterly embrace to include him during his short, sharp reinvention of her company's brand. Still looking after Wilf one day a week, she'd been baking an increasing number of goodies for the office as an excuse to pop in, and had a my-door-is-always-open policy at home. That meant she'd witnessed first-hand the work dynamic between Jo and Harry change from one of utter gratitude and relief on Jo's part to frustrated powerlessness, and from the just-playing-about-with-this-idea easiness of

272

Harry's initial pitch to the lethal alchemy of his skill: their recession-strangled cottage industry had suddenly sparkled like fireworks over a fairy-tale castle.

'Talk to him today,' Caro urged. 'I think he'll want to go for this.' Aware of how much Blue Barn meant to Jo, she wanted to help put the happy ever after within reach.

But Jo knew Harry: when he was hungry, his mood changed totally. Looking over her shoulder at him now, working his way through a huge portion of sticky toffee pudding and laughing with Ping and Roy, she was almost certain he'd lost his appetite for this one.

SATURDAY LUNCHTIME

The Market

No matter how bad-tempered Jo was being or how badly they'd parked, Harry always held the car door open for her. During their three years together, she'd staged a few independent uprisings of leaping out first, but she secretly loved the kindness of his gesture. Also, her pregnancy piles meant that standing up took time, so she was grateful for his outstretched arm as she stepped out into the bitter cold with a wince. She let it go to tug her hood drawstring tighter and pull her scarf up over her nose, eyes catching Harry's briefly through her fleece-lined hijab as she thanked him.

Sideways sleet was lashing its way from Rossbury's clock tower to the corn market as they armpitted their gloved hands and hurried between the stalls, like Arctic explorers checking the expedition's tents at base camp. They tucked supplies into bags, then ground on, heads down, hoods whipped back. Harry was determined to bulk-buy clutter to wreak revenge on Matt and Rowena for throwing so much out.

'How dare they junk all the old board games?' he grumbled, as he bought an armful of post-Christmas family-fun bargains from the toy stall. 'You can't go on holiday to a cottage in the middle of nowhere without KerPlunk.' He also added heaps of cheap scatter cushions featuring tapestry hunting and hare-coursing scenes, a hideous checked tablecloth and another owl necklace for Jo.

He rested his forehead against hers. 'I apologize for being

a bad-tempered shit.' He was inevitably the first to make peace offerings. Harry could argue black was blue, but he could also make the sun come out over the most bruising dark-cloud stand-offs. 'Let's forget yesterday happened. I want our 'to Morrow' back. Let me buy you an ironic Valentine's lunch at which I'll tell you I love the very ground you walk on without any irony whatsoever.'

Jo threaded her fingers through his, apologizing, too, as they shared a windswept kiss over thickly wound scarves, a wintry ritual of flirtatious making up. But she remained jumpy, all too aware of the open arguments, and tied to her promise to Caro that she'd speak with him today. Leaving Harry selecting duct tape in the hardware store with per-verted DIY relish, she darted back to the market to buy her own peace offering from the bedding stall, catching the owner packing up behind the flapping clear plastic tenting. She tracked Harry down coming out of the butcher's with two blue-and-white-striped bags, the handles straining weightily over his fingers.

'Venison for tonight.' He held them up.

'How much do you think we're going to eat?' She laughed.

'I got some pork pies and sausages to take back to Wiltshire,' he said, as they hurried towards the gallery café through thickening sleet. 'They sell the best veal, ham and egg pie in the world here, so I got one for us and one for your mum.'

'I'm too fat and pregnant for pies.' Jo was already out of puff, thinking guiltily about the sticky toffee. 'I need to exercise more.'

They'd reached the gallery now, and she was slightly offended to find that Harry, who would normally jump straight in and tell her she was perfect, was laughing. Then she saw the new signage and realized why.

Renamed 'Ab-stract', the gallery was now part gym, part organic juice bar, part exhibition space and totally customer-free. It was almost as cold inside as out.

'Let's eat somewhere else,' Jo suggested, eyeing a bench press warily. The art on the walls was a homoerotic mix of boldly coloured acrylics of six-packs, and splashy oils featuring suspiciously priapic shapes. It was hardly an ambient spot to talk to him about Caro's idea.

'Old times' sake,' Harry insisted, as a familiar figure sidled out of a side door wearing an Ab-stract logo hoodie and leg warmers matched with a scarf, fingerless gloves and a woolly hat stretched out of shape by the bun underneath.

'Today's specials are hot black lentil salad, egg white and wasabi omelette, and celeriac soup with arrowroot foam,' she intoned, as she showed them to a table.

'Brave choice.' Harry gathered up a plastic orchid, a cruet set, gym membership forms and a laminated menu shaped like a male torso from their table and moved it all to another. 'Any chance you can turn the heating up? My wife's pregnant and feels the cold.'

Rhona pointed wearily to a poster on the wall. 'The Ab-stract philosophy is that we lose fat keeping warm.' It read KEEP COOL, BURN KILOJOULES.

'My guess is the Ab-stract philosophy is more about keeping the heating bills down,' Harry said lightly. 'I can't say much for the art, but you're a very welcome sight, Rhona.'

She recognized him now, pink dimples embossing her cheeks. 'There's a DeLonghi in the office I can bring out.'

'You're an angel.'

Moments later, an oil heater was making dripping and creaking noises beneath the table, scorching their calves.

Jo pressed herself close to it and ordered the soup while Harry chose everything with carbohydrates in it from the menu.

'You called me your wife,' she said, after Rhona had wheezed off. It wasn't the first time he'd done it.

'Did I?'

'You said, "My wife is pregnant and feels the cold."'

'"Partner" is for cowboys or business start-ups.'

'I like "partner". It implies equality.'

'So does "wife".'

'This is for you.' She thrust her bedding-stall package at him, hoping laughter would lift them. 'I thought we should try out that foursome after all.'

He studied it, eyebrows shooting up, then flashed a quick smile. 'Thank you, Owl. That's beautifully perverted.' He set it aside, kissed her briefly and looked at the menu again.

'It's a duvet set with a naked couple printed on it,' she explained. 'It's supposed to be funny. You seemed to fancy the idea this morning.'

'Yes, well, that bedtime story backfired, didn't it?'

'I don't want to think about the glass-box couple while we're having sex, Harry. I just happen to think they'll be good tenants.'

'I got that without you needing to illustrate the point.' He turned the menu over. 'And I personally think they'd be lousy tenants. They told us they never let their cats outside. That's practically animal cruelty when you've got three acres.'

They were about to resurrect track one of the five-argument compilation-tape loop. Jo said nothing.

Not looking at her, he got up to study the priapic paintings. 'Christ, these are bad. We must get some for the cottage. Matt and Rowena will hate them. Which shall we buy?'

'We can't afford to make too many jokes like that at his expense,' she said carefully.

'Or each other's.'

She watched him wander around, louche and masculine. They were so constantly in each other's faces and at each other's throats at home and at work in recent months that she'd sometimes found herself yearning for the enforced separation that had once made togetherness so intoxicating: the houseboat days when he'd left their bed at seven a.m., donned a slick suit, hair still wet from the shower, laughed at her cannoning around making him the toast that he'd put into his mouth after he'd kissed her farewell and eat en route to the station, covering his long black coat with crumbs. She'd loved that coat, its formality over his suits, and remembered the tic it had triggered between her legs when she'd seen its silhouette pass along the little boat windows if she'd got back first and was waiting for him. She'd found it in a wardrobe recently and taken it out to admire, only to thrust it back when she'd spotted the label was an exclusive New York designer, a part of his previous life when he was married to Bree Hunter.

He'd stepped back and was looking up at the vaulted ceiling. 'This place has so much potential. We should have taken it on when the lease came up.'

'Business partners or cowboys?'

'Bonnie and Clyde, you and me.' He smiled across at her. 'Any business we try to run together would inevitably be High Noon.'

'Not necessarily,' she argued, although she knew recent evidence wasn't in her favour. 'We used to talk about running a business together all the time.'

But he wasn't listening, chuckling – that husky lullaby – at a triptych of male nipples now. 'This I like. *Scaramanga*.' He read the label with a snort of approval. 'We're buying it.' He snapped it with his BlackBerry. 'It's the perfect card, coaster, tea-towel all-rounder.'

'You'll never get it past Caro.'

'Not our problem much longer.'

Jo knew this was her cue, her moment to pitch Caro's action plan. But Harry was the one who was brilliant at pitches, rolling out the perfect green vista on which to bowl a new idea. Jo needed to test the ground first, investigate the scene, and establish there were no bodies buried under the wicket. 'Has Caro said anything to you?' she asked, aware that her voice had picked up gravel, like a police detective's car tyres swinging into a suspect's drive.

'Caro never stops talking.' Harry tilted his head to admire an abstract erection. 'Can you narrow it down?'

'About the Blue Barn offer?'

'We never talk business, you know that. "Why be Blue Barn bores when we can scoff scones and disagree on Europe, darling?"' His impersonation of Caro's deep, warm bray was spot-on.

Jo winced. It didn't do to dig up the pitch too much when you wanted your star batsman at the crease.

Harry was less impressed by Caro than she was by him. They were so politically and culturally opposed that they cancelled one another out. Most significantly, he still didn't like Caro looking after Wilf. Jo half suspected that was the motivating force behind his offer to help bring Blue Barn up to date. He had no great desire to reinvent greetings cards – the shop idea had never kept his attention, after all – but he did have a strong vested interest in reinventing their son's childcare. He thought that Wilf was too bonded with the Roachford brood and that Caro lavishing their baby with so much mother love was wrong. Harry was never going to be a house-husband – two weeks of enthusiasm for the novelty of home-keeping and baby-minding after he'd told his company director to get lost had proved his limit – so he'd hatched a flexible work solution at Blue Barn instead.

279

He called it the 'Nordic model', which meant he, Jo, Caro and Wilf moved seamlessly between the business unit, the Roachfords' farmhouse and the Granary. It brought Caro (and her baking) to the office more, reconnected her with her business, and reinjected some of Blue Barn's original reason for being. He'd persuaded Caro to produce some new work, to judge a competition on the website, and to let him restructure the way their card range was presented visually. He'd limited the range and introduced new packaging that brought cross-product continuity. Then he'd rebranded how Blue Barn was presented as a company, with a new logo and a fresh ethos.

It was perhaps inevitable that, once Harry started to get involved with the day-to-day running of Blue Barn, he wouldn't be able to stop himself taking over. With just a few deft strokes on part-time hours, and several heated arguments with Jo, he'd made the changes that made a difference. Online sales had rocketed. They now had ranges in retail outlets nobody had previously considered, from bars to spas to chocolatiers. Caro's iconic cosy Labrador cartoons that had personified the brand for twenty years suddenly soared in popularity. Harry was Midas.

Now Midas had worked himself out of a job, and quite possibly Jo too. A fortnight earlier, one of the biggest card manufacturers in the county had made an offer to buy Blue Barn outright.

Having witnessed Caro's Lottery-win reaction to the news, Jo was under no illusions. Caro's husband, David, was about to resign his army commission: they had long-held plans to move to Northumberland, where his family was based, and they wanted to set up a shoot. With the children all away at school, it was ideal timing. Even Jo's second baby slotted in perfectly: Caro would never cover another maternity leave. They had both been working on ways round that one, but Caro selling the company was one solution neither of them had seen coming.

Jo knew the Roachfords would take the offer on the table unless she could talk Harry into her way of thinking. From experience, that meant one flint thinking like another. They were both tough and came from different angles, and that was what made them spark. Jo anticipated sparks. If nothing else, it might heat up the chilly space they were about to eat in.

He was tilting his head to look at a bad acrylic of legs pounding a cycling machine.

Jo's legs jumped beneath the table, as though she was already at the sprint finish. 'Harry, Caro says she'll sell Blue Barn to us for less – a lot less!'

He let out a long sigh, straightening up and raking his hair. 'I thought she might. How much?'

She named the figure – far less than they were being offered by the big manufacturer, far more than Jo and Harry could afford. 'What do you think?'

He didn't turn round. 'Yes, bargain. Does she want our first-born son, the Golden Fleece and a cambric shirt without any seams, too?'

'Be serious for a minute, Harry. I know it seems a lot, but I've already spoken to a business adviser at the bank and—'

'I know what they said.'

'How?'

'Because the company has a twenty-year record of profitability. Banking is just maths. I know they'll back you. All they do is crunch the numbers – it's you who have to break your back making it work.'

'So what do you think?' In her heart, she already knew – he hadn't even turned to look at her and his voice was as husky as a rusty hinge – but she couldn't give up hope.

'Blue Barn's always been your baby,' he said carefully.

'And we've got *our* baby cooking in here, whose future depends on this decision.' She patted the bump and Thesis gave a few high kicks of support.

At last Harry turned to look at her, his eyes so clever and fearless. 'It's got to be your decision, Jo.'

She felt a needle of terror in her back as she understood it really was up to her. And she wasn't 'Owl', she was 'Jo'. Equals, but not partners. 'Don't shift it all on me.'

He rubbed his hair with his hands, making it stand up like wind-battered straw. 'I want you to be happy. But I've also seen first-hand how hard you work, and I know it will only get harder for you if you own the company.'

'If *we* own the company,' she corrected.

His eyes flashed. 'We don't work well together in an office environment.'

'Since when?' However many times she'd thought this herself, it seemed far more offensive coming from him.

'Since you become as risk- and criticism-averse as North Korea every time you have a key-card lanyard round your neck.'

'I do not!' She stood up. 'I take criticism very well. And wanting to buy the company isn't risk-averse. *You*'re the one who's hell to work with. You're totally top down. What about the rest of the Blue Barn team?'

'I'm loyal to *you*, Jo, not to them. There's too much dead wood. You've done an amazing job, but you're pruning a dying tree.'

'You said yourself that Blue Barn is profitable. The bank will back us.'

'They just look at past figures. We both know greetings cards will soon be a thing of the past, like telegrams and fax machines. The internet's driving them into extinction. That's why the big boys are buying out the opposition – not because companies like Blue Barn are too brilliant to ignore, but because the market's getting too small to sustain everybody. The only way to survive is to be small and to move fast. You either watch Blue Barn get sucked up, like plankton into the whale swimming towards the beach, or you take the risk and buy it, turn the tide and reinvent it. That's King Canute stuff. It's not easy.'

'You do it all the time.'

'Not any more, Owl. I'll find something new.'

'We need income!' She was shrill now, her desperation to save Blue Barn crashing against her fear of the unknown, frantic to safeguard a future for their children.

Harry didn't look frightened at all. His blue eyes were unblinking, flint free and entirely focused on her. 'I want you to take a break. You're exhausted. You have so much talent, Owl. Paint. Illustrate. Think about what you want to do, not what you've always done, day in, day out.'

'We have bills to pay.' She laughed incredulously.

'Let me worry about that. I've always been able to make money. It's like cooking, fucking or laughing.'

They had done none of those things lately, Jo thought.

'I'll ask around,' he went on, 'look into short-term projects. Ned said he might have something coming up.'

His faith in Fate terrified her. She knew he'd always been like that, an impulsive optimist who jumped without knowing where he was going to land. It was part of what made him amazing to be around, but it also made it impossible to plan a family budget.

Behind them, Rhona swept proudly out of the kitchen with a loaded tray, soup bowl and carbs steaming, wheezing hard as she set it down. 'Not being funny or anything, but you two are putting off other customers. Could you pipe down?' She shuffled back to the kitchen.

Jo and Harry peered around them. Nobody else was there.

Looking at Harry again, Jo waited for the husky laugh. It didn't come. He was watching her closely as they faced one another in the empty space, surrounded by gym equipment, homoerotica and plastic orchids.

'I've always been able to make money, Owl,' he repeated.

'Along with cooking, fucking or laughing,' she echoed. Things that came as naturally to Harry as breathing. When you boiled it right down, were they just arguing about money? One of their four cornerstones, which could bring everything down.

Her hands instinctively closed around her Thesis bump, and she longed to have Wilf's solid warmth there too. Seeing Harry step towards her, she pitched forwards, anticipating his reassuring embrace, only to find he was pulling out her chair and gesturing to her to sit down.

'It's snowing.' He pointed towards the big windows. 'It falls fast round here, so we'd better eat up to save ourselves being trapped with Rhona in Rossbury's answer to Muscle Beach.'

Jo gazed at the white storm outside. It wasn't just falling, it was billowing, flakes as big as confetti, already massing on the sills. Harry was now wolfing up his order, dedicating himself to the need to eat as single-mindedly as ever. She sat down opposite him and started eating her soup, which was surprisingly good.

Thesis was soon having a workout using her bladder as a dance mat, no doubt excited by the arrowroot foam heading her way. Escaping to pee, Jo felt a tic of regretful nostalgia as she headed along the corridor in which she and Harry had connected with knee-trembling unstoppability the first time he'd brought her to Rossbury.

Sitting on the loo, she recalled her plan back then. If she hadn't met Harry at Fi and Dom's dinner party that night, she'd almost certainly be a parent now, but there would have been no Harry in her life. There'd have been none of the love, laughter, rows, tears and tantrums, mutual support, sex and fear. And there would be no Wilf.

The thought shook her, making her hug herself in shock. There would be no Thesis growing. No squabbling Viv and Gerry, no high-drama Titch, no low-key Matt and his saviour Rowena, no high-flying rascal Ned or all the other friends Harry gathered in his wake wherever he went. There would no Hare and Moon and Rossbury Market once a year. There would be no Morrow. The thought was unbearable.

But the thought of having no Blue Barn was equally insupportable.

Would she still be facing the same career crisis right now as a sole parent, she wondered, with no Harry to insist that he'd take care of her, Wilf and Thesis? What would the pre-Harry Jo have done, the woman who had been so certain of her ability to embrace motherhood alone, to build a little family of two alongside her Blue Barn life, itself a surrogate family?

She knew without doubt that she would have done everything in her power to buy it. If the four columns of the life she shared with Harry were food, sex, money and laughter, Blue Barn remained the foundation. It was her career.

She hurried back. 'Let's do it!'

He put down the last corner of a panino, eyebrows raised. 'Do what?'

'Let's buy Blue Barn! We'll run it.' The idea sounded so right, so totally kismet, it felt like saving a life. And even though she knew Harry had his doubts, and even though it perhaps wasn't exactly what he wanted to hear, it *would* work.

'If that's what you want.' High colour stole along the deep

grooves in his cheeks. It was only the second or third time Jo had ever seen it. The effect against the rugged gold of his skin was stunning, like a vein of copper in a goldmine.

'It's what I want.' She laughed, arms folding over her head, liberated by the utter certainty of the decision. She wanted to dance around the gallery whooping. She stooped to kiss him, tasting basil and salty prosciutto. 'We'll run it together.'

He caught her scarf ends, drawing her back, eyes serious. 'We'll never be partners.'

'Of course we're partners.'

Shaking his head, Harry stood up, wrapping his arms around her. 'You'll be my wife.'

She caught her lip in surprise, tilting her head back to look at him, finding her heart racing ridiculously fast. 'Are you asking me to marry you?'

At last he smiled, eyes dancing between hers. 'Proposing on Valentine's Day in the worst gallery in Powys is not my style. Now finish your soup,' he held out her chair, 'because if we don't set off soon, we'll never get up the track to the cottage.'

Rhona gave them a hefty discount on the *Scaramanga* triptych, which Jo bought as a fortieth-birthday present for Harry, crossing her fingers behind her back as her over-loaded credit card was swiped. It held up, adding to her high, which was only slightly undermined by indigestion from eating too fast. Harry's mood was harder to read.

Racing home in a thickening blizzard, he drove freneti-cally, hands drumming the wheel to the Prodigy's 'Omen' while Jo's mind swirled as chaotically as the snow falling around them, thoughts about Blue Barn, about marriage and about their future. As they twisted and turned through an increasing white-out, the celeriac soup in her stomach started to swill and swirl above Thesis, who punched the ceiling overhead, like a disapproving basement tenant complaining about a bath running.

Jo was soon feeling extremely car sick. To her embarrassment, Harry had to stop the Jeep twice for her to throw up. He was incredibly sympathetic, but the finger-drumming, sky-glancing urgency to get on with it increased. The snow was falling so densely that her puke was discreetly covered by a gauze sheet the moment it landed.

The next leg was driven almost blind, the windscreen a riot shield for bombarding white flakes. Terrified, Jo held her bump in her arms as though reassuring it, thinking about Wilf, gripped by an illogical terror that she might not see him again, or her mother, who was blissfully unaware that her daughter was sliding around in a Jeep in swirling white nothingness right now. She'd never been out in a car in weather like this, least of all on a mountainside. Harry seemed to find his way by instinct, reaching across to hold Jo's cold, clammy hand in his warm, dry one and reassure her that they'd be fine.

'Wouldn't we be better sitting this out in the pub?' she fretted, as they climbed out of the village towards what looked like a wall of snow.

But Harry wouldn't hear of turning round. 'This is nothing. I've seen much worse. We're going to Morrow even if it takes all night.' Jo was reminded of her father at the wheel of the family Marina, exhaust fumes and traffic jam ahead of them, their holiday hopes packed on the roof rack, determined to get to his favourite campsite by nightfall. God, she loved them both.

SATURDAY EVENING

The Romantic Meal

As they drove uphill, the snow became deep and drifting. Tall white tides marked gateways and broken hedges, and started to fill the lane where it was exposed to the fields. The Jeep slowed to a crawl to push and creak through it, its four-wheel drive already struggling to keep a grip. The track beyond the cattle grid had disappeared, the ruts and potholes royal-iced into smooth, uniform white, the stream a barely visible black vein beneath its snow-clogged banks.

Jo tried hard not to panic, putting all her trust in Harry and his calm determination to get her to the warmth and safety of Morrow. He had to get out several times to shovel snow from beneath the tyres as they ground to a slippery halt again and again, his hair whiter each time he got back in.

The path to the cottage was already so deep in snow that it was over their ankles and required high-stepping care to navigate – Jo trod in Harry's footprints like King Wenceslas's page – and Morrow's door had already gathered an ermine hem. Inside, it was so warm it made their skin prickle, startling them afresh with its emptiness and pine-disinfectant smell, the half-painted walls so white they might have been in an igloo.

To Jo, it was the loveliest igloo she'd ever seen. Relief coursed through her as she hugged Harry. 'That was so brave.'

'It was bloody foolish.' He hugged her back tightly. 'Sorry,

Owl. Now I know how shit scared my father must have been bringing us all up here in weather like this. And that was in a seventies hatchback. I remember Mum threatening to murder him with the tyre lever if we all froze to death.'

'Isn't that a contradiction in terms?'

Pouring himself a large Scotch, teeth chattering, Harry waited for the kettle to boil so that he could make Jo a mint tea, watching her pale, drawn face. 'You look wiped out, Owl. Have a nap. I'll bring this up and light the stove so it's toasty when you come down. And I'll cook tonight – no argument.'

Jo had no intention of arguing. They had four arguments left now that they had settled Blue Barn and agreed a way forward. The thought gave her a shot of energy and excitement, along with Harry's comment in the gallery: 'You'll be my wife.'

'Thank you for today.' She put her hand up to his cheek, already coarse with silver-blond stubble. 'For letting me decide about Blue Barn,' she kissed him, 'and for being you.' Smiling into his eyes and melting in the warmth they gave back, she ran her thumb along his cheekbone and beneath the fold of his ear.

'I can deny you nothing.' He laughed, moving his mouth to hers. 'Keep doing that and I won't let you nap much, I warn you.' She could feel his groin stirring against hers. But apart from affection and guilt, she felt nothing stir in return, tiredness mugging her again. Beneath her scruffy jumper, the elastic waist of her maternity jeans was pulled right up to her tits for comfort. Her mojo was buried deep outside under the snow.

She stepped back, and they exchanged a brief look, the silent language of couples, one apologizing that she wasn't interested, the other irritably resigned and frustrated, neither wanting to make a scene about it right now.

Upstairs, the snow was a white tide already a quarter of the way up the low little windows, forming a curved frame in each casement like a Christmas-card cliché. Within minutes Jo was deeply asleep.

She awoke in the dark, disoriented and full of cramp. There was a mug of cold mint tea on the bedside table. She could hear music downstairs and smell onions and garlic frying.

Harry was cooking. It smelt delicious. Her mouth watered in anticipation.

This felt more like the old Morrow.

She stretched back and flexed her toes, relishing the new mattress and trying to imagine weekends to come at Morrow once they owned Blue Barn. It was important to take regular breaks from a busy life raising their family and running a business. Nothing much would change, she thought, in the way that nothing much was changing about the cottage, apart from a lick of paint and some much-needed mod cons.

She thought about Harry in the café, saying, 'You'll be my wife.'

She smiled, throwing her arms wide, breathing in the cooking smells.

'Mrs Inchbold.' She tried it out, then dismissed it. Viv and soon Rowena could share those honours. 'Ms Jo Coulson,' she said instead, 'mother of two, her own boss and wife to Harry.' She liked that. She wanted to contribute equally to the bread-winning, bread-making and bread-baking mix. She and Harry were a team. Even if he didn't want to help run Blue Barn day to day – which was a relief – she'd need his input and advice.

There was the issue of childcare, but Jo was determined to make the company more working-mum friendly, and overcome the reason its creator had lost control of it in the first place. She already had visions of expanding Harry's Nordic model at Blue Barn. They'd have a crèche with a qualified childminder on site, made affordable by offering it to other companies at the business park.

And perhaps, in a year or two, if she controlled it well and Harry fulfilled his promise to find a new role that brought in good money, they would be able to afford to move back to the Granary for keeps. The thought made her euphoric. She could even look at relocating Blue Barn to Wiltshire. Or perhaps she'd work from home three days a week. She could play it whichever way suited her best because she would be her own boss.

She couldn't wait to call Caro and tell her the news.

Rolling over, eyes adjusting to the darkness, she saw at least two more inches of fresh white rim on the little casement sills and remembered Roy's anecdote about the cottage guest who had been snowed in for weeks, forced to burn the furniture and eat pickled onions. There wasn't a lot of furniture left at Morrow to burn, but Harry had bought his own weight in pork pies and sausages in Rossbury.

As she headed downstairs, her mouth was watering again. The wood-burning stove was lit, candles puttered and the table was laid. Bon Iver's Justin Vernon was singing about his lost love for Emma.

Harry had moved the table and chairs in front of the stove and tracked down some plain white candles, which already glowed between the two place settings.

The kitchen was a bombsite, every chopping board in active use, every pan commissioned, a chunky venison fillet resting in foil while red wine, peppercorns and butter bubbled on the cast-iron skillet. Harry was wearing a walking-sock headband to keep his hair back as he threw green beans into boiling water, adding an indecent amount of salt, pinching up spilled crystals to toss over his left shoulder.

'You superstitious old romantic.' She watched him from the door.

'Less of the old, more of the super.' He held out a wooden spoon for her to try the sauce. 'I'm not yet forty. I have two days more to prepare for that landmark.'

'Delicious.'

'Of course it's delicious.' He stretched past her for the peppermill. He smelt of Scotch and chopped onion. 'Matt's very big on zero numbers, like he's running a birthday tombola. You wait till next week's family meal. He'll almost certainly make a speech and lead a toast. When we turned twenty he had a huge party at UCL and I was dragged into it in my official capacity of Drop-out Brother. I got so pissed I have absolutely no memory of it. One day I was a teenager, the next twenty.'

'That's usually how birthdays work – you wake up a year older,' she said, picking up a stray bean to crunch. 'D'you remember turning thirteen?'

'Thankfully, that specific detail is lost in the mists of my middle-aged decrepitude.'

'I was on a French exchange.' She fetched plates from the cupboard, grateful that Rowena's purge had spared the kitchenware so far. She loved the dated, rough-textured Denbyware, remembering Harry running his finger round and round the rim to catch the last traces of her sauce the year they had cooked the big fish.

He was standing close behind her now, his breath warm on her neck, voice low. 'I bet you were sexy at thirteen.'

She closed her eyes, not eager to play into any fantasy that cast her as a schoolgirl when she was heavily pregnant and lacking libido. 'I had very bad acne and a brace.' She moved quickly away to look for side plates.

They ate by candlelight, trying to avoid the four remaining arguments, aware that this year the Valentine's clichés might need to be called upon.

Jo had changed the music to INXS, still eager to tune into her teenage self, if not the spotty one with braces who had become a teenager on a French exchange and told nobody in her host family that it was her birthday. She hadn't wanted them to make a fuss, then had cried herself to sleep, racked with self-pity and homesickness. She needed to fast forward a few years to sixteen-year-old Jo, still shy and awkward, but with a bedroom alter ego who had almost accidentally discovered what pleasure the body held – the most exquisite thing she had ever felt. After that she'd looked at herself differently in the mirror, knowing she shared a secret with her reflection.

And she looked at Harry in the same way, knowing they held that same secret together, that they had given one another that pleasure many, many times and would again. She would feel it once more, however far away it seemed now.

'Why are you looking at me like that, Owl?' He laughed. 'Don't you like the venison?'

'I love it. It was a loving look.' It was supposed to be seductive, she added silently.

'You need to work on it,' he teased, pulling an eyes-wide face, then smiling.

She pulled an even goofier face back. Then, looking down at her plate, she felt bad, acutely aware that he'd gone to all this effort, with beautiful food and candles, while she was still wearing his jumper, her hair on end and not a scrap of make-up on her face, gawking at him because she'd forgotten how to look sultry. Glancing up, she was at least grateful to spot that he was still sporting the sock as a headband and had spinach between his teeth.

They ate on, laughter and anger rubbing together painfully, like arthritic joints, romance awkward and forced, yet gamely undertaken. With the advantage of two large Scotch aperitifs now chased with a bottle of Malbec, which was already at half mast, Harry was showing ever-greater largesse with those charming smiles and hard, sexy eyes. Jo guessed he planned a big bed scene later. The thought made her anxious. The food was sublime and she loved the conversational rhythm of birthday memories, snow stories and great movie moments, but her patter was rustier and more pregnant with pauses. She was unaccustomed to time alone together that wasn't passed in working, arguing or parenting. She was finally getting into her swing with a scene-by-scene breakdown of why Manhattan was a classic when she realized Harry was watching her mouth with the expression of a man no longer hearing what she was saying. She knew that expression of old.

His slow smile was pure seduction. 'Do you want pudding or shall we go straight to bed?'

Thesis kicked hard. Jo's piles throbbed. Indigestion was already starting to burn in her chest.

'Or perhaps we should take pudding to bed?' he suggested, in the irresistible voice she knew only too well, a voice that made everything sound like an order to strip off.

She shook her head. She craved that connection with him, yet her body felt latent and apathetic, even here at Morrow, scene of so many erotic encounters. She looked round for inspiration, remembering intimate moments all over this cottage. Surely there was one they could re-enact. The rug they'd rolled on was gone from in front of the stove; the sofa they'd knee-trembled their way on to had been jettisoned; the kitchen table would hurt her back too much. The fantasies didn't work for her right now, the 'Daddy Harry says' and 'Pose for me' slutty role-play as unappealing as bad porn.

Any stroking, massaging, body kissing or licking inevitably had a narcoleptic effect on her.

Michael Hutchence was growling and purring 'Never Tear Us Apart' over the speakers.

'Come here.' She looked up as Harry stood and moved to her side, offering her his hand. His eyes were heartbreak-ingly seductive, warm with intent.

'I don't want to go to bed just yet,' she bleated.

'I'm not asking you to go to bed.' He smiled, glancing towards the empty space where the sofa had been. 'I'm asking you to dance.'

She laughed.

'Shall we?'

'No way.' She shook her head, expecting him to share the joke now. His eyes didn't leave hers.

An almost forgotten sensation in the pit of her stomach made her start. Butterflies. It's not sex I need to get my head round right now, Jo realized, shocked. It's flirtation.

She felt a warm hand in hers, and as she took it she was aware of sixteen-year-old Jo – also a lousy flirt, but a big Hutchence fan when she wasn't singing along to Lloyd Webber numbers – standing up with her to take to the floor.

As snow fell harder outside, Harry and Jo danced. Heads together, breath shared, bodies folded ever closer around Thesis, they danced until Jo's sixteen-year-old self and her thirty-eight-year-old self were both breathless with laughter and swept up in the glorious romance of moving in the arms of a sexy-as-hell man with a sock on his head. Jo leaned against him, not caring if she couldn't remember how to flirt, not caring that the four remaining arguments were hanging around, like wallflowers at a disco, not caring that outside the car had disappeared beneath a boulder of white or that, inside, the washing up was piled high in the kitchen, and Harry appeared to have melted the plastic chopping board to the cooker hob. As they danced to INXS, then Lady Gaga, she knew tonight would go down in history as the most romantic Valentine's date of her life.

Eventually, when they danced past the dirty pans and kitchen surfaces to clean their teeth side by side in the bathroom, eyes meeting in the mirror, Jo witnessed her face doing something it hadn't in so many weeks. It glowed with anticipation, sharing its secret, eyes positively greedy with desire. Brushes clattered on to porcelain. Rinse. Spit. Splash hot face, register tight nipples, muscles rippling deep inside.

Stepping behind her as she straightened up, Harry looked into her eyes in the mirror and shared the secret. Running his hands up inside her top – his own old shapeless jumper, marking her as part of him – he lifted it over her head. She watched her torso appear, so wide and round, a favourite old bra battling to hold up breasts that were scattered with light veins. They'd been Wilf's domain until so recently, and were already preparing for another needy mouth. But tonight they belonged to the grown-ups. She reached back and undid the hooks to release them, realizing how little she looked at them any more. There'd once been a time when she'd been obsessed with their symmetry and the role of the Wonderbra to enhance them. As Harry reached round to cup them, thumbs running lightly across her nipples, she was amazed by how quickly his touch sent a message round her body that normal service had been resumed.

TUESDAY MORNING

Harry's Birthday

Morrow had been snowed in for three days. The only radio station Harry and Jo could get was in Welsh and played a lot of techno, but having switched it on hourly to listen to the news and weather after the pips, Harry – who spoke no Welsh – had confidently predicted throughout that it would thaw tomorrow. Jo's faith in his translation was minimal, but it was backed up when Harry finally struggled high enough up Mawr Vron to get a phone signal on the third attempt. He came back looking very pleased with himself and reporting that Di – who had insisted Wilf was having a whale of a time and that Wiltshire had only had a light dusting – had confirmed a thaw was on its way.

'Did you call Caro?' Jo had asked, having urged him to relay the news.

'I almost killed myself getting up there, Owl – the drifts were up to my waist in places. I wasn't going to start ringing round friends and family for a chat. It can wait.'

At first maddened with frustration, she'd forgiven him as their snowed-in siege became a love-in.

They'd argued quite a lot during their sixty-hour close-quarters confinement, battle recommencing on the four open arguments, but it was so much easier now. Talk of tenants and tenancies, Harry's nebulous career plans and Matt's precipitous wedding was interspersed with sex and laughter and short, snowball-fighting treks through thigh-high snowdrifts to raid the outbuildings for more wood, to feed pellets into the biomass boiler and to carry in the boxes of Inchbold paraphernalia that Harry was happily reintroducing to shelves and cupboards.

They found the decorator's paint supply in the outbuilding and painted a few walls – Harry was still on his primeval DIY kick – laughing and kissing and turning one another speckled white as they splashed 'I LOVE YOU' across the old yellowed whitewash in the bedroom, marking their territory before covering their tracks.

They'd played a lot of board games, and Jo was embarrassed to discover she was so competitive that she wasn't beyond a little low-level cheating. Harry was astonishingly incorruptible. Their diet was an appalling mix of fried breakfast leftovers and meat products – Jo wasn't sure she'd ever manage a pork pie again after this, although the sausages were sublime – and drank endless cups of mint tea, which was all that was left, much to Harry's consternation when he finished the last of the coffee. They carried piles of the outbuilding books upstairs and read for hours, Jo delightedly rediscovering George Eliot, Harry cackling over an old Clive James autobiography.

Mostly they'd stayed in bed. As the snow glittered beneath cold sun, then bright moon, they slept more, curled ever closer, and talked deeply about subjects beyond work, Wilf and family for the first time in months, moving backwards and forwards through nostalgia and daydreams, listening to their small collection of CDs or bed-boogying in time to the radio, fantasising themselves teenage techno fans, but more often falling over one another to turn it off, realising they were starting to get too old to call their tastes eclectic when ninety per cent of the playlist was too excruciating to endure.

This morning, for Harry's birthday, Jo had made him stay in bed while she hurried down to cook the last of the breakfast supplies, then carried them up on a tray. She had pushed a candle into a pork pie, which was acting as a cake. She also brought a large rectangular wrapped parcel under one arm. 'Happy fortieth!'

'I can guess what this is.' He grinned, having seen her buy the nipple triptych at Ab-stract.

'Open it, then.'

Jo pressed her fingers to his mouth in anticipation as he did so, hoping he wasn't disappointed.

Inside was a painting she had done of Wilf, smuggled here under the boot liner in the Jeep and slightly crushed at the corners as a result. It captured their chubby-cheeked rebel holding on to one of the kitchen chairs at the Granary as he tried out his determined wobbly walk, infectious laugh bubbling.

Harry stared at it for a long time.

She sat down beside him. It was the first full-sized painting she had done in years, almost all her artistic endeavours reduced to sketches and card illustrations these days. 'It's for your office, wherever that ends up being. Or our home, wherever that ends up being. Wherever you like.'

His arm went round her. He couldn't take his eyes off the canvas. 'You are incredible, Jo. Forget buying Blue Barn—'

'We *are* buying it, Harry.'

'Yes, yes, I know. But you will paint, Owl. You must paint. This is brilliant.'

'I will paint if you take photographs,' she said. Last night, ignoring his protests, she had brought in all his wonderful character photographs and carefully removed them from the broken frames to take back to Wiltshire.

'I'm officially middle-aged,' Harry lamented now. 'How did I get to be forty?'

'You mean you don't know?' Jo turned to him in mock shock.

He returned her gaze with a level of hangdog self-absorption that really needed to take itself less seriously, she felt.

'Well, this is how it happened,' she explained in her bedtime-story voice. 'About forty years and ten months ago, your mummy and daddy—'

He kissed her to stop her talking, and they celebrated life beginning with the novelty of middle-aged sex, which felt just as satisfying as the sex they usually had, especially Harry's spectacular finish.

'I'm glad you've got your Inchbold chutzpah back so soon after the shock of discovering you're no longer thirty-nine.' Jo propped her chin on his chest.

'A lot of my Inchbold chutzpah has entered your Coulson body this week. Good job you're already pregnant. Not that we'll stop after Thesis. We want at least four, don't we?'

She widened her eyes in amused horror. 'Only if you give birth to the rest.'

'If I could do that for you, I would. Unfortunately I can only impregnate you and wait patiently for the opportunity to do so again. Such a basic design fault. Stay there a minute.' He pulled on a sweater and jeans and bounded downstairs.

Jo picked up *Middlemarch* to read some more, then drifted in and out of sleep before waking with a start as she thought she heard a shout. Harry had been gone a very long time. She heard the cry again. She got out of bed and hurriedly started pulling on the nearest clothes she could find. Then she heard it clearly. It was more of a whoop. It was coming from outside.

She stooped down to the low window and looked out across the white landscape, cast yellow by a low sun. Through the snow-edged panes, she could just make out a small figure.

She wrestled with the latch, forcing the old window open.

Harry was waving his arms in the distance, wearing nothing more than wellies, a dressing gown and a woolly hat. In front of him, stamped out in letters as big as buildings, she read, 'MARRY ME'.

Jo dragged on as many layers as she could find and raced outside. Running through the snow, she turned loops and circles, kicking up big crunchy white kerbs as she replied, 'YES!'

FROM THE VISITORS' BOOK, FEBRUARY 2009

When guinea fowl make tracks in the snow, they scuff along like teenagers; pheasants are much daintier. Rabbits leave just three footmarks, their back paws landing so close together that they look like they've lost a leg. Foxes are light-footed, and when you walk in the snow around Morrow first thing in the morning, you'll see their tracks follow the others everywhere. The loo seat is wobbly.

Jo Coulson, Wiltshire

2010

*Music: Florence and the Machine,
Paolo Nutini, Larry Adler*

Car: Jeep Cherokee, very battered

Season: Summer, sunny

FROM THE VISITORS' BOOK, JUNE 2010

I like to think I own my past, but the truth is that we give ourselves away all our lives without knowing it. You're a rare soul if you can look back, wrist-flick and say, 'Owned.' Somebody else will always lay claim to a different memory. Let them. Just remember yours is your truth.

Harry Inchbold, Buckinghamshire

SATURDAY MORNING

The Indian Breakfast

Jo was sleepily aware of Harry moving around by her side of the bed as he deposited a cup of tea on the little table. He then lifted the duvet to kiss her forehead.

'Come back to bed,' she murmured, not moving.

'I'm driving to Rossbury to buy coffee from the bean man at the market. You sleep.'

She claimed her solitary lie-in gratefully, sprawling diagonally across the bed as she dreamed that she was trying to match a thousand greetings cards with different-sized envelopes before a courier arrived to collect them. She was largely oblivious to Harry's absence until he called up that a traditional Inchbold Indian breakfast was served on the picnic table by the stream.

Squinting tiredly as she wandered out into bright sunlight, hair on end, Jo was greeted by fresh mango, cold Indian takeaway, minted Greek yoghurt and honeyed crempogs, juiced blood orange and the best Arabica she'd ever tasted. As it exploded in her mouth and body-hugged her awake, she could understand why Viv and Gerry had been addicted to it for years.

Jo didn't like to admit that cold Indian takeaway for breakfast wasn't high on her getaway-treats list, given Harry had made such a big effort. She spooned a few small blobs on to a crempog to show willing, then discovered it was absolutely delicious. More blobs and crempogs followed.

Watched by a gathering crowd of hungry guinea fowl

from the woodland's edge, they were both still grazing and coffee-drinking an hour later, sitting on elderly recliners on the little mown patch in front of the cottage. It had been designated as a garden area for guests after online complaints that the wilderness surrounding Morrow didn't provide adequate 'outdoor entertainment facilities'.

In exchange for a bottle of Scotch, Efon the farmer now came and ran a brush-cutter around him like a whirling dervish once a week in the growing season. As a result the crop circle was more like sitting in the epicentre of a recent typhoon, but the furniture was comfortable, the views spectacular, and the big new fire-pit meant they could stay out long after dark. Last night, after an *al fresco* Ganges feast, they'd watched the stars until one in the morning, their fatigue so deep that going up to bed had been too exhausting to face until, eventually, falling into it had felt more like fainting.

'Why have we never done this before?' She gazed out across the valley, which looked as though it had been sharpened on Photoshop, every fine detail sparkling in the late-morning sun.

'Indian breakfasts are a summer-only tradition.'

'We were here for an Indian summer once,' she reminded him.

'You can't do it after blackberries and bonfires start.' He was staring across to the Black Mountains, as though planning a distant crusade. 'Too cold first thing.'

Jo breathed deeply, tipping her face up to the heat. 'God, I've missed vitamin D. You can almost hear the melatonin toasting.'

'Put sun cream on it,' Harry said vaguely.

'I was being metaphorical.'

As they lapsed into silence, Jo listened to the buzz and rustle of an insect world living on the breeze around her, and the deeper throb of the valley in front of her. The exchange counted as one of the longest conversational rallies so far on this visit. It wasn't that she and Harry were cooking ongoing arguments, as they had in previous years, or that they had nothing to say to one another. They were simply too exhausted to speak and too grateful to be there. Now, with the Arabica doing its magical narcotic things to their nervous systems, they were waking up to the reality that they were finally at Morrow again and that, despite the excess of soft furnishings labelled 'Hand Woven by a Women's Collective' and the scented reed sticks in the every room (which Harry had deposited outside the back door), it was Morrow and nobody was going to take their grown-up, work-free weekend away from them. Except their own guilt.

Having nipped inside to get dressed and make more coffee, Jo returned with her big work bag and drew out her laptop.

Harry was reading the visitors' book, now decidedly battered, every page crammed with comments and tips from a year's worth of holiday lettings. 'Listen to this: *we're so happy to have discovered Morrow, our very own secret hideaway.* Fucking cheek. My family found it. You just had to Google it.' He turned the page. '*What a shame there is no phone signal.* That's the whole *point*, Hilary and Graham Boswell from Ipswich.'

Jo found it curious that someone who was as generous a host as Harry hated sharing Morrow with other people. And while he claimed it was traditional not to spend time inside the cottage in summer, with the days at their longest apex – and Jo was only too happy to be outside now – she knew the truth was more complicated. He wasn't yet comfortable inside the cottage because it had been depersonalized, his favourite space accessorized with a welcome tray, fluffy towels, a basket of maps and walking guides, and a folder full of laminated pages explaining how to work the woodchip boiler and what to recycle.

Secretly, Jo loved most of the changes. The shiny industrial grey kitchen was a bit of a shocker, and there was a superfluity of sheep-themed art and sheepskin rugs everywhere, but the power shower in the bathroom was heaven, and she sensed Harry was starting to see past the tourist trappings to his tap root. They were there to rest and it was easier to do that without listening out for mice and the back boiler overheating. Morrow was the most restful place they knew and, beneath the fresh paint and furnishings, it was still an old shepherd's cottage perched halfway up a mountain. Being there felt like going native, for all it glowed like a show pony.

As he huffed and grumbled to himself over the visitors' book, Jo edged her lounger further under a parasol and opened her laptop, as frustrated as Hilary and Graham Boswell that her dongle reported no signal so she couldn't check the state of the order book, a compulsive twitch she'd developed in recent months.

Instead, she started composing an email to Caro, now living in the Borders and an eager correspondent. Bored by rural isolation, Caro sent lengthy emails complaining about David's family, which Jo barely had time to read, let alone reply to, beyond a few guilty lines promising she'd find time to write back with news soon. Now was that time. *We're all great! With H at Morrow right now. Big changes here – sister-in-law has maxed out on the ovine accessories, but it has lots of bookings, so popular with sheep lovers.*

Rowena had done a superb job of marketing Morrow – five-star write-ups poured in – and Matt had let her loose on his Barcelona apartment, now resplendent with a shiny red kitchen, Gaudí-inspired homeware and a reed diffuser in every room. They had plans to expand their holiday-property portfolio once they came back from their month-long honeymoon travelling through the Americas.

Jo tried not to dwell upon the fact that she and Harry had struggled to secure even this one weekend away together, an early honeymoon before a September wedding that was now mired in practical problems.

The wedding: just as somebody might put a DO NOT DISTURB sign outside a door in a hotel, this short break had an invisible DO NOT TALK ABOUT THE WEDDING sign somewhere near the cattle grid. They had come to an agreement and there was no more to say. And she wasn't going to share it with Caro, who was quietly piqued that she and David hadn't been invited to the family-only gathering.

Weather blissful, she wrote instead, eager to project an image of a woman enjoying the perfect work-home-escape balance. *This is being written from a sun-lounger in front of the best view in the world.*

Hearing her typing, Harry turned irritably. 'You're not working, are you?'

'No, just emailing Caro.'

'Tell her she should be banged up for VAT avoidance.'

Harry says hello, Jo wrote, tuning out the well-aimed dig. *He's still working on the shared commercial space project with his old friend Ned Whittaker – it's a short-term enterprise-funded project filling a big new West End space with a showcase of start-ups (a mixture of pop-up and brand that plays to Harry's strengths).* Even as she typed it, Jo didn't understand it, but she knew Caro wouldn't either, so it didn't matter if she'd got the details wrong. It gave her confidence to know Harry was back in his houndstooth check, wowing industry. So far he'd made no money from the business venture, but Ned had advanced him a lump sum – already spent on the upcoming wedding – and there was a lot of talk of a big pay-off coming soon, which Harry had mentally reinvested already.

His big plan is to start up a guerrilla street-food venture for the London Olympics called Flash in the Pan, she told Caro, *and Ned's already offered to put up half the money – he and Harry have the ultimate bromance.* Jo had always kept a respectful distance from the old friendship, which had its own codes, jokes and shared language. Their bond was so loyal it could be picked up and dropped at will. Right now it had picked up momentum fast, and not always to Jo's liking. Harry spent a lot of time after hours with Ned, who was newly divorced and seemed to confuse 'needs to talk' (Harry, apologetic, on his mobile at six p.m.) with the need to have a wingman at 'this fucking amazing party in Shoreditch House' (Harry, pissed, on his mobile at eleven p.m.). At first Harry had been bloody-minded about putting his hand up to Ned and bowing out so he could be back to give his new daughter her last feed and bring Jo a glass of wine in the bath, but it was a fine line, and given Ned was currently keeping them above the breadline (or the 'organic focaccia line', as she called it whenever she let Harry loose on ocado.com), Jo tried not to resent the ever-later homecomings, those night feeds and bath-time Chianti chats gradually replaced by a toddling, toy-finding, story-telling bedtime marathon she now ran alone.

The kids are on great form. She had moved on to safer territory. *Thea is a total duck and* so *easy, already walking and talking (admittedly 'want Peppa Pig' isn't the Dimbleby Lecture, but indulge a proud mummy here!) and tucking into Marmite soldiers. Still as blonde-haired and blue-eyed as her father, aw. Wilf's a live wire as usual – he misses you! We've done loads of drawings for you which I'll post up. He's totally* Thomas the Tank Engine *obsessed right now. The childmin-*

der is bit worried about his behaviour, but Harry insists it's an Inchbold trait for boys (and men) to shout and throw tantrums, so we'll suck it and see. The crèche at the Blue Barn office has been a huge success – it generated more net profit than card sales in the first quarter, ha ha. Was she sharing too much? She didn't have to check the online order book to know they were down on last year's June. Father's Day had barely registered as a spike despite a swathe of online advertising, but she didn't want Caro to think she'd handed over her baby to an incompetent successor at a bargain price.

'Are you explaining the plot of *War and Peace* to her?' Harry had located a pen and was writing his own entry in the visitors' book.

'I'm sharing.'

'I hope you don't share anything too intimate.'

He wants to know if I'm telling her why we can't get married in September, she realized.

DO NOT TALK ABOUT THE WEDDING.

'Every sordid detail of the dishwasher breaking down and the cost of getting the Jeep through its last service.'

Mum's looking after Wilf and Thea this weekend. She's not been in the greatest health, but seems to be rallying. She looked away from the screen, staring out at the valley, aware of her self-denial and her pragmatism locked in battle, one telling her all would be well while the other worried her mother was far more ill than she made out. Di had lost a lot of weight, was constantly tired and under increasing family pressure to go to the GP, but insisted that she was fine and that she'd simply been dieting – even adding gentle, jovial digs at Jo that she and Harry should do the same. But Jo was concerned about her, and had agonized about leaving the children with her this weekend in case it proved too much. Di's reaction had been a determinedly jolly: 'You give them to somebody else to look after, Joanna, and I'll

311

disinherit you! I am more than capable of looking after my littlest grandchildren. I don't see enough of them since you moved away.' Oh, the guilt.

Di was really looking forward to the wedding in September – she talked about it non-stop. In the past few weeks, it had made conversation increasingly awkward. DO NOT TALK ABOUT THE WEDDING.

My sister wants Mum to move to Harrogate to be close to her, she went on (thinking, Over my dead body – she doesn't know anybody there), *but Mum's undecided and we all hope we'll be able to live close together in Wiltshire again soon (although our tenants love the Granary so much they want to buy it, but that's another story . . .).* The lovely family whom Harry had convinced her they should choose over the glass-cube sexual-fantasy duo had become firm friends, and wanted to make the barn conversion their forever home, a dream Jo still couldn't bear to give up. Oh, the guilt.

For now, we're still living in Flatpack Heights. That was what Harry called their modern rental, a stop-gap that was as anonymous as a police safe house, but ideally designed for a family with two small children and close commutes. While Harry would always hate it for its lack of personality, Jo had grown to embrace the low-maintenance, low-cost practicality, and the memories its small, square rooms and handkerchief garden now held of Thea and Wilf. *There's a great community nearby, although I've been working most week-ends, which limits the social life.* And the sex life. They now needed two bottles of Tesco's Finest to get in the mood.

Harry tapped his pen against the visitors' book's cover while she shared news of the Blue Barn team, mutual friends and Harry's family, whom Caro had always called the Grinch Bolds after the Dr Seuss character because Viv and Gerry were so Christmas-phobic and curmudgeonly, despite Jo's great affection for their indomitable spirit. She kept her report unwaveringly positive, bigging up Titch's exciting bit part in *Casualty* and Matt's grand wedding, at which Harry had been a heroically generous and funny best man.

Matt was gearing up to return the favour in September, still unaware that his services would not be required in quite the same capacity.

DO NOT TALK ABOUT THE WEDDING.

Beside her, Harry had abandoned the visitors' book and was noisily flapping the copy of the *Guardian* he'd bought in Rossbury earlier.

I hope you've now recovered from election fever. You must be so pleased David's friend triumphed. Unlike Harry, who had thrown a cushion at the bedroom television when the Roachfords' Borders constituency, a marginal seat, had turned blue on the BBC's map during the early hours. He now blamed Caro and David personally for the Coalition.

The newspaper crunched pointedly.

'Would you like me to stop?' She sighed.

'Your laptop always make me think of an usherette in the cinema with her glowing tray of ice creams.'

'Now you're showing your age.' She smiled across at him.

'I was barely old enough to see over the seat backs – *The Rescuers, Watership Down* – and I wasn't allowed near those girls. My parents said they were tooth-cavity eye-candy. It marked me for life, and now I'm married to one.' His eyes teased her over the top of the paper.

She saved the message in Drafts and closed the lid. 'You were busy writing in the visitors' book.'

'I was *sharing*.' He put down the paper.

They sat in silence, staring out at the view. The braver members of their guinea-fowl audience had edged forwards, chuntering a few metres away now. Jo threw them some crumbled crempog. Harry ate a mango slice and batted away a wasp. A lamb bleat made them both stiffen; that *faux* child's cry still guaranteed a Pavlovian reaction.

'Thea will be going down for her nap now.' Jo looked at her watch, feeling the maternal pull like a bungee rope. 'I hope Mum's coping okay. Shall I call her?'

'No – she'll take offence knowing you're checking up on her.' Harry's voice softened. 'She'll be fine. She's Granny Cool, remember?' It was the nickname Di had coined for herself as the Coulson grandmother. Viv, rather alarmingly, had insisted she be called 'Viv', although Gerry had taken jocundly to 'Grinchpa'.

'The children could have come here with us.' She was still feeling uneasy about it.

His hand found hers across Efon's crop circle. 'Coming to Morrow is our weekend.'

They sat in silence again, and Jo studied a chip in her toenail varnish. It was a long time since she'd painted them. Like everything about her body, it needed touching up. Whenever she set aside time for pampering, it got eaten up by work or the children. She splayed her hand in Harry's, their fingers threading together.

'Did you tell Caro what's being going on at Blue Barn?' he asked.

'She's not really interested in it any more.' In five emails, Caro had made just two mentions of the company she'd founded.

'She never was,' he muttered.

Jo couldn't deny it. It had always been about friendship. When Jo had finally bought Blue Barn, Caro had admitted that the only reason she'd kept it going was because she knew how much it meant to Jo. When Jo looked at the way Ned and Harry worked, she sometimes saw Caro and herself. But Harry had always found Caro superficial, and thought she took Jo for granted.

'Do you two discuss David's cruel but shallow interest in slaying wildlife, playing cricket and late-night online poker?'

Despite his alarmingly accurate approximation of Caro's emails, Jo said, 'We just gossip.'

'So gossip with me.' He squeezed her hand.

'I told her about Wilf's nursery suggesting we seek a specialist opinion,' she started hopefully, eager to break one of their speak-no-evil silent caveats.

'That's not gossip.' His hand dropped away. 'I mean news like Dom and Fi's spectacular bust-up or Matt discovering Rowena's kids have different fathers.'

'Caro doesn't know them. I don't share things like that with anybody apart from you. And since when were you interested in gossip?'

'Since I heard Dom's new girlfriend and Fi have the same due date.'

Jo caught an edge of competitiveness as Harry proved he knew more than she did, just as his colds were always worse than hers and his work more important.

'Even DIY Daddy would struggle to match that,' she said lightly, closing her eyes. All couples did this. You had to look past it, she reminded herself. See the heart and ignore the burn. Poor Fi, another friend she'd sent a one-line holding email to. Oh, the guilt.

So many of their friends' marriages were failing. This decade was the *Four Weddings and a Funeral* era in reverse, now averaging three divorces and a love child per year. Who could have anticipated ten years ago, when she was enduring endless summer Saturdays sitting alongside Tom in draughty churches listening to Corinthians 13 and worrying that she was missing out, that those newly pronounced husbands and wives would have separate addresses on her Christmas card list by now? To her shame, while she was sitting through Matt and Rowena's wedding ceremony last month, she'd thought of those failures and wondered if they would join them.

The hand came back, landing tight in hers. 'I know what you're thinking about.'

'That fireworks display.' Two hundred guests had gathered on the Embankment to guzzle wildly expensive catering. Matt had arranged for his and Rowena's names to be spelled out in a flaming display of togetherness as the finale, only to discover his new wife's name had been mis-spelled as that of a popular steam-iron manufacturer. Thus MATT & ROWENTA had fizzed and sparkled in six-feet-high lettering over the Thames for fifteen minutes

DO NOT TALK ABOUT OUR WEDDING. Matt's was fine.

She closed her eyes again, thinking about September, the wedding plans that they'd spent so long making and debating and Googling and laughing and whooping and arguing about. They had been happy, excited, passionate arguments because it mattered to get it right for each other. Their decision to host a tiny quiet ceremony on the Greek island where they'd taken their first long holiday together had seemed so perfect. They wanted just their children and their closest family there – those who would never forgive them if not invited – the date carefully chosen to give every-body time to recover from Matt's London extravaganza and to avoid clashing with other family commitments. Everyone could come – Viv and Gerry, Di, Titch, Orchid, Matt and his new family, Jo's bossy sister and her brood. They'd used all Harry's cash advance from Ned to book flights for everyone and a big villa with its own private beach, complete with a romantic little clifftop guest annexe that they could escape to. It seemed utterly perfect.

Their carefully laid plans had only one flaw, but it was a big one. Jo's future husband had 'just impediment'. Harry, it transpired, was still married. He'd never checked. It was typical Harry. His oversights were inevitably ten times more dramatic than anyone else's, just as life with him was always in technicolour compared to everyday monochrome. Where other grooms might forget the ring or their speech, he'd forgotten to get divorced.

Bree had been so fast on the case with her family's lawyers when they'd called time on the marriage that he'd never imagined the divorce she'd set in motion wouldn't happen. He'd behaved, he believed, with total honour: he'd signed all the paperwork that had come through; he hadn't asked for any money. Yet five years later he remained technically married. The divorce had stalled as a result of the fifty-page pre-nup drawn up to protect Bree's family assets, which afforded Harry very little grace in the event of the marriage ending. What it did grant him – by virtue of omitting a crucial piece of legal wording – was his right to retain the company shares he'd earned through his decade's employment as a high-ranking Hunter Broadcasting executive, voting rights that Bree could use by proxy as his wife but would forfeit through divorce. In a company that had been fighting aggressive takeover bids for years, that was crucial leverage.

If Harry played tough and fought for his rightful settlement, he'd been advised, he could be very rich indeed. If he signed away his right to the shares, he'd be divorced by September and could remarry. Harry had wanted to sign away his rights without hesitation.

'You're my life now,' he'd told Jo. 'My old one has no value. I walked away with nothing and now I have everything I could ever want.'

But Jo had begged him not to sign. Her need for security – their children's future, the Granary, the evil spectre of money worries – had made her force him to go back on his word to his ex-wife and fight for what was his. Jo thought Harry hopelessly proud and foolish to want to make such a moral sacrifice: he'd worked incredibly hard for those shares. He had a new family now, and they needed that reward.

Harry hadn't signed.

He now faced a long and bitter fight for his right to the shares – there was no doubt that the Hunter family would throw the best-paid corporate and family lawyers at him while he was still struggling to find anyone to represent him in an international case of such complexity without a big-fee deposit on account. But he had promised Jo that he'd sort it. And Harry would do anything for love.

Oh, the guilt.

Jo squeezed his hand and he returned the pressure, his thumb slaloming softly around the mounds of her knuckles.

DO NOT TALK ABOUT THE WEDDING.

They would now host an exchange of promises in September, followed by a family party to end all parties, a Greek romantic getaway with a hitch that meant nobody would get hitched. They had yet to break the news to anyone, but Jo was certain they'd work it out. And despite Harry's deep desire to marry her this year, it was such a relief to have made a decision that a warm tide of deep affection pulled them tightly together as they drifted towards September, like castaways amid the financial shipwreck of his first marriage. The little family in Flatpack House, whose livelihoods depended on making blank cards and filling unused spaces, had no fear that this would shake them.

But now that she was able to pause from the punishing non-stop grind of combining work and toddlers, with Harry's warm hand in hers and a baking sun on her face, Jo felt a cold rush of remorse. In Flatpack House, money was a big deal. Here at Morrow it took on a different priority.

318

Harry would do anything for love.

She turned to look at him now, his dark blue eyes fixed on a spot on the far horizon, the softening jowls and widening crow's feet merely adding to his sex appeal as the silver fox took over from the urban one. He still made her stomach flip just as he had when they'd very first met, when he hadn't had a penny to his name, believing he'd signed it all away, and she'd taken him on those terms without hesitation. And here, at Morrow, where the petty squabbles of family life faded into the background, where they knew that their wedding was just a random date compared to the lifelong marriage ahead of them, where they held hands and stared across a thousand acres of valley fading into the mountains, sharing a moment of deepest connection, she realized that she would do anything for love too. Marriage meant so much to Harry. He was incredibly old fashioned about it. Her money-minded prudence felt all wrong as they sat here, gripping each other's fingers, an unspoken bond so loyal it hurt.

She turned in surprise as Harry slid off his sun lounger and got down on one knee. He kissed her hand, not noticing that he was kneeling on a plate of leftover crempogs. His eyes met hers over it, bluer than the sky behind him. 'Let's go to the pub and get pissed.'

The smile they shared came with one unspoken message: WE WON'T TALK ABOUT THE WEDDING.

SATURDAY, EARLY AFTERNOON

The Pub Lunch

'Half Inch!' Roy threw his arms wide at the bar. 'Looking good, boy – and the lovely Mrs Inch! Congratulations to you both! When was the Big Day?'

'We're not married,' Jo said quickly.

'Yet,' added Harry.

But Roy was already fishing a bottle of champagne out of his fridge. 'I've been waiting a bloody long time to open this for you two. You were the talk of the village when we had the snow in February last year. When it started to thaw, all you could see from Mawr Vron was "MARRY ME" and "YES". It lasted all week. There's even a photo on Google Earth – one of the local hillwalkers put it up. You're famous!'

Harry and Jo held hands and smiled gamely as two champagne flutes were placed in front of them.

Pouring the Moët, Roy wouldn't let it drop, telling them it was a story he never tired of recounting to the Morrow cottage guests, who wandered down the hill on Harry and Jo's recommendation to try out the local pub. He even had the hillwalker's photograph, which he'd printed off the computer and Blu-Tacked behind the bar. They both stared at it in silent horror.

'My cyan cartridge had run out so the grass came out yellow,' he explained, raising his glass. 'To the future Mr and Mrs Harry Inchbold!'

As Jo and Harry joined in with stiff smiles, she crossed

her fingers tightly against Harry's palm, hoping Roy would move swiftly on to his favourite subject. He didn't let her down: 'I take it Ned will be your best man? Seen much of him lately?'

But Harry's explanation of their commercial-space-sharing venture – even more confusing when he pitched it – left Roy head-scratching before he was back on the case with more toasts. 'To the better Halves! Fancy the Inchbold twins getting married the same year. You two always were competitive bastards. Is Matt's wife as gorgeous as this one?' He gave Jo the benefit of a comedy up-down-side-to-side eye sweep, which was just a thin smile away from earning him a handbagging. She'd become a lot quicker to jump to womankind's defence since she'd had a daughter.

'Definitely not.' Harry helped himself to a top-up, raising his eyebrows at Jo to calm her down, casting urgently around for a change of subject. 'Karaoke later, I see.' It was advertised all over the blackboards.

'Ping's a big fan. You must stay and sing. I've hired a new machine that projects a pop video on the big screen.'

The sensible thing, Jo and Harry realized much later, would have been to finish their drinks and head back to Morrow. But they were rarely sensible at Morrow. From the first time he'd brought her there, Harry had taught Jo the benefits of being totally irresponsible at least once a year. Nobody was going to stop them tonight.

Harry had always been a sociably unruly drunk, liable to burst into song and lead a riot; Jo was more self-absorbed and emotional, apt to quote Yeats and declare undying love. When they set out to get drunk together, they were a formidable creative and liberated double act worthy of a beatnik café in fifties Paris. Instead they got a small pub with its beer garden in Wales and its bar in Shropshire. To them, it felt perfect: the romance sunlit at the ultimate candle's angle, the backdrop as lush as a green velvet curtain, the bubbling stream and cawing birdlife a jazz beat, and the company that came and went a vibrant mix of doughty local and clever incomer. Jo knew she might sometimes grumble that she found Harry's fantasies out of hand, but on rare afternoons like this, when they were both lost in each other's worlds and eyes, work and family were so far from their minds that it felt like the most skin-tingling make-believe just to step off the hamster wheel for a few hours. The company came and went, the drinks slid down, alcohol made to seem innocuous with ice, sweeteners and straws, but gradually and inevitably taking its toll.

The first Jo noticed was that she laughed a lot, uncontrollable giggles taking over, so much so that she got a stitch and almost wet herself more than once. Needing to go to the loo a lot was another sign – she and Harry dashed relays back and forth along the rear corridor by the pub kitchens. Hunger took over too, the crisps bags gathering in the slats of their picnic table like shark fins. They lost sense of time, only moving inside when the midges started to bite, only realizing it was early evening when the campsite families started arriving to order supper. They lost their inhibitions – kissing and whispering sweet nothings, well aware that foreplay was under way.

To others around them, they weren't obviously drunk. They were both more than capable of his-and-hers wine-bottle nights at home, and could hold their drink admirably. They mopped it up with Hare and Moon steaks, mixed it with the sugar-rush puddings and pepped it up with coffee. The effect made them spark off one another more than ever, idealistically infatuated and hedonistic. But as the highball and wine glasses kept emptying, they were, in personal terms, bombed.

Jo only grasped the full extent of their inebriation halfway through the karaoke, a pastime she'd vetoed since her mortifying performance of 'Eternal Flame' as a student. The first giveaway was her over-enthusiastic use of wolf whistles, whoops and air punches when Roy summoned Harry to the stage with a lot of guff about Glass Half Full's one-hit wonder in the eighties. Smiling winningly – far better at hiding how blootered he was – Harry produced a perfectly pitched, crowd-pleasing 'Stand By Me', his handsome face captured on webcam amid a swirling background of stars and fireworks on the pub's sports screen above the fruit machine, along with the sing-along lyrics. Jo clapped out of synch and wept with pride.

But the true sobriety test came when Harry called on her to join him at the mic, backed up by loud audience encouragement and a rallying cry from Roy. 'Ladies and gents, I give you *the* most romantic couple in this place tonight,' he announced, then recounted the MARRY ME snow story for the benefit of the three people in the crowded pub to whom he hadn't already told it. Now the focus of an entire room's attention, Jo didn't hear the alarm bells in her ears or put up a self-conscious 'count me out' hand as she usually would. Roy was already cueing up 'Put A Little Love In Your Heart', and Jo had a whole lot of love in there for Harry, his blue gaze on hers, beckoning her to join him. Carried away with the hype, a long day's summer loving, and at least half a bottle of vodka in Hare and Moon cocktails, she arrived at the microphone, like Dolly eagerly joining Kenny. Holding hands, they turned to look up at the screen as the music started.

Even when the words began running beneath a close-up of her own sunburned, cross-eyed face, framed in a flowery graphic alongside Harry's, Jo felt no fear.

'Insert coins to play,' she sang with feeling, 'jackpot bo-nan-za . . .'

'You're reading the fruit machine graphics,' Harry muttered, through a fixed smile, as they head-bobbed between verse and chorus. 'It's okay, nobody's noticed.'

Drunken stage fright hit her like a spade. She felt sick.

Harry was singing again, his voice fabulously husky, fingers though hers. She closed her eyes briefly, trying to imagine that they were standing on Efon's crop circle in front of Morrow with an audience of guinea fowls. When she looked at the screen again, the words were in sharp focus, their message clear: love makes the world a better place. She could see her tomato red face glowing with happiness and her mouth moving to belt out each line – apparently in time and in tune – without the slightest idea how she was doing it.

And as the last bars of the song faded away, Jo glanced up at the screen to see her mouth still moving, voice amplified by the microphone in her hand. 'Harry, I want to talk about the wedding.'

SATURDAY, LATE EVENING

The Pub Flight

'Whose bright idea was it to walk back?' Jo wheezed, as she took another breather to look back down at the star-lit village, lungs bursting, head spinning, feet tripping over one another. She was pausing to 'admire the view' a lot, a transparent euphemism for trying not to pass out. Climbing a mile up an uneven, meandering forty-per-cent incline was a challenge in daylight, but in total darkness, stuffed with steak and swimming in a new cocktail Roy and Ping were trialling called No Thais – which Jo now suspected was a fusion of whisky, methylated spirit and embalming fluid – it was an open invitation to curl up in a ditch. Looking down, she saw she was standing in one. It was spinning very fast.

'Bloody Efon could have turned up tonight.' Harry helped her out. 'Apparently he's been having funny turns ever since Roy introduced him to online dating. He posted up a photo of himself on country-bumpkins dotcom not realizing it was a website for LGBT farmers.' He dissolved into giggles.

Jo was now riding the pitch of drunkenness that hard-wired compassion, and her heart went out to poor, lonely Efon and his quest for a wife. I want to be a wife, she thought groggily. 'Harry, we have to talk about the – argh!' She was lifted clean off her feet. 'What are you *doing*?'

'Giving you a piggyback. You're slowing us up, Owl.'

'You'll kill yourself.'

'I can think of no better way to die.'

Their old driving joke. They had so many.

'Fuck, you're heavy.'

'You're pretty intense yourself.'

When sober, Jo and Harry parented, worked, scrapped, fixed, cooked and cared. When pissed, they loved or warred. Tonight marked a ceasefire. Love ruled completely.

Somehow they made it to the cottage, from piggyback to walking backwards hand in hand looking up at the stars, dancing through ruts and chasing sheep in the darkness. They both knew seduction was in store: work-fatigued parents didn't put so much effort into getting drunk for no reason. The cottage glowed with subtle timer-controlled lighting, the last metres of path marked out with solar lights, like unseasonal jack-o'-lanterns.

'I miss you crawling around in that fuse cupboard.' Jo sighed nostalgically, flattening several solar lamps as they started pulling off each other's outer layers along the path.

'I miss those blackouts too,' he said, kissing her before she could question the slip of the tongue.

'Leave the lights off,' she urged, vainly aware of her sunburn and midge bites from the pub garden.

These days, when sober, Jo and Harry made love considerately and patiently, ever more body-conscious as the weight crept on, and often a little tiredly. When drunk, it was a selfish, uninhibited free-for-all, exhibitionist, gregarious, generous and clumsy.

Most of their clothes were off by the time they were through the door.

'Remember this?' Harry growled, backing her inside.

'Ouch!'

There was an occasional table where the old camelback sofa had been.

Laughing, they did a tangled tango of falling shorts

to one of the new Knole sofas that played sentry to the wood-burning stove, crashing over the coffee-table and jettisoning its perfectly fanned copies of *Shropshire Life* across the room.

The sofa was very small and high-sided with multiple scatter cushions. Jo and Harry were no longer as svelte as they'd once been. Contorted, kicking away underwear, they tried to find an ideal angle. They thrashed around briefly before, with heroic effort, Jo offered herself crossways and turned to cast a coquettish look over her shoulder, realizing too late that the sofa arm-protector was now on her head, like a wimple. She whipped it off.

Harry was backed up against an army of scatter cushions with nowhere to go.

She didn't need to see in the dark to know he was smiling widely as he stood up and clasped her hand. 'I'm taking you up to bed, Owl.'

Sitting up, fighting dizziness and giggles, Jo found herself face to face with his cock, barely more than a gleaming bow in the dark, yet magnificently animated as he reached back to steady himself and it swung from ten o'clock to two.

'You expect me to ignore that?'

'You have lately.' He gave a sharp intake of breath when, lovingly and drunkenly, she gave it her full attention, soon taking his long hand straight up to midnight.

When she finally tipped her head back for air, she said, 'I want to talk about the wedding.'

'Not now, Owl.'

'I want us to marry in September.' Realizing she was still gripping his manhood like the karaoke microphone, she hurriedly let go. 'Forget the shares. I want you, not your past.'

'Let's talk about it in the morning.' He helped her up and she went straight into his arms. They kissed the life out of one another, the midnight hour hard against her pelvis, Jo only vaguely aware that her bra was hanging off one shoulder, like an evening bag.

The steep stone steps caught their knees and shins as they ricocheted up them, spilling gratefully into bed and carrying on where they'd left off, in comfortable, cushioned bravado until the glorious finish.

SUNDAY MORNING

The Hangover

Jo woke painfully, eyes thick with sleep, mouth dry as dust. She could hear Harry snoring behind a bank of pillows. Turning, her eyes blearily focused on tufts of blond hair, her nostrils catching a tang of cigar smoke. Closing one eye, she vaguely recalled a drunken bet in the Hare and Moon involving a hand-rolled Sancho Panza and a Ben E. King number, but most of the evening was a blissful blur. She recalled more vividly several hours of unbridled love-making that made her smile as she cautiously unfolded aching sticky thighs and fanned back the duvet.

Harry didn't stir. It was a sign of a seriously good night if he didn't tip out of bed at first light in search of caffeine. She pressed a kiss to his ear, noticing more grey hairs threaded through the blond and loving the knowledge that she'd see them work all the way through his mane to season it with old age.

'I love you,' she whispered. 'And I haven't changed my mind.'

An arm came out and rolled her against him. 'Tell me that at home and I'll believe it.'

Parched, they pulled on T-shirts and tottered downstairs. Following Harry, Jo winced as she adjusted to being upright with her legs together after so much unaccustomed sex. She dissolved a fizzy vitamin C tablet and knocked back two paracetamol, determined never to get drunk again. Harry put on the kettle and drank two glasses of water while he waited for it to boil. Then they silently danced through the preparation of a Rossbury-market pastries-and-crempogs breakfast that they could walk off with their hangovers up Mawr Vron. As they did so, Jo thought about her last call to her mother to check on the kids, made from the pub payphone amid so much background revelry. Assuring her that all was well, Di had told her to stop worrying about the children and enjoy her time alone with Harry. 'It's the last chance you'll get before the wedding,' she'd insisted excitedly.

'I want us to marry in September,' Jo said, over a *pain au chocolat*.

'So you said.' He focused on his croissant, not looking at her. She knew Harry's trust had been severely tested. She had a way to go before she earned it back, however enraptured they had been in the Hare and Moon. But with every swig of grade-A Arabica and every mouthful of rich pastry, her certainty, resolve and love grew. She wanted to marry Harry with their children in their arms as they'd planned.

'Let's walk up to the Burf.' She'd propose there, on one knee if necessary.

After an all-new Morrow power shower each, they dressed and strapped on their walking boots; Jo grabbed her phone at the last minute despite her mother's orders not to call again.

As they set off, several guinea fowl minced away from Efon's corn circle where yesterday's Indian breakfast was still in evidence, upturned and raided. The sun was already high enough to stripe the trees. They trudged towards higher ground, soon sweating Hare and Moon cocktails and finding memories bubble up unpleasantly.

'Did we really sing together?'

'Yes.'

'Was it as bloody awful as I remember?'

'I believe so.'

Now within signal range, Jo's phone started beeping with missed-call notifications and text messages.

'Popular.' Harry leaned back against a tree as she started to check them, palely hung-over and impossibly handsome.

Far below, they heard an engine roar as a car bounced up the track towards the house.

Jo listened to the messages, her mother first, panicked and apologetic, making little sense, just repeatedly saying, 'I'm sorry, Jo. I don't know what to do. I'm so sorry.' Then her sister, harsh and frightened, telling her to call back. Her sister again, more demanding. A neighbour of her mother's. Nobody explained. They all just asked her to call. More messages from her sister, crackling on a car phone in the early hours.

Below them, the big off-roader had parked outside the cottage now, a figure jumping out. Jo recognized Roy's broad torso, the hand raking back and forth over his bald pate when he realized nobody was home, the stoop of bad news heavy in his shoulders.

Beside her, Harry watched too, his cheeks shot through with their rare crimson jet streaks, his eyes marble black. 'It's got to be one of the kids.' He was off like a shot, racing back down the path to the cottage.

Jo ran down the hill after him, phone still clamped to her ear, her sister's recorded voice pleading with her to ring, then crackling away as she lost the signal.

By the time she caught up with Harry, he was waving Roy off.

His arms went straight round her. 'We have to leave, Owl.'

'Is it Thea or Wilf?' She wriggled away.

He gripped her hands. 'Jo, we have to go back.'

PART THREE

2011

Music: none

Car: Jeep Cherokee, falling apart

Season: Winter, wet and windy

FROM THE MORROW LAMINATES FOLDER

In the interests of sustainability, we no longer have a visitors' book and ask that cottage guests fill in the online feedback form on the Morrow website instead. Be environmentally friendly. Go paperless!

Matt and Rowena Inchbold, 2011

FRIDAY AFTERNOON

The Supermarket Shop

Glyn Pugh was in full festive swing, discount fir trees trussed in nets playing sentry to the entrance, a skyscraper Jenga of crackers teetering in the foyer, tinsel decking the tills where queues were eight deep, trolleys overflowing. Assistants in Santa hats hurried around, restocking shelves crammed with special promotions of booze, chocolates, mince pies and biscuit selections while George Michael sang 'Last Christmas' from the speaker.

Jo put her head down and steered her trolley towards Ready-made Meals. She didn't want to remember last Christmas or think about this one.

She wished she'd stuck with Harry's instructions to go to Waitrose. His orders had been very simple: 'Buy your favourite food. Rest. Relax. Forget about me and the kids for a day or two.'

Instead she was in Glyn Pugh's in search of nostalgia, trying to time-travel back to a carefree era when she and Harry had kissed behind the bakery section and nothing had mattered but the here and now. Next week still hung over her like a day of reckoning.

She wanted Christmas cancelled. Did nobody realize there was no point any more? Santa Claus had ceased to exist for Jo years ago, but now that her mother wasn't there, it felt as though Christmas no longer existed.

Pull yourself together, she told herself firmly, as she lobbed in random selections. Glyn Pugh's ready meals were unappetizing at the best of times, and positively off-putting at this time of year when Turkey and Gravy Kiev, Cranberry Luncheon Meat Loaf, and Sage Stuffing Pizza vied for space with the usual array of faggots and pies. *Think about the children.*

Now four, Wilf was already maxing out on TV advertising and peer pressure, his whole life revolving around Santa's arrival with a Fireman Sam Rescue Set. Eighteen months behind him, Thea's favourite occupation was twilight car journeys where she could point excitedly at the flashing icicles, coloured rope lights and inflatable reindeer on houses shouting, 'Look, Mummy – buddy oofoes!' She'd picked up 'buddy oofo' from Harry, who had taken against their neighbour's blue outdoor Christmas lights and said his house looked like a 'bloody UFO'.

Granny Cool would have screamed with laughter at that. She had so wanted to see another Christmas. But the leaves had barely started falling from the trees when Di had lost her eighteen-month fight to survive cancer.

Her illness had been littered with mile markers that she'd battled towards: the wedding had been the first, although she'd kept silent about her diagnosis until after that, wanting everyone to enjoy it without the stress of her news. The terrible dash back from Morrow last year after her collapse had been waved away as overreaction – she'd soon be on the mend, she'd insisted. But by then, everybody had guessed a black shadow was about to cross all their lives. Di had been illogically ashamed of her condition in those first weeks, of it being cancer of the bowel, a body part whose purpose people of her upbringing found embarrassing to discuss, even a former district nurse. Then came chemotherapy, each session a tick in the diary towards surgery and remission. During that time she'd seen Harry and Jo's long-awaited move back to the

Granary, expedited by her illness and funded by Harry's shared-space venture finally paying off. She'd seen Wilf turn three and managed to be at Jo's fortieth a few days later, held in the London restaurant that Harry and Ned had taken the lease on.

Christmas last year had been written off by the chemo, making her so ill she couldn't get out of bed, but she'd met more mile markers with typical tenacity and good spirits. She had recovered strength for her surgery in February, coming to the Granary to recover, sitting in her tartan chair by the fire in a sparkling headscarf, Rathbone the terrier on her lap, watching the children play. She'd enjoyed a legion of visitors and endured the noisy rhythm of family life echoing through the vaulted living space. Insisting she loved it, she'd seemed to rally. For her sixty-ninth birthday in May, they'd taken her up in a hot-air balloon – a lifelong ambition – and she'd chattered about it for weeks. In June, she'd insisted she was well enough to move home, another mile marker. But then she'd started to drop weight again and they'd learned that the surgery had not removed the cancer. Its spread was now unstoppable. Between Thea turning two (a sun-drenched, defiant family garden party at the Granary, determinedly planning forwards to Christmas) and Jo and Harry celebrating their first wedding anniversary (a muted meal cooked together, trying not to talk about the darkest of approaching shadows), more weight had dropped off her, pain and exhaustion stealing her from them. In early October, she'd died at home with Jo and her sister at her bedside.

Jo concentrated hard on the sell-by date of a Sprout and Stilton Mini Quiche, feeling as though she'd just swallowed it whole, box and all, and it was lodged in her throat.

Her sister had been right to take her family abroad this Christmas, an all-inclusive bask in the sun filling the hollow space where Di's chestnut-stuffed turkey and all the trimmings had once taken pride of place in their childhood home. After their father had died, they'd needed to gather force there, supporting each other and their mother. With both parents gone, they clutched their little nuclear families as tightly as they could.

Having moved back to the Granary at the beginning of the year, Harry and Jo had been intending to host Christmas, but now that was shelved. Instead, they would share the festivities with Matt and Rowena's brood in their newly renovated house in Blackheath, a picture-perfect, sprawling Victorian villa that Harry had nicknamed 'The Doll's House', now prettily poised to store up a new generation's memories and traditions. Family gatherings there inevitably involved a compulsory tour of the villa's carefully preserved original features, the word 'authenticity' drifting from Matt and Rowena's lips as often as 'shoes off'. Jo was wearily anticipating candlelight, goose, parlour games and many pairs of gifted slippers. Now, staring at the fridges in front of her, she had a satisfying mental image of Rowena serving Glyn Pugh's Seasonal Favourites Party Bites on a silver platter.

Rowena always made Jo feel wholly inadequate, a selfish, bad parent with an unhealthy lifestyle, hopeless time management and no control over her own children.

Her lowest point had come in the last months of Di's illness when she was trying to care for her, look after the kids and keep Blue Barn going. Then, as now, Harry had been wrapped up in the new restaurant, and she'd been going demented. In the Inchbold family, it had been obvious for some time that Harry's father was no longer coping, MS robbing him of independence as he struggled around his impractical house, and he needed more help than Viv was willing to provide or capable of giving. Tasked with sorting something, Titch had dropped everything for an acting job and passed the mantle to Jo, who got Gerry on the waiting list for a local-authority needs assessment. Then a crisis point arrived when he found he could no longer get in and out of his wheelchair unaided.

Rowena had arranged for a winch to be fitted that day and a carer to move into the Inchbolds' basement within twenty-four hours. 'You should have asked for my help,' she'd told Jo puritanically. 'It's selfish to take everything on yourself.'

Jo went to the pet-food section to track down the right meat pouches for Rathbone; Di had been very fussy about his diet, lavishing care on her little 'Ratty', who had been Jo's late father's dog. Now he'd been bereaved again, poor little creature. Jo felt a close alliance with him. He couldn't relax around Rowena either, and had cocked his leg on her handbag several times, which meant he'd be banished to the utility room while they lifted eggnogs next week.

Coming away for two nights at Morrow the week before Christmas was another selfish act of which Rowena no doubt disapproved, especially as Matt's offer to have the children to stay in the Doll's House meant Wilf would be charging around breaking things and getting fingermarks on the chalky heritage emulsion. It was cuddly toddler Thea whom Matt and Rowena adored, their favouritism obvious. Poor Wilf got that a lot. His biggest champions, apart from his parents, had always been Caro and Granny Cool. Now one lived hundreds of miles away and the other . . .

Jo gritted her teeth, determined to get past the till without blubbing. She found displays of emotion in public places deeply embarrassing. Even crying in front of Harry could feel too raw and exposed, his attempts to cheer her out of it too abrasive. It had been different during those terrified, exhausted, hormone-racked first weeks of being a mother

341

when she'd lost her dignity but never her sense of humour. Now, in the first grief-stricken, disorienting, lonely weeks without her own mother, she'd surrendered all comfort and joy.

'You all right, love?' asked an elderly male bag-packer, sporting fluffy reindeer antlers.

'Fine!' Her artificial sing-song voice was like a stranger's. 'I heard we're in for a few frosty nights.'

'They say it's getting colder right enough.' He put her bottles of wine into a box to transfer into a trolley, then spotted several more rattling down the conveyor-belt and picked up another box with a knowing look.

I'm a grown woman, Jo wanted to shout. I lost my mother seven weeks ago. I'm hanging on to my business by a thread, my husband thinks he's going to be the next Gordon Ramsay, and I've left my children in the care of a recycling-mad, vegan overachiever. I'm allowed to behave badly. Just you wait until you see how much chocolate I'm buying. But that would be unkind, and she wanted to reassure him that there was peace on earth amid the reindeer antlers and sleigh bells. Which was why, to her shame, she found herself lying. 'Got a few old friends coming round for Christmas drinks.'

Who was she kidding? She'd not seen most of them for months, maybe longer. Moving house so often meant losing touch fast, and each Christmas served as a sharp reminder of her dwindling social circle and dying industry as the cards kept thinning out. Season's greetings were now dispatched by email to a spreadsheet list of names on which hers appeared, landing among the spam in her in-box with a few personal condolences and impersonal round robins.

The cards at her parents' cottage had always been hung from string along the old ceiling beams, like colourful bunting, row after row. Jo had driven there last week to open those from far-flung friends and old acquaintances unaware of Di's death, writing straight back when she had a return address to break the news, setting others aside to research when she didn't have contact details. Alone there, Jo had allowed herself to cry a great deal, briefly at one with the past. She was so rarely alone these days that she'd forgotten what solace it brought. Now the total privacy of Morrow beckoned.

FRIDAY, LATE AFTERNOON

The Arrival

Jo drove straight to the cottage, bypassing the Craven Castle takeaway and beer-flagon run, grateful for the satnav's monotone directions from its windscreen holder. Even after almost six years, she struggled to find her way by memory. It was already getting dark, the road gleaming with ice as she crawled cautiously up through the sunken lanes, then finally crossed the cattle grid. The track had undergone some serious patching to enable the holiday-makers to get their cars up it, but it was still brutal on her suspension, sheep scarpering as she roared up it using too much clutch, an ominous wrenching noise coming from below as she lost the front wheel off the track briefly on the steepest stretch. She was enormously relieved when Morrow came into sight, and surprised to find how much it felt like a homecoming.

Inside, the cottage was bitterly cold. Nobody had stayed there recently. The freelance housekeeper who racketed around all the local holiday lettings on changeover day, with her van full of cleaning equipment, loo rolls and miniature jam pots, clearly hadn't been in since she'd last done the beds and topped up the mulled-spice reed diffuser. If Jo breathed deeply, she could almost distinguish the familiar tang of damp and mouse cutting through the cold, sweet air. Stopping in the doorway, she smiled.

She went straight to light the wood-burning stove, already made up with paper and kindling for visitors more accustomed to flipping a thermostat than arranging Zip firelighters and logs. Holding a match to it, she remembered losing her eyebrows the first time she'd visited. Harry had told her she was beautiful even without them. She missed him, aware of a pulse deep within that always beat strongest at Morrow.

The fire took quickly and she slid the vents open to help it roar, watching Rathbone settle gratefully in front of it, then going in search of the binder containing boiler instructions.

Half an hour later she stood on a pitch-black Shropshire hill, shouting to be heard over the wind. 'How do you start the woodchip boiler?'

Standing outside a commercial kitchen door in central London, shouting back to be heard over traffic and evening service, Harry wasn't much help. 'It's in the book.'

'No, it's not. That just says how to manually refuel it if the hopper vacuum gets blocked. It's packed up totally and is stone cold. I tried to start it and now the power's gone.'

'Have you pushed up the red switch?' he asked distractedly, then broke off to talk to somebody else, returning apologetically to the phone. 'We've got three Christmas office parties in and half the waiting staff haven't turned up. I have to go. Let me call Matt as soon as I've done this and I'll call you right back.'

'No, I'll do it. Sorry. I'll be fine. I know you're busy.'

'You're more imp ... tant,' the line was breaking up. 'If you can't ... it started, go ... the pub. Roy ... help out.'

'I'll be fine! Morrow's still rocking and beautiful, and I've slept here through a power cut before, remember?' But the line was dead, the signal gone.

Jo climbed higher, struck by how odd it felt being there without Harry, a moment of loneliness washing through her, no matter how impossible she knew it was for him to get away right now, his working hours off the scale.

Harry was so determined to safeguard his family's future by making his new business a success that he lost sight all too often of their present needs. In the same way, he regularly lost all sense of time and his short temper, but he'd never lost sight of his 'Flash in the Pan' idea to roll out pop-up pavement cafés for the Olympics crowd next year, and now the plan was finally coming together. When he and Ned had re-invested the money they'd made from the commercial-space venture, they'd bought boldly, taking a short lease on a restaurant in the trendy heart of EC1. Renaming it Street, they'd quickly hired the best team money and favours could afford, including a maverick media-friendly young chef guaranteed to garner maximum attention for the brand. The tactic had paid off with maximum publicity, plaudits, a frantic social media buzz and a waiting list for tables, although Harry and Ned knew that the economies of set-up scale and fickle London foodies meant that, at best, Street would only ever break even. But the fifty covers a night served at the flagship restaurant had never been the main goal. Neither was it Harry's kitchen apprenticeship, the instinctive cook watching and learning from a trained young genius, both fascinated by and passionate about their subject. The main business idea – now renamed 'Street Food' – would be the most talked-about, must-have unofficial food bars at the Olympics, for which the restaurant was the perfect launch pad. The kerbside chefs were already being trained on site, the food tested on clients, the mobile kitchens trialled in the West End and on the South Bank, and the logistics all coordinated from the restaurant. It looked a sure-fire success.

Jo's initial involvement in the project, designing artwork and producing printed material, had dropped away to almost nothing during her mother's illness, any spare energy taken up in trying to keep Blue Barn running.

Harry and Ned were perfect business foils, one a bold and tireless ideas man who could read trends like shepherds read weather, the other shrewd and superbly connected with a fat cash-pot and a reputation for perfect timing. The bromance between the two friends, who had once shared their schooldays as well as a brief taste of fame, now shaped Harry's career. Both knew no fear. They were at once terrifying and inspiring.

Teeth chattering wildly now, phone battery running low, Jo called Matt.

'The kids are on great form.' His voice was terribly like his brother's, but without the husky edge that told of late nights and endless laughter. 'I think Thea's asleep, but Wilf might still be awake for a word. Do you want me to check?'

'No, it's fine.' Her jaws were clattering almost too much for her to speak now, her eyeballs so cold they were giving her brain-freeze. 'They'll only play up if they hear me.' Dying of hypothermia. 'I just wanted to check they were okay. And do you know how to start the boiler here?'

She knew she could rely upon Matt. As her teeth played castanets, her temples shrivelled with cold and she lost all feeling in her feet, he patiently explained the process for relighting it.

'The power's out. Is that a problem?'

'You'll need to reset the trip switch in the main consumer unit.'

'I tried. It just trips out again.'

'You need to—'

The phone battery died.

Cursing, Jo stomped down the hill to the cottage and searched unsuccessfully for the car-battery charger: Harry must have nabbed it again. She did, at least, find his Puffa on the back seat of the car, which she crammed on over her own and headed back into the boiler shed with a torch.

After half an hour, no longer able to feel her frozen fingers, she finally conceded defeat and headed inside to find Rathbone shivering on a hearthrug in front of the wood-burning stove, which had gone out. Reaching to open the cupboard that had always housed newspapers and firelighters, she found it was shut, a small hasp and padlock now securing it.

'What the . . . ?'

She took her torch to the table to study the laminates and found a polite note pointing out that a free basket of logs was provided and guests were asked to buy their own fuel thereafter.

'From whom?' she howled, hurrying outside to the log store and finding another padlock on its collapsing doors.

Back at the fuse board, no amount of trip-switch flicking would persuade it to stay up.

She picked up Rathbone and headed to the car. It looked oddly lopsided.

Undeterred, she got in and started the engine. As well as the frost warning, a whole row of other lights came on in front of her, like a buddy oofo, and the car refused to move, its high-tech American alert system screaming, 'Lock down.' Flipping through the manual, she read that, for her own safety, it was preventing her from driving.

Jo got back out and started, just very slightly, to panic. She was – as Harry regularly pointed out – increasingly intolerant, these days, but nonetheless an incredibly capable person who kept calm in a crisis. Little ever ruffled her, apart from post-partum hormones and the death of a loved one, but—

It hit her again, this time like a full body impact from a speeding car.

Her mum had gone for ever.

She was stranded halfway up a mountain in midwinter with no power, no fuel, no transport, temperature plunging, and her mum had gone.

She needed her mum. Every day. Not just this day. She needed her mum.

The tears now were on a whole different scale from those she had wept over letters written to friends of Diana she had never met, sitting at a kitchen table she knew so well, drawing comfort from her surroundings and their everyday familiarity. Here, in the cold darkness, she knelt down and howled.

FRIDAY EVENING

The Pub

With Rathbone zipped tightly into her Puffa, Jo hovered outside the Hare and Moon feeling deeply antisocial. She could hear carol singing coming from inside. She had thought about sleeping in the car by the cottage with the engine on for heat, but there was only a quarter of a tank of fuel left and she was worried it might snow. The walk down had been treacherous and icy enough.

Bracing herself, she pinched her cheeks for colour and pushed her way inside.

Roy was barely recognizable. He'd lost a huge stack of weight, along with his beard and what had been left of his hair, now shaved to a thuggish buzz-cut. He looked seriously scary, although his smile was as big as ever.

'Christ alive, Jo, you're frozen through. You all right, lovey? Harry with you?'

'He's working this weekend.' She took off her steamed-up glasses. 'Can I have a very large drink?'

'Pint, is it?'

She forced a smile, unzipping her coat to release Rathbone. 'Brandy. Small glass. No umbrella.'

'Coming up.'

She glanced across at the performers by the fire, two men and a woman in close harmony. It was lovely.

'Plygain,' Roy explained. 'They're old Welsh Christmas songs. Ping and I prefer the karaoke, but her mother's a traditionalist so we're having a Christmas folk night.' He shuddered, casting his eyes towards a small figure at the centre of a large gathering on the sofas. 'You want food? We've got a Thai special of cowpat moo – the mother-in-law's idea of a joke.' He looked at the figure on the sofa again, eyes narrowing. 'She won't pull one over on me.'

'Khao Pad Moo, fried rice with pork – delicious,' Jo told him, putting Rathbone on the floor. 'I need to make a call if that's okay.'

She huddled by the payphone, still wearing two coats and shaking with cold. As she waited for Harry to pick up, she watched Roy's diminutive mother-in-law get up from the sofa and take to the stage, whooped by her companions, among them the unmistakably blonde figures of Cerys and her sister Lowri, one as buxom and smouldering as the other was pierced and fierce.

'What's happening?' Harry demanded, over the restaurant chatter at his end. 'I've had Matt calling every ten minutes, convinced you'll be found frozen to the mountainside by morning. Why didn't you bloody call me back?' He always sounded cross when he was worried about her.

Jo inevitably overcompensated with brittle, witty fragility, needing upbeat, charming Harry and his soothing flirtation, not the brusque bark of his love and fear. 'I'm fine – my phone died. The car's broken down.'

'Christ, are you okay? Where is it?' His voice was still cracked with impatience, and she knew he was angriest with himself for not being there.

'At the cottage. It's fine. I've walked down to the Hare and Moon, so I'm fine too – brandy in hand!' She raised her glass as though he could see her. Doing so with a rictus smile was becoming her motif this year.

'Poor Owl.' At last she had the smooth sympathy she longed for. 'I knew you'd be fine, beautiful Owl. You're invincible. What's that noise? Have they got that Björk tribute act back?'

'I think it's traditional Thai music,' Jo explained, as Ping's mother started howling emotively by the fire.

'Good for you to get out and enjoy some culture. Take your mind off things. This weekend is about you, Owl.'

Jo needed to hear him say things like that. Not the intense stab of 'How are you feeling?' with those big, soulful blue eyes watching her and sharing her raw pain, but the 'You're a trouper, go get 'em' rallying cry, telling her how well she was doing. Right now if people asked Jo how she was doing, she cried; if they just told her she was doing brilliantly she felt stronger.

She and Harry had argued just last week when he'd accused her of shutting him out and begged her to let him closer to her grief, but mostly he trod carefully near her, respecting her need to wrap layers of good humour around herself, too busy to question it.

'I'd kill for a pint in the Moon tonight.' He sounded distracted now, shouting something else over his shoulder about the partridge needing to be faster. 'Are you sure you're okay, Owl?'

'I said I'm fine!' She wobbled momentarily, then pulled herself together. 'Who cares if there's no power or heat in the cottage and the car suspension's collapsed? It's three days before Christmas, and there's an open fire and carol singers in the pub.'

'Sound just like my first family trips to Morrow.' He gave an uneasy laugh. 'Now I'm even more jealous.' Somebody was shouting for him in the background and he hushed them. 'Beautiful time of year. The frosts are sensational.'

Jo watched Rathbone venture tentatively from her side to the fire, like a small grey mop-head, and settle in front of it with a deep sigh. She knew that, after a brief nap, he'd wake up with a start and go in search of her mother, as he always did.

Suddenly she couldn't speak for tears in her throat.

'Are you really okay, Owl?' Harry's voice. Husky and light.

Stop asking that, she wanted to yell, but words were still impossible as she hurriedly turned her back to the room, blinking and slow-breathing.

'Jo?' Angry and hoarse now, crackling in her ear.

'I'm fine,' she managed, although she sounded as though she'd swallowed a bag of gobstoppers. 'I'll call you tomorrow.' Ringing off and draining her brandy, she pinched her cheeks again and headed to the bar for another, grateful for Roy's small world in which her grief was entirely unknown.

He served this one in a goblet, placing a paper coaster beneath it. 'For my favourite London customer.'

'Not quite London any more. How's Ping?'

'Great. Upstairs with the baby. Another boy,' he said proudly. 'Rhys.'

'Congratulations. Is that Welsh?'

He grinned. 'It's good to see you. The drinks are on the house. We get a lot of trade down here from the cottage now, and we're very grateful for the recommendation – much appreciated – although we'd like to see more of you and Half Inch.'

'We'd love to come here more,' she admitted. 'Life's been full on this past year.' Terminal illness, another house move, new nurseries for the children, another change of career for Harry, scaling down my business yet again, death.

Death. The truth clenched her throat again, asphyxiating in its sadness.

'I know that feeling with balls on.' Roy was clearly thinking of his own busy year as he cast his eyes to where the

353

traditional Thai music was hotting up in a duet with Lowri on the mouth organ. 'I've spent most of the last eighteen months building a bungalow, a kit car and a fairy-light-decked pergola temple – all for Ping's mother. And what reward do I get? They put me on a diet and tell me the beard must go. Still, not bad, eh?' He patted his flat stomach.

Jo looked at him blankly for a moment, then realized he was fishing for a compliment. She told him he looked great, then knocked back the second brandy and shuddered, the heat finally starting to penetrate, along with the recollection that Roy had just revealed house building, electrical and mechanical skills. 'In fact, Roy, you might just be my dream man.'

'Steady on. I'm taken.' He looked terribly pleased.

'Can you fix a biomass boiler, a faulty fuse board and a broken suspension coil on a Jeep?'

'Not overnight,' he admitted, sucking air between his teeth, chest puffed heroically. 'But I can get you some help tomorrow.'

'In that case, do you have a B&B room free?'

'That I do.' He took her glass to top it up again, watching Rathbone pant up to her, having awoken in a panic, just as Jo had predicted. 'No dogs on the beds.'

'I don't know how to thank you.'

'Get onstage now.' He rolled his eyes towards the wailing duet. 'It's a walk-up mic, so they have to relinquish it for a new act.'

She laughed, then saw he was deadly serious. 'I can't hold a note or play an instrument, Roy.'

'Neither can she,' he pointed out. 'You can sing a carol, surely. We all remember you singing with Harry a couple of years back. Voice like an angel.'

'I was very, very drunk.'

'Have another.' He took her glass and filled it with one double brandy on top of the other, adding a cocktail umbrella for good measure. 'Harry always said you had nerves of steel and a heart of gold. I'll put a tenner in the charity tin if you do it.'

At that moment, she missed Harry so much her ribs felt dovetailed over her heart. Impatient, distracted, short-tempered Harry, who longed to 'cure' her grief, would have sung beautifully. The collection tin on the bar was for Macmillan nurses, she noticed, tears dangerously close as it brought back vivid memories of her mother's final weeks.

'Make it twenty and find someone to fix my car.' Opening the paper parasol, she slotted it behind Roy's ear, raised her glass and headed onstage.

Jo needed distraction and, with three brandies roaring in the pit of an empty stomach, flattered into performing, she knew no fear. Until Ping's mother stood aside with a gracious bow and she stood in front of the microphone, adjusting its height up a foot, politely introducing herself and asking everybody to join in 'The Twelve Days of Christmas'.

It started out well enough, although Jo made it more rap than melody to disguise the lack of tuning, and she was acutely aware of Cerys's unblinking gaze from the sofa.

But then it all got a bit muddled after 'five gold rings'. She struggled to remember whether it was six or seven geese and whether they came before the maids or the swans. By the time the ladies were dancing and lords a-leaping, her stocktaking was in total chaos. The audience tried to help, but she was unravelling fast.

She saw Cerys mouth at Lowri, 'Pissed.'

Eyes narrowed, she gave her turtle doves both barrels. At least she could relax every time she was counting back from five rings to the partridge, relieved to be on safe ground. Until, that was, her mind wandered and found itself thinking of how dedicated and generous the True Love was, giving the singer all those things. Like Harry bringing her armfuls of gourmet treats from the restaurant; like her father, who had always embarrassed his family by the number and eccentricity of his gifts, especially for his beloved Di.

No more Dad.

No more Mum.

"'On the twelfth day of Christmas, my true love gave to me ...'" Was it pipers or drummers? What had she done last time? "'... twelve pipers drumming, eleven drummers piping, ten lords a dancing, nine geese a-milking ...'"

She imagined Harry bringing in ever-more extravagant armies each day to entertain her, to laugh away her sorrow.

"'... fiiiiive goooooooold riiiiiiiiings ...'"

The crowd joined in eagerly, grateful that she knew her way from there.

But the calling birds, French hens, turtle doves and partridge were flying around like a Hitchcock thriller in her mind now.

Mum's dead.

Before she knew it, Jo was doing Sinéad O'Connor tears. But not a pretty, doe-eyed, tuneful one. A great snotty, snorting, flat-singing one.

Rathbone hurried from the fireside to sit supportively on her foot and lean against her leg, which set her off even more.

The applause was one of great relief more than admiration.

Mortified, she hurried back to the bar to ask Roy to show her to her room. He was putting fifty quid in the Macmillan tin, she noticed, and there were tears in his eyes. Did he know about her mother?

'Funniest thing I've seen in years, that – you're a comedy natural.' He mopped his brow with a sigh of delight. Clearly not. 'You seen much of Ned lately, by the way?'

Lying upstairs with Rathbone tucked under one arm and twenty-four-hour news playing loudly on the television to drown out the sound of singing and bar talk, Jo registered that she had just experienced her most mortifying moment since taking to the school stage aged thirteen to collect an art prize on Founder's Day. She hadn't known that her arch enemy, Julian Black, had tucked her skirt into her tights while he was standing in the line behind her. That had been a humiliation in itself, played out in front of eight hundred pupils and their parents, the entire teaching staff, governors and the local mayor, all of whom had been granted the full spectacle of her sagging grey woollen behind through which her lucky Kermit knickers gleamed with a froggy-green thumbs up. It hadn't been Jo's mooning woollen backside that had made the occasion so mortifying, though, but her reaction to it. When third-year art star Joanna Coulson had realized that at least a thousand pairs of eyes were staring, including those of her proud parents, she'd lost it.

The tears had been as instant as those she'd just shed downstairs. There had been no warning, no chance to control them. Prize-winners were lined up on a bench at the back of the stage through long speeches and the school song. Jo had wept there uncontrollably until eventually, far too late, she'd been helped from the stage by the kindly Deputy Head into her mother's arms.

Knowing she'd never feel those arms again, she curled into a tight ball now, longing for Harry, whose comforting hug she had shrugged off so often lately.

SATURDAY MORNING

The B&B

By seven Jo was wide awake, showered and dressed, pacing between window and door. It was still dark outside. Rathbone was fast asleep. She cursed herself for leaving her phone in the car at Morrow when she could have borrowed a charger for it here. She needed to solve the problem of the non-working broken car, the boiler and the electricity without delay. That meant looking up numbers and making calls, but she felt embarrassingly light-headed and panicky after the spectacle she'd made of herself. Having not eaten since the previous morning, she could hear her stomach growling furiously.

She glanced in the mirror, appalled at the puffy eyes behind her black-rimmed nerd glasses.

A polite tap took her to the door. Tiny Ping was holding a tray weighed down by the mother of all fry-ups, clustered around which were plates of toast, pastries and fruit, along with yogurts, jams and juice with a cocktail umbrella in it. 'I hope you don't mind this intrusion. Roy thought you might like breakfast in bed.'

'That's so kind.' Jo was overwhelmed, battling a fresh wave of tears as she stepped back to let Ping carry the tray to the little table beneath the window.

'There is fresh coffee, but I can bring you tea, if you like?'

'This is all just perfect. Thank you.' Jo wasn't sure if she remembered sharing a sticky toffee pudding when they'd been pregnant with Gethin and Thea. 'I'm Jo – we met a couple of years ago.' Ping looked no different but Jo felt about a century older. 'And congratulations. I hear you've just had another little boy.'

'Three weeks old.' Ping nodded politely, pouring the coffee. She had barely a trace of baby bump left, Jo noticed. 'You want meet him?'

'Oh, yes, please.'

'I bring him down later. Roy said there was a phone call last night, and another this morning, but caller said not to wake you. He wrote down messages here.' She handed a piece of folded paper, then backed politely out of the room, muttering, 'No dogs on the bed.'

One of Rathbone's enormous grey eyebrows lifted sagely as he watched her go, then he yawned and body-crawled across the duvet towards Jo, anticipating breakfast. She was reading and rereading the note.

12.15 a.m. Harry on way.
6.35 a.m. Problem with bike on M5, Harry says.
Will call after 8.

She took off her glasses to rub her swollen eyes, fighting tears again as she imagined him setting out heroically for Shropshire on his motorbike after the Street kitchens closed. It was gloriously, impractically, bloody-mindedly Harry. No doubt the bike – an overpowered Italian crotch rocket, which he insisted cut down his journey times – had broken down again, grinding to a halt on a freezing hard shoulder at God knew what early hour. Harry had to be in London for lunch service. She wouldn't even see him. The thought made her hollow with disappointment.

She shared breakfast with Rathbone, longing to be sharing it with Harry too, although not if she cried all over him. The crying *had* to stop.

Carrying her breakfast tray downstairs, she found the kitchen deserted, along with the pub bars. She crammed the last of her coins into the payphone and called Harry, going straight to voicemail, then Matt, who picked up in a single ring.

'Jo. Thank God!' He was crackling on a hands-free in the car. 'I take it you heard?'

'Heard what?' She watched Rathbone and Sinbad the pub dog make formal, bottom-sniffing introductions, both stiff-legged and respectful.

'Harry was lucky not to get busted. Nobody else involved, thank God. I'm on my way to pick him up now. Are you okay?'

'Fine – what do you mean, "busted"?'

'He should never have set out.' His tone was as disapproving as that of a father on his way to collect his bombed teenager from an ABC party. 'They'd had the wine supplier in yesterday afternoon with a stack of samples, although he swears he stuck to Coke throughout service. From the sound of the crash, I doubt it. The bike's totally written off – he went across all six lanes and two sets of barriers and ended up in a pig field.'

'Oh, God, is he okay?' She covered her mouth, black-blinkered with panic.

'Bulletproof, trust me. You know Harry.'

'I'll come right there. Where is he? I'll get a taxi.'

'He won't thank you for it.' Matt was brusque. 'He says he's barely got a scratch and he feels a prat, which he is. Christ knows, he's a lucky sod. He stood straight up and walked back to the services he'd just passed, booked himself into the motel, took a bath, slept it off and called me. He'd even somehow had the presence of mind to mend the fencing so his little pig friends didn't get hurt. Of course, we still have to pay off the farmer and arrange for the bike to disappear.' Matt's tone was acerbic. 'There's no one else to cover him at work and he insists he's fine to do it. I wish I could pick you up too, Jo, but the turnaround's too tight. How are you coping? I can't imagine it's a lot of fun tackling Morrow's winter glitches.'

Jo looked around the pub, briefly clammy-skinned as she relived last night's bleeding heart, then regrouping, breathing in the smell of woodsmoke and warmth, her no-tears rule intact. 'All under control. Tell Harry I'll get everything sorted here and come straight back. Roy and Ping are being a great help.'

'You are amazing. Give everyone my regards. Call me if you need me.'

'How are—' But he'd hung up before she could add 'the children?'

Jo put the handset down slowly, then jumped as the phone immediately rang. It was Harry, breakfast television in the background.

'I admit it, I'm a numbskull.' His voice was huskier than ever.

'What happened? Matt says it was a six-lane slide!' Her hand was already shaking so much at the thought of it that his reply was vibrato in her ear.

'The bike did that. I rolled in the opposite direction and ended up in a gorse bush. Unforgivably stupid. Riding too fast.'

She felt a flash of anger, then guilt that he'd been speeding to get to her, then deep-vein affection, hugging the receiver tighter. 'Are you really not hurt?'

'My leathers will be ground deep into the M5 tarmac until it's resurfaced, but I stood up okay.'

'Thank God,' she breathed, and added, before she could stop herself, 'Matt said you'd been drinking.'

'Matt thinks a chocolate liqueur is reason enough to take

a folding bicycle to a restaurant. He can fuck right off. I was sober. Knackered, distracted and worried about you, but sober.'

'He's just protective,' she reminded him. 'He loves you. He's driving out to get you right now.'

'That was his idea. I could have caught a train home. He likes to play the hero.'

'*Touché.*'

'Are you really okay, my beautiful Owl? Did you manage to sleep at all?'

For once, the question didn't trigger a tearful, defensive insistence that all was wonderful. 'I'm bearing up.'

How would she feel right now if Harry had succeeded in his heroic quest? Jo wondered. Probably jittery and tearful because he'd already be about to leave again.

She'd slept like the dead after her mortifying stage show, purged of tears and day-to-day responsibilities, uninterrupted by wakeful children or late-shift husband, a small warm body nuzzled comfortingly in her arms. Harry rolling up in the early hours would have been a heart-stopping gesture, but a sleep-wrecking one – and if he'd hoped for an erotic reunion, he would have found himself grappling with a red-eyed wreck. Lately they'd both mistaken her need for comfort as a need for sex; they still hadn't really negotiated that one. It was often drunken and, to Jo's shame, she'd lost interest halfway through more than once, her mind drifting to such a degree that she'd wished she'd left Radio 4 on. She'd hate to think of him biking three hours from London expecting passion and eager for a snuggle, only to find her watching BBC News in geek glasses with a brandy headache and dirty teeth.

Yet ironically, from this distance, she felt suddenly exhilarated by his late-night ride, by the thought of a sexy after-hours reunion of petrol-head, leather-jacketed passion. 'I miss you.' She pulled the receiver closer to her cheek.

'Me too.' The huskiness in his voice drew the tiny hairs in her ear aside, like a curtain, and she recognized just how much he meant it. 'I love you, beautiful Owl.'

'I love you, Harry.'

They said it in full so rarely these days – accustomed to the universal couples' sign-off *Love you xx* that covered all bases without feeling its foundations. After Jo had put the phone down, she kept her hand on it for a long time, those foundations deep enough for her to wish she could pull it out by the wires and find him hanging on to the end.

Hearing a polite cough, she looked round to see Ping hovering in the doorway marked 'Private'. 'You okay to meet my boys?'

'Please!'

Along with baby Rhys, Ping was accompanied by toddler Gethin, and her tiny, smiling mother, whose name Jo didn't quite catch, although she thought she heard it as Pong. She wanted to ask her to repeat it to make sure, but Possibly Pong went into an elaborate bow, mirrored by her grandson, before both of them hurried into the kitchen to make coffee.

'Roy don't like my mother being here,' Ping said, in an undertone, plonking herself down on one of the sofas, which she patted for Jo to join her. 'He say every woman grow up to be like her mother. He say he marry me at twenty-six, but now he live with me at forty-five too!' She cackled. 'Every day he see old lady I will become!'

Realizing she was much closer in age to Ping's mother than to Ping, Jo smiled stiffly. 'She's still in her prime.'

'She have new boyfriend in Rossbury. They at it all the time. Karl the Car Breaker.'

'Can he get hold of spare parts?' Jo asked hopefully, thinking about the Jeep's suspension spring.

'He got name because he break into cars when he was a young man.' Ping handed her the baby, still fast asleep.

'Oh, he's beautiful.' She gathered up the warm, newborn weight of him. 'He looks so like you – and your mum. Wilf, my eldest, is his father's double, but our daughter takes after my side of the family. We named her Thea after my maternal grandmother.'

Ping looked confused. 'Your grandmother midwife?'

'My mother's mother,' she explained.

'Your mum very beautiful lady like you, I'm sure.'

'She was,' she said tightly, pressing her lips to the baby's warm, downy head and smelling his milk-sweet newness. 'She died recently.'

'I'm sorry.' Ping touched her arm.

'It was very quick.' Jo cuddled the new baby to her chest. She was never sure why she felt compelled to say that, given it had felt like the longest year of her life, a year of loving more than ever, living more than ever, caring more than ever, laughing more than ever, hugging more than ever and now crying more than ever.

'You still very sad, I think.' Ping's kind eyes darkened. 'Roy is a lovely man who treat me well, but a mother's love so much more forgiving than a man's. I need my mum.'

'Your English has got a lot better,' Jo said brightly, to mask another rush of tears.

'I can even say "Sorry, that was clumsy thing to say."' She dipped her head self-consciously, peeping up.

Jo covered her hand with a grateful squeeze and they shared a warm smile that ignited into a furnace of laughter when Possibly Pong emerged from the kitchen carrying a coffee pot laden with crackling sparklers. Beside her, little Gethin carried a milk jug, like a sacred urn. They both struck a pose.

'Miserable big lady not wet!' Possibly Pong trilled, indicating Jo.

Jo tried to look politely delighted.

'Her English is crap,' Ping explained. 'What she means is that you are very beautiful and she wants you to laugh, not cry.'

Jo tried very hard not to as her tear-prevention supporter, Rathbone, came to sit on her foot, looking up at her through thick grey brows.

'Funny dog!' Gethin pointed.

About to say that he'd belonged to her mother, Jo switched to, 'Harry calls him the family dogma.' The joke was lost on her audience, but she felt a deep tug of affinity through the nearby telephone wire.

SATURDAY AFTERNOON

The Chill-out

Walking back up the track to Morrow, turbo-charged with coffee and buffeted sideways by the wind, Jo met a Land Rover towing her Jeep on a rusty car trailer. The unfamiliar driver raised a flat cap, as she and Rathbone clambered on to a hillock to let it pass, but didn't stop to talk. It was only after she'd raised her bobble hat in return that she realized her phone, clothes and food were being towed away with it.

'Wait!'

It was too late, her voice an anonymous bleat among the sheep as the engine roared into the windswept sleet below.

She hurried on to the cottage, where Roy was wearing a very clean boiler suit and drinking the Morrow welcome tray hot chocolate while talking to a man lying inside the cupboard under the stairs with only his legs, clad in jodhpurs and riding boots, visible.

'You've had water leaking into your boiler controls apparently – it would stop it working and trip out the power,' he explained. 'George here thinks he's fixed it, but you'll need to let it dry out for a few hours. He's just running a few checks before he pushes off to whip in with the Union. Best not start the boiler until this evening. I brought you some firewood to keep you going.' He nodded towards a pile as big as the sofa. 'I'll come back later to get that boiler going, if you want me to.'

At last, Jo sensed her warm, soulful retreat so close that

she could already smell its smoky sweetness. 'There's no need. This is honestly fabulous.'

'Dai's taken your car to fix. He can't do it here because he needs a compressor. Your food's in the kitchen. Made us laugh, classy lady like you going to Glyn Pugh. You know there's a Waitrose up at the Castle?'

'I like to support local retailers.'

'Glyn Pugh's family live in Marbella. Most of the crap they sell is imported, but never mind. Just don't eat the Scotch eggs. My aunt lost three yards of gut from those. If you have any trouble, use this.' He handed her a klaxon. 'George's lot grabbed it off a bunch of antis they caught skulking around the estate this morning. It puts the hounds off so, for God's sake, only use it in an emergency. If you stand on high ground, chances are we'll hear it in the pub, as long as Ping's mother's not caterwauling.'

'Thank you so much.' She hugged the klaxon to her chest. 'I can't believe you're being so kind.'

'Ping likes you,' he said. 'She's not got a lot of friends round here.'

'I like her.' She smiled. Then, the memory of her smirking audience at last night's carol-singing fresh in her mind, she couldn't resist asking, 'What about Cerys and the gang?'

He made a *pfft* sound. 'Half Cut only comes back here to ruffle feathers.'

After she'd waved off Roy and George, insisting she would repay the favour, Jo gathered the peace around her like an old friend. She lit the wood-burning stove, which Rathbone settled in front of with elderly gratitude as Jo changed into sloppy joes: her favourite comfort joggers matched with an old fleece of Harry's, hair scraped up, thickest socks pulled up nerdily and glasses wonky on her nose as she went in search of her sketch pad and ink pens, packed as a last-minute afterthought, but now brought into use as she did a cartoon sketch of Roy and his family in front of the Hare and Moon as a thank-you, then another for George of a horse and rider sailing over a crouched figure with a klaxon.

The occupation wasted a couple of hours while the house warmed up and her busy mind settled. Being alone was alien to her these days, but she embraced it wholeheartedly, talking all the time to a small, sleeping dog.

Her CDs and phone playlists were all still in the car, so she rooted around the small collection stacked up by the stereo and found a Fleetwood Mac *Greatest Hits* album, which she put on. There was a television at the cottage now, which only played DVDs because there was no aerial signal, and Jo knew it would be Inchbold sacrilege to watch anything, although the sight of *Out of Africa* among the collection was sorely tempting. She knew it so well that she cushion-hugged minutes before the romantic scenes and cried before the sad ones. But there were too many sad scenes.

Instead, she selected a book of poetry – the first she'd read in years. Seamus Heaney. Her mother had loved poetry, always prodding Jo to read something beyond thrillers and racy romances. She read half a dozen poems now, reciting some out loud to Rathbone, her heart lifting. Yesterday she would have wept over the lost conversation she'd now never have about them. Yet here, in Morrow's silence, something had changed: she talked to her mother as though she was sitting next to her. It felt entirely natural and cathartic. Even Rathbone joined in with the book-club spirit, skittering up on to the sofa to lie exactly where Jo imagined Di's knees to be.

Feeling surprisingly hungry, despite such a mammoth breakfast, she went to raid her Glyn Pugh selection. Roy was right. It was crap food, yet strangely bolstering as she ate a cold mini-quiche and cracked open a bargain wine as accompaniment; this was her holiday and it was almost Christmas, after all. When 'Songbird' started playing, her grief reflex kicked in and she hurried back to change the CD to one she'd never heard of. Its artist struck a self-conscious pose in a beret on its jacket and his lyrics spoke blandly of feeling good, dancing in Manhattan and looking at life sunny side up.

Without Jo noticing, her mother slipped quietly out of the room.

From late morning until late evening, Jo ate, drank wine, sketched and listened to every unfamiliar CD on the Morrow shelf, feeding logs into the stove at regular intervals, feeling at ease for the first time in months. It wasn't pleasure, or really relaxation. It was total, tearless, thought-free numbness. Whenever an emotional thought threatened to penetrate the detachment – her mother, the children, Harry, the future – she reminded herself to stop, eat, refill her glass, top up the fire and dance around the room, if necessary.

She suffered a brief spike of guilt and worry that she couldn't call Harry to check he'd got back okay, or ring the Doll's House to ensure the children were all right, but putting on a Sage Stuffing Pizza and cracking open another bottle of wine saw her through the dip. Me-time, she reminded herself. Family orders.

She started the boiler at six, grateful to hear it roar into life.

The cottage was still bitterly cold, apart from the furnace-like sitting room, where she'd taken up residence on the bigger of the two sofas. It doubled as a pull-out bed and Jo decided to try it. After a brief, panic-stricken moment trapped in the spring-loaded jaws of its metal mechanism, she created a new nest and lay back to christen it with hot seasonal pizza and more wine.

She was now down to the CDs she knew, a minefield of tracks likely to make her cry. She selected a Welsh radio channel instead, delighting in the voices speaking a language both lyrical and incomprehensible to her, interspersed with very bad country-and-western music. Had she spoken Welsh, she was in no doubt she'd have heard the show's hosts droning on boringly between tracks about Nashville versus neo country, but as it was they sounded as though they were speaking from their souls.

She napped for a bit, woozy now, awoken by a fiercely needy bladder. Cannoning around in the bathroom, a haven of eau-de-Nil tongue-and-groove these days, she realized she was really quite pissed. To her recollection, she'd never before in her life got drunk alone. It was liberating. Being at Morrow alone was a revelation. No wonder Harry had always advocated it. She could spend the evening running around naked, shouting obscenities, masturbating furiously and drinking more wine if she wanted to.

Instead, she curled up with a novel, pulled from the shelf at random, a modern fable about two free-spirited sisters that grabbed her attention for three chapters before lashing out to pinch her painfully in the tear ducts by giving one a terminal illness and the other an impossible decision. Jo hadn't seen it coming and snapped the book shut, feeling betrayed.

Hungry from all-day wine-sipping, she shared the Turkey and Gravy Kiev with Rathbone, both pleasantly surprised by its tasty succulence. Glyn Pugh could relax on his Marbella sun-lounger with pride, she reflected as she chomped it from its metal tray in rebellious isolation, unaccompanied by veg.

Standards slipping fast, she relented on the DVD moral stance, although Meryl and Robert remained off-limits for emotional reasons. Instead, she chose an innocuous-looking kids' animation.

Two hours later, she was a wreck. Who could have known that something about an Armageddon trash truck and a floating Android could be so emotional? She needed more wine and blank space.

She had lost all sense of time, darkness being such a constant. She had a vague feeling it was the winter solstice. She remembered being there for the summer one, sitting outside with Harry on Efon's corn circle. Harry had hated being inside the cottage. He found the changes hard to bear. Jo loved being in the cottage without its memories. It was just perfect by her. She looked at her watch. Almost midnight. How had that happened? She must go up to bed and sleep.

But first there was *Out of Africa*. She had to go there . . .

EARLY HOURS OF SUNDAY MORNING

The Arrival

Jo woke with another overfull bladder, the room lit by the glow of the DVD menu screen, which featured a photo of Meryl Streep looking determinedly aloof in front of a bloodshot African-sunset backdrop. There was another light illuminating the walls, one that moved and brightened. A car was coming up the track. Rathbone was barking.

'Shit!' She rolled off the sofa, head throbbing, and peered from the windows. It was just rounding the corner by the woods, very cautiously tackling the big bumps before the last sharp ascent.

She rushed to the loo, cursing how long it took to empty out three-quarters of a bottle of cheap sauvignon. Stretching for the sink, she grabbed her brush to clean her teeth while she was sitting down, removing the tell-tale wine breath, although she suspected the telltale wine stumbling would give her away, if the visitor hung around for long. As would her sofa-bed slut-nest.

Who the hell was it?

Back in the sitting room, she looked around in despair at the student-digs bombsite she'd created in just one evening. Her wine-slewed brain wasn't at its sharpest, but she made a guess that it was either Roy, prodded by an anxious Ping to check on her, or a sex-crazed local alerted to the fact that, among several hundred sheep on Mawr Vron, there was a woman on her own with a geriatric dog. Either way, being in fake-sleep lockdown seemed the best policy.

Unable to find the remote, she pulled the television plug out at the wall to darken it, killed the last of the lights and hid beneath the window, holding tightly on to Rathbone, her hand gently round his jaws to silence him.

The car engine approaching had the most extraordinary lion-cub roar. It was a sound that had accompanied her twenties and thirties behind the wheel on the road. She peeped briefly above the sill. It was a Mini. And the blond glint of hair as its driver got out was unmistakable.

Rathbone was released, his renewed barks drowned in Jo's cry of joy.

She wrenched the door open and raced out, not caring that she was welcoming Harry in her scaggiest joggers and specs, reeking of her white wine and junk-food binge.

He gathered her into a kiss that almost turned her inside out. 'I couldn't bear to think of you so unhappy and alone here, Owl.'

Inside, he didn't seem to notice the food-strewn sofa-bed, open DVD boxes or the spilled-wine smell. As soon as they were through the door, to Jo's shrieks of protest, he slid an arm around her back, the other dropping behind her knees to carry her straight up to bed.

'You can't!'

Harry was very strong, but he'd come off a bike at speed the night before, he was dog tired, and she was two pregnancies heavier than she'd once been, plus slewed with binge-eating, drinking and movie-watching.

'You're right, Owl. I can't,' he said, after a brief tussle, letting her back down with a groan, defeated by her leg-kicking protests about bad backs and needing to floss and moisturise.

Instead, they took turns in the bathroom. For once, Jo didn't mind that Harry came in to pee while she was washing her face – two long restaurant shifts, a killer amount of coffee followed by four hours on the motorway were taking their toll. In six years together, she'd never quite got used to how unselfconscious he was compared to her, but tonight her inhibitions had been lowered by her hours on the sauce. In fact, she decided, it was high time to redress this balance by undressing.

Not pausing to think what she was doing – or remember that she was wearing two fleeces and a polo neck – she pulled off all her top layers in one go, cursing when they got stuck near her ears, inverted, forcing her to lurch around blindly with her arms in the air wrestling free. As she did so, kidnapped by her own lust, her self-critical mind was already at work, telling her she was mistaking sex for comfort again, reminding her that she was repeating herself by getting her tits out in this bathroom. But when she finally burst free, Harry seemed delighted.

'You are so beautiful, Owl.'

Facing her now, he was wearing an old hooded fleece over his crumpled front-of-house suit and the driving glasses that they joked made him look like a serial killer, but he was still the best-looking man she'd ever known, and Jo's insides turned to liquid at the thought of a night alone together at Morrow. She didn't care if the sex was muddled up, she needed comfort and joy.

Ricocheting through the dark cottage, they tripped upstairs and fell on to the bed amid the still-folded square piles of fluffy towels and complimentary lavender pillow pouches.

We still have it, Jo thought giddily, as they kissed, giving it her all, still channelling Karen Blixen reunited with Denys in the Kenyan heat and dust.

To her dismay, the warm heat pressing her into the mattress lifted as Harry stood up. 'Hold that thought.' He stooped to kiss her again. 'Christ, you're sexy tonight. I have to fetch something from the car.'

Jo tried to hold the thought and hold consciousness, but it was hard with the room spinning around her like a baby's mobile, especially when Rathbone scrabbled into bed with a groan of effort and sneaked beneath her arm, like a teddy bear. The lavender bags smelt delicious. She closed her eyes and breathed deeply, amazed at the soft, fragile hammock of happiness that had lifted her from her grief-filled bed of nails. She was only vaguely aware of Harry coming back up. Now almost asleep, wiped out by wine and excess, she half believed she'd dreamed his arrival.

'Hold that thought,' she slurred, shifting to make space for him.

She felt his arms around her and his lips on her, and she was vaguely aware of Rathbone growling beneath her arm, but she was already bobbing out to sea alone. Then, as she sought out a warm slot to stow away in, she heard a sharp breath, opened one eye and saw the naked torso she was snuggling against. It looked as if Turner had been trying out his stormy-skies palette on it.

'Oh, my God, you're black and blue!' She straightened up. 'Did you go to A and E?'

'Of course not. It's just a bit of bruising.'

Totally bombed by wine and tiredness, Jo tumbled out of bed and clattered around in search of her washbag. Finally she located it and applied arnica to Harry's bruising with cross-eyed tenderness, covering all the blackest areas. 'There. How's that?'

'I love you.' He kissed her gratefully as she collapsed back beside him, tube still in hand. 'I'm sure having ...' he prised it from her '. . . cracked-heel cream on them will make a huge difference ... Jo?' He nudged her awake as she nodded off with her forehead pressed to his recently anointed chest.

'Ready for action!' She looked up, fighting a yawn.

Harry drew her gently towards him to rest in the crook of his arm. 'You need to sleep.'

'Rubbish.' She rallied with effort, woozily horny and determined to keep the happiness hammock swinging. The door of the old wardrobe that sat drunkenly on the elm floorboards had swung open, she saw, its speckled mirror reflecting them in the half-light. Harry loved having sex in front of mirrors.

She sat up groggily to straddle him, her voice throaty and enticing. 'Look at us.'

They turned. Two very rounded pink figures stared back, one with a paunch, the other a significant rear end.

'Christ, is that really us?' she said, in a frozen voice.

They looked from the mirror to each other. Then, collapsing into laughter, they curled together like two tightly fitting fat commas.

As she drifted off dozily, a thought made her stir. 'What were you getting from the car?'

'The keys. It's not mine.'

'Whose is it?'

'Yours.'

She fell asleep before she'd digested his answer.

FROM THE VISITORS' BOOK, DECEMBER 2011

Forget the unromantically crap nature of
the cottage's part-owners, I have bought
Morrow a new visitors' book for Christmas.

Wishing all who stay here in 2012 a joyful
visit. The guinea fowl like porridge oats. The
wood-burning stove hates the Daily Mail.
Please stop stealing the corkscrews.

Harry Inchbold, Wiltshire

2012

Music: Mumford and Sons,
Ed Sheeran, Glass Half Full

Car: Mini Countryman

Season: Spring, wet

FROM THE VISITORS' BOOK, APRIL 2012

Morrow never deals the same hand twice. But she warms them every year.
   She's less forgiving of cold feet. Bring socks.

Harry Inchbold, Wiltshire

FRIDAY AFTERNOON

The Diet

Jo and Harry arrived at Morrow with three Waitrose calorie-controlled ready meals, a packet of crispbreads and half a dozen big bottles of mineral water, along with a small bar of chocolate that Jo smuggled in and hid behind the many herb jars left by guests, which now crowded the shelves above the cooker. As she rearranged them to cover it up, she discovered Harry had already hidden a bag of jelly babies there.

It didn't bode well for their detox-and-diet boot-camp weekend at the cottage if they were both already cheating. Perhaps they had overplayed it with the 1000-calorie-a-day limit. Rathbone had more food in the cottage cupboards to keep him going than they did, and his Mighty Meaty Meal pouches looked considerably more filling than their lean turkey quinoa crumble.

Shamed by how much they usually ate – and drank – during their parsimonious stay with Matt and Rowena (whose small portions and restrained measures of fine wine had left them sleepless with sober hunger), Harry and Jo had made a new-year pact to go on a much-needed diet. It had come with one condition: they had to do it together. They'd both agreed that their children needed parents who didn't sleep-walk through early mornings and nap through playtime, that their jobs needed sharper minds than ever to bring home the bacon – not eat it all – and that they owed it to each other to show more willpower.

To start with, Jo had envisaged coquettish games of tennis, smouldering workouts in the gym, and lots of great sex as their bodies hardened in all the right places. In her mind, they would spend hours cooking together – they'd be like two sexy kitchen whippets waving around delicate little olive-oil sprays and trendy griddles instead of knobs of butter and sauté pans – followed by gazing lustfully at one another over their tiny, exquisitely arranged platefuls, appetite focused upon eating one another.

Instead, the diet had created a competitive environment of self-denial, turning a good patch into two cross ones: they sulked through crispbread breakfasts, nit-picked on chocolate-ban days and grazed their way through salads like two angry rhinos. As their mutual love affair with food was driven into lonely secrecy, suspicion and defiance grew in its place. Jo now knew the exact contents of the fridge and cupboards and could tell if Harry had raided them, while finishing the children's leftovers gave her a frisson as thrilling and shameful as flirting with a stranger. It was the only flirting on the cards. Wine sanctions inevitably led to a complete sex drought: whenever they started making cabbage soup, they stopped making love.

Both Harry and Jo knew that in theory if they detoxed, dieted and streamlined, they should be at it like rabbits, newly beautiful bodies inspiring all sorts of erotica, but they had always been hopeless at delayed gratification, and the diet pact had been plagued by disaster from the start.

Four months later, after several false starts and the unnecessary purchase of three low-fat recipe books (unread), a juicer (unused), two pairs of running shoes (unworn) and a case of de-alcoholized wine (emptied down the sink by Harry after one sip), they had come to understand that they were guilty conspirators in a far longer-standing pact to eat, drink and be merry: they loved cooking, they fancied one another fat or thin, and they both comfort-ate like crazy.

When a crisis struck, their habit was to sit up late at night, the third bottle of wine and the contents of the fridge spread out as a smorgasbord, determinedly seeing the bright side (Harry), finding the irony (Jo) and wishing for an easier life (both), however lousy it made them feel in the morning. Harry's energy and positivity, largely fuelled by cabernet sauvignon and cheese, was something Jo drew far more strength from than the dial on the scales moving left. Her calm kindness, often enhanced by chocolate brownies and caramel cappuccinos, inspired him to be more compassionate and less headstrong.

This year, there had been a lot of late nights spent sitting at the kitchen table. Still dealing with the devastation of losing her mother and now tackling the practical complexities of sorting out Di's estate – including an ongoing row with her sister about the sale of their parents' cottage – Jo found it hard to get through an evening without a large glass of white and at least one secret fridge raid, but that was nothing to the calorie-blowing drama in Harry's life.

Their first major diet failure had come not long into the new year when a rival company had copycatted Harry's Street Food idea and poached his maverick chef to front it, his departure from Street a devastating betrayal. The rip-off rival, 'Street Fair', had secured official Olympic approval, thanks to its fair-trade credentials and a percentage of its profit going to charity. Now the original Street Food brand faced law suits at every turn if it continued trading. After lengthy consultations with lawyers, Ned had cut his losses and was urging Harry to do the same. But Harry couldn't afford to. With six months left on the restaurant lease, he remained determined to reinvent Street. He had a new concept, a few loyal team members still with him and had already secured crowdfunding. It was a huge risk, and his creditors were baying at the door. He'd needed a lot of comfort food to get through January and February. With Blue Barn limping through the recession on an ever tighter margin, Jo had shared the biscuit tin with him. They weren't sleeping much.

And in the past month they'd failed spectacularly on the diet again as another unexpected crisis had arrived. As before, neither of them had seen it coming, but they could reach for the corkscrew together blindfold.

When Gerry and Viv Inchbold had calmly told their three children of their intention to divorce after forty-six years of marriage, three-bottle nights had swiftly returned at the Granary. Wine glass in hand, Harry had talked and sniped and raged, mostly about Nita, the quietly spoken, middle-aged live-in carer, whom all the Inchbold children put squarely in the frame for causing a much-patched marriage finally to come unstuck. Gerry now intended to live out his days with Nita at his side. To everybody's initial shock, Viv seemed incredibly relieved.

The Inchbolds' decision to divorce so late in life had come as a deep shock to Harry, who insisted it wouldn't be happening if 'Maneater Nita' hadn't been introduced into the family by his nemesis, Rowena. But in recent weeks so many more historic truths had started tumbling out about the Inchbolds' marriage that it was harder to see how it had survived almost five decades than why it was ending. There was the twenty-year discreet friendship between Viv and a married male work colleague, which continued to this day, along with Gerry's gambling problem, for which he still received help and which had once almost cost them the house, his hushed-up affair when the twins were very young, and the unfortunate time Viv had been held in custody for criminal damage to her husband's car. Jo didn't have to read between the lines too closely to imagine how traumatic the marriage had been at times, particularly for Viv. The whole family was struggling to come to terms with the existence of this secret history, although the husband and wife who no longer wanted to be together put it very simply: 'We haven't loved each other for years, but now we don't even like one another much.'

Having spent a shocked month drinking himself into laughing, ranting and weeping it out of his system, Harry was now determined to purge the bloat and get the diet back on course, announcing that he no longer wanted to talk about his parents at all. He was uncharacteristically tight-lipped as a result. The self-improving self-punishment that marked this year's break at Morrow was, Jo was certain, far more to do with what was going on between Gerry and Viv than their own tetchy marriage and expanding waistlines. But her overwhelming desire to protect and comfort him through the end of his parents' marriage was being challenged by his renewed obsession with getting fit.

Jo had hoped coming to Morrow would help him heal and bring them closer. It was normally such a place of forgiveness, laughter, tears, love-making and mutual indulgence that reminded them they loved one another, warts and all.

Instead, he'd come up with the idea of an intensive detox, a brainwave pitched on the fast lane of M5. When Harry fixed upon something, he wanted it here and now, his determination unflagging. Jo was willing to give it a go – her muffin top wasn't going away – but she knew they were in for a tough few days. Morrow was all about excess and relaxation, not ab crunches and starvation. Harry was always bad-tempered when he was hungry, and this level of self-denial could take it to new heights, particularly given that he had so much more to be angry about. And, these days, they inevitably caught bad moods from one another, like head colds.

By bedtime they were both so grumpy that they could barely bring themselves to speak, largely conversing through Rathbone, who looked pleasantly surprised to be getting so much attention, less so by the strenuous exercise of two vigorous walks already that evening.

Having grown accustomed to his same short outing along the local footpath twice a day during his six-month gig as Inchbold family dog, the elderly grey terrier was already in shock at the amount of yomping involved in a visit to Morrow. It was in sharp contrast to his last stay, which had largely involved sharing a bed and a lot of junk food with Jo.

Now confined to his basket on the bedroom floor, he watched wisely as Jo pulled on warm layers to sleep in, the no-sex bedtime uniform of the off-limits wife.

'Rathbone thinks we're both looking slimmer already.' She tried to inject some cheer when Harry came upstairs from brushing his teeth.

'Rathbone has cataracts.' He climbed into bed and picked up his Hilary Mantel book with a huff. 'Everybody looks like the marshmallow man to him.' Up came the barrier of his back as he turned away, intensely crabby, determined not to talk.

When Jo slipped downstairs to clean her own teeth, she checked the jelly-baby bag concealed behind three jars of mixed herbs, just a paprika refill away from her chocolate bar, like a Mexican stand-off. Both were still unopened.

It was going to be a long two days.

SUNDAY MORNING

The Walk and Talk

Jo turned on the kitchen radio while she set off two Special K porridge breakfasts in the microwave, then fed Rathbone, noticing jealously that his food pouch was three times the size of theirs. The DAB reception at the cottage currently offered the choice of two radio stations: testosterone-packed rock or vintage pop.

Leaving pop blaring cheerily, Jo went to the bathroom where Harry had just left wet towels everywhere, a line of scum around the tub. Opening the window irritably to let out the steam, startling a roosting guinea fowl, she sat down to wee. They'd barely talked or touched all weekend, both too bad-tempered from hunger, shattered from an excess of exercise, and prickly from avoiding the subjects of work, money and his parents' marriage to make the first move. Now that Harry had slept eight hours straight and was freshly bathed, she wondered if they should try to have sex. It might cheer them both up. But the idea remained abstract, the actions of a more energetic version of her without the grumbling stomach, aching legs and hot head.

Then she heard the music change in the kitchen and any seductive plans vanished. Harry had come down and flipped channels to grinding guitar rock.

She sidled out, checked he'd disappeared back into the

sitting room and switched back to Katrina and the Waves singing 'Walking On Sunshine'. She badly needed her chocolate fix, but when she checked the jelly babies again, they were still unopened, and she couldn't let him win.

Peering out of the window at grey drizzle falling between the wet tree trunks, she willed the sun to come out. Rathbone scuffed up behind her with a scrape of dried mud and sat on her foot, sharing the wish.

Rathbone was a placid and sedentary soul, adored by the children for his long-suffering good humour and generally agreed to be an unfortunate result of a love match between something short-legged like a dachshund and something very hairy like a bearded collie. This meant he was essentially a low-slung mobile fluffy duster, currently sporting a skirt of mud, burrs and brambles gathered on his many vigorous Shropshire walks. He clattered around the Morrow flagstones like a clogged vacuum-cleaner attachment. The sound drove Harry mad. Everything was driving Harry mad this weekend.

'Why did you change stations?' He stomped in to switch it to a gravelly bass screaming about needing a fix.

She snapped it back to feel-good Katrina. '*You* were the one who changed stations.'

'It was tuned that way first thing this morning.'

They glared at each other.

'Rathbone loves eighties pop.'

'Rathbone's practically deaf.'

'Then I'll turn it up.' She did so childishly, until it was too loud to speak.

Harry helped himself to the last of the fresh coffee, deliberately not offering her any.

Halfway through their breakfast of diet porridge with skimmed milk and three grapes – their first calorie intake for twelve hours – the radio DJ introduced a 'golden oldie

388

that a few of you who were teenagers in the eighties may remember'.

As the music struck up with a strum of sentimental synth chords and a husky voice started singing, Jo closed one eye. 'Is this Lloyd Cole?'

Saying nothing, Harry stood up to switch it off.

'Leave it playing!' she pleaded, suddenly realizing what she was listening to.

He let it run on for a few more bars before slamming the power button.

As he wandered around hopefully for crumbs, Rathbone's matted coat, making its scraping and scratching noises, sounded disproportionately loud in the sudden silence.

'I can't listen to that dog's bloody din a moment longer, sliding around like an Ugg boot.' Harry marched towards the door to pull on his walking boots. 'Let's climb up to the Burf again.'

Within minutes they were panting at speed up Mawr Vron in thick Welsh mist.

Despite being tempted to stay behind listening to eighties music, a competitive spirit and intense curiosity drove Jo uphill again. Keeping up a breathless half-jog to stay upsides Harry, Rathbone at her heels, she suspected it was an entirely different 'bloody din' that had propelled Harry outside.

'Was that Glass Half Full on the radio?'

'Yes.'

'You never told me the title of the song you had a hit with.'

'You never asked.'

'Isn't it a Philip Larkin poem?'

'That's "fuck you up". Ours was good clean teen pop.'

'With muck?' she echoed the title.

'I think "shit" was the word Ned used to describe the

orchestral strings and choir the producer added to the track.'

'I thought it sounded good.'

'Ned wrote it as a dystopian exploration of oppressive parents thwarting a *Romeo and Juliet* love affair, but basically it was five kids singing about how pissed off he was when Mummy and Daddy Whittaker divorced and moved away from the girl he fancied next door in Chelsea. He must have been a bloody poet to make it work as well as it did.'

Harry never usually spoke about Glass Half Full: he and Ned treated it like a mortifying rite of passage that was now buried. Burning her way up the hill beside him, grateful that they were talking in more than monosyllables, Jo suspected there was more resonance to the lyrics than that. 'You were the one who sang it like you meant it.'

'I sang it like I wanted to get out of bombing my A levels. Pity I couldn't look twenty-five years into the future, eh? Ned and Larkin were right. Clean or mucky, it's a family fuck-up.'

From what Jo could gather, now that the senior Inchbolds had decided to end their marriage, Viv and Gerry had been on the verge of divorce many times over the past four decades. She wondered how close they'd come during his Half Glass Full days.

'Don't they say the greatest tragedy about *Hamlet* is that actors only really understand how to play him when they're too old to do it?'

It was one of the first times she'd heard him laugh all weekend. 'Jo, if that song was *Hamlet*, A-ha sang the entire *Ring Cycle*.'

'Well, they *were* Norwegian.'

'That was my point. Keep up.'

Uncertain if he was referring to her legs or her brain, Jo said nothing. The more stressed out Harry was, the more quick-thinking he became, as though his mind needed a pressure cooker to plump up ideas. Jo's, by contrast, preferred gentle poaching in a long sous-vide bath.

'Glass Half Full's second single would have been even more prescient,' Harry bent his head against the thick mist, 'but, of course, that never got released.'

Jo thought about Ned pulling the plug on the band, the shock they must all have felt. Her pent-up anger directed itself on to his expensively barbered head. 'I don't know how you ever forgave him. Now he's just let you down again, dropping out of Street when you need him most.'

He put on a burst of speed. 'I was the idiot who fucked it up, hiring the wrong chef.'

Blisters throbbing, Jo sped in his wake, hating the angry silence through which she made sporadic attempts to inject positivity, uncomfortably aware that she sounded like a breathless Olympic coach whooping up a marathon runner too far into the zone to hear. 'Wow, I can feel the burn already! Just think how energetic and sexy we'll be when we're lean as whippets.'

'Whippets have no sense of humour,' Harry said, through gritted teeth. 'Ask Rathbone.'

'Rathbone doesn't know any whippets.'

'Exactly. They're no fun.'

Jo glanced back at Rathbone, now dragging half the Shropshire countryside on his coat hems, like a road-sweeper let loose in a farmyard, eyes bulging with the effort of keeping up.

Clanking through a kissing gate, hands inadvertently covering each other on the latch, bodies pressed close as it swung back on a spring, Harry and Jo briefly leaned their weight together, a cantilever of puffed-out irritability. Later, Jo would realize that had been the moment when they should have laughed. They could have passed a few minutes catching their breath and comparing eighties pop songs to great tragic works of theatre and opera, or musing on which breed of dog had the best sense of humour. That would have got them back on track, Jo and Harry in classic form: competitive, flirty and inclusive.

But Jo was fed up with Harry's constant bad temper, his clammed-up tension, the way the high dramas that always followed him had yet again so immediately and totally eclipsed hers. She was fed up with the punishing self-flagellation of diet and exercise through the one weekend a year they shared together.

So instead of humouring him, she humbled him: 'I know it's awful that your parents are divorcing, but at least they're both still alive. It's only their marriage that's died, Harry.'

Harry kept the gate closed, trapping them both in it. 'So why the fuck couldn't they have shown the dignity to keep all this under their hats until they peg it, like most decent people would?' he raged. 'If they've stayed together for our sakes, why not see it through? Why bail out now?'

Jo was watching Rathbone wriggle his way through the gate, then wander off to sniff a tree and leave a marker.

Still trapped with Harry, she felt cold rage. Living cheek by jowl with somebody as long as Jo had now lived with Harry meant that, as well as knowing how to flatter his ego, turn him on, make him laugh and comfort him, she knew how to cut him down. 'Ask them! You can still talk to your parents, Harry. You have that right.' The tears undercut her words without warning. 'Do that instead of sulking. If they stayed together for your sake, maybe they've got tired of waiting for you to grow up.'

He turned away with a wince, and Jo knew he felt the same knife through his tendons she'd experienced so recently, cutting away the sense of belonging, the blithe Harry optimism that looked backwards and forwards through life and saw equal lengths of railway track stretching into the distance.

His happiest childhood memories were safeguarded here at Morrow, those that were not so happy distanced by time. She remembered him telling her that his parents had walked up Mawr Vron to have arguments where their children couldn't overhear them. Had they argued in this spot, she wondered, hurling insults through their own midlife crises because each believed they felt their own pain more acutely? Had that been the beginning of the long, bitter swansong for Viv and Gerry Inchbold? Would she and Harry follow the same pattern?

Pity and pathos drenched her. She reached out for his hand, but he'd already turned away.

'Let's leave it there.' The gate creaked in his wake as he stormed along the track his family's feet had bounded up through the earliest years of his life, head down, chin set.

Jo raced after him, but Harry was already leaving her behind on the hill, pushing himself hard, not looking back at her as she slipped through deep mud in his wake. Now that mutual animosity had taken over, he didn't wait for her at the stiles, powering ahead until he disappeared into the mist altogether.

Defeated, Jo took a breather on a stone boulder, fishing in her pocket for a Bonio for Rathbone, who flopped down gratefully at her feet.

The first time Jo had walked up here, Harry had tried to have his wicked way behind every bush, she remembered. A year later, they'd held hands through the entire climb. When they'd walked up in high summer, they'd carried a cold box to the top and got tight on prosecco before almost rolling down to the pub for Sunday lunch. On a more recent visit, they'd squabbled their way up, admired the view and declared peace before coming back down. Standing on top of a hill where the air felt thin and the world below looked tiny put life into perspective, far beyond domestic warfare, wiping out the irritation over one another's inability to change loo rolls, get up for a crying child or empty the dishwasher in turn. Mutual irritation and self-doubt faded that high up. Even the big dramas usually paled briefly into insignificance, emotional baggage unpacked and dropped like hot-air-balloon ballast. Not this year. This was the third time they'd walked up the hill in thirty-six hours, and Jo felt as though she was carrying heavier burdens than ever.

Her phone rang in her coat pocket. Please let it be Harry calling from higher up the hill, she prayed, as she fished it out. But it was Rowena's healthy, wholegrain complexion on the screen, her contact photo possessing the kind, stern look of a headmistress about to administer a sharp telling-off.

'All well here,' Rowena reassured her in her deep, flat voice. 'We're making Easter bonnets. Thea's asked for a princess tiara and Wilf wanted a fireman's helmet with eggs, but we've agreed on something more gender neutral and on-theme.'

'Crown of thorns?'

'A nest.' She sounded shocked, never certain how to take Jo's humour. 'Do they eat falafels, by the way?'

'You can try.'

Thea was a pasta addict and Wilf currently only ate fish fingers, Tuc biscuits (not the sandwich sort) and one brand of fruit yoghurt that came in a squeezy container shaped like a space rocket, but Rowena remained determined to win them over to what the kids called her 'brown cooking'. Her linseed and black rice Christmas log was now family legend.

'I promise they won't starve. How's Harry?'

'Tense,' she said carefully. 'What word from Highbury?'

'The ramps are all in, so they're just waiting for the kitchen to be delivered.'

The question of who would live where had dragged on for weeks. A seventy-something MS sufferer with an adapted living space, like Gerry, could hardly leave his wife for his mistress in a midnight flit with a note propped on the mantelpiece, particularly if his mistress was the live-in carer who occupied the basement. Now Matt had stepped in with his building team to divide up the house.

The senior Inchbolds had been in surprisingly good spirits about separating their lives and living quarters, relieved, even. Now it had been agreed that Viv would occupy the top two floors of the Highbury house while the adapted ground floor was incorporated into the basement flat, where Gerry was already staging a rebellious love-in with carer Nita.

Rowena was asking what time they planned to pick up the children.

'Not too late, I hope.' Jo turned to gaze up into the white mist, beyond which Harry was no doubt storming onwards, like Ares on the warpath. She knew it was wrong to take it all so personally. They owed it to the children to make friends before going home, even if it took sharing a small bag of jelly babies and a chocolate bar.

'Make it as late as you like,' Rowena insisted. 'I'll get them into PJs.'

Ringing off, Jo set out in pursuit again, the mist thickening with every step. It was still only late morning, but the wooded hillside was darkening as though evening was drawing in.

She came to a fork in the track and looked down at Rathbone blankly. Now a hovercraft floating on a forest of detritus, he looked back at her blankly too.

She opted for left and walked purposefully for a few minutes before the track turned almost back on itself and started dropping dramatically downhill. Turning back, she found herself at another fork she didn't remember. She aimed uphill, but that started dropping away too. Trying to retrace her steps, Jo realized she was totally lost. Close behind, Rathbone let out a couple of agitated barks.

'This is where you run off into the forest, find Harry and bring him here to lead us to safety away from the man-traps.' She shivered and pulled up her hood as mist turned into pelting rain. Edging under a tree, she pulled out her phone and found she had no signal. Rathbone hugged himself to her shins, shivering.

Feeling hungry, she groped through her pockets and discovered she had three Bonios and a small bag of dried goji berries to last them until the rain lifted. Here, on the Shropshire-Powys border, that could be days.

'We'll have to have another go at finding our way out,' she told Rathbone.

Jo trudged on, head bowed, already soaked as she tried to find higher ground, certain that was the secret to breaking out of the tree line and spotting the Burf. As she walked, she thought about Harry, who knew this hill so well but had been lost all weekend, his memories mugged.

Rathbone was lagging behind, starting to lose faith in her, his waterlogged undercarriage weighing him down.

She picked him up and hugged him closer, too wet to care that it was the equivalent of throwing herself face down in the mud. He was her connection to her parents, she thought, with deepening compassion, just as Morrow would always be Harry's connection with his, and with the happy years before their marriage had died.

The rain was driving so hard it kept catching in her eyes, half blinding her.

'Harry!' she called, holding her face up as Rathbone licked it encouragingly. 'Harry!'

All she could hear was the rain drumming and dripping. It was hammering now.

She sheltered under another tree, thinking again about Viv and Gerry arguing on this hill all those years ago, imagining herself in Viv's shoes, enduring the drama that surrounded her husband, from near financial ruin to a devastating illness. Viv's reaction had been to protect herself with a career that gave her self-worth, a discreet lover and many lifelong friends.

It was more than could be said for Jo, these days, her increasing detachment from Blue Barn mimicking that of Caro in its early years, reading her children's bedtime stories a far more precious use of her time than checking her order book. During her mother's illness, she'd taken on an assistant to cover her long absences, and she still worked at home with the kids three days a week, reluctant to reclaim the day-to-day grind. But this meant that while she put in just as many hours, she now took a fraction of the income. She had dark moments when she contemplated selling it, but even assuming she could find a buyer, Harry's business was too vulnerable to guarantee their family's future. She remembered Viv telling her that being the breadwinner was no fun if it was half baked, especially as a wife and mother. Unlike Viv, she wasn't the primary source of family income, but she was shackled nonetheless, running home and work in tandem – a push-me pull-you uphill bicycle ride.

Would that one day make her as dispassionate as Viv was? she wondered. What if Harry, so cruelly afflicted, found love in his twilight years? Her breath shortened as though she'd been punched in the chest. 'I would kill him,' she breathed, the fierceness of her love suddenly alight. She would never have stood aside. She would have chased Maneater Nita up the wheelchair ramps and kicked her bony arse straight out of Highbury. She'd fight with every blood cell in her body to regain Harry's loyalty. She needed him like she needed air.

She suddenly felt the full force of his anger possess her. She was almost brought to her knees by it.

'Harry!' She stumbled out into the rain again, slithering through the mud. 'Harry!'

She ran on blindly, Rathbone tight in her arms.

'I love you! Harry! Jesus!' She tripped over tree roots, felt brambles across her face and arms, and was whipped by branches. 'Harry!'

The rain started to abate as she found higher ground, mist replacing drips.

'Harry Inchbold, I love you!' she bellowed.

They were climbing hard now, the way ahead a hazy wall of white, yet totally clear to her. She and Harry were for ever. She was absolutely alive with love.

'Harry!'

'There you bloody are.' He stepped out of the mist, making her shriek in shock and almost drop Rathbone. He looked as irascible as he had when he'd disappeared earlier, as though he'd merely stepped out of shot to have his frown lines re-pencilled by a make-up artist. 'What's wrong?'

'Nothing!' Still bursting with love, Jo couldn't stop smiling, 'You appearing like that is a bit Jack Nicholson, that's all. You could have waited for me. I lost you.'

'I went up the Burf, then realized you weren't there. The view's terrible.' His eyes, intense as will-o'-the-wisps, danced between hers. She recognized the flints of hunger in them, along with a blaze of relief that told her he'd been a lot more worried about her disappearance than he was letting on. 'Let's go and dry off in the pub – it's only a couple of minutes' walk from this side of the hill.'

'Can't we just go back to the house for warm clothes and a cracker or two?' She was already planning the hot, shared bath, the reconnection, the return to intimacy. She longed to hug him, but Rathbone was still shaking in her arms, and Harry had already set off downhill, beckoning her to follow.

'The pub has an open fire. And we'll pig out on two bowls of rambler-reviving soup. Just don't let me eat too much.'

Jo and Rathbone exchanged delighted glances. Harry needed hot food. He didn't need to lose weight. She loved every last inch of him.

SUNDAY AFTERNOON

The Hare and Moon Lunch

'I think we should bring my parents here,' Harry announced, as he set two pints of soda water on a table in a quiet corner. The place was already filling up with damp walkers refuelling on Roy's ramblers' lunch package, feet plunging into foot spas.

Jo looked at him curiously. 'You think they'd want that?'

'*I* want that.'

She absorbed this slowly. It never did to overreact with Harry, particularly when he had an empty stomach. 'How do you propose to do it?'

'First, we have to get rid of Maneater Nita.'

'By what means?' She eyed him warily, not liking the way his blue eyes were stretched wide or the excited smile on his face. She hadn't see him look so alive in weeks, his hair tumbling heroically across raised brows, the long, dimpled grooves in his cheeks deepening with laughter. Jo had always found it scary how sexy he could be when he was on a mission, even a misdirected one. When he wanted her onside, he was at his most passionate, funny and fiery, a hair trigger away from explosion.

'Pay her off. How much have we got?'

'Nothing, Harry. We're flat broke, you know that.'

She'd almost forgotten what it felt like to check their online balance without a cold sweat of trepidation, to watch two regular salaries adding up instead of constantly counting backwards between the overdraft and zero-interest credit-card balance transfers. Harry's coping mechanism was never to bother checking. Instead great wads of fifty-pound notes appeared sporadically, along with wildly generous gifts, like the Mini he'd bought her for Christmas. Then he would be having to borrow cash for weeks on end. Any attempt Jo made at getting him to be more organized with family finances ended in a huge row, then more wads of cash. In her wilder moments, she wondered whether he was covering up a gambling habit, like his father, or laundering money through the restaurant, but she knew the truth was far simpler. Harry wasn't frightened of money. While Jo panicked constantly that it was about to run out, it held absolutely no fear for him. Harry worked as hard as he did for more than remuneration.

'I'll find something to pay Maneater Nita off with,' Harry said, through gritted teeth.

'If you could pay the mortgage first, I'd be grateful.' She sighed.

'Or we could lay a honey trap.' He wasn't listening. 'Or have her killed. How much do hitmen cost?'

Jo was spared the need to answer as Sinbad, the smiling pub dog, came lumbering up to be reunited with Rathbone. Caught napping, the little terrier leaped out from beneath the table, like a snarling mud cake, to defend his pack.

Harry grabbed him just in time, holding him out of reach. 'Do that to Maneater Nita and you'll earn your weight in Bonios, little chum.' He laughed in surprise.

Grateful that he was finding a streak of dark humour, Jo watched him set down Rathbone, now waggy-tailed once more and eager to make amends with Sinbad.

'Although not if you do that to her.' He observed the two dogs bottom-sniffing appreciatively. 'Or that,' he muttered, as their little grey mud-ball stretched up to lick the big dog's ears. 'And definitely not that.' They were already curling up together in front of the fire.

Jo saw so much of Wilf in him: their beautiful little dynamo possessed a vivid imagination, determination, and a fierce temper that could never be controlled.

'What if Nita really loves your father?'

'Of course she doesn't. He's a vulnerable old man. Relationships like that are always about a trade-off. Look at whatshername here, Ping,' he said, in an undertone. 'She only married Roy for—'

'Half Inch!'

'Roy!' He stood up for the man-hug. Hands slapped backs hard enough to loosen teeth.

Roy was wearing his chef's whites, a tea-towel thrown over one shoulder, face glowing red. His beard was back, a sharp-edged chinstrap that made him look as though he'd drawn a line round his face with an orange marker pen. 'Thought I heard your voice. You well?'

'Never better.' Harry caught Jo's eye and they shared a silent alliance: bad news and bad tempers stayed between themselves. 'Terrific to be here.'

'I hear you're in the restaurant trade now.'

'I dabble.'

'Business good?'

'Excellent.'

'Cerys brought in a review for your place she found in a newspaper last year,' Roy said eagerly, still back-slapping. 'Bloody brilliant it was. Got Ping to cut it out and pin it on the fridge as inspiration.'

Harry looked at Jo over Roy's shoulder, both knowing that in London, being last year's news was the worst of all sins.

'I still remember your cooking from years back.' Roy

stepped back. 'Those Half Moon Gang feasts camping up by the Burf. Your Mars Bar fondue was the best thing I ever tasted.'

'I'll add it to next week's menu in your honour.' He forced a smile. 'And I hope I can cook for you again one day.'

'My kitchen is your kitchen. Looking lovely, Mrs Inchbold!' Roy gave her a kiss, eyeing her pint glass disapprovingly. 'Let me fetch a cocktail umbrella for that.' He headed to the bar and brought one back, along with a Scotch for himself. 'I've got five minutes. Seen much of Ned lately?' He pulled up a chair.

Jo and Harry glanced at one another again, trying to hide their horror at the prospect of a friendly grilling when they were currently living life under fire. The secret alliance strengthened.

'Not very recently, no,' Harry said, eyes flashing briefly into Jo's.

'Where are you two living now?'

'Wiltshire.'

'Pretty part of the world. Happy there?'

'Very.' The secret alliance looked at their hands. They loved the Granary, and living there had helped them all cope with Di's death, a way of keeping her memory alive as they looked forward to the future in the area where she had led such a full and kind life, where the schools were good and Jo had old friends with children close by. Affording life there was another matter. They'd already taken the maximum number of mortgage holidays.

'How are the kids?'

'Great! Fantastic. Wilf starts school next autumn.'

'Another brainy Inchbold boy, no doubt.'

The alliance narrowed their eyes at one another across the table.

The GP, whom Jo had alerted to Wilf's sometimes

aggressive and hyperactive behaviour at nursery and at home, had suggested he had ADHD and wanted to refer him for more assessment. Jo was eager to get things moving so that Wilf had maximum help from the start of formal education, but Harry – who hated boxes with a pathological loathing – was dragging his feet. He thought Wilf was too young for diagnosis, and argued that growing up with a hastily applied label in exchange for funds would stigmatize him in the same way that Titch's dyslexia had always set her apart, giving her a complex long into adulthood that she was slow and inadequate.

'Wilf is very much his own man.' Harry was putting on a good show for the alliance 'Thea is a total diva. Yours?'

'Number three on the way. A girl. Seren. That's Welsh,' he told Jo proudly.

'Congratulations.' She smiled.

'Ping will be sorry she missed you. She and her mother have taken the kids to Shrewsbury.' He wiped his still sweaty face with the tea-towel. 'I could use the help but, to be honest, any day away from the mother-in-law is a bonus, eh, Harry?'

Harry smiled briefly, worried eyes on Jo, silently asking if she was all right as Roy enquired after his family. 'Your parents in good health?'

His eyes were still boring into Jo's and she reached out to take his hand, his fingers closing firmly around hers, like warm battle armour. 'Rude health, yes.'

'Titch still the wild child?'

'In Spain with a new boyfriend.' Harry's jaw was tense. Of all Viv and Gerry's children, Titch was the one who had really fallen to pieces over the news that they were separating. She had refused to come back to England while that was going on.

'Matt still dabbling in property?'

404

He nodded. 'He specializes in snapping up bargains from unwitting pensioners. Currently converting a nice Islington house into two maisonettes with an eye to long-term capital growth.'

Jo looked away, saddened that the situation was driving an even bigger gulf between the brothers.

'And how's his lovely wife?' asked Roy.

'She's a bitch.' Harry's hand tightened around Jo's.

'Right-oh.'

Jo returned the pressure. 'Harry's mad because Rowena's trying to turn our children into wholemeal vegans who think Blackheath aerials can't receive CBeebies.'

'I'm mad because she's a bitch with bitch friends who prey on vulnerable old men.'

'She makes Matt happy,' Jo insisted.

'She's making him miserable.'

'I'd better check on the kitchen.' Roy stood up with an embarrassed laugh. 'You ready to order yet?'

'Two minestrone soups,' Jo said firmly.

'And then?'

'Beef.' Harry looked at the board.

'Just soup for us both,' Jo insisted, remembering her promise.

Roy grinned. 'You're pulling my leg, right? You both love my roasts.'

'*Soup*,' Jo growled.

He stepped back. 'You sure about this, Harry? It's prime Hereford topside.'

'Soup.' Harry sighed, a whisper of murder in the sound.

'Could you bring it quickly?' Jo pleaded. 'Preferably piping hot.'

As Roy hurried back to his kitchen, Harry picked up her pint of water by mistake. He didn't notice, staring at her fiercely over the brim, its cocktail umbrella tickling his nose. 'We definitely have to bring my parents back to Morrow.'

'I have to work tomorrow.'

'You know what I mean. Let them find love again here.'

'Harry, with the best will in the world, I don't think that's going to happen.'

'Why do people say that?' He slammed the glass down, all the suppressed anger needing a vent. '"With the best will in the world." What shit! It means nothing – like "at the end of the day". With the best will in the world, Jo, my parents found happiness together here at the end of the day. We all did.'

'That was years ago.'

'You and I still do. We find it.'

Jo stared at him, wondering whether they really did. She'd thought she'd found it in the mist in the woods, but now she wasn't so sure. 'Happiness' wasn't a word that described how she was feeling right now. Exasperated, concerned, supportive, yearning for the closeness they knew was there, and very hungry, but not happy.

'We find it, Owl,' Harry repeated, and she could see in his eyes that he wanted it as badly as she did.

She looked at him questioningly. 'Where is it this time?'

'It's been a difficult year.'

'They're all difficult years, Harry. What are those things always listed as most stressful in life? Giving birth, getting married, moving house, a divorce, a bereavement, having no money, changing jobs. We do two or three a *year*. We go through them like other people go through socks.'

He sat in silence, glaring at the window.

'I just want a year of socks, Harry.'

'I'll do my best.' He glared up at the blackboard.

'Have the beef,' she said, before she could stop herself.

He glanced back at her irritably. 'I'm not that weak-willed.'

'You're a lot nicer to be around when you eat.'

His eyes flashed, an alchemy of anger and amusement. 'I'm even nicer when I drink.'

Jo opened her mouth to remind him that that definitely wasn't allowed in his detox rules, then changed her mind. Let him fight his own battles.

'I'll drive home later.'

'I'll order at the bar.' The expression on his face changed and he slowly turned to look at her, eyes darkening and sweetening, voice crackling with seductive husks. 'We could stay another night, set out at dawn. There's nobody booked in the cottage next week. Let the wholemeal bitch keep the kids hostage in the Doll's House a few more hours while we remind ourselves how we made them.'

Jo looked away. He was at his most selfish when hungry. But then he leaned across the table and took her hand. 'Eat with me, Owl. Get drunk with me. Come to bed with me before we go back. I miss you.'

She looked at him again. His eyes were raw with honesty. And lust.

He lifted her fingers to his mouth, breath warm against her engagement and wedding rings. 'We'll have every pudding on the menu and burn it all off in bed later.'

For a moment, Jo felt her body rev up, sharing his hedonism. She smiled at the thought of such recklessness, letting her hungry gaze slide away to the board, reading through the puddings list, and imagining bingeing out on Death by Chocolate and Irish coffee before tipping back up the track to make love on a boozy sugar high. Then her smile froze as she remembered the sweet treat waiting for her at home, along with less savoury ones.

Wilf needed the ingredients for chocolate Rice Krispie cakes to be assembled for his first cooking session at nursery tomorrow – he was hopelessly excited about it, already sharing his parents' love of food. The quarterly Blue Barn accounts were due; she had artwork deadlines on Tuesday; she needed to speak to the printers urgently about their price hike; Blue Barn's card agent was coming in for an annual review this week and she had a lot of preparation to do ahead of it; she and her sister had a meeting with the probate solicitor on Friday. She wanted a year of socks.

'We've both got busy weeks,' she told Harry, without looking at him. 'Besides, Wilf will be waiting for us by the Doll's House window already.' The image made her throat tighten, already anticipating his car-crusher hug, her guilt at leaving him, Thea bundling in sleepily with her favourite cuddly toys gathered in her arms to join in the group hug and welcome them back.

She could tell Harry was watching her face.

'Soup for you, then,' he muttered.

'That's what I said.'

'Fine.' He stood up and stomped to the bar.

Jo rubbed her face tiredly, trying to stay positive. All was good. They had detoxed and slept a lot; she and Harry didn't need forty-eight hours of rampant sex to know they loved one another. Arguments were purging – a part of the detox.

SUNDAY EVENING

The Departure

Jo packed quickly for the long trip home to Wiltshire via London, where Harry would stay on with Matt and Rowena for the short hike to EC1 in the morning, while she took the children to the Granary.

Harry started off lying on the bed watching her, then on the sofa watching her, then sat at the kitchen table watching her, chin propped in his hands, trying hard to talk her back upstairs. Three pints up and full of hot food, his dishevelled, charming, blond admiration made his company just about tolerable, despite the dodgy porn-movie patter, delivered in his huskiest drawl.

'The way you move is so sexy, Owl. We can stay another hour. What can I do to excite you? What will really turn you on?'

'You could start by lending me a hand,' she muttered, wishing the food had made him helpful, rather than just hornier. 'Loading the car, maybe.'

Jo gave Rathbone a hasty bath while Harry grudgingly packed the car. She was trying to wash out the mud, which had given him beaded dreadlocks, feeling the little dog cower at the techno rock now booming from the kitchen radio, interspersed with bangs and curses as bags and boxes were taken out. Martyred Harry was deliberately making as much noise as possible, annoyed that he couldn't devote himself to physical pleasure. This would be the first year that they had ever stayed at Morrow without making love.

The pang of regret was followed quickly by a twitch of irritation that he was being insufferable.

'He'll snore all the way back, trust me.' Jo kissed Rathbone's head. He looked so ribby and fragile when wet, all the big-coat bluster removed, dark eyes anxious. She felt a hard prod of guilt for all the wet, angry walks he'd endured followed by long fireside silences. Her mother would be furious that he'd been given such a miserable time. Jo was reminded painfully of Rathbone's feistier brother, Turtle, who had loyally endured so many angry stand-offs in the Crouch End flat. At home in Wiltshire, Rathbone had a routine he understood and the children, whom he adored. She'd been banking on the magical Morrow effect. 'We're normally nicer than this when we're together here,' she whispered reassuringly. 'We're like this.' She pinched finger and thumb together and laughed as he sat down in the bath with a splash, anticipating a treat. Gathering him in a towel, she carried him through to the kitchen for a Bonio, only to find Harry had blitzed the cupboards and shelves, even removing her hidden emergency chocolate supply and his jelly babies. She suppressed a hot body-flash of embarrassment at being rumbled, hoping he was too tight to notice.

'All loaded.' Harry put his head round the door. His eyes hardened when he saw her towel-drying Rathbone on the table. 'I thought you were in a hurry to go.'

'Almost done.'

'You never wash my hair.' He moved closer.

'You never ask.'

'We could do it now, Owl.'

'I've no time to wash your hair.' She reached back to cuff him, knowing he was getting tired and silly, like Wilf after a long day.

He stepped in tightly behind her, breathing beer fumes on her neck. 'I wasn't talking about washing hair.'

Correction – tired, silly and still horny. 'Not now, Harry.'

He put his hands around her waist and drew her back against the denim bulge of his erection, as though imagining she would swoon feverishly at the feel of it between her thighs, instead of glancing tetchily at the clock and then apologetically at an anxious-eyed Rathbone.

'We have to get back.' She side-stepped.

He side-stepped with her. 'You used to love fucking on this table.'

'I wasn't grooming a dog.'

'So lose the dog.' He picked up Rathbone, who gave an indignant squeak as he was deposited on the floor before shaking gratefully, a small revolving carwash brush of drops.

'Another time, hey?' Jo reminded herself that Harry was trying to blot out what was waiting for him in London: elderly parents divorcing, business in crisis. Be kind, she told herself, however much he's pissing you off. 'It's me. I'm not in the mood.'

'C'mon, Owl.' His hand snaked under her belt, knowing her body so well, practised fingertips sliding a well-worn route from dimples of Venus to the hollow above her pelvis. Jo's libido gave a brief echo of response, as sentimental as it was sensual, then nothing, just impatience that he wasn't getting the message, that they had a long journey ahead and a killer week beyond it.

'Get off, Harry.' She tried to laugh, but as his hand delved further, her fingers clamped round his wrist faster than police restraining cuffs on an unruly demonstrator.

He bellowed in pain.

'Shit, have I hurt you?'

'No, the fucking dog's bitten me.'

As Harry hopped off to a chair, Jo stooped to find Rathbone glowering beneath the table.

When they lifted his jeans hem, Harry's ankle was sporting neat toothmarks, one or two jewelled with blood. 'That dog's always had it in for me. I'll need a tet jab.'

She cuddled the tired, wet, traumatized little terrier to her. 'He was just frightened.'

Glaring at them both, Harry stood up and limped outside.

Jo closed her eyes. 'I lied,' she whispered, into a soft, damp head that still smelt of wet Shropshire walks. 'We're not so nice when we're here.'

Opening her eyes again at the sound of the door slamming, she saw two long legs striding back towards her and flinched. Rathbone growled in her arms.

A box of Bonios and a bag of jelly babies appeared at eye level as Harry stooped down with a peace-offering, blue eyes huge with shame. 'I'm going to give us a year of socks, Owl. Just watch me.'

FROM THE VISITORS' BOOK, APRIL 2012

When it has lots of logs on and the vents open, the stove lights up the carpenter's marks in the beam over the fireplace like a secret code nobody can figure out. The guinea fowl dance on the roof when you take a long bath. Cuckoos are already calling. The microwave door sticks.

Jo Inchbold, Wiltshire

2013

Music: Bowie, Arctic Monkeys, blues

Cars: Mini and Range Rover

Season: Spring, sunny

FROM THE VISITORS' BOOK, MARCH 2013

You can never fully escape the world outside, and as that world gets smaller and more complicated and quarrelsome and wirelessly data-connected, it becomes ever-harder to say genuinely, 'You couldn't have got hold of me if you tried.' To this end, I've marked up the map in the laminates folder with all the places where you still stand on this hill and know that absolutely nobody can penetrate your peace of mind unless they're standing right beside you. If they're doing that, you have only yourself to blame.

Harry Inchbold, Wiltshire

FRIDAY EVENING

The (Thwarted) Arrival

Jo's phone glowed on the pub table, its recent IM+ message bright on the screen:

19.57 Setting out now. No time to shop. Wait for me in pub. H

She scrolled back to her own messages, most recent first.

17.49 Forgotten handbag with cottage keys and money!!! Can you food shop? Love you. xxx

14.18 Stuck in London traffic, argh. Looking forward to tonight. Love you!!xx

12.34 Dropping kids with Matt and Rowena now. Love you! x

As she read them, she saw she'd added a kiss and exclamation marks each time. There had been no kisses in return, she noticed. But, then, Harry had always been a three-kiss charmer in person and a brutally basic messenger.

She fed Rathbone a chip under the table and looked at her watch. It was past eight. Even with his pedal to the metal, Harry would struggle to get here by last orders. They had both promised they would make a big effort this weekend, but her forgetfulness and his bad timekeeping already made it feel like a run-of-the-mill quarrelsome week night.

Safe journey! x she replied, cutting back on her lip-smacking abbreviation, then adding a pedantic **PS: There's a Waitrose at the Michaelwood Services now. We need loo roll.**

Harry hated smart phones, always preferring the immediacy of a voice in his ear, while Jo would happily tap at a little screen keyboard all day. Here in the Hare and Moon, with its free Wi-Fi and lack of phone signal, it played into her ingrained habit. And she had a fellow collaborator, who was always equally happy to hide behind a screen.

She messaged Matt, trying to ignore the little heart leap that inevitably came with selecting his name from her contacts now, his profile photo reassuringly grey-haired, direct-eyed and grown-up. **Hope the kids are behaving?**

His reply came within seconds. **All good. Pizza. Pingu. Fast asleep. You okay?** He always communicated in abbreviated sentences, encouraging her to do the same.

Wide awake. In pub. Running tab. Left my handbag on your kitchen table. Harry late.

Plus ça change. How is the Moon?

Same old same. *La lune ne garde aucune rancune*.

The moon holds no grudges. 'Rhapsody on a Windy Night'. Windy and cold here too.

Matt and Rowena loved T. S. Eliot. They had encouraged Jo to read *Prufrock and Other Observations*, a favourite of Rowena's, which Jo was now using as the basis for a series of greetings cards. She'd chosen to focus on the imagery and lyricism rather than the themes of middle-aged fear and misery that Rowena apparently dwelt on when discussing the piece with her Sharing Menopause Group.

How's the weather there? Matt chased.

She started typing **cold** then stopped, tempted to throw in a **tropical** to test his response time.

Her brother-in-law was a lightning messenger who demanded total attention when live online but lagged if thrown a curveball, and switched off instantly if Rowena was around. Tonight was one of Rowena's therapy nights, part of a punishing ongoing schedule of self-help in her determination to see her way through the Change naturally. Matt was finding it hard to cope with the intensity of his wife's anger – much of it directed at him – and had confided in Jo about it in recent weeks, in return for which she'd gradually admitted her concerns about Harry's increasing indifference.

Any faces in that I'd know? Matt messaged impatiently now, cutting through her tropical versus cold deliberation.

Jo squinted short-sightedly across at the sofa where Cerys was laughing overloudly with her sister Lowri, both crammed in among a crowd she vaguely recognized as local, although she was struggling to make out individual faces.

Can't really tell. My glasses are in my handbag! Forgetfulness was a new thing, along with overuse of guilty exclamation marks.

How could you see to drive?! Matt was becoming incongruously punctuation-addicted, too, in the same way that she mirrored his abbreviated sentences.

Contact lenses.

Why take them out?

This was getting too pedantic. She had no desire to go into detail – however abbreviated – about the stye she'd felt forming while in contraflow traffic on the M40, blinking painfully all the way, whipping her contacts out gratefully upon arrival at Morrow only to remember that her bag, with her glasses in it, was still in London – along with the cottage keys.

Must go. Food going cold! Thanks again for being the Carb Uncle, ha-ha.

She turned the phone over on to its face, forcing herself to stop, and rubbed her sore eye. Her crush on Matt was small, comforting, occasionally irritating and very much under control.

The deepening friendship between them dated back to a big family Sunday lunch in Wiltshire last summer when Thea had fallen from the swing in the garden. Shamefully, the only family member sober enough to drive to hospital was Matt, who had ferried his niece and Jo to A and E where a hairline fracture was diagnosed and Thea's arm plastered. The nurses kept calling Matt and Jo Mr and Mrs Inchbold, which had made them laugh. They did nothing to correct the mistake because those were their names.

That wasn't what had triggered the crush, however, or even the heroic hospital dash: it was a brief moment of collusion when Jo had thanked Matt for his help as they'd driven home, trapped in traffic from a nearby sporting event, Thea asleep in the back.

'Good excuse to get away for an hour or two,' he'd said, in his terse way.

She'd laughed. 'Are my Sunday lunches so bad you need to escape?'

'They are heavenly, Mrs Inchbold.'

'Thank you, Mr Inchbold.'

What had been a silly joke in the hospital waiting room became uncomfortably clumsy and coy in the close confines of the car. Glancing across at him, Jo had seen the colour streak through his cheeks, so similar to Harry's rare damson stain, the face leaner and hollower, the brow higher.

'You have no idea how much I look forward to your lunches, Jo.' His voice had been controlled, but the blush-banded cheeks were a giveaway.

Jo stared at the back of her phone now. The gratification she'd experienced at hearing that was still oxygen into the bloodstream all these months later. The moment he'd said it, she'd known Sundays would never feel the same again.

'Harry hates them,' she had admitted at the time.

'That's because Harry hates Rowena.'

'Not at all!' she'd protested too heartily. 'He thinks I'm far too competitive in my quest to beat her perfect port *jus* and Hasselback potatoes.'

It irked her that Harry saw cooking Sunday roast – her only big culinary gig, these days – as little more challenging than a television meal. He also resented his one day off being hijacked, whereas Jo had become increasingly family-oriented since her mother's death.

Harry's bad temper at Sunday lunch had become something of a running family joke; his bad temper the other six days of the week was less easy to live with. It was one of the reasons Jo looked forward to those Sunday lunches too.

The Inchbold clan met fortnightly. Tactfully balancing the political cross-currents in their parents' complicated marital situation, they alternated between the Doll's House in London – where Gerry would bring carer-turned-companion Nita to spend time with all his grandchildren in Blackheath – and the Granary in Wiltshire, where Jo and Harry would host and Matt's mob would arrive crammed in his Land Rover Discovery with Granny Viv long-suffering and car sick in the front. These days, the senior Inchbolds preferred to break bread at separate tables unless it was Christmas or a landmark birthday, at which it was a free-for-all, often with Titch, Orchid and Jo's sister's brood, everybody mucking in. Jo relished orchestrating these high days, her sense of belonging never stronger than when twenty were gathered around the ridiculously long refectory table in the Granary's reception hall. She loved the children chattering, the criss-cross conversations, the oohs and aahs over a vast side of meat coming in to be carved. In a way, she knew she was competing with Harry's new restaurant two days a month.

That day in the car after Thea's accident, Matt had become her secret Sunday-lunch ally. 'You are a wonderful hostess and cook, Jo. Harry's very lucky to have you.'

The correct response at this point, Jo had realized afterwards, would have been to point out what a wonderful hostess Rowena was. Alternatively she could have said that she and Harry were lucky to have one another, although she sometimes questioned that amid the fire and ice nowadays. Instead she'd glowed at the compliment and, without thinking, had said, 'And Rowena's unbelievably lucky to have you.'

'I only wish she shared your enthusiasm.'

'Of course she does.'

'Trust me, you're alone on this one, Jo, actually.'

At this, Jo had sucked the corner of one lip for a long time, debating whether she'd just heard a polite, diffident 'Jo, actually' or a reference to their first meeting at a dinner party years ago, when he'd introduced her to his brother as 'Jane' and the very first Joactually/Basicallyharry nicknames had formed, long since cast aside. Had Matt hijacked an old pick-up line?

She still didn't know. But in a stuffy car in a traffic jam, she had felt as if she was travelling back in time, the buzz of mutual attraction too obvious to question the provenance.

In the long, awkward pause that had followed, they'd both known they had just stepped through an invisible air lock, the atmosphere totally different. Until then, Jo and Matt had never spoken about anything more emotional than a film plot. Her brother-in-law was among the most awkward, repressed men she knew, and yet that day she'd seen Harry in him so vividly that she'd felt a deep scar of affection opening up into a fresh, vulnerable wound.

He'd hurriedly turned on the stereo, but they'd both remained self-conscious, particularly as the music was a hopelessly romantic piece by Satie.

Jo pushed the phone away now and looked up at the ceiling beams, low and black, like the bars of a cage. The pub was filling up. She glanced across at the sofas again, seeing Cerys's arms flung wide as she described something that reduced her companions to shrieks of laughter. How different would Matt's life have been had he married the love of it? she wondered.

Matt's marriage to Rowena had always seemed the perfect fit, the ready-made family, and intelligent, wholemeal super-wife creating Utopia in the Doll's House. Compared to Jo and Harry's disastrous lurches between feast and famine, their epic rows, slapdash parenting and impossible work-life balance, Matt's life seemed effortlessly off the peg.

But she now saw how irritating they found each other. As Matt's secret ally, she'd learned just how disparaging

Rowena was about his family, especially of Harry, whom she thought completely out of control. While Matt and Rowena's marriage bore none of the obvious tensions of her own – when she and Harry were cooking a roast and a row, the kitchen at the Granary would be a no-go zone of flying insults and utensils – their brand of warfare was far more deadly, a battle of silent stealth. Jo now knew what a terrible time Matt's three stepchildren had given him, and that Rowena refused to admonish them, seeing it as part of their grief process for their father, insisting that Matt was in the wrong if he stood up to their anger and resentment. Jo knew about Matt's insomnia and loneliness. She'd heard all about the fasting and obsessive exercising that Rowena did to stay in shape, the compulsive cleaning and tidying to keep the Doll's House perfect. Rowena's high standards set an impossible bar. When she'd gone into teeth-gritted battle with her hormones, armed with no more than soya milk and red clover, Matt had ducked beneath the cross-fire, retreating to the safe bunker of work. And messages to Jo.

She picked up her phone again and looked at them now, rolling up through three months, all accompanied by that wise, greying, direct-eyed avatar. Her stomach twisted with the need to be safe.

Listening to Satie on that first crush day, as they'd crawled back from hospital along a road clogged with 4x4s, panting dogs in the back, Jo had rewound her memory through the many gatherings between the families and seen them in a new light. She recollected Matt's obvious pleasure in her company, the way he so often sought her out for conversation.

Matt's admiration was a light that she'd allowed to glow dimly and reassuringly ever since. Although nothing outwardly had changed between them, the crush stayed intact, a quiet background frost protection that saw them through every Sunday lunch with increasing ease. There was absolutely nothing improper in it – it was the politest mutual crush possible – but it helped immunize Jo against her own increasingly dysfunctional home life.

Returning to Harry's message string, she studied his profile photo, a mad-eyed, bearded blond blur of laughter and unpredictability. Without her contact lenses or glasses, she had to hold it very close to her face to focus, seeing a huge white smile bursting from a lot of bristle. The beard had been last summer's invention, sported when he'd finally offloaded the Clerkenwell restaurant and taken over the lease on a converted church in Bath, determined to be closer to his family. Having loved its unreconstructed novelty at first, Jo had been glad to see it go when it was shaved off for Church's opening night. Friends said it was totally Brad Pitt, but it caught food and scratched the kids' and Jo's faces, and her thighs on those very rare occasions that they'd had the sort of sex where he got a visual of her clitoris. That certainly hadn't happened since the Big Row.

She rubbed her sore eye again. Every week she matched and folded twenty-eight pairs of socks. She'd counted them. That was almost three thousand socks in a year. When she'd asked Harry for a year of socks, that wasn't what she'd meant at all.

The evening that she and Harry had started having their biggest row to date, she had been folding socks. Not that Harry had noticed, marching around, wine glass in hand – champagne flute, she corrected herself – ignoring her protests to keep his voice down in case he woke the kids. Against all odds, he'd just made a lot of money from the sale of Street. They should have been celebrating. But his decision to invest most of his profit straight back into another restaurant venture without discussing it with her had been devastating. Another huge risk. More crazy work hours. A marriage increasingly divided into his and hers, with so little in their lives that they shared: time, conversation, social life, children, money, sex, life-changing investment decisions.

Her Year of Socks had got lost in the whitewash. She was livid about the broken promise.

'You want more time to finish? Oh, it's you, Jo!'

She looked up short-sightedly to see Ping, who had come to collect her plate, its contents now cold, congealed and barely touched.

'Hi! I'm full, thanks – please take it.'

'Something wrong with it?'

'It was delicious but I'm doing it no justice,' she apologized, rubbing her eye. 'My no-carb diet was trashed by too many Haribos in the car.'

'I need that diet. You are so slim!' Ping slid in opposite her, glancing towards the bar and whispering, 'What is your secret?'

Jo had stuck with self-denial over the past year, shedding the stones that she'd put on with each pregnancy. She stood up straighter now, walked taller, felt healthier and spent far too much money on clothes, although her confidence remained vulnerable, and she still couldn't pass a deli counter without the urge to body-slide along it straight into a ripe Brie. The quiet crush had helped her stay focused, along with Harry's ever-longer absences as he dedicated himself to his new restaurant. They always put on weight eating together and she'd lost it by eating apart.

'Stress.' She smiled at Ping, who looked exhausted and bloated, her normally bright eyes dulled. 'How's Seren?'

'Daddy's girl.' She sighed. 'Roy dotes on her. But I say no more babies. I want him to take measures,' she whispered, as she leaned across the table to confide. 'He on nookie ban until he agrees. It's six weeks now and it's driving him mad.'

Jo smiled weakly, aware that her own lacklustre nookie ban had driven Harry mad for far longer. Sex was something she had to plan towards these days, once a month or so, like a dinner party one secretly dreaded organizing but knew would be fun once it got going: she'd start with a trip to the waxing salon, then have a rootle through her undies drawer for a shortlist seduction selection, and put a couple of bottles of wine into the fridge. To her shame, her sex drive increasingly relied upon a fine balance between the domestic situation and fantasy – her libido seemed hard-wired to the state of the dishwasher and the romantic content of Sunday-night television.

She could count the number of times they'd made love in the past six months on one hand, which needed no fingers to mark the number of times she'd reached orgasm. Neither had she been sober once. This weekend, she was determined to make amends. And stay sharp. That meant she was waxed, flexed and body-scented, and for every alcoholic unit she consumed, she'd decided to match it with caffeine. She knew that wasn't exactly treating her body as a temple, but their detox at Morrow had been a disaster, and she had no desire to be holier-than-thou. This weekend they were leaving Church behind, after all.

Hearing Roy shouting for her from the bar, Ping stood up. 'You want pudding?'

'Just coffee.' Most of Jo's friends drank nothing stronger than mint tea after midday nowadays, but Jo had never kicked the need for a caffeine buzz after a meal out. She blamed Harry's bad influence. They might not have regular sex any more, but at least twice a month they could still be found sitting up until two in the morning with an espresso and an Armagnac. They were less likely to put the world to rights nowadays, more likely to be box-set bingeing in onesies, but it gave her hope that they could find their way back to their good place. That was what coming to Morrow was all about.

Her phone buzzed with an instant message and she snatched it up in the hope that Harry was eating up the miles, already pit-stopping at Michaelwood.

But it was Matt. **I can't stop thinking about you tonight.**

She 'felt heat prickle up her body, looking guiltily away to find herself staring myopically at Cerys, wide-eyed and laughing over something her sister had said. She must have been exquisitely pretty as a teenager, Jo thought. Like a china doll. Perfect for a Doll's House.

Matt had messaged again. **I wish I could keep you company.**

You are.

All weekend.

'Too much,' she muttered, turning the phone face down again, then flipped it up.

Cerys is here. She winced as she sent the message. The screen darkness that followed was telling.

Matt had never once talked about Cerys, but he was clever and sensitive enough to guess she knew the back story. Jo often caught herself trying to hurt Matt deliberately – cruel taunts to force him away and spare them both – while Harry, who drove her so mad, was forgiven anything eventually. Even the Big Row. Only this morning she'd fantasized about murdering him for the way he'd rolled up the garden hose. Now she was willing him to get to her as fast as he could.

She eyed Cerys again, astonished that somebody she didn't know at all could throw such a shadow over her life: someone with whom Harry had fathered a never-born child and whom Matt had loved first and strongest. She was one of those infuriating women who remained dimple-charming and baby-faced even though she was over forty, her hair still as blonde and thick as ripe corn, teeth white as a cloud, sky-blue eyes edged with the finest laughter lines that Jo's bad eyesight blurred flatteringly.

Cerys caught her gaze before she could look away. Both women smiled, bright and defensive.

She is the only one who has been where I am now, Jo realized, with sudden clarity. Celibate with the Saint and carnal with the Sinner.

'It's Cerys, isn't it?' She made her way over, trying not to let her sore eye wink twitchily.

'And Lowri? Jo.' She held out her hand to shake theirs, knowing too late that this was stupidly formal, especially as both women were soft-eyed and silly from drinking.

'You remember *Jo*, Cerys,' Lowri said, in a carefully enunciated voice, loaded with meaning. 'Married to Half Inch. What a lovely dog!' She leaned down to greet Rathbone.

Jo introduced the little terrier as he went into a well-practised back flop of stomach exhibitionism at the suggestion of any attention, freckled belly proffered, old white teeth smiling. Jo stooped down to tickle him too.

'Harry not with you?' Cerys watched her closely, on eye level now.

'He's on his way. He was working late.'

'Still in the restaurant game?' asked Lowri.

'We've just opened one in Bath.' She nodded, far more aware of the proprietorial 'we' than they were. 'Harry was meeting a rare-breed meat supplier in Somerset today. '

'I thought he owned that place in London all the trendy shlebs love?'

'He sold that.' Harry, the eternal ideas man, had re-invented the ill-fated Street restaurant at the eleventh hour, creating Street Meet, which bought into the idea of social media and online dating, creating a venue at which young, unattached Londoners arranged to hook up, flirt on- and offline and eat great food. A pick-up joint with its own app, it was the first example of what was now known as 'app-er-tainment' and was currently huge. Street Meet's success was so prodigal that by the time the Clerkenwell lease expired, Harry had already clawed back much of the year's losses. With a cynical disregard for his own invention, he'd then sold the brand to repay the rest of his creditors, making an almost embarrassing profit that he'd ploughed straight into Church like guilt money, not thinking to dis-cuss it with Jo first.

Grilled by Cerys and Lowri – who insisted she cram into a tight corner of the sofa and share news of the Inchbold Saint and Sinner – Jo felt as though she was being inter-viewed by two tabloid gossip columnists eager for tales of wealth and glamour, but all that she had to offer was a broadsheet business-section summary. Her garden hose death-wish story remained strictly under wraps. She man-aged a bit about Matt's property empire and Harry's new restaurant, although the truth was that she knew more about her brother-in-law's marital spats than his portfolio, and she had minimal involvement with Harry's new res-taurant. Its very existence had been the cause of their most catastrophic row to date, a two-week mutual meltdown during which they'd both said things that could never be retracted. Even months later, the after-effects of the Big Row still reverberated, and was one reason why they were determined to be nice each other this weekend.

The Bath project couldn't have been more different from Street. Harry was determined to turn the converted church into a Michelin-starred restaurant and cookery school. Still basking in the glow of the fast-track success of Street Meet, he'd got a horde of investors on board, and had promised Jo that the venture would earn them retirement at fifty. He'd also joked that if it went belly-up, he would turn it into another pick-up joint called the Pull Pit, but Jo struggled to see the funny side, however much heart he threw into it. It was his new mistress. As always with Harry's enterprises, it took up all his time and energy, leaving her spinning in his wake.

And however quickly Harry charmed others into backing him, Jo was already counting down until he got bored with it.

The Jones sisters had lined up more drinks. Cerys lurched off to the loo.

'Is Harry still friends with Ned Whittaker?' Lowri asked, with such deliberate cool that it was obvious the question was as loaded as a New York cop's gun. 'Man, that boy was bad.'

Jo laughed. She'd already been asked the question by their landlord that evening. 'Ned certainly made an impression round here. I'm starting to think Roy has a crush on him.'

She'd never really fathomed Ned out, a commitment-phobic, slightly geeky overachiever whose big, soulful eyes reminded her of the nocturnal tarsiers she'd once seen in Borneo, ever watchful and suspicious. He and Harry gambled red and black on the same table in a bid to break the bank, their joint ventures relying upon Harry's flair for ideas, charm and inexhaustible dedication, matched with Ned's well-connected ability to make deals and money, although his predilection for bolting the moment the heat was on – a trait he demonstrated in his marriages as well as his business deals – meant Jo mistrusted him. Both men showed little interest in each other's family lives and never mixed them. Yet they were intensely loyal to one another, and as well as combining forces in business, they still had occasional lost weekends together, which involved vast quantities of malt whisky and machismo, an Opus Dei to which she had no access.

'Ned's pretty rock and roll still,' she told Lowri, 'and he's criminal at making money – not literally,' she added quickly, explaining that he had now invested in Church. She was better at glossing over truths nowadays, having learned spin from Harry, but her innate honesty inevitably let her down. 'Why is everyone around here so interested in Ned Whittaker?'

Lowri's eyes flashed, checking that Cerys was still out of the room, and she rolled her lip beneath small white front teeth, the piercing rattling. 'You seen my sister's tattoo?'

Jo remembered the night she'd lent Cerys mascara, a word on the back of her neck surrounded by stars. 'OWNED'. Her husband had been rugby thug Owen. She'd assumed it had to be to do with him.

'She added the "OW" when she got married.' Lowri's ringed eyebrows nudged up.

That left NED, Jo realized. 'I thought Cerys was Matt's girlfriend.'

'She was. She's the reason the Inchbold twins got known as Saint and Sinner.'

Jo looked away, face burning. How little she really knew of the secret history here. 'So what happened with Ned?'

'It's all in the song,' Lowri muttered, then made a shushing noise as Cerys came back across the room, red lipstick and black eyeliner redrawn with Lichtenstein precision. 'Rys! Jo here says Ned and Harry have gone into Church together.'

Cerys's eyes widened as she sat down. 'You are so fucking kidding.'

'It's the name of their restaurant,' Jo explained vaguely, still trying to work out how Ned's song about his parents' divorce could relate to a tattooed teenager on the Welsh borders, and how Harry fitted into it.

'Ha!' Cerys reached for her drink. 'Dad'll love that.'

'How is Efon?' Jo asked. She hadn't seen him in over two years.

'He's not been well,' Lowri explained. 'We're back here to look after him.'

'He's had a stroke and his liver's packing up.' Cerys put it more bluntly. 'They gave him six months tops six months ago. We think they were pretty much right.' She and Lowri exchanged a brief, tortured glance before the hands shot out in unison to grab glasses.

'We're keeping the farm running for now,' said Lowri, 'although it's a toss of a coin if it goes under before Dad does.' The sisters exchanged another look. This time their eyes held for a long time without blinking. Jo could almost hear a penny drop between them, and she had a hunch picking it up might not bring luck.

'Are you thinking what I'm thinking?' Cerys asked her sister.

'I'm thinking it.' Lowri smiled.

They turned to look at her in unison.

'You want more coffee, Jo?' Cerys asked brightly.

'Fuck that.' Lowri stood up. 'I'll get a round of Jägermeisters in, Rys.'

'I'm fine.' Jo held up a hand, reluctant to be hoodwinked into whatever plan the sisters had in mind. 'I need some fresh air, so I might walk up to the cottage and wait for Harry there.'

'Stay!' Cerys gripped her arms. 'I have a proposition.'

'What proposition?'

'Harry can buy the farm.'

'Your father's farm?' Jo's sore eye started throbbing. She pressed a finger to it to ease the burning. When her mother's cottage had been sold and Jo had paid off the mortgage on the Granary with her share of her inheritance, Harry had talked again about buying out Morrow, although the owners were all now sensibly hanging tight as the holiday-let money rolled in. The neighbouring farm, which was twice the size, and ten times as decrepit, hidden in another fold of wood further down the valley, would no doubt be perfect compensation in his eyes. It would also probably bankrupt them.

'Will you promise to ask him about it?' Lowri asked eagerly.

'I really don't think that's a good idea,' Jo told the Jones sisters firmly, holding her palms up, highly protective of the fact that her joint account with Harry was in the black for the first time in five years. 'Why not try asking Matt? He's the property man.' Her quiet crush glowed.

'Half Bold doesn't deserve it,' Lowri rolled her eyes. 'Tell her, Rys.'

'You're a nice woman, Jo,' Cerys slid closer on Jo's other side, 'and you know Harry better than either of us, but you didn't know Half Inch. The rhyming slang was wrong. He'd never steal something that didn't want to be taken. He just took life as it came and made the most of it. What is it they say? Give him an inch and he'll take a mile.' She raised her brows. 'Not that Dad's land is a mile. Give him an inch and he'll take a hundred acres. We'll sell it to him for buttons.'

'Why do that?'

'What she's trying to say,' Lowri leaned forwards, stage-whispering, 'is that Harry earned this.'

'We'll be forced to sell the farm for buttons at auction after Dad dies anyway,' Cerys said, her jaw clamped with tension. 'He knows he's not got long left.'

Instinctively, Jo put an arm round her. 'It's like waiting for a train to crash, knowing you can do nothing. But the train doesn't crash, I promise. You know when it's going to stop. You're ready.'

On her other side, Lowri's voice was a tough little growl of repressed emotion. 'You've been through it?'

Jo put an arm round her too. 'Twice.'

'*That* calls for a fucking drink, whatever you say.' She wriggled out and headed to the bar.

'I'm worried about Lowri.' Cerys watched her go. 'Dad's all she's got. We have different mums, you see, and hers isn't around any more. Mine lives in Shrewsbury and hates Dad's guts, but at least she's there for me.'

'And you're there for Lowri.'

'I grew up with Dad. She didn't.'

'Was her mother the one who ran off with the sheep shearer?'

'That was mine. It didn't last – she's allergic to lanolin. Lowri's mum ran off with a married teacher. You know what happened, surely.'

'I wouldn't be asking if I did.'

'Christ, they play it close to their chests, the Inchbolds. Lowri's mum had an affair with Gerry – must be thirty years ago now. It was a big, big thing.' She turned guiltily as a phial of herb liqueur was thrust under her nose.

'She's talking about my mum and Gerry Inchbold, isn't she?' Lowri crammed in next to Jo.

'Yes.'

'They took me with them, then dumped me on my nan. When Gerry went crawling back to Viv after a fortnight, nobody came to get me. Mum just kept on running all the way to Canada. He broke her heart, you know. All Inchbold men do that.'

'Jones men are worse,' Cerys countered. 'Look at Uncle Huw.'

Jo listened as they ran down various male family members, her stye twitching. She felt her phone buzz in her pocket. Was it Matt or Harry? Her heartbreaking Inchbold men. She had a sudden unwanted image of herself running away with Matt, of losing her children and Harry. Their marriage was a mess, but the thought of abandoning it was unbearable. The crush and the messages had to stop.

By the time Roy was ringing last orders, she'd drunk enough coffee to make coughing a dangerous pastime, her loo trips severely interrupting the flow of conversation, along with messages from Harry that she read in the cubicle.

Glyn Pugh now 24 hours! We have faggots and black pudding! H

Going to Ganges now!! H

His explanations were marked. Despite absent kisses, she felt a thread thrown out to her, spinning him towards her.

Cornered by Roy, who asked if she was staying on for a 'moonwatch' lock-in, she thanked him and shook her head, looking at her vibrating phone again.

Christ, there's a queue. Takeaway could be a while. Will fetch beer. Can't wait to be with you! H x

His first kiss of the evening. The invisible thread was pulling hard now. She hurried to say farewell to Cerys and Lowri.

'You promise you'll talk to Harry about buying the farm?' Cerys entreated.

'I'll try,' she hedged. They had a lot of talking to do.

Heading towards the door, Rathbone at her heels, bad eye closed, her thumb worked faster on screen than Rumpelstiltskin's when he was spinning straw into gold. **I'll be waiting at the cottage – can't wait to be with you too!! xx**

She paused in the pub's porch, flipping back a screen to Matt, feeling the familiar pinch of guilt. **The Moon holds no grudges. This must stop here.** She sent it before she could think about it too hard.

FRIDAY EVENING/SATURDAY MORNING

The Arrival

Jo hurried up the track with Rathbone, forced to press a palm over one eye because the cold air against her stye was making it water like mad. Her Cyclops navigation made her zigzag over the ruts and into the stream bank so it took longer than ever to get up, her legs aching. A Shropshire hill was far harder going than the gym treadmill's Matterhorn setting.

When she finally reached Morrow, she slid her back down the front door gratefully, letting Rathbone hop on to her lap, relieved that they'd beaten Harry there: she needed the sweat to cool and her breath to catch as her heartbeat dropped from three figures to two before she saw him. They were going to turn over a new leaf, she reminded herself. This weekend they were going to put Jo and Harry together again.

She drew solace from the familiarity of her surroundings, the quiet darkness of the cottage's solitary lair gradually revealing the life teeming all around it. The guinea fowl roosting in tree branches chattered irritably at the intrusion, a fox barked and black bat spectres darted in her peripheral vision, like eye floaters from staying awake too long.

Still on a caffeine high, her mind raced through the things she wanted to say, the shortfalls she wanted to make up for, the irritation that had made her shut him out so much since the Big Row. In recent months, she had thrown all her love and energy into the children. When

Harry complained that she showed no interest in Church, she usually retaliated that he showed none in his family and home, but that wasn't entirely true. He was a great father when he was around, but on those rare occasions he had spent time at home, she had retreated into her own work and her quiet crush. They were emotional shift workers.

These days, she often found herself dwelling upon the decade Bree had held on to Harry's loyalty, wondering at that marriage's inner world. She still remembered his honest summary when they'd first met: 'We both started drinking too much, flirting with other people, destructive patterns ... The fights were toxic.'

She felt cold fear whenever she ran those words back through her head, wondering whether history had repeated itself. She'd talked about it with Matt, who claimed Harry had stayed married to Bree long after the rot had set in as a result of his gilded cage – luxury and sexual excess – but Jo knew Harry was too feral to be kept: he had simply loved her. Harry worked tirelessly for love.

Covering her watering eye with her hand, she found the other was weeping too. She mustn't cry, she told herself firmly. This was going to be a happy weekend. They both deserved it. They would eat, drink and be merry. They would stay in bed all day making love. They would walk up Mawr Vron holding hands.

An owl screeched, making her jump.

She squinted at her phone to read the time. It was almost midnight. Where *was* he?

For a brief, heart-stopping moment she wondered whether he'd been in an accident. He always drove too fast in the luxurious, gas-guzzling Range Rover he adored, bought with the Street Meet money, and cause of another argument because Jo thought it impracticably large, expensive to run, and it always made Wilf hopelessly car sick. Now she imagined it mangled on a blind bend, blue lights, cutting equipment, paramedics fighting to save him . . . She forced herself to stop, knowing it was the same illogical panic that gripped her when he was late back with the kids and she envisaged them all wiped out together.

Another ten minutes passed, then became twenty, which stretched to half an hour. Her stomach rumbled. The queue at the Ganges must have been huge. She was starting to feel seriously cold as well. Rathbone was shivering in her lap.

She got into her car to warm up, tuning into a late-night radio phone-in. As the warm air wafted round her and the voices lulled her, she closed her eyes.

A horn made her jerk upright. The dashboard clock said it was after one. She could hear the big roar of Harry's car.

Its xenon headlights arcing up the track made her heart-beat accelerate again as she got out. She could hear the Arctic Monkeys booming from the stereo. She closed her eyes briefly, one swollen, the other twitching with tension, mustering kindness.

'Owl!' He laughed as he climbed out, arms already wide.

'At last!' She cannoned into him and he briefly gripped her, more of a body slam than a hug.

'Don't tell me Roy had the cocktail book out again.'

'I'm blind, but not drunk,' she explained. 'I have no glasses and a stye.' She showed it to him beneath the deeply unflattering porch light, moths dive-bombing all around.

It wasn't the most romantic of starts, but Harry rallied valiantly. 'Poor Owl.' He cupped her face and kissed her lightly. 'I'll be your eyes this weekend.'

She could smell beer on his breath. 'What took you so long?'

'I got talking to the landlord at the Six Tuns. Amazing guy. Used to be in restaurants.'

Jo counted to ten. Do *not* rise. Leave the arguments at the door. 'Let's get inside.'

As soon as his key slid into the lock, their shoulders dropped in relief. When they stepped inside, they breathed in deep lungfuls of Morrow, its woodsmoky dampness reclaiming the air a little more with every passing year, smiles digging into their cheeks.

He turned to her. 'I've been looking forward to this all year.'

She pressed her hand into his. 'Me too.'

When they switched on the lights, the Morrow décor was even more minimalistic – an off-season deep spring-clean, ordered by Rowena, had eradicated yet more pictures and crockery – but as soon as Rathbone marched in and flopped down expectantly by the stove, it felt like the forever home from home they loved. While Jo lit the ready-laid fire, Harry slotted his phone into the iPod dock and soon the sexiest steel-string blues was filling the room. Looking back over her shoulder, Jo found his eyes sparkling down at her, the long-anticipated Morrow seduction already under way.

He held out a hand to help her up. 'Let's have a drink. We'll get the stuff in from the car.'

But as soon as they stepped outside into the chill, tired irascibility nipped at them and they squared up to each other by the car boot, searching through a rubble of disorganized Glyn Pugh shopping in ripped carriers for a bottle of wine. Despite the cold, the frozen food had softened to mush.

'You obviously had more than a few drinks at the Six Tuns while I was shivering my arse off up here,' Jo muttered.

'Sorry about that.' He handed her a brace of sauvignons. 'I lost sight of the time.'

Inside again, they sought out glasses and corkscrew in

silent accord, eyes catching, heads ducking away from the cupboard door, amused and apologetic. It was ridiculously late, but the rituals were there to be observed, and they were well practised in boozy after-hours vigils. Harry poured two glasses brimful of wine. Jo had only the briefest of guilty moments before they clinked dribbling rims and drank an inch.

'To us.'

'To here.'

Their smiles were knowing and expectant.

Outside, Harry slid a pungent, leaking takeaway box from the front seat while Jo picked up his weekend bag from the boot, talking through the dog grille, tetchy again.

'Didn't you think I might be getting cold waiting here?'

'I told you, I didn't realize it was that late.'

'I waited over an hour!'

'I thought you were in the Moon. They always have a lock-in on a Friday night.'

'I texted you to say I was coming here.'

'I didn't get it. I've said I'm sorry. Let's eat this before it gets any colder. Please stop winking at me.'

'I told you I have a stye. And I'm past being hungry,' she protested, following him inside, where Rathbone had already moved into position beneath the table ready to hoover up scraps.

Emptying the contents of the box randomly on the table, Harry dived into the cartons, eating straight from them with a fork.

We used to lay them out on trays in front of the fire and feed each other, Jo remembered wistfully.

Yawning, she picked out a few small nuggets, put them on her plate and ate them slowly. 'Mmm, this is good.' She helped herself to a few modest spoonfuls. 'I always forget how good Ganges is.' Finally, abandoning her plate, she binged from the cartons, too, eyes lifting to meet his with amused concession. 'My diet's blown.'

'You can afford to blow it. You look great.'

Jo tilted her head so her puffy eye was away from him and gave him a smouldering look, rusty from lack of use. 'I thought you were too devoted to work to notice me any more.'

'Forget Church. You are my religion. I'm a solipsist.'

'That means you think only you exist.'

'What's the one where God's in everything?'

'Pantheism.'

'I'm that.' He smiled. 'A panther.'

Harry had led sexier flirtations, but he was trying hard. Jo still had her head turned so her bad eye was hidden. She was getting a crick in her neck. They exchanged another hot look, acknowledging that sex was on the cards.

They grabbed the last poppadum at the same time.

'You have it,' she offered, letting go.

'No, you have it.'

Laughing, they split it.

'Let's go to bed.' He looked at her levelly and the thread of hope running through Jo tightened, her libido triggered.

But the sex was among the least connected they'd ever had. As they ran their gamut on Morrow's guest-friendly Egyptian sheets, generous and vigorous, it felt like a never-ending performance. Still pumped with caffeine and giving it her all, Jo found the curry shifting like ballast in her belly as she bounced on top then beneath, in front and behind, long legs folding every which way, battling indigestion and wind. Harry kept changing position, blond hair everywhere, so it felt more like circuit training than love-making. Several times, she suspected he'd lost his erection, but it came back as he manhandled her around the bed, getting harder again, manipulating her into a new position, like a gymnast performing a floor programme. Jo thought he would never come; she didn't even come close.

He fell asleep almost straight afterwards.

Jo lay awake, a buzz humming in her ears alongside his snores, profoundly unsatisfied. Her bad eye felt swollen and itchy.

'I bumped into Cerys and Lowri tonight,' she muttered.

A deep snore and a grunt.

'They say their father's dying.'

Another sonorous nasal rumble.

'They want to sell you his farm for buttons. Apparently you earned it.'

This time the snore roared right into his sinuses, and he rolled over with a low-level fart, but at least he stopped snoring.

Jo fanned the duvet and reassured herself that she had done her duty.

An arm swung back in the darkness, making her duck in surprise as Harry tugged the duvet from her grip and settled it down again, covering his bare back.

She crept downstairs to fetch a glass of water, clean up and pee, checking her reflection in the bathroom mirror. It wasn't pretty, the eyelid swollen and red as though it had been punched. Soaking a flannel in hot water, she pressed it to her eye and wandered back out.

Harry was sitting in darkness at the table, his face glowing in the light of his phone screen.

'What a lot of messages.' His tone was flat.

'Is it to do with Church?'

He didn't seem to be listening. 'There's satellite Wi-Fi here in the cottage now. It's faster than we've got at home.'

'Yay! Let's Skype Orchid in Australia.' She yawned.

'Matt's quite the poet when he gets going, isn't he?'

She froze, trying not to give herself away. It might not be her phone. 'Is something wrong?'

'Matt certainly seems to think so, and I quote: **What's wrong?**' he read out, thumb tapping the screen. 'Before that, we have: **Do you want me to come there tonight or not? We must talk. I can't bear the thought of you with Harry.** Nice one, bro. Although **I want to be alone with you so much** is the most revealing line here, I feel.'

Jo closed her eyes. It was definitely her phone.

'You should put a better screen-lock on this. Wilf could crack it in ten seconds flat.'

'He does.' She sat opposite him, prayer hands over her mouth. Then, indignantly, they became two fists at her temples. 'How *dare* you read my messages?'

'It kept buzzing by the bed and woke me up. When I saw Matt's name, I thought it was an emergency with the kids.'

'He's going through a bad time with Rowena.'

'I couldn't give a shit about Rowena. It's his relationship with *you* I'm interested in. Why the fuck did you invite him here tonight?'

'I didn't!'

'**I'll be waiting at the cottage,**' he read out huskily, '**can't wait to be with you too!! xx.**'

'That was meant for you.' She groaned. Oh, God, she'd sent it to Matt in error and triggered some sort of emotional outpouring because he thought she'd asked him to come and spend the night with her at Morrow.

Harry's eyes bored into hers above the phone's glow. 'What exactly is going on?'

'We message. He needs to talk.'

'And you are very easy to talk to, Jo. People confess things to you.'

She looked at him for a long time, trying to work out whether he was being sarcastic or not. 'Talking's good.'

'Don't hold back.'

The phone screen locked, plunging them into darkness. It was eerily silent, just a soft burble from the fridge and the distant squeak of Rathbone having a dream upstairs.

Jo put her hands palm down on the table. 'What do I have to say to convince you that I love you more than I've ever loved another soul, that I want this marriage to work, that I know we've had a shitty year or two – or three – but we've come through them and we deserve to try, for each other's sake and the children's sakes? What do I have to say to make you believe that Matt just needs to sound off about Rowena, and that, yes, we've grown fond of each other but I love *you*, Harry? I want to be with *you*, Harry. You're selfish and obsessive and lousy with money, and sometimes you act like I'm not even here, but I've chosen to share my life with you and you'll have to try a whole lot harder at being a crap husband to make me change my mind. What do I say to make you see that?'

He stood up to fill the kettle. 'That's certainly a start.'

They talked until close to dawn, drinking endless cups of tea that made Jo's caffeine jitters no better. Some time after three, Rathbone joined them, pacing, yawning squeakily and scrabbling as he tried to settle on the uncomfortable kitchen floor, finally giving up on them and sloping into the sitting room to heave himself on to the sofa.

They talked about everything they had busily ignored in the past year: they voiced their frustrations at home, confessed resentment and deep anger in their work lives, revealed their worries for the children, their fears for his family, and the grief that Jo still couldn't get through a day without feeling.

They talked in a way they so rarely did, yet they let each other down totally. They were calm and articulate – Jo only cried once and Harry shouted only a few times – but they weren't always as open and as honest as they believed, and although the long tête-à-tête made them feel happier and more secure, it brought them no closer to understanding how the other felt or thought.

Because while Jo and Harry talked themselves hoarse, they didn't listen. They simply waited their turn. It was yet another performance. Too busy trying to voice their own thoughts to take each other's to heart, they were tired and united in their customary best-behaviour roles – Harry as funny, forthright and heartfelt as Jo was earnest, fair-minded and sardonic. They spoke as passionately and politely as two students at the Oxford Union: 'This House Believes This Marriage Can Be Better', an old-fashioned Inchbold family debate made by two opinionated people who wanted something for the good of all, but without conceding a point.

As the dawn chorus burst out, they cooked breakfast in the half-light, still talking, exhausted but calmer, flipping bacon as sunlight stole through the trees and into the kitchen in broad stripes. They ate gratefully, a companionable silence finally settling between them through the shadows of a night they'd rather forget.

'You promised me a year of socks.' Jo watched a long leg of sunlight point its toes across the table.

'I never give socks. Fucking unoriginal.'

They went upstairs and made love again tiredly, no longer trying to run through a potted medley of their best marital-bed highlights, but simply make the connection that words couldn't. It was no more of a success. This time Jo got frustratingly close to coming, her body at melting point, unable to tip the fraction further and let go. Harry was determined to take her there, as he had so often before, but they were both shattered.

447

'Let's not worry about me.' She pulled him down towards her. 'I want you inside me.'

'I can't. Too soft-hearted, -minded and -dicked.' He kissed her and rolled away.

'We'll try again after we've slept.' She spooned up behind him, wrapping her arm round his reassuring bulk.

'Sure.' He patted it.

Jo lay awake, watching the early-morning sunlight's minute hand slide across the room, knowing Harry was still awake too. It was as though they'd missed some vital point, something that might make all the difference to a night of white-noise talking and lacklustre lovemaking, the key to making their marriage work. She felt uneasy and slightly sick, a bad headache kicking in. Her eyelids were heavy, one throbbing.

'I love you.'

'I love you too.'

FROM THE VISITORS' BOOK, MARCH 2013

This is my favourite time of year at Morrow, the white hedges on the hillside teasing you that snow's still here until you approach them and see that it's blackthorn blossom. You never know whether you'll open Morrow's door to frost, sunshine, rain or snow. But if you know where to look, you'll see chiffchaffs and skylarks, hares and pipistrelle bats, whatever the weather. Unless you've forgotten your glasses.

Jo Inchbold, Wiltshire

2014

*Music: Paolo Nutini, Hozier,
Sam Smith, Mungo Jerry*

Car: mud-splattered Mini

Season: Summer, heatwave

FROM THE VISITORS' BOOK, JULY 2014

I will be here the same time next year, and every year.

Harry Inchbold, Wiltshire

FRIDAY EVENING

The Takeaway

Jo was watching the last poppadum on the plate like a lioness watching a kill. Harry's hand hovered over it, then withdrew to his chin, rubbing the stubbly beard, blue eyes searching her face. From the speaker, Paolo Nutini sang 'Looking For Something'.

Ask me if I want it, she willed. You've had four, I've had one. Ask me.

Jo often set silent challenges now, regressing to childhood insularity – if these stairs have an even number of steps, I'll be happy; if we can get through an evening without starting sentences with 'Listen' and doing the opposite, we'll be happy. She also wished on stars and new moons. Far beneath the deep-frozen cynicism, a child was still playing Loves Me, Loves Me Not with flower petals. If Harry helps himself to the last poppadum, our marriage is over.

'We'll get another dog,' Harry said, refilling his beer mug.

'I don't want another dog. I want Rathbone back.'

Rathbone had been missing for three months, disappearing the day Harry and Wilf had driven to a nearby beauty spot to take him for a walk and burn off some Easter eggs during the holidays, happening upon kite flyers on the ridge and staying to watch and join in. Entranced, Wilf – who had been proudly in charge of holding his lead – had let it go without Harry noticing. They'd only realized that the little dog was no longer with them when they'd got back to the car. Days of searching and ringing around rescue centres had proven fruitless, along with posters, adverts and his own dedicated Facebook page. Their funny, woolly, lazy little wire brush had vanished miles from home. Jo couldn't bear to think of how frightened and lonely he must have been, or of the fate that might have befallen him. The guilt she felt over her parents' small, kind-natured old dog haunted her. She tried to comfort herself by imagining him rescued by a kindly soul like Widow Tweed in *The Fox and the Hound*, but it was a fragile fantasy, easily shattered by her pragmatic inner voice, which was increasingly shouty. Her spoken voice was muted by contrast, strangled by the tourniquets that stopped her feelings bleeding everywhere.

'I don't want another dog.'

'I heard you the first time. But I've promised Wilf a dog of his own.'

'He's not even seven yet. And what if Rathbone comes back?'

'Then we'll have two.'

'It's not fair leaving them, given the hours we work. I can't take two into the office with me.'

'Are you talking about the dogs or the children?' He laughed, earning a hurt look.

After a brief period of very contrite apology, Harry had moved on. Excited that the loss of the old dog meant the acquisition of a new one was on the cards, Wilf had moved on even faster, showing no remorse whatsoever. But Jo remained grief-stricken, still hoping against hope that the little grey dog would come back. And Thea, so diligent at almost five, always sensitive to her mother's moods, drew new posters and searched the garden every day. Team Rathbone had formed versus Team New Dog. In their increasingly male-female divided house, Rathbone – their neutered, neutral go-between – was now a martyr figure.

If they were going to get another four-legged mediator to talk through, Jo feared they'd belong to a pair of divorce lawyers.

She was exhausted by Harry's anger, his volatility and constant need for change; the children were increasingly disoriented and sensitive to the rows they struggled to hide. There was absolutely no sense of routine with Harry, no way of predicting his movements or mood from one day to the next. Now that he was expanding the Church brand, he sometimes disappeared at dawn, calling her late at night from Glasgow or London to say he might not make it back until tomorrow. Equally, on other days he didn't go into work at all, very often when Jo was working from home and frantically trying to catch up on Blue Barn paperwork, only to find televisions booming sport in every room, the fridge and larder emptied of a week's worth of food. He thought nothing of eating all the sweets and chocolates she kept as special rewards for the children.

Perhaps she could forgive the disorganization and greed if it wasn't for the anger.

He never blinked when he shouted, she'd noticed.

They hadn't made love in months, they hardly talked any more and they had almost completely different social circles, these days. They avoided one another as much as possible. If called upon, they could still put on a good united front, but it was an enormous strain. Just as the happy mask they wore for the children all too often slipped.

Perhaps she could forgive the neglect and carelessness, if it wasn't for the anger.

Last week she'd counted ten minutes of Harry talking without blinking, his voice getting louder and louder. Then he'd broken a cupboard door by slamming it, and accused her of not listening.

Jo knew that one should never fight out relationship

differences through one's children, but Harry's deep-set, hot-blooded defence of Wilf was hard to see past. Like his father, Wilf was outspoken, impulsive and regularly off piste. Unlike his father, he still needed an education, and having been excluded twice from school for aggression in his first year, his concentration span almost non-existent, he clearly needed more support in class. Harry refused to accept that there was any difference in their son from his peers, despite the school pressing hard for outside agency involvement that might enable extra funding. Jo was worried that Wilf was being bullied, that his anger stemmed from fear, but Harry called it high spirits and cordoned Wilf in his care as he took an increasing back step from the Church restaurant, no longer his only religion. Wilf, his doppelgänger, was currently at the centre of everything. Jo loved Wilf with a fierceness that always shocked her, as she loved them all, but Harry currently wanted total exclusivity. His interest in Thea, meanwhile, was minimal, flirtatious and condescending.

Perhaps she could forgive the partisan parenting, if it wasn't for the anger.

Harry often broke things during arguments. The house was patched with repairs, although it was hard to tell where Harry's wall-punching damage started and Wilf's toy-crashing, pinball path ended.

Jo knew she should be pleased he cared so much – Wilf needed all the champions he could get – but she was worried about how long it would last. Harry was already eyeing new horizons.

'Ned's putting up the money to buy the Oratory in Edinburgh,' he told her, as he refilled his beer mug. 'He wants to make that the second restaurant, with the ones in Oxford and Leeds coming a year later.' Ned liked buying religious buildings, saying they brought him closer to

God than the skyscrapers he built as a day job. 'We think London's too risky, but Brum is predicted to be the next Michelin-starred hotspot, although I'm trying to steer Ned away from the mosque idea.'

He was spooning up the last of the rogan josh now, along with the butter chicken sauce and the lemon pilau, scraping out the foil tins, offering her none. There had been a time when the leftovers created a lavish brunch the next day, but Harry ate more now, like a man attacking his last meal.

'Do you want that poppadum?' she asked, but he wasn't listening.

She stared at it. It was no longer on his radar. Neither was she. He was talking at her. Harry did that a lot when he was uptight.

He knew how bad things were. They both did. But it was easier to ignore it than deal with it.

Perhaps she could forgive being talked at if it wasn't for the anger.

He'd broken two mobile-phone screens throwing them down in frustration when she'd hung up on one of his rants.

'Good to leave Col and the team flying solo at Church,' he was saying, talking about his head chef. 'They're machines. I'm going to restructure the management team so they have total autonomy.' He scraped the final dollops of sag aloo and dhal on to his plate and eyed the poppadum briefly.

She tensed.

'I'm ready to take a back seat in Bath, sock puppet a load of five-star reviews to crank up the value, and find something new.'

'What about the Oratory?'

'Mmm?' For a moment he looked perplexed.

'You were just talking about expanding the franchise to Edinburgh and beyond.'

'Ned'll get a team in to do that.'

'It's your brainchild, your business.'

'I've just about had it with restaurants.'

Perhaps she could forgive the inability to stick to one work project for more than a year if it wasn't for the anger.

Harry's latest mobile phone was pristine. He called her less often now, although he shouted just as much.

Jo looked away, blinking hard, her mind already ahead of any tears, cutting them off at the pass. She couldn't pinpoint the moment she'd retreated into herself so deeply, addressing her own anger at inanimate objects, hating Harry for a discarded pair of trousers, a dropped towel, a forgotten date on the calendar, yet no longer confronting the big issues. The high drama that always surrounded him no longer terrified her if she focused on the minutiae.

'Be good to have a sabbatical,' he was saying. 'Ned's keen on a big boys' rugby trip. Matt still wants me to get into golf, but that's the final frontier. I need to shift this.' He smacked his thickened middle. 'I'll start running again.' The final quarter of naan bread was whipped on to his plate, drenched with raita and lime chutney, then washed down with beer.

She half listened, glancing at the wood-burning stove and remembering the first weekend he'd brought her there when they'd eaten from the cartons on their laps, feeding each other while enjoying the insatiable urge to feast on one another.

They'd made love long before making friends. They had always made peace at Morrow. Their eight years together had brought one drama and crisis after another, life-changing personal earthquakes through which they had kept standing, thrown closer together even, only to be felled by a year in which nothing more dramatic had happened than losing one small, elderly dog on an afternoon walk.

Harry's business had made money; both children were healthy and well; Orchid had landed a television presenting job; Matt and Rowena struggled on; Jo no longer messaged her brother-in-law, but the alternating Sunday lunches remained an institution; Titch was expecting a baby with a gay friend; Viv and Gerry continued to live happily separate lives under the same roof; Blue Barn was now stripped to the bone and paid Jo a smaller income than ever, its survival a metaphor for her own.

But the short marriage of Harry and Jo Inchbold was about to collapse. At home, they constantly bored, irritated and sometimes hated one another. Now at Morrow, where peace should reign, it felt like the lull before a war.

He was talking trainers now. 'Adidas are good basics, but to cover serious miles you need Cloudrunners or Salomons.'

Since when had Harry become so dull? He used to reduce her to tears of laughter daily. Now they were tears of boredom.

She dovetailed her fingers together under her nose, knuckles on her septum. They had two children they adored more than life, a home they'd fought for, a lifestyle of hard work that they soldiered through from angry alarm-clock slap and toxic hangover to late-night arguments and sex avoidance. Weekdays were all about work, childcare juggles and exhaustion; at weekends they became two children's entertainers, counterbalanced with wine-induced apathy, greed and movie nostalgia after dark. Family holidays revolved around the kids, food and alcohol.

Theirs was like a hundred thousand other middle-aged, middle-class marriages, straining at the seams.

Friends of Jo who were leaving theirs – and there was an increasing number – were outwardly blossoming, liberated and adrenalin-pumped, but the scars ran deep, the practicalities tough to endure. Would it make her and

Harry any happier to join them? Those she knew who had stuck valiantly together found coping mechanisms, turning themselves into comedy double-acts or weary business partners, living through the children or work. Single friends who had never settled down still searched hopefully, along with the second-time-arounders – some third. Giving up on love only ever seemed to be a short-term option.

The music from the speakers was the sweetest, simplest of love songs: 'Someone Like You'.

Perhaps she could cope with the mutual boredom if it wasn't for the anger.

Jo had trained herself to tune out his shouting; most of the time it was just noise.

'I could think about doing some half marathons, maybe.' Harry was already imagining the lean running machine he was going to become, his vision ever positive. He would no doubt do it, throwing himself into yet another short-lived obsession that led to a flurry of new friendships, social circles and bromances before he tired of them and it, dropping friends and deleting accounts without a backward glance.

By contrast, Jo had looked up a lot of old friends recently – Facebook was her new ally. She'd caught up with Caro, deep in Northumberland shooting lunches amid the country set, and with Fi, now living in the Cotswolds with her two children and dating a new man. She found herself looking back through her life more than forwards towards her future. She'd even looked up Tom, still a lost cause despite working for good ones. He was divorcing amid bitter wrangles over money and pet custody. They had met for lunch, both gratified by how much the other had aged and grown cynical. It had been an awkward and stilted encounter, and they'd talked mostly about dogs. Afterwards, she'd felt emotionally bottomed out, unable to stop herself wondering whether she and Harry would one day end up so completely detached from each other, repelled even. When she'd talked to him about seeing Tom, he'd been typically dismissive: 'Rather you than me. The only Bree I want to see over lunch comes baked with fruit chutney.' He never talked about his first marriage; he only ever talked about his childhood and the future, both idealized, the colour and contrast turned up to maximum by Inchbold spin.

Right now, he was fixed on the road to fitness: 'I can't see the point of driving to the gym and running on a glorified hamster wheel when you can run in open country.' The music had stopped playing, but he hadn't noticed and Jo didn't say anything, grateful for the peace. He loved the latest hits – 'Take Me To Church' by Hozier was an obvious kitchen favourite in Bath – whereas Jo's taste had always been retro. She'd stopped listening to music lately because it made her too emotional.

'We'll come here more often, bring the kids, run, walk the new dog.'

Caro, who wrote regular long, funny emails about the mid-life crisis David was having, which involved a sports car, a tennis club and too-tight trousers, thought Harry was going through the same. Fi was more embittered, her personal experience bleaker: she had suggested he was having an affair. But Jo knew Harry had always been like this – capricious, obsessive, domineering, dependent. It was the eyes she was observing him with that had changed as she'd got older: just as she needed reading glasses for small print nowadays, so she needed thick, rose-tinted lenses with scales on them to see Harry's attitude to life in a positive light, despite the idyllic family shots and restaurant scenes she posted online while looking up old friends.

The internet was a dangerous place for the discontented. One pretended everything was marvellous on public time-lines and revealed the sordid truth by direct message.

She picked up her phone now and sent one:

Shut up and listen.

'Cycling might be better, and that way, Wilf can ...' Harry checked his phone, then cast it aside. He fell silent and rubbed his fingertips across his eyebrows, looking at her between his hands.

'Aren't you worried about our marriage?' she asked.

'Where did that come from?' He laughed.

'I am. I'm so disappointed in us.'

The laugh died, eyes widening.

There was a long pause. She could see his clever head assessing the situation behind those big, shocked blue eyes. He'd known this was coming, surely.

'Of course I'm worried about you, Owl,' he said eventually, chewing a thumbnail, 'but we've weathered worse. This dog thing is really not—'

'I'm not talking about the dog thing! And it's us, not me – it's *us*! I'm talking about the fact we don't get on any more. We don't laugh or make love or make plans. The money situation terrifies me. The fact that you still waste your talent pisses me off. The fact that I'm still having to work night and day to get us through the lean patches makes me sad sometimes because I'm missing out on so much of the children for an ever-decreasing return, but I could weather that if we didn't argue all the time and I didn't feel exhausted all the time.' Now the floodgates were open, she couldn't stop. 'I want the children to have the best of us. Our kids are growing up with parents who don't respect each other any more.'

462

He stared at her in shock, starting on the other thumb-nail. She'd never seen him chew his nails before.

Why wasn't he angry? He should be angry.

But he was wide-eyed. Such heartbreaking eyes. 'Our kids are growing up with a father who thinks their mother is brilliant and beautiful. I love you, Owl. I love the way your mind works. I fancy you all the time.'

Accustomed to his quick charm, she closed one eye and looked away with a cynical huff. Why wasn't he angry? She needed him angry. His anger was what hurt most, what justified this. 'Well, I don't fancy you.' *That* would make him angry.

She glanced at him again.

He looked as though he'd been shot, taking the bullet, still staring at her.

'Not tonight anyway,' she added, glaring at the pop-padum.

'I've said I'll start running, Owl.'

'It's not physical. I mean, that's great, but that's not it. It's . . . ' She pushed herself to say it, frightening herself but unable to stop. 'I think we need some time living apart.'

Jo hadn't planned what she was going to say until that moment. Now it felt totally right, a burst of tremendous relief. A break. Time apart. Time to breathe. She braced herself for the explosion. But it didn't come.

'I won't let it happen,' he said quietly. He was on his third nail now.

'You can't stop it, Harry.'

'I won't let you do this to the kids.'

'You want them to grow up with us hating each other?'

'*I* did.'

She braced herself again. Now he was about to get angry, she was certain.

But his gaze moved around the room, Morrow's old stone

463

walls witnesses to a lifetime of family highs and lows, its memories decluttered away. He just looked incredibly sad.

Where was the anger?

'It's just for a bit.' Jo stared fixedly at her hands to stop herself crying. 'See how it feels.' She knew it would feel better. Her whole body was lifting up at the thought. She was possessed with a strangely calm sense of rightness. But the lump in her throat was strangling her.

'It's not all just about your fucking feelings, Jo.'

She didn't look up. The anger was so close she could smell it. 'So how do you feel?'

He stood up and started clearing the table. 'I feel fucking tired. I want to go to bed.'

'We're still talking, Harry.'

'I'm not, Owl.' He was stacking plates and foil trays, as quick and efficient as his best waiting staff. Domestic martyrdom was another avoidance tactic they both employed to avoid a fight, like movie fugitives catching the side of a freight train to hurtle away to safety. Jo had cleared enough plates when he was shouting angrily down the table at her to recognize it. Why wasn't he angry now?

He was reaching for the plate with the poppadum on it. Jo stared at it with frozen, hawk-like attention. It had taken on a significance all of its own, her symbol of their brittle, broken marriage. 'I'll put this in the breadbin for tomorrow.' She watched him carry it off.

She wanted to be mad at him for not being angry, but she suddenly felt totally emptied out and exhausted. It was past midnight.

She grabbed the rest of the empty foil trays and followed.

It amazed Jo that she and Harry could always line up side by side in the most practical of tasks – brushing their teeth, breakfasting and dressing the children, defrosting the cars – after blistering arguments, without acknowledging the poisonous atmosphere that lingered like napalm. It was a complicit enmity. Now it seemed more shocking than ever, yet they stacked the dishwasher, recycled, and pulled washbags from weekend cases without any high drama.

Later in bed, she curled as far away from him as possible, cocooned in her own unhappiness, missing the children, missing the routine, her too-tired-for-truth normality, missing Rathbone's bed-making scrabbles in his basket, listening for the telltale snore that meant Harry was asleep.

Instead she felt a warm hand on her shoulder and flinched, momentarily terrified.

'Lonely,' he breathed. 'I feel lonely.'

Covering his hand with hers, Jo found she could hardly breathe for tears. 'Me too.'

Their fingers briefly locked. Then they slid apart to be tucked beneath their pillows, like wishes, as they lay in silence, listening to the owls shriek and the sheep bleat, too proud and shocked to break the silence again.

SATURDAY MORNING

The Cooked Breakfast

The poppadum was still in the bread bin, like a battle-marked shield, when Jo prised out Glyn Pugh's best crusty loaf to make fried bread. Hozier was singing 'To Be Alone' on the stereo. Its words went right through her.

Harry was in the same bath she'd soaked in earlier, the bubbles popped away from scrubbing the bad night's sleep off her skin, now soaking the rancour from his. He had already cooked the bacon and mushrooms, left warm beneath the grill as she took over. They had the routine off pat.

The bathroom door opening made her jump as though a gunshot had gone off.

'Good bath?' She didn't turn, terrified of seeing him so clean and blond and familiar.

'Cold but fine.'

The polite awkwardness strained like a ship's sides under pressure but held fast.

Hozier sang 'Work Song' as they ate. Harry read the visitors' book in silence, no longer sharing the jokes and pique. Jo flipped irritably through the local paper, looking at the property section as usual, imagining a life here, wondering if it would have been any better had she taken up the challenge he'd laid down so passionately at the start.

She started uncomfortably as she read the caption 'MORROW FARM – 100-acre Shropshire Smallholding for Complete Renovation'. The photo showed a stone house with a sagging roof and a familiar jaw-dropping view fading away into the Welsh mist behind it.

She closed the paper hurriedly, glancing at Harry. He was writing in the book, totally focused.

Outside the sun had already blistered the dew from the bleached grass

They stuck loyally to the programme, not knowing what else to do. They drove to Rossbury, music blaring from the stereo, to shop at the market in baking sun, buying gifts for the children, Welsh lamb, Shropshire Blue, vegetables and more fresh bread. With engrained syncopation but barely a grunt of agreement, they headed in tandem to the side road off the high street and found the gallery once again reinvented, now an arty tea shop called Crempog. The old joke should have made them laugh, but it didn't. It was as empty as ever.

Rhona's bun was freshly hennaed, her eyes brightening in recognition, her breath shorter than ever. 'Usual table?' she greeted them eagerly.

Jo watched Harry launch into a charm offensive, less flirtatious than usual but no less kind, finding out all the latest news: that Rhona had inherited some money and bought the gallery lease, after its latest disastrous incarnation – a nail art and tattoo bar that they had thankfully never seen – and that most of the work now on display came from local artist friends. There were a lot of curvaceous nudes.

'I'm familiar with this style.' Harry admired them one by one, stepping back, blond head tipping this way and that.

'Mine.' Rhona blushed happily. 'You bought one years ago. I've never forgotten you for it. It paid my rent and gave me faith. '

It was *The Wimberry Nude*, which hung in their spare room at home, Jo remembered, rescued from Morrow after a flood of visitors' book complaints. They had to swap it for the Klimt print whenever her sister stayed because she complained it gave her bad dreams.

Rhona watched them indulgently as they found a table in their usual spot. 'I'd love to paint you both one day.'

'Better hurry if you want to do us together,' Harry muttered, looking at Jo.

She snatched up the menu, her throat aching because the choke in it was now so big.

Harry ordered every panino on the menu as usual. Jo ate a tuna baguette, which stuck in her mouth like sawdust.

She wouldn't take back what she had said, but that made saying anything almost unbearably painful. She needed him to get angry, however much she dreaded it. And she sensed it approaching all the time, like a gathering storm.

SATURDAY AFTERNOON

The Pub Fight

In the Hare and Moon beer garden, there were Thai pergolas dotted everywhere, crammed with families from the nearby campsite seeking shade from the blistering sun. The pub was crawling with perspiring ramblers, and more campers heading outside clutching trays of drinks, ketchup bottles and cutlery sets wrapped in paper napkins. There was barely a local in sight.

'They stay away this time of year now!' Roy told them, after the usual back-slapping hug had loosened Harry's fillings. He was sweating heavily in his chef's whites, the chinstrap beard now a centimetre wider all round, like an oval orange picture frame. 'Bloody madness it is. Two pints.' He handed them across the bar. One had an umbrella.

So many old jokes, Jo realized. At home there were hundreds. She always forgot the ones here until she found them afresh, year after year. She stole a glance at Harry. He was looking at the umbrella in confusion. 'What's that about, Half Mast?'

It's my joke with Roy, Jo thought. Harry has never got it. 'Thank you.' She raised her glass. In day-to-day life, she would no more dream of drinking a pint of real ale than she would sniff glue, but at Morrow it was ritualistic. Just as getting drunk on a Saturday afternoon with Harry here felt normal, talking to the campers, who drifted to and fro, eating the vast steaks, catching up with Ping, who brought their desserts, another big bump to the fore. Her face had aged more, her body softened, the bags bruised dark beneath her eyes.

'Another boy.' She mustered a smile. 'Rhodri. That's Welsh.' She shared the joke with Jo on the ghost of a wink.

'How's your mum?' asked Jo.

'Living in Rossbury with her boyfriend. She and Roy fell out. The council want us to knock down bungalow because we have no permission. She's very mad about it.'

'I'm sorry.'

'Seeing you makes today a happy one.' Ping smiled again. A nearby table of walkers were shrugging on backpacks and finger-clicking for the bill, and she retreated with an apologetic nod.

Jo knew Harry was scrutinizing her face closely. It made her skin prickle guiltily. Please be angry.

She stared up at the blackboard, blinking hard. 'We're missing Folk Karaoke Nite next week.'

He followed her gaze. 'Next week's a long way off.'

There was a time Jo had watched other couples in restaurants and pubs and wondered at their lack of interaction, the fact they barely spoke or looked at one another, like strangers in a waiting room. She and Harry had become like that, she thought sadly. Drinking too much, watching the action around them, muttering the odd caustic comment.

She tried hard to pull out something to soften the discomfort as the beer mellowed her resolve. 'I wonder when the storm will break.'

But getting drunk was having the opposite effect on Harry, the polite charm slipping away as he snapped, 'I was under the impression it broke last night.'

'I was talking about the heatwave. It's unbearable, isn't it?'

'Is it?'

For the first time that day, she saw he was wearing a sweatshirt. Everybody else, including her, was wilting in cotton Ts. But Harry looked cold, his face drawn and his knuckles white.

'Summer pudding!' Roy steamed up, plonking two bowls in front of them, their contents resembling bleeding hearts. 'Sad news about old Efon, eh?'

Jo gripped her spoon tightly, thinking about the farm-auction notice in the newspaper. Behind it was a tragedy she'd been too self-protective to acknowledge until now.

'Very sad.' Harry drained his pint. 'I was fond of Efon.'

'Farm's being sold.'

'I heard that was the plan.'

'The girls don't want to run it. Cerys is back in Cardiff and Lowri lives with her . . .' he lowered his voice '. . . lady friend, doing something they call "upcycling". I'm not sure what it is, but mountain bikes aren't really my thing.'

Jo turned the spoon round and round. Looking up, she found Harry watching her.'You knew?' she asked, after Roy had gone.

'You told me last year.'

She remembered her duvet-flapping confession, the night of the bad-performance sex. 'I thought you were asleep.'

'I went down to talk to you about it' – there were hot sparks in his voice – 'but something else came up.'

She turned the spoon the other way. Matt's messages. Her own hot sparks flared. She missed his friendship. Not the crush, which had always been awkward, but the affinity, the ally within the family. They were gawky dance partners in the Sunday-lunch-group reels again now.

They lapsed into a long silence, those sparks catching

and smouldering out of sight. Jo pushed her pudding round and brooded furiously about the practicalities of trying out living apart, from Sunday lunch to the school nativity play. Harry ignored his and glared up at a light fitting, as though it was personally to blame for everything.

They drank on steadily, pouring alcohol on to those smouldering fires, not wanting to be alone together. They said little, but what they did reminded them of why; both trading quiet, low blows in a public bar, anticipating the bare knuckle punches ahead.

'You should have stuck to your DIY Daddy plan,' Harry muttered at one point.

'At least Wilf would be getting proper support if I had,' she hissed, a hydra attack from the bottom of a pint glass.

The light fitting Harry was staring at should have combusted long ago.

Jo's summer pudding was a bloody battlefield. 'I can't bear being this unhappy,' she breathed, unaware she was saying it out loud.

'Don't lay that one on me. You were unhappy when I met you. Default lies with you.'

'I knew what I wanted when I met you.'

She didn't need to say more: they both knew it wasn't this.

Later, Roy produced Jägermeisters on the house, and they drank far too many.

When the last-orders bell rang and Roy came up to tip the wink about a lock-in – 'I haven't asked you about Ned yet, Half Inch. You seen him lately?' – Harry politely declined and he and Jo walked in a straight line with effort, spilling outside.

'God, I miss Efon. May he rest in peace.' Harry pitched across the bridge towards the car park. 'I'm not bloody walking.' He pulled the keys from his pocket.

Seeing the Mini's hazards flash, Jo snatched the fob from him. 'You're drunk. We're walking.'

'That's my decision!' He tried to wrest them back.

'My car.'

'I paid for it.'

'Since when did that give you the right to take it back?'

'Since I bought it.'

'Who's bailed us out through six years of feast and famine, thanks to your bloody restaurants?'

'And I've listened to you fucking whingeing about it. I've worked my butt off trying to make amends for it.'

The anger broke now, already a red-hot furnace, the petrol of repressed emotion meeting fresh air and exploding.

'You fucking bitch!' he howled. 'You fucking stupid fucking beautiful fucking bitch! Do you know what you're giving up here?'

'Yes! This!'

She watched him prove her point, raging out of control, slamming the wing mirror clean from the side of the car with his fist, smashing its window with a rock.

He thinks of the car as me, Jo realized in shock. It's like me when I find his unwashed mugs littered around the house or his clothes abandoned on the floor or his unopened bills in a drawer and I want to jump up and down on them.

Without warning, she threw herself at him and started to fight. Slap followed grab and push. Pent-up aggression came out, as if a dam had burst. She was so skewed on beer and Jägermeister that she was mostly air-guitaring and sky punching, like a bad disco dancer, but when she hit home, she threw her heart and body behind it, tears running, pain as raw as that from a machete cut.

'What are you doing?' He stepped back.

'GIVING UP!' She threw a wild punch, hearing an irritated 'oof' as it landed among his ribs, no more painful than leaning over a knee when putting on socks.

'Stop it, Owl.' He laughed.

It was a red rag. Furious, Jo lifted her knee to his groin, missing by miles. Even more livid, she summoned her inner ninja, arms and legs flailing in unison.

For a long time Harry stood and took it, looking cross and hurt and – increasingly – in pain, as punch after pinch after kick hit home. Then, like a baited bear, he roared with anger, lifting her clean off the ground and depositing her in the stream.

The cold water was a body slap ten times as forceful and sobering as those she'd been raining down on him. As she surfaced, spitting and cursing, her mind whirred emotional slides, trying out guilt, shame and laughter. No, she was still angry. Angrier than ever.

'Sorry, Owl, but you were hysterical' Harry was looking down at her, arm outstretched.

Refusing his help, she clambered out. 'I hate you.'

'And I love you.' He picked up the keys she'd dropped in her kick-boxing frenzy, heading to the car and holding open the passenger door. 'Come back for a bath. We'll talk.'

Why wasn't he still angry too?

'Fuck off!' She stormed towards the cottage track.

Don't drive, don't drive, please don't drive, her head chanted. However incensed she was, however much she wanted him to feel pain right now, she was terrified he'd hurt himself if he got behind the wheel in his current state.

When an arc of light began bobbing in the distance behind her, approaching fast, Jo's heart thrashed with fear and disappointment. Then she turned. She couldn't hear an engine. Just hard breathing and hammering feet. He was running, carrying the super-bright Maglite she kept in the boot of the Mini.

Rage engulfed her again. He's beaten up my car; he's thrown me into the stream; I am *not* going to let him get to the cottage first. She had to win this race.

'Nothing like starting the fitness programme straight away.' She gritted her teeth and broke into a run too.

As the torchlight grew closer, it cast her shadow ahead of her – a long, lurching Grim Reaper silhouette occasionally throwing up childish, drunken Vs that soon became a short munchkin with clenched fists, then disappeared to nothing when he drew level.

Saying nothing, they pounded along side by side. Jo's lungs were bursting, a stitch slicing her in two. Harry had found a rhythm, feet beating a relentless tattoo on the ground, as angry and unforgiving as the shouts she'd taught herself to blot out. She should be the fittest one, but he'd always had reserves of inner strength that pulverized the opposition. She started to fall behind, legs leaden with lactic burn now, toxic from so much alcohol and mule kicking. Nausea rose in her throat.

'C'mon, Owl. Keep up.'

'Don't patronize me!' She stopped in her tracks, hands on her knees, feeling faint. She looked up through a fog of giddiness. 'I am *not* your fucking owl!'

The torch swung back, blinding her. 'What's wrong?'

'I just prefer to run alone.' If she was going to throw up, she didn't want Harry around to witness it.

'You should have taken me up on that lift.'

'Fuck off.'

She sat down on the grass bank, head between her knees. Her heartbeat was so deafening in her ears she took a while to notice that Harry had gone, leaving her in pitch darkness and silence. Arms wrapped around her knees, forehead pressed to their bony nubs, she concentrated on her breathing, nausea lifting.

There was something eerie about the night's stillness. There were no sheep. No bleats. No white ghosts. Efon's flock had gone.

An owl hooted overhead.

'You can fuck off too.' She looked up.

It hooted again, a dark shadow crossing a moonlit cloud.

She pressed her eyes down on to her forearm, stemming a spring of tears. She'd always loved Harry calling her his beautiful Owl. She was suddenly freezing cold.

She stood up with a squelch, knowing she had to set off, dry off, and tell Harry where to get off. This has gone beyond wise words, she reminded herself. He dunked you in the stream; he smashed up your car.

As she trudged uphill, shoes slipping and wet clothes clinging, outrage seeped through Jo's bones like acid. She had half a mind to do an about-turn and stay at the pub to regroup, but the embarrassment of walking back in soaking wet was too much to face, and Ping had enough on her plate without the Inchbolds' marital break-up played out between bed and breakfast. She also wanted to hit Harry again. Badly. Illogically, she kept thinking about the poppadum, imagining him scoffing it right now, their marriage crumbling.

When she finally stomped into Morrow, eternally grateful for its warmth, the cottage was deserted. A bath was running, and a glass of brandy sat on the kitchen table. Sam Smith was on the stereo singing 'Money On My Mind'. Harry's hallmarks: bath, booze, music.

Stealing herself, she opened the bread bin and almost broke down when she saw the poppadum still there. Not because she'd thought he might have eaten it, but because she had actually checked. She was gripped by the sort of madness that meant her marriage hung on a deep-fried Indian cracker.

She sank down at the table, head in her hands, distinctly remembering Fi telling her that towards the end of her marriage she'd been tempted towards mariticide by the way Dom squeezed the toothpaste.

Still cold to the bone, head racing, she drank the brandy. She had to get out of her damp clothes, now clammily stuck to her and reeking of algae. The deep bath was too hot to resist and she plunged into it briefly, like a sheep into a dip, warming and disinfecting at warp speed, wary of being vulnerable for long.

Dried and dressed in pyjamas, she looked for Harry again, only realizing how bombed she still was when she found herself in the outbuilding by the biomass boiler, searching behind the boxes crammed with Inchbold memorabilia, as though imagining he'd be cowering there, like in a game of hide and seek. Harry never cowered. She leaned against the top box, taking deep breaths to try to sober up. It was open, filled with old vinyl and cassettes.

Her eyes focused on a home-made label, the handwriting spidery and teenage: 'Glass Half Full Sessions, Summer 1988. Morrow'.

She picked it up, clutching it to her chest, bursting with affection and annoyance for the boy whose talent had been so wasted, and whose fifteen minutes of fame had simply been a way out of flunking his A levels. She was starting to panic, terrified that she might have driven him into doing something stupid.

She hurried back into the cottage and found her mobile in her sodden jeans pocket. The screen was dead. Without thinking, she went into the kitchen, fished out an open bag of rice left in the cupboard by a previous holiday let, and pushed it inside.

She slugged out more brandy, then tipped it down the sink, aware that she mustn't get any more thick-headed. At home she and Harry could crack guiltlessly into a third wine bottle on a Saturday night, cushioned by a routine of bad habits and mutual dependence, but now the broken edges of their marriage needed sharper focus. She started to make coffee, then abandoned it, too fuelled by nervous energy to wait for the kettle to boil.

She paced the cottage instead, irritated by the new holiday homely touches she spotted amid the neutral minimalism – wicker hearts, letters spelling out 'PEACE', gingham cushions and more discreet laminates asking that dogs be kept off the sofas. Rathbone had scrabbled his stiff-legged way up on to the Knoles to the last, she remembered proudly.

Sam Smith was singing 'Stay With Me' now, the album playing on a loop. Harry had bought it for her, along with a chunky necklace that rattled on her collarbones and caught her hair in its clasp. Jo had played the CD a few times in the car, liking this track, but had never really listened to it. Now it went right through her. A one-night stand that craved more; she'd had eight years more. She hurried to the stereo to switch it off, then saw it was Harry's iPhone that was playing. She plucked it out.

His screen lock stayed open. She flipped to texts. Hot guilt licked her cheeks, but this was an emergency, she reminded herself. They were in the middle of a marriage bust-up here, and he was missing.

Funny, pithy, kind. Nothing incriminating. So many to her. He hated messaging, but he made a huge effort for her – they took up almost half his sent list. Her heart burst a little.

His music list was still a mystery tour, she thought, as she flipped through it, recognizing almost nothing. Reselecting

Sam Smith, she clicked it back into the pod and started pacing again.

She must have covered almost a mile, criss-crossing flagstones, quarry tiles and floorboards, when he finally appeared through the door, red-nosed and -eyed, hair in vanilla-ice-cream peaks. Jo turned to face him, ambushed by relief and anger. 'Where have you been?'

'I walked to the Burf.'

'I was worried sick.'

'Don't be polite. You were fucked off.' He headed through to the kitchen. 'I'm famished.'

'Me too.' They'd always been ravenous in a crisis.

Jo heard the bread bin lid rattle up. She watched from the doorway as he pulled out the poppadum, broke it into pieces and crammed each into his mouth without offering any to her.

As she watched him sweep away the crumbs and pull out the loaf to slice, her chest was a fireball. She wanted to laugh, but the tears were so close behind that she looked away, holding the door frame, focusing on her thumbs against the wood, two determined digits that gave double ups when Wilf and Thea came out of school, that hammered the computer space bar by day and the phone screen by evening, that smudged charcoal on laid paper and tears from eyes, sauce from plate rims and creases from school collars.

She put her thumbs together now, fingers splayed to either side like a bird taking flight. It was never about the last poppadum. She'd always known Harry would eat it without thinking to share it. What she'd needed to figure out was how she could change life for the better. Morrow had given her that answer. It had been here from the very start.

Harry had made two ridiculously doorstep sandwiches,

snarling at the mouth with Shropshire Blue, honeyed ham and lamb's lettuce. He carried one across to her now, holding it up as a peace-offering.

'So what do you want to do, Owl?'

'When we first came here together,' she said, wishing her voice was less strangled and tearful, 'we agreed to give it a year together. Now let's give it a year apart.'

Their eyes met.

EPILOGUE

2015

Music: blues, Abba, Glass Half Full

Car: battered Mini with duct-taped wing-mirror

Season: Spring, cold and bright

SATURDAY AFTERNOON

The Arrival

Jo had asked a friend to make the booking online so that her name didn't appear on the Morrow Cottage database. She knew she was probably being overcautious, given that it all went through an agency, but she didn't want any of the Inchbolds to know she was there.

She didn't want Harry to know.

Same time next year. It had been written in her diary from the start, an ever-approaching landmark. But Harry had welshed on their deal. She'd wept bitter tears about it in private all month, but her public face was one of steely calm. That was the face Harry got most often now. The nonchalant nod was her secret weapon.

This had originally been Harry's weekend to have the children, so when he'd left a message a few weeks ago to say they needed to juggle dates, she'd already had secret plans in place for Wilf and Thea to stay with friends so that their parents could get together at Morrow. Instead, he'd told her he was going to be on a buying trip to Ireland that he was typically vague about (probably snapping up another church with Ned, who had quite a collection now), so perhaps they could move the dates around. The exchange had been increasingly irritable, largely conducted by text because nonchalant nods didn't work in phone calls. Harry still hated texting, his answers short and crabby. Jo's answers were even more so: she was terrified of crying in front of him.

Telling him she and the children already had plans, she'd gone straight online to check the cottage's availability – it was free from today, so she knew Harry wasn't cooking up a secret romantic coup – then called her friend to reserve it for her.

She extracted the keys from beneath the flowerpot, as instructed in the booking email. She still had her own key, but it felt wrong to use it somehow.

Frustratingly, the cottage lettings agency only took Saturday to Saturday bookings online. She'd just wanted the weekend, and would no doubt have got it if she'd used family influence, but she was too painfully, proudly aware that she had been waiting for this weekend all year while Harry had moved on.

She'd deliberately avoided all the rituals – there had been no supermarket or takeaway detours, her minimal groceries already packed in the boot of the car when she'd set off from Wiltshire. It was still light, the cottage glowing in a low gold flamethrower of a sunset that seemed to cast a light at ankle level, making shadows infinite.

On opening the door, the smell of woodsmoke hit her, and she felt a surprising rush of happiness. Where she'd expected misery, there was comfort. She'd come back to Morrow. Now she felt as though she was letting out a breath she'd been holding since setting out from Wiltshire.

When they'd separated, Harry had wanted to move to Morrow – there'd been a huge fuss about it at the time with Matt and the other co-owners outvoting him: the cottage earned a healthy income, had won awards and was booked out months in advance, as Jo had learned to her cost when trying to come here this month.

Living apart had been agony at first, growing pains they'd barely had respite from. The counselling, the family interference, the spats and silly grievances that turned into

486

sleepless feuds, the united front for the children. And the gifts, both of them absurdly generous in their guilt and desire for reconciliation. Harry had dropped weight like a jockey, at first flattering, then worrying as his ever-leaner look went from striking to shocking, his temper often as black as the smudges beneath his eyes. For months, they'd swung between love and hate like two lousy trapeze artists, rarely catching each other in the same mood.

But gradually they had found a rhythm. No longer wrapped in a deep-freeze of married misery, Jo still tried to keep her cool around Harry's hot head but a genuine warmth between them was starting to melt that more and more often. Harry was eating again, looking good, the sharp humour and generosity back in force. They spoke on the phone whenever he called the children, shared long coffees when she dropped them off or he picked them up at weekends and school holidays. They'd stopped marriage guidance because of Harry's work commitments, but the counsellor, with a constantly running nose and an obsession with their sex life, had irritated them anyway. And they'd started flirting over the odd glass of wine instead.

Harry's work and home life remained as complicated as always. He still dabbled in ecclesiastical restaurants with Ned, but his new baby was spearheading Country Mile, a high-end grocery-delivery service that traded on its ability to source the best local produce across the British Isles with minimal food miles. Head-hunted for the role by a West Midlands entrepreneur from his old branding days, Harry had even negotiated himself accommodation with the contract, staying in one of the central Birmingham penthouses his tax-exile CEO kept as investments. Give him an inch and he'll take a . . .

The children both adored Daddy's 'footballer's flat'

with its amazing views and two-minute stroll to the Sealife Centre. Jo rather liked it too: it reminded her of London in the nineties when canal-side developments had started springing up and her trendier friends had rented studios in Shad Thames, before property there had become a commodity traded between the Far and Middle East. As ever, Harry seemed to be growing older backwards. It was a very sexy flat. They'd flirted in it more than once when she'd brought the children there, her nonchalant nods melting into spontaneous laughter, their eyes talking to each other in secret again.

In the build-up to this weekend, Jo had believed they might just make it back together, older and wiser, scarred and toughened, but together. Instead, she was here alone. She'd kept her word, but coming here was about much more than that. It was about reclaiming the cottage for its good memories as well as bad.

She lit the wood-burning stove. Then, for the first time ever, she settled with the house-manual folder, a cup of tea and a biscuit from the welcome tray, reading instructions on how to switch on the immersion heater, work the television and Wi-Fi, and where to buy the best local lamb; a proper paying guest.

She turned to the visitors' book, which Harry had loved to hate – her first leather-bound gift to the house long since replaced by many successors as comments filled each up – a gilt-edged new hardback with just half its pages filled, the first entry dating back eighteen months. She flicked through, pausing as she found last year's entry. *I will be here the same time next year, and every year. Harry.*

Jo felt tears prick and pushed them back, looking up to summon self-control, indignant and angry. His broken promise wasn't going to make her cry again.

After it came a long rant from a guest from Kent . . . *My*

wife cooked rice from the store cupboard. We were shocked to find, when served, that there was a mobile phone in it . . .

That's where I put it, Jo remembered with relief. When she'd she got home, she'd pulled out what she had taken to be her phone from her pyjamas pocket, but it had turned out to be a cassette tape. Oh, that awful, awful night.

She pulled the ribbon on the visitors' book, which fell open on the last entry. Dated today, the handwriting instantly recognizable.

Great place! We made ourselves right at home. Sorry about the state of the bed . . . Harry and Clodagh, March 2015

She stared at it for a long time, not taking it in, a portcullis of shock slamming down, a drawbridge of denial pulling up. Then the boiling oil of anger landed on her head.

'Bastard!' she growled. 'Bastard, bastard, bastard!'

Harry had a new woman and he'd brought her to Morrow. They had left just hours before her arrival.

Illogically, she hurried upstairs to examine the state of the bed, but it was immaculately laundered and counterpaned, a welcome posy of grape hyacinths on the bedside table. Fresh towels had been laid out on its tartan throw.

Harry was in here and inside someone else last night, she thought bleakly – probably this morning too. Had they shared a fried breakfast? Had he taken her to Rossbury Market? Were they still in the pub after a long lunch?

She thundered downstairs, rage seething, picking up the visitors' book again. *Harry and Clodagh.* Same time next year, and every year. He'd kept his end of the bargain too, it seemed. Just with somebody else.

She hurled the book at the wall.

Jo pulled on her running shoes and headed outside. Harry had been right: Salomon's were by far the best off-road shoe. How could she ever have thought him dull on the subject? Since taking up running she'd become a shoe obsessive.

They were both much healthier apart. Had she been here with Harry, they would have cracked open the ale flagon and started a row by now, conspirators in an endless feast. Jo had found better ways of dealing with stress, helped by the glamorous divorcee army who filled an increasing proportion of her address book. But despite the solidarity, she remained married; she felt married. There had been no one else in her life. The children came first, and the hope that Harry and Jo might one day be put back together again. Until today, she'd carried it everywhere.

She pounded up the path towards Mawr Vron, her sunset shadow creating a long, thin line into which she ran. She remembered the first year she'd walked up it with Harry, making love against the Burf stone like sex-mad pagans; she remembered the year she'd wandered round the woods after a row, lost in the blank whiteness of a Welsh mist, shouting at Harry that she loved him.

The woods were striped with sunlight and dark shadow today. It was like running through a strobe.

'Clodagh? Clodagh!' A distant shout. 'Where the fuck are you?'

She slid to a halt. She'd know that voice anywhere.

Harry was here. He was having a row with the new girlfriend. Her eyes narrowed.

'Clodagh, please come back.' The voice was closer, softer and more conciliatory now. 'Come to me, baby. Come to Daddy.'

Ah, the Daddy fantasy. Bastard!

Jo heard the undergrowth cracking nearby and hurriedly edged behind a tree, trying not to breathe too loudly. After a moment, she heard something else breathing loudly. And it was standing right behind her.

Swinging round, she found a small dog looking up at her. She stared back down at it in wonder. It was Rathbone in miniature: a smiley, low-slung grey rug on legs with a comedy swagger, rolling over now to proffer a pink belly.

'Hello, you.' She stooped to rub it, seeing that Rathbone's micro-clone was female.

'Hello, you.' A familiar husky voice.

She straightened up as a silhouette stepped out of the shadows, topped with a mop of silver and gold. As well as losing weight, Harry had gone a lot greyer in the last year. It suited him. He looked very grown-up.

'This is your dog?' she realized.

'Jo, meet Clodagh.'

Harry's guest is a *dog*. Jo suddenly felt incredibly stupid as the little dog leaped up, bounded towards him and writhed lovingly around his legs.

'You stayed at the cottage last night?' She straightened up.

'Just one night.' He looked at her intently. 'You?'

'Just one night.'

They looked at one another in silence, letting this sink in.

'I sailed back from Wexford with this girl yesterday.' Only Harry could make it sound like a swash-buckling adventure involving tricorn hats, smuggling and tall ships. 'You knew I was coming back from Ireland last night.'

'Somehow that one missed me.'

'I told you very clearly.' His voice had a snap of anger in it.

Jo fell back on a nonchalant nod, her mind racing. It must have been lost in translation amid the crabby exchange of texts about who was having the children this weekend. But he'd said nothing whatsoever about Morrow. She would have remembered.

The little dog was scrabbling at her legs to be picked up. 'She looks just like Rathbone.' She lifted her, finding her nose licked enthusiastically.

'Glen of Imaal,' he said, with authority.

'I thought she was called Clodagh?'

'It's a terrier breed – very rare. When I went in search of a dog like Rathbone, I found his mirror image online. Seems he was from noble stock all along.'

Jo felt the gesture rub against the raw blister she still carried for poor Rathbone, and her responsibility for letting him and her parents down so appallingly, along with Harry's part in that. She put Clodagh back on the ground.

'He was a one-off,' she said, her voice harsh because she was trying to hide the fact she was upset. 'I don't want her, Harry. She's lovely, but this isn't about romantic gestures. We agreed.'

'She's for the kids, Owl, not you.' He picked the tail-wagging terrier up.

Now Jo felt even testier, protective of their little divided family and its confusing demarcations. 'That's really not fair on them. Or her. You live in a top-floor flat with no garden.'

'I live in a canal-side penthouse with a wraparound roof terrace one minute's walk from four parks.'

'In the Jewellery Quarter. It's hardly the Wicklow Mountains.'

'Birmingham has more canals than Venice, more trees than the Bois de Boulogne, a symphony orchestra, a ballet, a Selfridges, the best cricket ground going and a chocolate factory. And it's Ladywood, not the Jewellery Quarter. I know my way around now.'

He's happy with his new life, she realized painfully. The Harry Inchbold positive spin has bedded in. He has all new horizons. She felt suddenly very cold. Dusk was gathering. Birds had started to roost in the trees overhead, a group of starlings chattering higher in the sky out of sight. Jo had always loved the sounds around Morrow. She remembered the summer's day when they'd held hands on sun-loungers for hours, just listening to those sounds. She didn't want to flirt with Harry over coffee made on his high-tech Jura in the footballer's apartment once a fortnight. She wanted to find what they'd had here at Morrow.

But they couldn't even get that right.

'I waited for you last night,' he muttered.

'If you'd actually told me you were going to be here, I might have stood a better chance of knowing.'

'We agreed it a year ago. Same time next year. I didn't think you'd need reminding. We came here on Friday the fourteenth.'

'Today is the fourteenth, if you hadn't noticed. It moves on one. Yesterday was Friday the thirteenth.'

'It felt like it.' He was looking seriously pissed off now. 'Why are you always so bloody practical?'

'You used to love it when I was practical. And I think the word you're looking for is pedantic. The devil's in the detail.'

'The devil's in the mind.' He caught her eye over the little dog's head.

Clodagh really did look incredibly like Rathbone. Poor Rathbone, who had seen the worst of their arguments and brooding silences. No wonder he'd run away. Life with Harry had become one long, exhausting war of wills. She couldn't go back to that. She'd been crazy to carry around a year's worth of hope that she could.

What hope did they have when they couldn't even agree on the date?

With only a split second's warning, Jo knew she was going to cry. She didn't want Harry to see her cry. She stepped back out on to the path, the sun out of sight now, a red glow beneath her where the woods opened out on to the grassy hillside, dropping away to the valley. She walked towards it.

'Where are you going?' He stalked after her.

'I'm cold. I have to get back to the cottage.'

'We meet out of the blue here and you're just going to walk away?'

'We meet every fortnight, Harry.' She turned her head away so he couldn't see the tears.

'If you're upset about the dog, I'll take her back.'

'It's not the dog.' She clambered over the stile at the edge of the woods, snagging her running trousers on a piece of wire.

He released them with an elastic snap. 'Then what is it? What have I just said?'

Now they were out in the open, the sky was darkening fast, but not with nightfall. The bird sounds were extraordinary. Clodagh started to bark excitedly.

They both looked up.

'Starlings!' Jo gasped. It was a sight she'd never thought she'd see again.

Just as they had the first time Harry had brought her to Morrow, the starlings had gathered in their tens of thousands, a sparkling, chattering, ear-piercing smoke cloud that swirled and billowed with eye-defying geometry above the valley, sweeping along the ridge that ran down from Mawr Vron to the village. A murmuration that danced for them in the gathering twilight, the most extraordinary show of nature's ability to stun and confound.

Harry laughed as the starlings gave one last fly-by, like a giant black ghost, before starting to disband. 'Is your conscience clear?'

Jo remembered the local myth that if it wasn't the devil would take you within the year.

She hugged herself tightly, thinking about the visitors' book, broken-spined on the flagstones at the cottage, in it the story about her phone being boiled with the rice. She'd taken home a cassette tape instead, an original session tape made by Glass Half Full. It had been months before she'd listened to it – she didn't have a tape player – but she'd decided to get it digitally copied as a gift for Harry at the peak of their present-swapping phase. Copies of 'They Muck You Up' still existed, now selling for 99p on eBay, but the band's debut album had never been pressed, nor its second single, languishing on a master tape in the archives of their erstwhile recording label. But she'd listened to it now.

Her conscience wasn't very clear.

'Come back for a drink. Where's your car?'

'At the pub.'

'That puppy's far too young to walk all the way up here.'

'She's six months old – and I'm carrying her. Look.'

'That's still only three and a half in dog years.' She couldn't look at him.

'I was running all over this hill at that age. We're too soft on kids, these days.'

She set off again, heart thudding into her belly, like a fence-post driver, not at all certain this was a good idea. At home in Wiltshire, she could control herself; in Birmingham she was magnanimous; at Morrow the rules had always been different. She had no idea what they were any more. But she had to tell him what she knew.

Harry was talking about Wicklow. 'Man, but it's beautiful there. Makes this place look flat. Clodagh's breeder lives halfway up a mountain called Lugnaquilla. I saw a pottery for sale there. Can you imagine the life? I've always fancied being a potter. How would you feel being married to a potter?'

'Better than I'd feel being separated from one,' she muttered, as Morrow's roof came into view, smoke still curling from the chimney. She hadn't meant him to hear, but from the way he fell silent, she knew she had.

*

It seemed so familiar, him throwing logs on the stove while she made coffee and raided the chocolate supplies.

They settled on adjacent sofas, Clodagh asleep on the hearthrug.

Jo and Harry hadn't been alone together in months. They had been with the children, with family, with fellow drinkers in a busy wine bar, and with mediation, but the intimacy of Morrow, so far from another soul, made them both awkward and stiff-jawed, like fifties movie stars in a war drama, trading polite confessions as they sheltered from German gunfire in a barn.

'I took something from here,' Jo admitted. 'Last year.'

'I'm sure Rowena has it noted in the inventory.'

'It was a Glass Half Full session tape.'

'Ah.'

'Half the songs are about Cerys. One's even *called* "Cerys".'

He nodded, staring into his mug. 'That was going to be the second single, although the label changed it to "Kerry" which they thought had more pop-tastic appeal. You can imagine Ned's reaction.'

'He wrote them all?'

'Ned had a bit of a thing about Cerys. A teenage crush. But he wrote bloody good songs about it.'

'You'd be mistaken for thinking from the tattoo of his name on the back of her neck that the feeling was mutual.'

'God, no – at least, only briefly, and that was after everything had blown up between her and Matt. Ned was far too well brought up to make a move while they were together. It was me who screwed everything up on that front.' He cleared his throat uneasily.

'But Ned and Cerys did get it together?'

'Like I say, only briefly. She'd always seemed to think he was a bit of a knob – in fact, her dislike of him probably helped fuel all the lusty teenage angst in his lyrics. Why do you want to know?'

'It helps explain the songs. Humour me. When was it?'

'The year Ned went up to Cambridge. He'd come into his trust fund and suddenly had a lot of money. He made a huge play for Cerys, all power boats and gate-crasher balls. When you're seventeen, that sort of thing is a lot more impressive than it should be. He was down here all the time, posing in his dad's Porsche. Cerys fell for it briefly. Roy fell for it totally.' He grinned. 'He still thinks Ned's the coolest thing since *Miami Vice*.'

'And this was after she split up with Matt?'

He nodded. 'It can't have lasted more than a month or two. More of a rebound thing. And a good example of why you should never get a tattoo with a lover's name on it, unless they're called "Love" or "Peace". What's this got to do with the songs? The band was over by then.'

'I think something happened between them when she was still with Matt,' she said. 'I think it was Ned who got Cerys pregnant, not you.'

'I was there, remember?' He shook his head with a gruff laugh. 'It was me my brother caught in bed with his girl-friend.'

'You say yourself you have no memory of it.'

'This isn't St Elmo's fire, Owl. I know you want me to feel better about all this, but cooking up a conspiracy theory isn't going to help, trust me.'

'When their father was dying, Cerys told me that she owed you, big time.'

'That hardly proves anything.'

'The night of the party, she'd argued with Matt because he refused to sleep with her. She knew she was pregnant by then, and that if Matt found out, he'd realize she'd cheated because they hadn't actually done the deed. She didn't want anyone to know it was Ned's, least of all Ned, whom she didn't like or even trust very much. In a panic, she climbed into bed with you, knowing you were bombed enough to oblige, honourable enough to take responsibility and discreet enough to keep it secret. But then Matt walked in and caught you both. There was no way Cerys was going to tell the truth and make herself look even more of a slapper. The fact she got it together with Ned further down the line makes total sense. It wasn't about the fast cars and flash cash. It was about the guilt. That's why she got the tattoo.'

'This is all total bollocks. Cerys would never have put out for Ned when Matt was in the picture.'

'She did! There's a song about it on the sessions tape. "Rock Gig". It happened at the Free Nelson Mandela concert at Wembley stadium. Your record label had got you a stack of backstage passes. Cerys came down on the train specially, but Matt didn't turn up to meet her.'

'It was the day Titch got knocked off her bike on the Holloway Road,' Harry remembered. 'We were all at UCH waiting for her to come round. Matt went spare trying to get a message to Cerys.'

'Ned chaperoned her. They shared an E and did it in one of the loos when Whitney Houston was on stage. And because he was young and selfish and besotted, he didn't explain exactly why Matt wasn't there until afterwards, when he begged her to dump your brother and go out with him instead. She told him she'd cut his balls off if he ever breathed a word of it to anyone, and that she didn't want him ever to sing about her again. So, being Ned, the first thing he did was come here and write a song about it.' She looked around the room with a sigh. 'Then he made the ultimate sacrifice. He pulled the plug on the band. All the songs that were about her vanished. Soon all that was left of Glass Half Full was one forgotten pop single and a few home-made cassettes nobody ever listened to.'

'Until you. You got all this from a song?'

'Lowri helped point me in the right direction. That and the tattoo. Like you say, Cerys was seventeen and impressed by fast cars and speed boats, but she was genuinely humbled by somebody sacrificing fame and fortune for her. She'd never told him about being pregnant. You'd nobly taken the fall for that. She and Matt were over by then. She decided to give Ned another chance. Several drunken nights out with a bunch of posh teenagers – and one regrettable tramp stamp – later, and she realized Ned was never going to float her boat, however many speeds it had, so she settled for the rugby-loving Owen. Meanwhile Ned went on to have a series of dysfunctional relationships with women who looked like Robert Palmer backing singers. And Harry Inchbold was spared a tedious spell of stardom, supermodel girlfriends, private jets and possible drug abuse.'

'We weren't that good. I might have got to open a shopping centre.'

'You were still a victim of circumstance.'

'I'm no victim, Owl.'

'You're no Sinner either.'

Harry looked at her for a long time, smile widening, small dog snoring in his lap. 'Christ, I love the way your mind works. I love you. That story is almost certainly total rubbish, but the fact that you've thought it all through, that you care so much to make sense of things, that you've done all that just to make me feel better about something that happened a lifetime ago, I love you for it.' His eyes glistened.

Jo flushed proudly, glad that she had told him about it, and thrilled at the number of I-love-yous it had provoked, although the 'total rubbish' hurt. She'd lain awake night after night trying to make sense of it, listening to an awful lot of badly recorded eighties pop featuring her husband as a young man rasping on about being in love with Cerys.

It had always bothered her that Harry was cast as a Sinner to Matt's Saint when she knew he would lay down his life for those he cared about.

'What a love story.' He leaned closer, eyes playing with hers.

'Better than ours. Harry and Jo meet at dinner party, shag a lot, have two children, marry, argue a lot, separate.'

'You forgot the twist at the end.'

'What's that? Kill each other?'

'Get back together.' He picked up the visitors' book from the coffee-table, flattening out the battered pages before reading his last entry. 'This is a lie. I didn't make myself at home last night. I missed you too much. I didn't sleep at all. Do you miss me?' He looked up.

'Of course I do. We've said it enough times in—'

'I'm not talking about the "right" answers we gave in counselling to please the sniffy pervert. Tell the truth.'

'I don't miss the arguments,' she admitted, then thought about it. 'Okay, sometimes I even miss the arguments. And I miss the sex. Most of all, I miss the laughter.'

'Christ, I need a drink. Don't you really not have any wine here?'

'None. You're a lot healthier without me.'

'I can think of nobody I'd rather die of a heart attack with. Or live with.'

'My weak milky tea drives you mad.'

'There is that. And your fifty bottles of perfume with one squirt left in them.'

'That's nothing on your random loose-change piles.'

'Your disposable contact lenses stuck to the side of the washbasin.'

500

'You coming to bed late and waking me up to help you find your reading glasses.'

With no more than the welcome tray of tea and coffee to plunder, the embryo of friendship, conceived at Morrow, finally started to kick its way into life as they listed the things they missed about each other and the things that drove them mad, so often the very same things. Not noticing the fire go out or the last streaks of light fade from the sky outside, laughing and flattering and insulting affectionately, they embraced the rare joy of familiarity.

Jo felt the sexual thrill running alongside, their eyes lingering and remembering. The moment was so perfect, it frightened her. It felt new and special. She didn't want it spoiled by another argument, by pushing too hard.

'You should go. It's a long drive.' She stood up eventually, snapping on lights, revealing holiday-let Morrow in all its biscuit-toned neutrality.

'Want to get rid of me?'

'No.' She looked at him levelly. 'Yes.'

He stood up reluctantly, knowing they'd talk on the phone tomorrow; they'd see each other next week. They had a rhythm now. They'd got it so horribly wrong before that they couldn't risk hurting each other or the children by doing it again. 'Same time next year?'

She didn't hesitate. 'Yes.'

It was dark outside. A Welsh mist had rolled in, hiding everything beyond the fence line. Clodagh bounded enthusiastically into it, disappearing totally.

'Do you want me to drive you to the pub?' Jo asked.

'You'll never make it back through this. It'll be clear by the time the stream dog-legs. We're in a cloud.'

She went in search of a torch, the only one she could find a wind-up basic. When she came back, he was crouched

501

over the visitors' book, amending his entry. He snapped it shut.

'I'll see you with the kids next weekend. We could all spend the day together, maybe.'

'Yup.' She handed him the torch. 'I'd like that. They'd love it.'

The kiss was an awkward jaw clash, eyes averted, hearts pounding. As soon as it was over, Jo wanted to try it again, to feel his lips against hers, to reach her hands up to his face.

But he'd already vanished into the mist, the little dynamo whirr fast disappearing along with a more distant bark.

She closed the door and pressed her forehead against it, breathing in woodsmoke and an unidentifiable sweet top-note that she thought she now recognized as hope.

She opened the visitors' book.

I will always love you, however long it takes.

She settled down in front of the fire and hugged the book tightly to her chest.

'Me too.'

Then she heard the unmistakable sound of a dynamo torch winding its way back towards the door. Smile bursting across her face, Jo leaped up to throw it open.